Anna
and the Tale of the Wolf
By A. C. Nicholas

authorHOUSE®

AuthorHouse™
1663 Liberty Drive
Bloomington, IN 47403
www.authorhouse.com
Phone: 1-800-839-8640

© 2010 A. C. Nicholas. All rights reserved.

No part of this book may be reproduced, stored in a retrieval system, or transmitted by any means without the written permission of the author.

First published by AuthorHouse 11/15/2010

ISBN: 978-1-4520-2050-1 (sc)
ISBN: 978-1-4520-2051-8 (hc)
ISBN: 978-1-4520-2052-5 (e)

Library of Congress Control Number: 2010915354

Printed in the United States of America

Certain stock imagery © Thinkstock.

This book is printed on acid-free paper.

Because of the dynamic nature of the Internet, any Web addresses or links contained in this book may have changed since publication and may no longer be valid. The views expressed in this work are solely those of the author and do not necessarily reflect the views of the publisher, and the publisher hereby disclaims any responsibility for them.

Dedication

Family is important,
both the one that you are born into
and the one that you help to create.
Daughters and sons,
Mothers and fathers,
Brothers and sisters,
Friends, always good friends,
And Claire.

Acknowledgement

This story would not have been told had it not been for a number of circumstances that occurred and a number of people who worked with me, and of greater importance listened when I had questions and comments.

Ever since I was in my early teens, I have wanted to tell stories. You might say it was a secret desire of mine. Having spent over thirty years working with students, I found little time to pursue that guarded goal. Between teaching and counseling students there just was no time. And then with the birth of our son and daughter, free time became even more rare, so I would take to writing down scraps of ideas and saving them in my desk, hoping that some day they might be taken out and grown into stories.

When the time came that I was presented with the opportunity to retire, I began speaking to my closest friends and family members. It is to them first, that I owe acknowledgement. Carmela, the literary lioness whose virtues are, what else but Patience and Fortitude, acquiesced to be my proofreader. Michael, my good friend who convinced me that retiring and writing could actually be done, and then was pleasantly surprised when he read the first draft, may still be ruing the day he offered such encouragement.

I would like to thank Sophia for reading the story and seeing a cover I didn't see, and her mother, Regina for creating it and putting up with a string of "what if we…" type questions.

I would like to acknowledge Claire, who read, smiled, asked for more, read and smiled some more and all throughout this first adventure, believed in me.

Finally, I would like to acknowledge my parents, who started me on the journey by letting me buy used books for a quarter at the Farmers Market.

Table of Contents

Part I

Chapter I	Fire and the Night	1
Chapter II	A Request	13
Chapter III	The Banquet	21
Chapter IV	The Red Ribbon	35
Chapter V	A Little Detective Work	51
Chapter VI	Anna, the Little One	91
Chapter VII	Preparation	119

Part II

Chapter VIII	A Visit	137
Chapter IX	Chelsea Goes to the City	141
Chapter X	Conversations	151
Chapter XI	Life Lessons	157

Part III

Chapter XII	Palermo: There and Back Again	173

Part IV

Chapter XIII	O Canada	189
Chapter XIV	Merry Christmas to Us All	193
Chapter XV	A Visit to Yesterday	211
Chapter XVI	Local Lore	227
Chapter XVII	Meditation and Revelation	249
Chapter XVIII	Resolution	265
Epilogue	Gina's Story	275

Part I

Chapter 1
Fire and the Night

My grandfather never spoke that much. Often, when we would come to visit at the little farmhouse in upstate New York, he would smile faintly and retire to another room as my parents spoke in animated tones with my grandmother. This would have been around 1965. My sister and I were usually sent outside to play in the yard that stood just in front of the vegetable garden. Sometimes we would see him from a window, staring vacantly out or pondering, deep in thought, over a chalk portrait that hung on the wall in the back bedroom.

The portrait was of a lovely young girl with deep brown eyes, and long hair the color of burnished walnut. Her small, sad smile was, in a way, reassuring, especially for one so petite as she. We had been told that she was our great-aunt, my grandfather's sister, and that she had died in an accident before he immigrated to America from Sicily in the 1920s. We were never told any more than that. "Nonno," as my grandfather was called, would stop or change the subject and walk away.

When we were very young, we never really thought much about it. Then one year, late in the fall, my parents (who were both teachers) were asked to attend an educational conference, and my sister and I were sent to spend the weekend with my grandparents. While we enjoyed the thought of spending time with my grandmother, we were, even then, at the ripe old ages of fifteen and thirteen, reluctant to be with Nonno. We loved him, inasmuch as granddaughters love their grandparents, but the deeper bond that sometimes arises between the generations never had formed.

By the time we arrived, the evening had already grown cold and dark. Pockets of wind swirled leaves into frantic little games of tag all around us as we marched up the front walk, suitcases in hand. In the small living-room fireplace, my grandfather had built a fire. Its flickering blaze, although not very big, was a great contrast to the moonless chill outside. As the hour was late, we all sat down to dinner. My parents had already left, dropping us off and continuing on to the airport for their flight to the conference. After dinner, Nonno returned to the fireplace, stoking it back to life. Nana gave us fruit and popcorn to nibble on as we all sat around the revitalized fire.

"I know!" exclaimed my sister, Tina. "Let's tell stories ... scary ones!"

"No," I said. "Tell us about Sicily."

Perhaps it was the wine that he had been drinking, perhaps it was just his mood, but Nonno put down his glass and looked at us. As he raised his hands to help conjure up pictures of the old country, his eyes glistened in a way I'd never seen before. I couldn't tell if their wide, animated gleam was a reflection of the flames in the fireplace or some inner torchlight.

"The town of Arcamo is a parched, old place," he began. "The hills are dry and empty, with patches of woods here and there as you go deeper into them. Maybe a few wildflowers grow, but even they fade into the dust at the foot of the hills. The only water in the town comes from a well outside of the baron's villa."

"Who's the baron?" asked Tina. At her age, one would have expected her to be beyond the stage where every little detail had to be spelled out, but such was not the case.

"The baron owned a lot of the workable land in and around Arcamo. What I mean is, his family owned a lot of the land, as they had for generations before him. In Sicily, the title of *baron* comes with the ownership of a lot of land, and the title is always given to the oldest son. If he marries, the wife's title is *baronessa*." Then he stopped. He turned and looked into the fire, his eyes seeming more wet and annoyed. Lifting his glass, he drained the remaining wine, spilling a little onto his chin.

"Papa," my grandmother interrupted, "let her go. It's been so long. She's happier."

I looked at my sister, with the reproachful stare that only an older sister who has achieved the lofty stage of know-it-all-ism can give, and whispered, "See what you did, Tina? You interrupted him." She returned my glare with the classic *you're-not-the-boss-of-me* sneer, but before we could bring it to the next level, I turned to my grandmother and said, "Nana, who are you talking about?"

"Well, Anna, you know that you had a great-aunt."

"Sure. Aunt Rose. She's great!" Tina chimed in.

"No, girls, not your aunt Rose. An aunt is the sister of your father or mother, like your mother's sister Rose. She is a great person and an aunt, but she is not a great-aunt. A great-aunt is the sister of your grandfather or grandmother. Nonno had a sister who lived with him in Sicily. Her name was Gelsamina."

"She's the girl in the picture, isn't she, Nonno?" I asked.

"Yes," he replied with wistful sadness.

"Tell us about her, Nonno." The distant look in his eyes softened. He looked at each of us with melancholy and relented.

"Outside of the town, past the well and into the hills, was the baron's villa. It wasn't a big one, like the castles that you see in the movies. But it was pretty big for Sicily, and to us, it was enormous—certainly more grand than the church in Arcamo. And it matched the baron very well. His name was Leonardo, and except for some servants—he called them his men—he lived there alone. He was the only child of parents who died when he was very young. From that time on, an uncle raised him, only to abandon him on the day he turned eighteen. We all thought that there had been an argument over money, but the uncle told people in the town that the family had been cursed. He refused to say any more and left angrily.

"In those days, the baron was a good man. He was young and just. He gave the people of the town permission to take water from the well whenever they needed it. And in bad times, he would often help them by offering the protection of his estate. That was until … well, I must tell you that the baron was a hunter, but he did not hunt for sport. Most nobility hunted for sport in those days. They had falcons or visited hunting lodges where they could catch and kill much bigger game. The baron had only one quarry: wolves. You see, in those days, wolves still lived and hunted in Sicily. In fact, packs of wolves lived in the woods and forests of most of Europe. In the north lived big, furry wolves with dark brown or black fur that changed to white in the snowy winters. Here and in much of southern Italy, the wolves were a lighter colored brown or tan, to blend in with the tans and browns of the hills that surrounded Arcamo and towns like ours that were away from the coastline. Smart animals, cunning and hungry, always hungry. There aren't so many now, but then the woods were full of them. And where there were farm animals that could be killed, there were wolves to kill them. And when there was no more livestock on the farm, well …

"And that is why the baron hunted wolves. There was once a story that wolves, a great pack of them, had killed his parents late at night, in the hills outside of the town, but the uncle told everyone that it was a storm at sea that took them. That would explain why their bodies were never found. Still, people love stories. Maybe that's why the baron grew so keen on hunting the wolves. He could always tell when they were near. And he would never shoot to kill with his first shot. I had heard many stories of how he would wound the animal first, just to see it turn on him and try to attack, only to meet his eyes and then turn and run in desperation. Once, he tracked a wounded wolf for two days into the hills just to watch it slowly die. It was as if his rifle was not enough. He had to hunt it with his gaze to prove that he was its master. That is how the baron D'Arcamo came to be known as the Master of Wolves."

"Nonno," declared my grandmother, not needing to say more.

"But," he continued, "Sicily is an old place, and hardly any wolves live there anymore." Taking his cue from Nana, he looked down at his watch. "Oh my, look at the time. Girls, it's time to get ready for bed. No more stories tonight."

With a chorus of *awww*'s and *noooo*'s, we begrudgingly left the room—but not before getting Nonno to promise to finish the story the next night. And so it was with some anticipation that we went off to the beds that Nana had made up for us, filled with visions of some dark, heroic, windswept figure standing at the parapet of his villa, gazing vigilantly at some distant point in the hills of Arcamo where the baying of a wolf could be heard.

The rain continued all that night and into the next day, as we read the books and completed the schoolwork that we had brought to keep us occupied and away from my grandparents for at least a little while—

all the time looking toward that magic time after dinner when Nonno could finish the story.

We both wore heavy sweaters—Tina wore two—so as to keep warm and cozy in front of the fireplace. Nana brought her knitting to work on as Nonno, now settled into his chair, finished his last pieces of fruit and cheese, and drank his last sip of wine. He wiped his mouth with the back of his thumb, looked to us, and began.

"Tonight, I need to tell you a little bit about my sister, Gelsamina." As he spoke the name, it sounded melodic. "My father, your great grandfather, used to say, 'In Italian, some names are meant to sound like a song.' Gelsamina was a few years older than me, and as you can see from the picture in the back bedroom, a beautiful girl, just like your nana." We both looked at my grandmother with appreciation, searching for the face of the pretty young girl that my grandfather was describing, and now only he could see.

"You know, girls," he began, "farm work in the twenties was very different from farm work today. And I'm not talking about the little things that Nana and I do here. In order to make a living, Gelsamina and I had to get up between four-thirty and five o'clock in the morning, feed the animals, get the eggs, and milk the goats—and this was all before breakfast. Then I had to go out and, using the rain water that we'd collect in barrels, irrigate the crops (you know, water them) and weed, and I guess just basically take care of them."

"Nonno, how did you get the water from the barrels to the crops?" Tina interjected.

"Well, we had a small cart and a donkey. I would load a barrel onto the cart, and each barrel had a hole cut out near the bottom and plugged up with a cork. I would stop the cart by each row of crops and unplug the cork so that a stream of water would run into the ditch along the side of the plants."

"Oh," said Tina, satisfied at the answer.

"After all, these crops and our extra eggs and goat milk were our livelihood. If anything happened, we'd lose the farm. The farm was all that we had; it's what our parents left to us." For a young girl growing up in the suburbs in the sixties, it was difficult for me to comprehend the reality of people running a farm. My parents were teachers. They worked, essentially, with their minds. This was a very different scenario.

"One day, long ago, toward the end of the summer, my sister and I were tending to our chores," Nonno continued. "The day was like any other day; Gelsamina fed the goats and chickens while I worked at the crops that we had planted in the spring. This is what we hoped to sell at the market in town in the weeks to come. It was a bright, clear day, so sunny that the work seemed to go quickly. Soon, with our chores finished, we were on our way to town, where I would buy some fish for the night's meal. Now normally, my sister would not come into town with me—she would stay at home and shell peas or weed the flower patches that we had planted in the front of the house—but this was such a lovely day that she decided to join me on my walk. We held hands, and arms swinging, we joked along the way. She used to make fun of the expression on my face, which for a boy, just seventeen years old, always seemed angry. In Italian, we call this *faccia brute*, a hard face.

"Well, as I remember it, the fish had just been brought in. We made our choice, paid for it, and had it wrapped in leaves and then paper to keep it fresh for our walk home. Now, as nice as the day seemed so far, it became just as dark on the way home. Not dark meaning no light, but dark as if we had a feeling that something was going to happen. We were about halfway home when we heard the crack of a rifle shot, followed by the clopping of galloping horses' hooves and the thumping of men running along with it. No sooner did we look up than we saw the baron and two of his men charge up and cross our path. As they did, he brought his horse to an abrupt halt and looked at Gelsamina, first with the angry eyes of one who hunts and then with the smitten eyes of one who is hunted, although perhaps not for the same purpose. She returned his look with a shy innocence; he froze for a moment and then continued on with his hunt.

"His quarry had been a wolf, a great brown monster with red glowing eyes. I sometimes wonder whose eyes were more frightening, those of the wolf or those of the baron. He tore off down the road, following a set of bloody tracks that were his doing. But it was what happened next that eventually became his undoing."

Perhaps it was because the fire was beginning to die out that our eyes opened as widely as we could get them, feeling a small shiver of cold as we did, but I don't think that it was entirely to compensate for the lack of heat and light. The silence that accompanies anticipation was thick as Nonno turned toward the fire and, with a poker and another log, rekindled it. Fire lit, he reached down to the side of his chair for the wine bottle. After pouring himself a small glass, he sipped and then continued.

"Not thinking much of the incident with the baron, we were both walking on our way back to our little farmhouse when, along the side of the road, we heard some muffled noises, like whining or whimpering. Gelsamina went first, curious at the sounds. Sure enough, behind a mound of rocks were two small wolf cubs. They seemed to be crying for their mother, who was nowhere to be seen. We presumed that it was the great beast the baron was now putting to an end. Thinking only of the animals, Gelsamina adopted them, right there and then. She stretched out the apron that she wore over her skirts and held it like a basket as I placed the two pups delicately inside. She had a crazy idea that because they were so young, they would take to her. She wanted to tame them to be pets and guardians. Girls, I want to tell you something that I hope you will always remember: A thing that is wild must always be wild, and a thing that is tame can never be anything but tame. No matter how hard love makes you want to change, you can't. To change something that nature has made is to go against the power of everything in the world all at once. In the end, you will lose, and the thing that you tried to change will die—sometimes out of confusion, sometimes out of a broken heart, but it will die. Your great-aunt didn't know this, but she was young; we all were. And she raised those two cubs as if they were puppies. In no time at all, they grew. One was a rust red male that she called *Fiero*, for fire; the other was a black female that she named *La Notte*, the night. They had much in common, these two wolves. For one thing, they were big—as big as a mastiff (and remember, they were still young). Also, at sunset, their eyes would reflect the light and glow with the color of blood on fire. Finally, they loved my sister as if they were her children. And in a way, I suppose they were. Members of our family, aunts and uncles from neighboring towns, could all visit because she showed them affection. But no one could ever come anywhere near the house without the wolves standing on either side of her, backs bristling to defend. It was an eerie sight. A sight made worse on the day that the baron crossed our path again.

"We were by the well, getting water for the night's meal, when he trotted his horse over to water it. He saw her and their eyes met as if there had been no time between their last meeting and now. They exchanged pleasantries, and he left. The wolves stood at her side and gave a low growl, staring at his every move until he finally turned and walked away. I had seen him stare down animals before. In fact, there were stories all over the town of his ability to turn a snarling beast into a whining head-bent creature on the strength of his stare alone. But today, Fiero and La Notte returned his withering gaze, as if they sensed something about him that Gelsamina could not see. And they didn't calm down until the baron was completely out of sight.

"That night, after our evening meal, a messenger came to our gate. He was from the baron, informing me that I had been invited to the villa to discuss the sale of some of my crops, and the baron would be pleased if I brought my sister along. He even mentioned her by name."

"Nonno, how did he know her name?" I asked.

"He was Leonardo, Baron D'Arcamo. What he wanted to know, he found out; and what he wanted to own became his. There was no way we could refuse his invitation. He had given the town so much, and now he wanted to have business with us. Even if I had to bring Gelsamina with me, at least I could be there to watch over her."

"But what about the wolves?"

"Well, bringing a wolf to Villa D'Arcamo was like bringing a lamb to slaughter. But he had already seen my sister's pets at the well, and as fierce and protective as they were, she would be their guardian there at the villa. As long as she was a guest of the baron, no harm could come to them. Or so we thought as we made our way the next day to the villa."

Seeing the sleepy expression on my sister's face, Nonno picked up his empty glass and said, "That's enough of our story for tonight, girls. But I promise to tell you the rest before you leave tomorrow." My grandmother got us dressed and into bed, and while my sister was accepting her fate a bit more easily than me, I turned and asked Nana if she ever thought that Nonno missed his sister.

"Oh yes, especially when the moon shines brightly over the fields." I didn't understand what she meant about the moon—why that time would mean more than any other time—but I could appreciate his missing her. I mean, as annoying and bothersome as my sister was, I felt more comfortable when she was around. After all, she was my family. They all were.

We woke the next morning to mixed news. A storm had been crossing the state, and while rain and wind were pelting the farmhouse in sheets, the area where my parents were staying had fared far worse. A storm of hurricane proportions, a Nor'easter, had torn down trees and power lines with ferocity, stranding visitors and tourists in their hotels for at least the next forty-eight hours. At this time, according to the radio reports, there was no telling how many roads were flooded out or blocked. We would have to stay at the house with Nana and Nonno for a few more days, snug and dry with the fireplace and the story of my great-aunt, the baron, and the wolves.

Breakfast completed, my grandmother shepherded us into the kitchen with our plates and had us wash and dry everything. My grandfather, dressed in an old yellow slicker, went out into the rain to inspect the house. He returned some twenty minutes later with his report to Nana: A big branch had come down from the apple tree, and all of the chickens were skittish because of the storm. There would be no eggs that day. But other than that, we seemed to have done all right through the night. Later on in the day, Nonno let us help him feed the pigs and chickens out in the barn. He knew that we were a little bored and were really waiting for our time after dinner by the fireplace.

As he worked in his workshop in the basement, mending some birdhouses, I sat on a stool next to the workbench. "Nonno, what happened to your mother and father?" I asked. Now that the door had been opened, so to speak, I wanted to discover more about my ancestors—my family. I had been trying since last night to put the pieces together.

"I was wondering when you'd get around to asking me that," he answered, anticipating the way my mind was working. "Your great-grandparents had started the farm in Arcamo and were really making it work. My father started teaching me farming when I was about ten. And for the next few years, I couldn't have been happier. During the day, my father and I would work in the fields and with the animals; and at night, after supper, my mother would teach us. She was a very intelligent woman. Because of her, my sister and I learned to read and write. We learned the basic arithmetic that was needed to run the business part of a farm. And if there was time, she would tell us stories."

"Stories?" I asked, wondering if his mother told him stories like the one he was telling us.

"Oh yes, stories. My mother would tell us about ancient Rome and the Roman Empire. Did you know that Rome was founded by two brothers, Romulus and Remus, and they were adopted by a she wolf who fed them and made them strong? Before Rome, there were empires in Greece: Sparta, Troy, and Athens. Each of them brought things to the people that have been handed down to us—roads, accessible water, government, even education … oh, and taxes to pay for them all. She even told us about Garibaldi, who devoted most of his life to uniting Italy. You know, some say, even to this day, that he was responsible for bringing the Kingdom of the Two Sicilies to join the rest of Italy."

"There were two Sicilies?" I chirped. I couldn't imagine a second island called Sicily and thought that he was playing with me.

"No, my little one, there were two kingdoms that were ruled by one king. The two kingdoms were both in Southern Italy. One was the Kingdom of Naples, and the other was the Kingdom of Sicily, but back then, according to a political treaty that dated back over a hundred years, it was called the Kingdom of the Two Sicilies. Well, at any rate, Garibaldi helped bring them both together, and there were people at the time who even wanted him to become the king of the Two Sicilies, but Garibaldi was a patriot, and he openly offered all of the land in both kingdoms to Victor Emmanuel II, who became the first king of a united Italy."

"Wow!" was really all I could say, being fairly impressed with my grandfather's knowledge.

"Yes, my mother was a pretty smart lady. But in the first decade of the new century, everything changed. People began to come down with a disease called influenza. Now we call it 'the flu,' but then it grew to deadly proportions. It became a plague, and it took many people. I can't think of any families that I knew who didn't lose at least one person to it. And sadly, first my mother, my wonderful mother, and then my father fell victim to it. I must have been fifteen when she died and maybe sixteen when he died. My father had taught me many things about farming and would have probably taught me more, but by my sixteenth birthday, what knowledge he had given me (really, they had given to us) was all that I had; Gelsamina, too." He ended his story with a sad sigh—a sigh that spoke volumes about the human spirit's need to continue despite the misfortunes that rise up to crush it. "When my father died, she was just short of her eighteenth birthday, a time when a young woman often thinks about having a boyfriend. In fact, the only difference between then and now was that back around 1910, it wasn't unusual for girls in Sicily to get married at eighteen. But my sister was not like any other girl. She looked at the farm as her responsibility, and while she cared for me, it was more like we were caring for each other. To us, when we looked at the farm or each other, we saw our parents, and we could never let them down. As long as the farm stood, in some small, spiritual way, they lived."

I was filled with a number of emotions. I was glad that Tina was upstairs with Nana, in the kitchen, because I didn't want these moments to be interrupted. This was so much more information about my grandfather and his family than I'd ever heard before. He was opening up a part of his past that I felt as if he'd sealed off from people for a long time. I felt honored that he chose to give this time to me. And I felt sad that now, with the exception of Nana, Mom and Dad, Tina, and me, he really had no one. And when I think about actual full-blood relatives (like brothers or sisters), he had no one at all. I had one more emotion lurking inside. "Nonno, did your mother ever tell you stories about the wolves?" I asked, letting out a little of the anxiety that I had, as I was adding together all the pieces of story that I had accumulated so far.

"You, my little Anna, have my blood in your veins," he said proudly. "You think like a Del Forno. Yes, she told us stories about the wolves, but never to frighten us. To all of us, at that time, the wolves were just a fact of life, like a storm or people you had never met before and really just didn't understand. With wolves, one needs to learn, and having learned, one needs to adapt. Tell me, have you ever seen those monster movies where a man is dressed up with muscles and claws, and fur all over his body, and fangs, and he hops around and growls? Have you ever seen anything like that?"

" Oh yeah, I've seen movies with stuff like that," I responded. "You mean werewolves."

"Exactly. Well, let me tell you, wolves are nothing like that. Wolves are sleek and beautiful, about the size of a German shepherd, you know, the dog, but sometimes smaller. They're loving and protective of their own, and when they hunt, they hunt because they are hungry. The only other time that you'll see a wolf growl or bare his or her teeth is when they feel threatened. You can't even say that about people. In fact, even a house cat will kill something just for sport."

"So you did learn about wolves from your mother?" It sounded as if he was defending them, annoyed at the horrors that they were being portrayed as these days. Up until now, I hadn't even equated the two as one entity, but the way that he spoke made me wonder.

"My mother had seen them, and my father, but the wolves never raided our farm. It goes back to what my mother had taught us: 'You learn, and having learned, you adapt.'"

"How did you adapt?" I interrupted, like my younger sister would have, now becoming hungry to hear more. I was thoroughly immersed in Nonno's story.

Smiling at me, he answered, "Whatever my father put out for the goats, he put out for the wolves, along with whatever meat scraps we had from our last meal. And he wouldn't put it near the house or the sheds. He put this out at the corner of the field nearest the woods. When he passed away, my sister and I continued to feed them. Now, I can't say for certain that he or even we were feeding the wolves, but the food was always eaten, and the wolves never bothered us. In fact, there were times when I would see one or two of them in the hills, and they would see me and just continue on with what they were doing, as if I were just one more member of their society. I remember the first time that this happened, I felt pretty good about myself, as if I had been accepted."

"Nonno, time for supper," came the familiar voice at the top of the stairs. "Come upstairs and wash up. And Anna, bring a pound of macaroni and the big bowl with the flowers on it. You'll find both of them in the pantry."

"Okay, Nana," I replied dutifully, as my grandfather put away his tools and wiped his hands. We climbed the stairs and prepared for the meal that Nana and her new helper, my sister, had made—a simple meal of macaroni and fall vegetables in a light olive oil with onions and minced garlic. The garlic, when browned in oil, tasted almost sweet and had a wonderful effect on the rest of the ingredients. I didn't speak much during the meal, mostly because I wanted to find out what happened to my grandfather, but more so because I wanted to find out what had become of my newly discovered great-aunt and her wolves.

Chapter II
A Request

There were still four or five logs in the log crib next to the fireplace after Nonno built the small fire, and as we settled in, dinner dishes done, he poured his glass of wine and waited as Nana brought in a bowl of fruit, just in the event that we wanted something sweet for dessert. He took a sip and began.

"Now, where was I last night?" he asked.

Tina responded quickly, proud that she had the answer. "You and your sister were invited to visit the baron."

"Well, we went the next day, through the town and past the well to the gates of Villa D'Arcamo. A man waiting there, one of the baron's men, let us in. My work clothes were clean and neat (my sister always saw to that), and Gelsamina was wearing a dark skirt and a peasant blouse with pretty red ribbons laced up and through the front of it. My sister loved red ribbons. She loved to wear them in her dresses and sometimes even in her hair. She had quite a few colors, but her favorite color ribbon was red. Her pets, Fiero and La Notte, who had been trailing behind for most of the walk, had now moved up and were at her side. The man let us in warily, and as we approached the great circular staircase at the front of the villa, he ran ahead to announce us to the baron. He ran up the staircase, opened the great doors, and entered—and by the time we were at the staircase, the baron stood on the upper landing, his hand raised not in a welcoming wave but as if he was beckoning us to approach.

"The house itself was a great rectangular building with smaller rectangular buildings attached at the left and right. At the front, on the ground level, was an enormous set of wood and glass entrance doors, the type that someone would enter for a formal dinner or an elegant reception. But surrounding this door was a twin set of curved stairs made of marble, one to the left of the entrance door and one to the right. The railings of these staircases began and ended with large marble vases filled with ragwort, a flower that looks like the big yellow daises that grow in your grandmother's front yard, and sulla, another golden-color flower that grew wild in Sicily. In between them all were bluebells, another local flower. The yellow and blue colors set against the white of the staircase and the house made it all look very stately, almost regal. The same flowers surrounded the staircases on the ground, making for a grand picture, one I don't think I'll ever forget. But, as I said, the baron wasn't standing at the entrance door that led to the grounds. He stood at a second entrance door, on the upper floor, that opened to the top of the twin staircases. This made the picture even more stirring.

"As we climbed the stairs, I could hear Gelsamina giggle a little, as if she were some type of fairy princess. The wolves stayed at her side, now visibly a bit more tense.

"'You'll forgive me if we speak out here. I have a strict rule about pets,' said the baron as he thanked us for coming. He almost bit off the word *pets*.

"'I understand that you have a strict rule about *wolves*, my lord,' replied my sister, adding a bit more courage to her voice.

"The cordiality faded a little from the baron's expression at hearing this. He was not used to a haughty attitude, especially from one of the townspeople, albeit a pretty one. However, he quickly recovered. 'Come, let us take a walk.' He was after all, the baron, and he deemed it his pleasure for us to climb the stairs, his stairs, and then walk down them again, in conversation with him. Whether it was to remind us to whom we were speaking with after my sister's comment, or just to take more time to talk, I couldn't say. But as he said this, he bid me to walk at his side, and it was clear that his eyes were on Gelsamina. She walked one or two steps ahead of us, giving attention to the floral arrangements as we descended the stairs. Although she wore a simple skirt and blouse, she looked as if she had come down those stairs a hundred times before. The baron was dressed in a chestnut tweed jacket with perfectly tailored matching trousers; a cravat was neatly tucked into his vest. His boots were also of chestnut brown, but of a leather so polished that you could see your face in it. As he spoke, he moved his hands about, and it was then that I could tell his shirt was a pale, handwoven fabric with three-button cuffs. I could also see the gold ring with his family's crest on it. It seemed to me that the baron had more on his mind than merely to engage me on a business affair. I don't recall ever having seen him dressed so impeccably for such an everyday task. But, as you may have guessed, my thoughts were straying, and I needed to listen more carefully now that the baron was speaking to me.

"'I have been told, Signore del Forno, that here in Arcamo your skills as a farmer are becoming quite a topic of conversation, particularly for one of your age. Your father trained you well.'

"'You flatter me, my lord. I am a humble farmer. We have been blessed with good crops this year. I can put food on my table,' I replied respectfully.

"'Good, because putting food on the table is exactly what I wanted to talk to you about. I will be sponsoring a feast here at the villa, and while I have sponsored the feast in town during the day, I will also be hosting a dinner for honored guests in the evening. I would like very much to send my man around to your farm to purchase some of what you have harvested so far. Do you think that you could spare, say, twenty bushels of your freshest produce?'

"'For you, my lord, gladly,' I stammered. 'You honor me with your request.'

"'Good, good. Now Giacamo, ehm, may I call you Giacamo?'

"'Of course, my lord.'

"'Giacamo, I wonder if I could ask you and your lovely sister to attend the dinner that evening as my guests?'

"Although my sister was close enough to hear his request, she pretended to still be concerned with the flowers. I bowed courteously and assured him that we would be glad to attend his feast '... in honor of, umm?'

"'Well, you know, the feast of Saint Andrew of Avellino is not for another few weeks, but I don't think anyone will mind if we celebrate his piety a little sooner. Oh, and Signorina Del Forno,' he coyly added as he turned to my sister, 'I must ask you to leave your pets at home that evening. As the warm sun brings out the faces of the gentle flowers, so too do you bring out the gentle nature in your *little ones*,' he said eloquently, gesturing to Fiero and La Notte, who had now returned to her side. 'But I fear that we may have some guests who have an aversion to the flowers that your sunlight beams down on.'

"The baron was playing a game with my sister, and by her actions, she had accepted the challenge. At the time, I really wasn't sure what the stakes of the game were, but we were young, and neither Gelsamina nor I had ever really experienced love, especially as the game that courtship can sometimes be. I realize now that the baron was falling in love with my sister, and I think that she liked him, too."

"Nonno, who is Saint Andrew Av … Av …" asked Tina.

"Saint Andrew Avellino is the patron saint of Sicily," answered Nonno.

"Naples, too," interrupted my grandmother.

The mock competition between my grandfather's beloved Sicily and my grandmother's Naples was often the topic of dinner-table discussion among the adults. Whenever the extended family got together and a conversation that held more than one opinion ensued, the final comment from my grandfather was usually something to the effect of, "Well, what do you expect? That's what they do in Naples!" In truth, I think that my grandparents adored each other, and whatever ancient tribal differences existed generations before had virtually vanished at our family level here in America.

Nonno continued, undaunted. "Anyway, he performed miracles during his lifetime and even after he died. When he was a very young priest, he was sent to a house where people sinned all the time, doing as many bad things as you can think of, and he changed it into a convent." In later years, it always struck me as interesting that my grandfather took great pains, for our benefit, to describe a brothel without actually saying the word *brothel* or even including the concept of intimacy for pay. My sister and I spent a great deal of time concocting all sorts of evil and malicious doings, without ever considering a house of ill repute. We wouldn't have understood it at the time, but in his story, to the two of us, it all made sense.

"They say that when he died, the people in the town where he lived came to see him one last time and were allowed to touch him for a blessing. From far and wide, people came to touch him before he was buried, and each one who touched him, upon looking at their hands, saw blood, although there was no blood on his body. To this day, they say that the blood of Saint Andrew Avellino causes great things to happen," Nonno stated proudly.

"Like what?" asked my sister.

"For that, we'll have to wait until tomorrow, because it's late and you two need to get your rest." And with that, he took a final sip from his glass, and the magic of the fire and the night dissipated until tomorrow.

The weather the next day was quite a bit better. We came to the breakfast table to find my grandmother speaking on the telephone to my parents. They might be able to come and collect us by that evening, but more probably by tomorrow. Although we missed seeing our parents, we really wanted to hear the rest of Nonno's story. This was actually the first time that we realized a deeper side to my grandfather than we were ever allowed to see before, and I must say we treasured it.

That afternoon, around the kitchen table, my sister and I asked if we could continue the story then. To our surprise, he consented, but before he could continue the story, he look at Nana, and with her silent approval, returned his attention to us. "Did I ever tell you what happened to the baron's parents? Or why he grew up at the villa with his relatives?"

"You said that they were killed by a pack of wolves," I replied, "and he was raised by his uncle."

"Exactly—but what I didn't tell you was that when his parents were killed, he was with them. The legend in Arcamo says that the baron, as a young boy, suffered from very bad dreams. These nightmares caused him to remain awake through most of the night, only sleeping in short fitful naps out of sheer exhaustion. After a while, he became sickly, and in those days, one of the first people parents went to see would have been the local priest. They had just gone to the church in town, where there was a priest who had been to the shrine of Saint Andrew Avellino, and who had been rumored to be able to pray for Saint Andrew's help in curing illnesses. The priest put his hands on the young boy's head and then his heart, and as the story goes, when the priest removed his hands, there, in the center of each palm, was a spot of blood."

"Did his hands hurt?"

"I don't think they did, Tina. In fact, as the family was walking back from the church—they had sent the coach on ahead because it was such a beautiful day—they were in such good spirits, what with the young boy having received such a blessing, that they took no notice of the fact that the day was coming to a close. As they reached a particularly isolated part of their journey, they were attacked by a pack of wolves. For some reason that no one can explain, both the mother and the father were taken by the wolves, but the young boy remained untouched. Frightened, he ran from the site, but stopped some steps away. Something caused him to turn and look at the scene he'd just run from. It was then that the second strange thing happened. The wolves and his parents were gone, vanished back into the hills and woods around the road."

My grandfather stopped here, just long enough to register the looks of surprise on our faces, before continuing. "Now, there was yet another legend that had its start around this time, and you have to keep in mind that legends are built from stories that are added to in the same way that a group of people help in the building of a house. Different people each add bricks and stones, and sometimes in their own way. But the one thing that I can tell you for certain is that every legend is built from a foundation of truth.

"The legend that I want to tell you about has to do with what happened that day long ago. For years, there had been talk among the people of Sicily that the wolves living in the wilder parts of the countryside, realizing that their numbers were dwindling, had appealed to the darker spirits of the earth for help. I can't say how it happened, because I really don't know, but I have heard that in the town of Arcamo, they say that when a wolf is killed, the remaining members of the pack can attack a victim in such a way as to mix their blood with that of the victim, and in doing so, make the individual who was hunted a member of the pack of hunters."

Seeing the incredulous looks on our faces, he restated his point. "They 'die' to being a person, but live on as a sort of wolf. In Italian, we call it *figli del lupo*, the 'children of the wolf.' Now as I said, this was just a legend, but it wasn't long after that, that relatives came to the villa to help raise the boy, now the young baron D'Arcamo, and also to protect him when in the evenings, especially during a full moon, he heard the wolves howling. Some say it was *l'anelito*, 'the longing'—his parents were calling him, some say to save them, some say to join them. Who can tell? But when he was old enough to hunt, he began. That is why he would stare down his quarry before shooting the animal. He had to know if this one was one of his parents. And until he found them, he would kill more and more wolves."

"But Nonno, what if he found them?" I asked, wondering if his parents had really been killed.

"Anna, that is the big question. Would he kill them? Would they kill him? Would he become one of them? Could he? Sometimes, we get a question that is so full of possibilities that, when we finally get the answer for it, we find that it has sprouted five more questions." He turned and looked at my grandmother, who had not sat down with us. She was busying herself around the kitchen, half listening and half, perhaps, not wanting to listen to this part of the story.

"Nana, come and sit with us. Looking at you helps me to remember."

"Soon," she replied, "but not now. I still have some things to do. All my helpers are busy right now, sitting with their *nonno*, so I have to do all the work alone." We knew by the manner in which she spoke that her gentle jibe wasn't really true. It seemed to me that her remark was masking something else. Perhaps she knew what would come next in the story and didn't want to hear it.

Chapter III
The Banquet

"The next two weeks passed very quickly. The baron's men had come to our farm to collect the bushels of eggplant, tomatoes, artichoke, and zucchini, and paid us handsomely for them. Because the baron had purchased so much produce from our farm, my sister and I didn't have to set up a table for the feast. Now this was a rare occurrence, because on the days of a feast each of the local merchants and farmers set out a table or a booth to sell things to people who attended. Butchers might set up a booth where they cook and sell their sausages, usually on a half loaf of bread with locally grown peppers. A local artist or one of his students might come and set up a table where he would make a chalk portrait of you for a small price. Another booth might sell candy for children. I can still remember one time, years before this, when my father bought us *torrone*, which is a hard candy made from nougat and almonds. It was as hard as a rock but as sweet as honey. In fact, I think that it was made with honey. At any rate, the booths were all decorated with bright ribbons or cloths, the most decorated ones being closest to the church.

"On the third day, usually the last day, twenty of the strongest, most trusted men in the town were chosen to go into the church and carry out the statue of Saint Andrew Avellino on a special wooden stand that they rested on their shoulders. This was called a *giglio*, and it was a very impressive and festive sight to see. People lined the streets as the *giglio* was carried around the town square and then set down on a special platform built to fit the stand that the men carried it on. After it was set down, some ladies decorated the platform with flowers and ribbons. People stood in front of the statue and, after saying a little prayer, offered a donation to the church in honor of Saint Andrew Avellino. Sometimes they would even pray to ask for him to intercede on their behalf."

"Nonno, what does that word mean, *intercede?*" Tina asked, getting back into the story.

"When you pray to a saint," Nonno began, "he or she will carry that prayer to God for you, sort of like having a good friend who knows the boss and will ask the boss to help you out. People in Arcamo would pray to Saint Andrew because he was their patron saint. He was the one who looked after Sicily."

"Wow," gushed Tina. You could see the wheels turning as she formulated her next question for my grandfather. "You mean saints get assignments?"

"Oh yes," came the answer. "Sometimes two or three assignments. Saint Andrew was in charge of Sicily and Naples … and a death that comes suddenly." As he said this, my grandfather turned from us again and looked in the direction of my grandmother. He then took the wine bottle that was always on the sideboard table just within reach and poured himself a small glass. After clearing his throat, he sipped. His eyes moistened a little, but I don't think that the wine had much to do with it. In fact, as I think of it, he was probably using the wine to hide his feelings. It was as if he was swallowing a great sadness along with the wine. And when it would come up again, he'd take another sip.

He turned back to us, smiled that sad smile, and continued on with his story. "Word had gotten around in the town that among the people, certain honorees had been invited—the priest from the church, the baron's uncle, Captain Vincenzo Martoni (a local retired naval officer who knew the family before the tragedy), some of the town's merchants and their wives, and finally Gelsamina and me. There were some ten or twelve others, but I can't remember them all. Now you'd think that this would be a wealthy, fancy-dress affair, but I have to tell you, Arcamo was not a wealthy place. The people were hardworking, but whatever we had didn't go to the purchase of fancy clothes. While the retired captain wore his military uniform, the rest of us wore whatever our neatest or special-occasion clothes were. I had a suit and a green tie that I'd worn once to a wedding. Gelsamina wore her special dress, a lovely yellow dress with red ribbons running through the sleeves and the hem. She even had red slippers to match the sash, which, at that time, was considered very daring for a young girl to wear.

"As we were preparing to leave for the banquet, her pets became restless. Fiero wanted very much to go with her, whining and pawing at the front door of the house. La Notte acted differently. She seemed to sense something outside, growling in that low growl that animals give when they fear something but cannot tell yet what it is. Finally, as Gelsamina opened the door, Fiero began yapping and barking wildly until both he and La Notte bolted from the house, running to the field nearby. I certainly had no time to find them and bring them back, so with a few words of reassurance that I would get them upon our return, we left.

"The road to the baron's villa seemed unusually still that evening. No one from the town was on it. In fact, there was no buzz from the insects or calling of birds. It was strangely quiet. And outside of the rising of a full moon, there seemed to be a stillness that sometimes comes with anticipation. The only sound that could be heard was the soft crunch of our shoes on the dirt road beneath our feet.

"As we approached Villa D'Arcamo, we could see lanterns glowing brightly at the entrance and all along the walk to the great house, even though the sun was still settling down behind the hills. It gave the old house an air of fantasy and wonder, as we could see the baron's servants welcoming guests amid the flickering flames of ornate wrought-iron candelabras. By the time we entered the grounds, the lights seemed to form an oasis for us, making us feel safe and secure within a vast expanse of growing darkness.

"Finally, when all the guests had arrived, had their wraps and cloaks taken, and been offered refreshments, the baron made his entrance. He was announced by one of his men and descended the inside stairway from his private rooms on the second floor. It has always struck me how some people, even in the simplest clothing, can appear to be elegant. The baron, dressed in a simple dark-blue vested suit, showed the grace of not wanting to lord his wealth over his guests, but in doing so, appeared all the more noble.

"The banquet was a lovely affair. The merchants, all of whom I knew, made little jokes and polite conversation, all pretending to be in a class of people that we really only sell our wares to, but doing so in a sincere and pleasant manner. As we stood and chatted, first about the weather, then about business, and finally about the generosity of the baron in hosting the day and night festivities, it became more and more obvious that, even from across the room, the baron's attention was drawn to my sister. It was easy to see that she was the most attractive girl at the banquet, and the way that the flames from the candles played in her eyes made a number of men take notice, especially the baron. Never stepping out of character, he maneuvered in and out of conversations throughout the room until, at last, he was face to face with Gelsamina.

"'My lord, you do me an honor by inviting my brother and me to such a lavish time here in your home,' said my sister with a slight bow of her head.

"'Please, call me Leonardo. My name is not often used these days, but when you say it, signorina, it will sound as if it belongs on your lips,' came his eloquent reply.

"'My lord,' said my sister again, not wanting to appear too forward, 'you flatter me.'

"'Signorina, after dinner, when I am able to steal away, may I walk with you in the garden?'

"'As you wish ... Leonardo,' she answered, hesitating before speaking his name.

"I must admit that I was an overly protective brother, or I would never have strained from halfway across the room, with my back turned, to hear their conversation," said my grandfather with a guilty smile.

"Dinner was announced, and we were escorted into a dining room just off of the reception room. The dining room, like all of the rooms in the villa, had a high ceiling painted in a soft white that allowed for the light from the numerous iron candelabras to play off of the gold-flecked woodwork and trim. I must admit that this was the first thing that caught our attention as we entered. At either end of this room was a fireplace with an opening the size of a man. While the mantle over each was white with gold flecks, above the mantle at the rear of the room was a marble statue of Diana, the Roman goddess of the hunt. She stood defiantly on a stone, bow in hand, with a quiver of arrows on her back. The rendering of Diana was so beautiful that, although it was marble, the gown she wore appeared to almost flow in a nonexistent breeze. She looked out over the room to the other mantle, above which hung the baron's crest. In this size I could now see that the banners encircling it held the family motto, 'Consentitemi di Vita e Morte Il Danza, Faccia a Faccia e Braccio in Braccio,' which translated from the Italian is 'Let Life and Death Dance On, Face to Face and Arm in Arm.' You know, I still feel uncomfortable when I think of that motto.

"High-backed chairs, tufted with red velvet cushions, surrounded an enormous table of some dark, hard wood that glistened at the legs. The legs of the table were really all I could see of it. A fine linen tablecloth had been laid out. On it were plates and silver the likes of which I had never seen before—simple, not ornate, but of a quality that didn't exist among even the most prosperous merchants seated at the table. The goblets were of a heavy crystal, like the two goblets that your grandmother has in her china closet. We were all seated, and servants, dressed in clean dark coats, began serving us a light soup made of chicken stock and carrots.

"As we dined, I leaned over to Gelsamina, who was seated beside me, and I whispered, 'I hope that you know what you are letting yourself in for. The baron is 'The *Baron*' and he can be a dangerous man.'

"'Something about his manner, his eyes ... ' she answered. 'I can't really explain it, but they remind me of Fiero.'

"'The same Fiero who he wants to kill, along with La Notte,' I added.

"'Giacamo, don't worry so. As long as I live, my pets are safe, and I think that the baron would very much like me to remain alive,' she countered with the smile of a girl falling in love.

"When we had finished our first course, the bowls were removed. Great platters of hen and roasted veal were then brought out, presented with my vegetables, served roasted or sautéed in olive oil. Cheeses from some of the local farms in the region were added—a great wheel of salty Maiorchino, a hard cheese of sheep and goat milk rumored to have been rolled all the way from Messina by the baron's men, and a fifteen pound step, err, a big block of golden yellow Ragusano cheese (this was known as the king of Sicilian cheeses). Olives from nearby groves were set out with the cheese, bright greens and darker brownish blacks, tangy from brine and oil. The table overflowed with wonderful sights and smells, all from the merchants and farmers from around the region that our town was a part of, and all under the watchful eye of our host and benefactor, Baron D'Arcamo. And we were just beginning to be served! It was truly a feast, so much so that for a short time, my sister and I forget our concerns and enjoyed the party.

"When our meal had ended, we were invited to repair to adjoining rooms for *aperitivi* and coffee, the ladies to one room next to the great room and the men to the reception salon itself. There we were offered a fine smooth grappa and espresso, dark and rich, in little cups called *demitasse*, also like the ones that Nana has in her china closet." We looked at her proudly. Throughout most of the telling of the story, she stood by or sat with us all quietly, not adding too much, mostly looking at the expressions on my grandfather's face, knowing more about his feelings than either Tina or I did. And it was nice to hear her included, especially when Nonno spoke of the fine things at the baron's villa.

"While we were talking and drinking," Nonno continued, "I took note of two things: First, I noticed that the baron was no longer in the room with the men. I had to presume that he and Gelsamina were taking that walk in the garden. And second, I heard the baying of wolves. One minute, there was the happy, noisy bravado of talk in the salon, and the next, the howling—*l'anelito*—that drew a hushed silence from us all. Before long, the baron returned, seeming a bit out of sorts, but then reacquiring his dignified cordial personality, engaging his guests in conversation as he poured liberally from a decanter of grappa. It's a congenial sign when the host himself pours you a glass instead of having his servant do so. And yet, I remembered the look on his face when he returned. As the night drew to a close, and he bid his guests farewell, the baron took my sister's hand and kissed it, saying that he hoped he might be allowed to call upon her in the future, as he found her conversation very enjoyable. At first I thought that there was nothing much to the words between the baron and my sister, merely a warm bidding of the evening and some pleasantries, but that look led me to believe that there was something unfinished between them. Not wanting to see us have to make the journey home in darkness, the baron offered the services of his coach. As we rode back, Gelsamina seemed in bright spirits. When I asked her about this and their parting words, she answered coyly, 'Make nothing of it, we walked in the garden and spoke of this and that.'

"'Didn't you hear the wolves baying in the night?'

"'Of course I did; they were mine.'

"'Fiero and La Notte?'

"'I have no others.'

"'But we left them home … '

"'They love me and will always protect me. They were there in the garden, watching our every step.'

"'But how?'

"'I don't know; I don't need to. It just seems that every time I'm near Leonardo, they appear.'

"'Leonardo?' I asked. This was the second time his first name was used, and I have to admit, it did seem a bit too forward and fast moving for my taste.

"'Leonardo. The baron wishes me to call him Leonardo.' My sister was putting less emphasis on the presence of her pets and far more on the chance of a budding relationship with the baron. When we arrived back at our little farm, it was late, but Fiero and La Notte met us outside in the small front yard, as if nothing had happened and they were two playful pups.

"Some few days later, when things had returned to the normal work and chores of the farm, a messenger came from the baron's villa. The envelope that he delivered bore, in its wax seal, the crest that I had seen over the mantle. In a beautifully handwritten letter, the baron asked for my permission, as Gelsamina's brother, to call upon her and offer a ride in his carriage on the next day. One sidelong withering look from my sister was enough for me to make a decision. 'Please let the baron know that my permission is given, and he may call upon my sister,' I announced in as formal a tone as I could muster at the moment. My reply was formal because, you see, in those days, permission was asked for and given between the men of the families on behalf of the women, and even though my sister was older than me, the rules of courtship had to be followed."

"I think they're silly," said Tina.

"By the way that we think today," Nonno responded, "those rules are different, but one of the main reasons that they were done was to show everyone in the town that the woman in question, in this case my sister, was a woman of honor." Again, as I think of this story, I'm reminded of how careful my grandfather was to keep words like *virginity* away from us and out of the story.

"The following day, some time after noon, a black carriage drawn by a single horse came trundling down from the direction of the villa, on the road through the town. The driver was one of the baron's men; I had seen his face before, most recently at the banquet. He got down from the carriage and opened the door, from which the baron stepped out. Smartly dressed as always, he walked up to the door of our farmhouse and knocked at the door, just like any other young man from Arcamo. Being inside and watching this, I was a bit surprised and a little pleased to see him treating the situation with the respect of a local and avoiding the privilege of nobility for once. Gelsamina had risen early that day in order to complete her chores and still have enough time to primp and prepare for her afternoon. She wore her yellow dress with the red ribbons laced across the front of the corset that, while it appeared simple enough, suggested her attractive figure. As he was let in and set eyes on her, it was clear to see that the effect was not lost. Although gallant in gesture, he seemed a bit tongue-tied, as he presented her with a single flower, one similar to those in his garden. He then escorted her to the carriage, and with a few short words to the driver, they were off.

"Now you may be wondering where my sister's wolves were during that time the baron was at our home, and he and Gelsamina went on their ride. Well, I must tell you, they were nowhere to be found. It was a concern of mine that morning, but as the moment arrived, they had completely slipped my mind. In fact, nothing was said of them until after Gelsamina returned from her drive with the baron some hours later. They sat at the back door of the house as if they were waiting for her. She came into the house clutching the flower and looking sad. Not wanting to be too far away when she returned, I had busied myself with some little work inside the house. She entered and took a chair in the front room. There, looking forlorn, she talked about the story of his life, of losing his parents and hating the wolves that he blamed for their deaths. She then rose and walked out to the back of the house, where she knelt down and hugged her pets. She whispered to them that no one, *NO-ONE* would ever hurt them while she lived. They whined a little, almost in sympathy for her feelings, and licked her face. She then stood and came back into the house, turning to me and saying, 'The baron will not be calling on us anymore.' Her voice was firm but with a twinge of sadness.

"'What happened?' I asked her, having noticed the change in her voice.

"'Sometime during our ride,' she began, 'the driver stopped, came to the door of the carriage, and informed the baron in a discreet tone that there was a wolf following us from within the woods across the road. The baron ordered him to drive on. As we went out into the open spaces of the hills, from time to time I looked out the window and saw not one but a pack of wolves following the carriage, staying as hidden as they could behind rocks or ridges, and always staying a distance away. Once, when one got too close to the carriage, the driver slowed, and almost as if he had rehearsed the moment, the baron reached down to a box stored at his feet, retrieved a pistol, cocked it, and aimed at the wolf. If I hadn't jolted him, he would have killed it.'

"'Gelsamina, you know of his hatred. Why did you ruin the shot?'

"'I thought of my pets, and I remembered how he had killed their mother. I could never love a man with a heart like his. In a heart so filled with hate, there could be no room for love.' And with that, she went to her room and stayed there until the next morning. From time to time, throughout the night, the sound of sobbing could be heard through the door to my sister's room.

"A few days later, on my travels into town to sell crops, the market was noisy with talk of a renewed hunting of wolves. The baron had posted an announcement in the town square saying that he would host a contest for all of the hunters in Arcamo. Declaring the wolves to be a plague that destroyed our livestock, frightened our women and children, and ruined the quality of our lives, he would hold a competition in two weeks to see who could hunt and kill the most wolves, the prize being a hunter's cup filled with silver coins given by the baron himself. All participants must sign their names on a scroll at the baron's villa by sunset the next day. The contest would run for three days and nights, and wolves could be hunted anywhere from the sea at the north to the hills at the south. Of course, the first name on the scroll, written in big bold letters, belonged to the baron himself. My sister, at hearing of all this, grew crazy with anger. She felt that he did this purely to punish her for saving the wolf. She tried her best to keep Fiero and La Notte in a backyard shed, or in the house or anywhere that she could keep them safe and fed. But by the last day they had become skittish and pacing, anxious to be out and free, even if it meant danger. When she came into the shed to see if they had food and water, they leapt for the door.

"'It was as if,' she said later, 'they were waiting for me to open the door, just so they could escape.' They ran for the woods and hills, in the general direction of the town, but it could have been in any direction really, as the villa lay beyond the town in that area. Throughout the day, and at the start of the evening, there was an occasional bark of a rifle, and the pungent smell of the gun smoke that was thick in the air, but no sign of her pets.

"As it grew dark, the fear and tension became unbearable for my sister. She left the house wearing a cloak, with a hood to protect her from the night air. I asked her where she was going. 'Out,' she replied, 'to save my pets … or the baron.'

"I never saw my sister again. There had been talk from people that we knew in town that she had been seen that night, walking on the outskirts of town near the hills, looking for Fiero and La Notte. Within a few days, the talk grew to say that she looks for them still. But a few others say that a strange thing happened that night. I heard from people who lived nearby that the baron and his men had gone off into the hills north of the villa, and they came upon Fiero and La Notte, now easily recognizable to the baron, his anger of them being as strong as it was. But with them was another wolf, a young adult female with white fur and eyes the color of Gelsamina's. The three of them looked at the baron—Fiero and La Notte standing shoulder-to-shoulder, fur bristling and eyes aflame, in the low growl of defense that wolves are known for. The third wolf stood back behind them, resilient, almost defiant to the impending danger that would mean their end. The baron's man handed him his rifle, fully loaded and kept as a spare in the event of a misfire. Baron D'Arcamo stared at them and then the single wolf beyond them, hoping not to see what he feared he would. As the story goes, he raised his rifle and took aim, his eyes fastened, his hands a little damp, and one could see a shaking in both of them as he stared down the rifle barrel at his target. After what seemed like an eternity, he cocked the hammer back, held his breath, and then lifted it to the stars and fired. Fiero and

La Notte fled and were soon followed by the third, but not before it slowly trotted up to him, bowed its head, turned, and joined them.

"I searched for signs of my sister for days and nights on end until finally, many months later, at the urging of a priest at the church, a regional magistrate from Palermo had her declared dead. I wanted to believe that she had run off, as no one ever found a body or even a remnant of her clothing. The only reason that I even mention the unbelievable story that I told you was that for the next two years before I came to America and met your grandmother, from time to time, in my sadness, I would take a small ribbon from the beautiful dress that my sister would wear and lay it outside at the back door where her pets, when they lived here, would rest. And from time to time, they would appear, coming at sunset from the hills nearby. Upon seeing them, I would kneel down and they would come up to me, licking me and playing as if no time had passed since that night. But they would never touch the ribbon. And yet, the following morning, the ribbon would be gone. At first, I thought that it might have been birds, looking to line a nest, so I stayed up one night, all through the night, looking to see who or what might take the ribbon. Then sometime after midnight it happened. A wolf—long, sleek, and white-furred—approached the ribbon that I had laid outside on the spot near the door of the house. It looked to be a female, smaller and with less muscle bulk than a male. As it approached, I watched silently. In its eyes, I saw my beloved sister. I softly whispered 'Gelsamina' as the wolf looked up at me, knelt before the ribbon, and gently took it in its mouth. It rose, turned, and retreated back into the darkness.

"No one from the town saw much of the baron from that point on. I read in a letter from some old friends that he had become a recluse, never leaving the villa. The letter also said that he had given up the hunt, choosing instead to leave table scraps outside of the gates of his property at dusk. One of his men told a story of how he would sit alone, up in his bedchamber throughout most of the night, waiting to hear the baying of the wolves, hoping to see them. But he never did. One evening, some few years later, he put on his shoes and clothing and, opening the gates to the villa, took a walk, not toward the town, but instead out into the hills where no one lived. They found him the next day, near a thicket of trees, dead—his body covered with bite marks, presumably from a pack of animals, probably wolves. The strangest part to the story is that in his hand, which was the only part of his lifeless body that was untouched, was a single red ribbon."

There are times when a person gets so caught up in a story that the little everyday things that take place during the telling of the story become invisible. I hadn't noticed the tears in my grandfather's eyes before this, so I couldn't say when they first appeared, but I realize now why the retelling of the story, however fantastic, made him weep. Only something as oddly unrealistic as this could have been kept locked up inside such a stoic heart as his. The ringing of a telephone broke the sad enchantment of the moment. It was my parents, telling us that power had been restored sometime early in the morning and they were already on the road. They'd be there within the next two hours to pick us up. For the rest of the afternoon and into the evening, my sister and I were quiet, not really knowing what to say. But when it was time to go, something happened that I don't think I'll ever forget. My grandfather hugged me with more emotion than I ever remember. Then he pressed something into my hand as we left. I put it into my pocket, and once in the car, away from my grandparents' house, I took it out and examined it. It was a small red ribbon.

A Note to the Reader

Throughout Europe, especially on the mainland, there were once great populations of wolves. Hunting alone, but more often in packs, they were the stuff of legend for centuries. Although they were carnivorous, they were survivors, and as such could subsist if need be on many combinations of things. Eventually, though, they had to return to a carnivore's diet; at some point, a kill for meat was needed. However, with the increase in the human population and the urbanization of more and more territory, wolves were gradually hunted down from their once great numbers. This, coupled with new and more virulent diseases, left much of Europe, especially the island regions of England, Greece, Sicily, and Corsica, largely free of the animal that was once a main character in many children's stories and folktales. Before the start of the twentieth century, when such stories still filled the human mind, imagination filled in the gaps that science had not yet claimed. And yet, when one sees an old photograph or hears an animal howl during an evening with a brightly lit moon, one cannot help but let the imagination loose once more.

Chapter IV
The Red Ribbon

Fifteen years passed. My life was eventful enough to push my recollection of the story into the background, where it probably would have stayed, had it not been for the turn of events that next took place. My grandparents had both passed—first Nana in the early seventies and then Nonno at the start of the next decade. He had spent his last years largely alone, save the occasional visit from one of us. Mostly because of his age and loneliness, the farm fell into a state of disrepair to the point where, after his death, the one aunt from my grandmother's side of the family took residence, surveyed the work required, and gave up all intentions of renovating in the span of two months. What little livestock Nonno owned had been sold long ago, and the unplowed fields yielded only random plants left over from seeds of crops sown in previous years, now intertwined with thick green and brown thatches of weeds.

Upon their retirement from teaching, my parents had moved to Ocala, Florida. It had been a dream of theirs ever since they first visited the place on their honeymoon. And Tina was working for one of the big hotels in San Antonio, Texas, where she had married and was starting a family. I was busy trying to keep my job with a small publishing company in New York City and not having much success at it. So when the time came and I was let go, I didn't have much in the way of options. With the skills and degree that I had, I applied for and got a job in Binghamton, New York, with the State University, some twenty miles north of my grandparents' place. The pay was quite a bit lower, but the job still had benefits, and after speaking to my father and getting permission to stay there for a while, I took up residence at the old farmhouse, promising to make repairs and keep the place up in return for my stay. If the job panned out, I'd try to either buy it from the family or at least help in its sale. That was the least I could do. The house itself was not a big farmhouse, although it sat on five acres of land. It had, just as I remembered, a shed and a small barn on the property, and except for the two-and-a-half acres set aside for field crops, the rest of the property was untouched woodland. As it was posted, no one hunted on it, so life at the farmhouse was peaceful to say the least.

Most of my grandparents' furniture was still there at the house, with the exception of an occasional end table or lamp that an aunt or a cousin had remembered and asked for. There were beds and dressers in all three of the bedrooms. Being the sole resident, I slept in the master bedroom. And there across the hall, in one of the smaller bedrooms, hanging on the wall over a Majestic floor-model radio, was the portrait. The face of my great-aunt in that portrait that had been etched into my mind some fifteen years ago looked out at me as if I had just bumped into an old friend—or more accurately, an old relative.

All things considered, the house was dusty and unlived in, but it was still sound and the roof didn't leak. The kitchen still had a few remaining tools in the drawers, certainly enough for me to make my meals with, and the kitchen table and chairs were still there and still intact, albeit a little older and a bit more creaky.

My job was at one of the colleges at the University. I would be in charge of all publications both on campus and for mailings to prospective students, and with a staff of three full-time workers and a dozen student interns, I soon found myself ensconced in a world that I was well accustomed to. Deadlines were met, supervisors were pleased, and both my workers and my student interns were happy working for me. My first few months progressed without a hitch.

My evenings were quiet, usually spent fiddling with some minor decorating or repair to the farmhouse. I cleaned, repainted, and refurbished the kitchen. I'd always been told that the first room that needs to be worked on is the kitchen, and the second room is the bedroom, because one will always need to eat and sleep. Not seeing too much that needed doing in the master bedroom, I skipped over it.

That is not completely true. It would be more accurate to say that in memory of my grandparents, I chose not to change the room from what I remembered it to be. To be honest, it took me a few nights to get up the courage to even claim it to sleep in, but it was the biggest bedroom. I also stand corrected with another room. Depending upon how one looks at it, the bathroom also takes a place of importance in the list of rooms to refurbish. Fortunately, the plumbing and fixtures, old as they were, still worked well enough to be serviceable.

I then turned my attention to the living room, painting it and having the fireplace cleaned. I can recall the odd feeling the first time that fall when I built a small fire in it. It was mid-October, and a real chill had set in. I built the fire and, between its warmth and the smell of the burning wood, old feelings from the past were also rekindled. The next time I stopped in town, I bought a bottle of inexpensive red wine specifically to be enjoyed with my evening in front of that fireplace. But between deadlines at work and repairs to the farmhouse, it wasn't until about two weeks later that I actually got to build that next fire and then open the bottle of wine and a good book. It was one of those moments that a person feels, now and then in their lives, when they can breathe a sigh of contentment, having accomplished some goal and rewarded themselves with a brief respite before taking on the next set of tasks they are presented with.

That was when I heard it. Having had some experience on the farm, both now and in the past, I was used to the quiet sounds of wildlife out in the woods nearby, but this was a new sound. This was the baying of an animal like a hound or maybe a wolf. There was, coincidently, a full moon in the sky that night. I believe that it was referred to as "the hunter's moon," but I just saw it as a fairly romantic thing of beauty, having noticed it rising on my way home.

Since my move from New York City to the farmhouse, I really hadn't had much time to think about a relationship. I'd had a series of minor flirtations in the past, all ending in a similar fashion, with one of us saying something like "It's not you, it's me"—that being the most recent catch phrase to end things in a less hurtful manner. But in the end, the result was still the same: bittersweet, a little sad, and ultimately, moving on. The sight of the full moon pushed my thoughts into that seldom tread-upon direction, but all thought dissipated with the baying sound.

I really didn't know what to make of it. It caught me off guard, and as a result, I was a bit unnerved when, in the morning, on my way out the front door, I stepped across what appeared to be a scrap of red ribbon, laid just at the threshold. I knelt and picked it up, and it became the focal point of my drive to work. Normally, this drive would be an uneventful experience—mostly highway, a few left-hand turns, one right, and then the staff parking lot—but I suppose that I was so engrossed in thought that I almost caused an accident, first coming off of the highway, where I didn't stop at a crossing and almost hit a school bus, and then again in the parking lot itself, where not noticing two people exiting from a car, I almost hit them. Jamming my foot onto the brakes in both instances and apologizing profusely, I meekly made my way into the office and began my workday. I didn't think much about it during the day, and it wasn't until dinner that evening when I reached into my handbag for something and inadvertently picked up the ribbon again.

I began to remember the story, bit by bit this time, alone in the house. The details came back, at first slowly, then in groups as if one memory spurred another and then two more until I was even remembering the words that my grandfather spoke in Italian. The first being *l'anelito*, when he talked about the baying of the wolves and their longing. I wondered if this was the type of howling he'd heard those many years ago. In all honesty, the events of the previous evening and this morning could very well have been a series of interesting coincidences, sparked by a fire, a full moon, a single woman, and a bottle of wine (that I must admit, came close to being emptied). The thought gave me some comfort during the remainder of my dinner, and for a good deal of the evening up until the time when I prepared for bed. It was well after eleven o'clock, and I was thinking about the work that would be needed for the next day's meeting at the college when I heard it again—the baying. It seemed more clear this time. I couldn't really say if it was closer or not, but it seemed to be more clear, as if it was calling out to me. The moon was still fairly full and the sound continued for a good fifteen to twenty minutes. I tried to listen as carefully as I could. Not too close to the house, but it might have been coming from somewhere near the barn. My sleep that evening was fitful at best.

I awoke the next morning determined to think clearly. Nothing had physically bothered me, the farmhouse was still intact, I had a reasonably good job with decent benefits, and the morning sun has a tendency to strengthen one's convictions. So it was with a renewed sense of resolve that I dressed, breakfasted, and left the house for work … only to find, lying in the driveway that stands halfway between the house and the barn, another scrap of red ribbon, clean, neat, and very much like the one found previously.

There are many trees on the property. Varieties of oak, maple, the occasional stand of pine and cedar, not to mention the half dozen apple trees that Nonno had planted decades ago just beyond the barn, in a line bordering the north end of the fields. In the spring and summer, the woods were filled with the sounds of birds nesting in those trees. Everything from the smallest sparrow to robins and blue jays, some cardinals in the pines, and I think I saw a hawk's nest in one of the really tall oaks at the edge of the woods. Between them and the owls that I heard from time to time in the evenings, I would imagine that the nests were built from hundreds of scraps of whatever the respective birds could find, both here and on neighboring properties. These thoughts were running through my mind on that second day as I drove to work. Mercifully, no one was endangered by my mental exercises to regain control on this day. In fact, just like the day before, my work took center stage, running well and without incident.

The next few nights passed by without event, and later in the week, I even took some time to stop by one of the University libraries to check on something I'd been mulling over at the time. I remembered hearing somewhere about how certain agencies and organizations kept track of the migratory movements of wildlife—herds of deer, flocks of different types of birds, that sort of thing. And it made me wonder if any such research had been done on the wolf in central New York. The library had several studies and reports, mostly printed in the seventies, on the success of bringing back wolf populations in the northern Great Lakes area, and of the continued presence of the gray wolf in Ontario and Quebec, but there was no mention of any pack presence in central New York, or any other part of New York for that matter. According to all reports, the wolf in the regions that covered New York and Pennsylvania had been hunted to near extinction by the start of the twentieth century. From time to time, an incident was turned in describing a sighting or the discovery of the remains of a deer that had earmarks similar to those of an attack by a wolf pack, but by and large, such reports were unfounded.

At first this information calmed me. I found it comforting to presume that the sounds I heard at night and the scraps of ribbon were really all just the stuff of a fertile imagination, rejuvenated by my return to the farmhouse. But after a day or so another thought entered my mind. A silly, self-centered, bizarrely romantic thought: what if I was being singled out? It was the same sort of notion that one gets when, as a youth, one finds oneself considering entering an abandoned house with some friends. Realistically, it is a dusty, creaking old building without light, thereby causing any flashlight to cast unique and suggestive shadows.

Yet there remains an aspect to the concept itself that appeals to the one standing, now, at the front door—the possibility of making contact with someone or something from somewhere other than here who, even with the accompanying sense of danger, is there specifically to appeal to that one individual. In short, there was a part of me that almost wanted to believe that I was being sought out. That part of me was touched yet again when, on Saturday, having decided to build a fire in the hearth, open a bottle of wine, and curl up with that book, I heard it again, the howling, the baying, *l'anelito*. But this time, for a reason that I can't really explain, I was not nervous. It actually gave me a sense of being safe—that someone or something knew where I was and was watching over me. I returned to my reading, but found within the hour that I was wondering more about my would-be protector than the story I was reading.

As the fire slowly died out, I finished my last sip of wine and returned to the bedroom, hoping to make yet another discovery of a red ribbon in the morning.

It was probably my thoughts of the evening that accounted for the restlessness of my night, or at least that is what I believed, until I fell off into a tossed and turned half sleep. I remember dreaming that sort of dream where one feels as if one is still awake, but when one tries to move, it is discovered that one is incapable, and as a result is trapped until one actually awakens.

And that is when she appeared: the girl of the chalk portrait, Gelsamina, my great-aunt. In my dream, I was sitting in the easy chair in front of the fireplace. The fire had been rekindled into a small steady blaze. She walked calmly and gracefully out of the kitchen and into the living room, taking the chair next to mine in front of the fire. She wore the dress that I'd remembered from the story, the one that was laced with red ribbon. She seemed young and warm and beautiful, and acted as if she'd known me all of her life. Immediately, I felt that I knew her too. She opened her mouth to speak, but her words were in English, not Italian. At first this unsettled me, but after all, it was a dream, albeit a surprisingly realistic one. Looking at me, she smiled and said, "Hello, my little one. I have been waiting so long to see you."

I tried to speak but couldn't. I tried to move my arms and legs but felt paralyzed. I felt such a deep familial love for her that I began to weep. "I love you too, my little one. I knew that you were my own since the day I first saw you. That feels like so many years ago. Your grandfather, my lovely Giacamo, my *faccia brute*, knew it too. He loved you, Anna. He loves you still. And your nana does too." The tears flowed freely from my eyes. I so wanted to throw my arms around her, to feel her holding me in return. In this dream, I felt as if I were younger, maybe fifteen years old again. I yearned for the comfort I'd felt when I was that age.

"You know, there are times that I can still hear my pets. I imagine that they are calling to me. The old country no longer welcomes them. But here, here there is still so much space for them and their young, and to the north, up in Canada. So much room for *mi figli*. It is like the days long before me." At this memory of some distant vision, her voice quickened with emotion. "I am glad that you have come back, but I knew that someday the world would bring you back to your *nonno*'s house. Now rest, little one, there is still much to do before I see you again." I looked at her, imploring with eyes trying to communicate in the only manner that was left to me.

She read my thoughts as clearly as if I'd spoken them. "Of course you will see me again, but before you do, you must find the key in Nonno's workshop." Again I looked, filled with questions, especially with regard to her last words. "Oh, my dear little one, there is so much to tell, but first, find the key. The key is now yours!"

The next morning when I awoke, the muscles in my arms and back felt sore, as if they'd been restrained for hours. My mind was alert, but I was in desperate need of a good strong cup of coffee. I trudged down to the kitchen, half expecting to see her there, but with each step into the morning sunlight realizing that it was all a dream—an interesting yet melancholy dream.

Coffee brewed, I took the first few sips from a cup and brought it back with me to work on in between the various parts of my morning routine: washing, changing, making up, pouring a second cup, and returning to make up the bed. I stopped as I leaned over to pull the pillows before drawing and smoothing the sheets, as I uncovered yet another red ribbon underneath where the pillows were. This ribbon was very similar to the others except that it had, scrawled in cursive, the word *ricordi*, which translates from the Italian as "to remember." This single item made the time from the previous episodes, right up to the dream, all seem more and more believable. My collection of red ribbons had now grown by one more, all lovingly kept in a small velvet box on the dressing table.

Finishing my task, I returned to the kitchen and had a small breakfast of toast and jam. Coffee mug and toast in hand, I stood at the back door and looked out over the yard and the fields that surrounded it. One could tell that this was once a proud little homestead. The enormity that I remembered as a little girl had been replaced now, in adulthood, with an orderly setting of buildings and grounds enhanced by fruit trees and the occasional shrubbery. The fields beyond, now fallow, once boasted what seemed to me then to be a never-ending bounty of crops, all cared for and tended to by my grandfather. Here, in the yard, on this property, there lived love. Here, in this house, under this roof, there too was love. But here too lived sadness and perhaps mystery, albeit something quite out of the ordinary. To dream of a story told to a fifteen-year-old so long ago, of a girl who disappeared and was rumored to have been taken by wolves, was far-fetched, though in a peculiar way romantic; to think anything further just bordered on the macabre.

She looked just as I imagined she would. She was lovely, and her beauty was the kind that an ungainly teenage girl would have looked up and aspired to. Not that my own mother wasn't attractive, but her beauty was of a different style. Her hair was honey blond and her eyes blue. My father would joke that for an Italian American, she must have been smuggled in by gypsies. Gelsamina was more of a classic Italian beauty. Her dark brown eyes were soulful. They alone could tell stories, evoking deep emotion. Her hair was dark, rich, and lustrous—thick, like the mane of a lion—and her features were like those of a Botticelli painting. She was one of those women who looked as if she had makeup on when, according to my grandfather, she wore none. In my dream, in my imagination, she glowed like fire, delicately flicking fingers of heat into the night with an air of intimacy that was masked by her open charm.

While my grandfather was alive, I can recall visiting him and sitting in his workshop many times, mostly because that had become a special place for us to talk. I'm sure he loved Tina as much as he loved me, but it always seemed like Tina belonged to Nana, always in the kitchen, learning recipes and telling stories. My place was with Nonno, downstairs in the workshop. And for all the times that I was down there, I never remembered seeing a key of any kind. He had drawers filled with tools, handsaws hanging on hooks, shelves of screws and nuts and bolts, but never did I see a key down there. Since it was Sunday, and I had nothing planned for the majority of the day, I resolved to go down to the workshop and hunt around, partly to satisfy my curiosity and partly because I still wasn't sure what to make of all of this. Up until now, the events of the last week or so were harmless; at best, the stuff of a somewhat interesting series of coincidences and maybe just the product of being alone a bit too much. To tell the truth, I still had my doubts. Maybe it was all just me.

I brought the last cup of coffee downstairs with me and sat on Nonno's stool at the workbench. I had come down here only a few times since moving into the house, and then it was just to find a brush or get a screwdriver to pry open a can of paint. But here I was sitting and looking at his world, his sanctuary, the place where he shared his thoughts with me while he made things or fixed them. I looked around. If there was one, there had to be thirty little drawers just at the table alone, filled with small tools and assorted hardware, all neatly assembled in order of accessibility. Surrounding the drawers were an equal number of cubbyholes, some housing boxes filled with screws or washers, some with baby-food jars that had been emptied and cleaned out to fill with other saved or reclaimed bits that he had presumed would be useful at some point in time. My grandfather rarely threw anything away, and for the first time in my life, seeing this workshop with the eyes of an adult, I was seeing where for all those years, everything that he had saved was being stored. The idea of going through everything in this workbench, let alone the rest of the shop, was beginning to look daunting.

I sipped my coffee and began, starting with the lowest drawers and cubbyholes on the left and slowly, methodically, moving to the right. The drawers at the bottom were the deepest and widest. They held saw blades and pipe wrenches, moving on to hammers of various shapes and sizes, then planes, from small box planes on to grander and more elaborate ones. On the next level were pliers and wrenches, then screwdrivers. Finally, the last batch of fifteen held cup hooks and little clamps, toggle bolts, lag bolts, and a variety of screws that I could not name. Throughout all of this, I saw no key.

The coffee had been finished long ago, and I could tell from a nearby basement window that the sun was no longer high and was beginning its descent in the west. I must have been down there searching for most of the day. And there were still stacks of wood and the old freestanding electric saws and sanders to look through. It was it this moment that I realized that I was searching through my grandfather's workshop because I'd been told to in a dream. The more I sat and thought about this, the more ridiculous it seemed. I was a single thirty-year-old woman who, having changed career paths, was trying to make a life in a new place with new people, all on the shoulders of a part of my family that had been gone for years, and now instead of going out and becoming a part of the world that I lived in, I was searching for something that I dreamed was in my past.

I stopped and climbed the stairs back up into the main floor of the house. I turned on a radio just to end the silence and then went into the kitchen to make myself some dinner. A chicken breast pounded flat, dipped in egg and then breadcrumbs, and fried in olive oil in my grandmother's old cast iron skillet made for a nice entrée. I added peas and onions and poured myself a nice glass of a dry red table wine. Its nose reminded me of the red table wine that my grandfather was so fond of, although I must admit I could never remember its name. I ate quietly and watched the sun set over the woods beyond the fields as the radio played some barely memorable pop song. I resolved that, starting Monday, I would make a point of socializing a bit more. It was about time that I did something in that direction.

I took another sip of the wine and finished the last bit of chicken.

It struck me that I had been sipping wine and thinking of Nonno and cooking from the skillet used by Nana. Whether I liked it or not, I was, at this point in my life, inextricably linked to the past. I poured another glass and took it and my book down the hall to the bedroom. Curling up on my bed, I began to read. All things considered, the day had afforded me the opportunity to think about where I was in my life and where I would like to be. Feeling somewhat contented with this progress, I began reading, becoming engrossed in a very short amount of time. Before I knew it, the clock in the bedroom showed ten minutes to twelve. I got up, put on my bedclothes, and reached over to turn out the light. It was only then that I saw her again.

Gelsamina was sitting in the chair near the foot of my bed. Her clothes were the same as in the dream, but this time she looked sad, as if she had been hurt. "Little one, why do you give up on your legacy so easily? The key is yours. My brother saved it for you and you alone. You sleep in the bed of Giacamo Del Forno. You cook with the tools of his wife, your nana. You even think of them as you raise the glass to your lips. What more proof do you need that the key is yours to find? The key is yours, little one." And having spoken, she rose to leave the room, but this time, not before I could speak. I called out "Zia Gelsamina [Aunt Gelsamina], wait! I looked, but I found nothing. How can I live today if memories of yesterday haunt me as they do?"

"Little one, yesterday and today are not as different as you think they are. Find the key. It is the key to your family, your legacy," was her reply. Her words were imploring but firmer than before. Once again, she walked away, but this time into the bedroom where her portrait hung. This time I wasn't dreaming. I followed but when I looked in the room, she was gone

She seemed so real to me, yet fragile, almost ethereal. She wanted me to find a key. I turned on the lights and padded back into the basement, across the floor and into the workshop. I started this time with the lumber piles, turning each plank over, hoping to discover some glint of metal. Having no success, I tried the table saw, checking at all of the metal recesses, even in the box that held the sawdust that the saw blade kicked up. Coming up empty again, I repeated the process with his sanding machine, first the disc sander and then the belt sander, still finding nothing. Some two hours later, long after two in the morning,

I found myself sitting at Nonno's workbench in frustration, staring blankly at the drawers and spaces that I'd searched throughout the day. I slapped the bench, open-handed, in anger at my inability—and in doing so heard the rattle of a spring from the side of the bench.

Unlike all of the loose bits of hardware in all of the drawers and all of the jars in the workbench, this sounded like a spring that was attached to something. I slapped my hand down again and heard the spring sound again. I did it a third time and a fourth and continued until I could isolate the sound. It seemed to be coming from the underside of the workbench, somewhere on the right. And then I found it. On the right side of the workbench, some four inches below the table surface, was what looked like a wide, shallow drawer with no handle. Between specks and splotches of paint, dust, and the aged wood itself, it was easy to miss this secret compartment. I tried pulling on it but to no avail. I tried jiggling and then pulling it down, but it wasn't until I pushed it in that I heard the spring click, recoil, and release the drawer.

In it was a large envelope. My first thought was that I'd succeeded in discovering a secret compartment, but still would find no key. Both the envelope and its contents looked very official. Opening it, I saw a single sheet document and, although it was written in Italian, I guessed that it was of a formal nature because of the thick parchment-like quality of the paper, the red wax seal at the bottom, and the raised gold-leaf key emblazoned at the top of the page. I wondered if this was the key I'd been searching for. As I couldn't read Italian, I could only surmise. I did notice that the wax red seal at the bottom of the page was the crest that my grandfather had described to me in his stories, and the name alongside it read "Leonardo, Baron D'Arcamo" in an elegant script. The date that this had been signed read 30 *Ottobre* 1924.

I was excited. I climbed the stairs quickly, document in hand. In the two rooms that were still lit, I could see from a wall clock that it was now three in the morning. I'd be lucky to get three hours of sleep even if I wasn't this excited. Things had happened quickly and most of them were inexplicable, but they all ended with a factual component, this document. It was as if I was unraveling clues to a mystery. I climbed into bed and lay awake in the darkness, trying to make sense out of the pieces I held. Nonno's story was, I'd believed, just a story, even after he handed me the ribbon. The next ribbon could have been a coincidence, until I got the third ribbon. The chances of them both being a coincidence were too remote, made even more so by the dream. The dream could have been the product of a fertile imagination, a return to the farmhouse and perhaps too much wine. But with the fourth ribbon the next morning? Finally, the events that took place this evening leading to my discovery of this document.

Some people believe only in that which they can reach out and grasp. Some choose also to believe in that which they can touch with their hearts. I have to admit, this sounded like a feeble attempt to explain something that I couldn't explain, but here I was, holding a document that was signed by Leonardo, Baron D'Arcamo in 1924. It could have been anything, but I had been led to it, and it was now mine. I slowly fell off to sleep.

The next morning was a blur. I was tired, and although I had responsibilities at work, I couldn't help but think about the document. I thought about bringing it to work to make a photostat of it, but I decided to copy it after dinner and find someone at the college to help me translate it. It was a fairly delicate fifty-six-year-old document, and I just didn't want to take a chance.

My work that day was performed as if in a trance. My heart was not in the work. Print publication is an exacting career, requiring focus and a genuine "eye" for each project. Today, I was extremely fortunate. My biggest project was a text publication for graduate admissions; all in all, fairly dry material. If this had been a color-spread presentation with photos and graphics, I would have had to go home, claiming illness. There was still a part of me that wanted to, but I wasn't ill; maybe a little anxious and certainly tired. And who could blame me? What I was experiencing had gone beyond an interesting family story. It had started moving in the direction of creepy. But then I remembered the document and my after-dinner project. The hours dragged on until five o'clock when I said goodnight to the secretary at the front desk and got into my car to go home. Funny that I was referring to it as *home*.

Once inside the house, I dropped my bag on the couch and went into the kitchen. I found the ingredients to make a respectable salad, and with some toast and a glass of diet soda (one glass of wine at this point and I'd have fallen asleep in my salad), I ate and started to copy the document. The document was written in a cursive print that was easy to read and copy. Some forty minutes later, both my copying and my dinner were complete. I cleaned up the dishes and went off to my bedroom. The sun had already set, now that each day brought us deeper into November and the heart of autumn. I lay on the bed and simply breathed a sigh. Before I knew it, I was asleep.

At some point during the night, I dreamed that I was outside, standing between the fields and the surrounding woods. It was this time of year, but I was younger. The trees in the woods were ablaze with gold and red, with an occasional flicker of rust. The fields had been harvested and now stood with bare stalks, having surrendered their bounty. The scene before me was familiar and reassuring. I heard footsteps crunching on the stone path near the shed, and I turned to see my grandfather. He was carrying a basin with some food scraps and a rabbit that he must have recently killed. "I'm glad that you've come by, Anna," he said to me as he approached. "Have you gone into the house yet?" he asked.

"No," I answered, "I just got here. Where are Mom and Dad?" I was trying to fathom why I was at the farm without my parents.

"They're not here. They're with Tina," he answered, as if this was a completely natural occurrence. I felt so much at home that I didn't consider it any further.

"Come with me, Anna. We have to feed them." He walked slowly by me as he said this. It seemed to be just one more chore that needed to be done, but I had to ask.

"Feed who, Nonno?"

"Anna, you know—my sister's pets. We have to feed them." And then he stopped and turned to me, saying, "Anna, you have been feeding them, haven't you?" I said nothing, but looked sheepishly at the ground, kicking a nearby stone. "Little one, if we don't feed them, how will they know who we are? Come and walk with me. We'll feed them together." There was comfort in his voice. It was a comfort that I had come to know ever since that weekend when he first told us the story. As we came to the end of the fields, there was a clearing in the woods, sheltered by a thicket of young pin oak trees. He set the basin down and emptied its contents there, near some rocks. As he finished, he rose up, and with the basin under one arm, he put the other around me. We walked for a minute or two in silence. Then he looked at me and said, "My soul is here in this land, in this house, and with these creatures. Your nana is here, too. My soul is with her. Our spirits live here. Do you believe, Anna?"

"Believe in what, Nonno?" I asked.

"Oh, in spirits," he answered.

"I suppose so," I replied. I wasn't sure what he was going to say next, but here walking with my grandfather on our way back to the house, I felt so completely happy that it just didn't matter.

"Where your heart is happiest, your spirit will live," he announced.

"Then I guess my spirit is here too," I decided.

"I thought so, little one. No matter where a person is, here and now, their spirit will always return to the place where their heart is happiest. And if you are blessed or patient or both, you might be surprised at what you see." He finished his sentence just as we stopped at the steps leading to the back door of the house.

"Nonno, I don't understand. I don't know what you mean. Help me with all of this, Nonno," I said, raising my voice a little as he ascended the steps. As he reached for the handle of the door, I awoke. If the dream had any meaning, I was at a loss for it.

In that early morning twilight, somewhere between waking and still trying to remember the bits of dream that one has just experienced, I found myself thinking about Nonno and his religious beliefs. There are times when one confuses spirituality with genuine religious faith. I suppose that it happens as often as it does because of the similarities in the positive aspects of both. I find that a spiritual person often adheres to many of the primary tenets of the basic world religions (don't kill others, don't steal from them, treat others as you would want to be treated, think about these things and try to see the essential good in others). It's when one begins to learn more of the specific do's and don'ts of any particular religion that things begin to get a little sticky.

I never viewed my grandparents as overly religious people, but I did think of them as spiritual. In spite of the fact that they were knowledgeable of saint's days, and always kept and referred to their Bible, I don't recall them attending any church services on a regular basis. I know, from conversations with my parents, that they were Roman Catholic, but as an adult it seemed to me that their beliefs were more a combination of spirituality and ethnic tradition than a genuine religion.

That may be why the questions that I remembered from my dream were not as disturbing as one might consider. I think that people, in general, try to build a logical structure on those aspects of their beliefs that they hold to most strongly. At least, this was my perception of some part of my grandfather. At best, I was being given yet another message—perhaps even an additional piece to my ever-growing puzzle.

Chapter V
A Little Detective Work

It was seven-thirty in the morning, and I had slept soundly through the night. Feeling physically refreshed, I performed my morning rituals and went out into the kitchen for breakfast. Two cups of coffee and two slices of buttered toast later, I grabbed the copy that I'd made of the document, stuffed it into my handbag, and headed to work. As I drove, I looked over at the paper peeking out of the bag on the passenger side of the front seat. I remembered when I had bought that bag. It was a Coach handbag—thick, soft leather in a style they don't make anymore. I believe now it's referred to as "vintage." And big? The only way I can describe it is as sort of a gate-mouth satchel. It was one of those bags that we women are notorious for storing enormous amounts of very necessary things in, or at least that's what I've been told. As far as I was concerned, it held everything that I needed on any given day, sometimes even my lunch.

I got to work about thirty minutes early to give myself time to look up a person who might be able to translate the copy for me. I found such a person in Natalie Genova, an adjunct professor who, on overhearing me describe my plight to the language department secretary, volunteered her services and translated it right there at the desk in the office. She read my copy, and after commenting on the language used, she explained that this was an early twentieth-century version of an informal will. "At least, that's what the wording implies, from what you've written," she reported as she read my writing. "I've never seen an actual Italian will from that time, but it seems to me that this Leonardo person wanted, in the event of his passing, to deed all of his land and properties to Giacamo Del Forno, ' … in light of the events that have transpired involving Gelsamina Del Forno.' Geez, something must have happened to this guy, this baron, that he really felt guilty about. It goes on to describe a villa and all of its holdings, fields and all rentals thereof, and the water rights to the well." Natalie ran her finger over the next line or two, mumbling to herself as if putting the words in order mentally before speaking.

She continued, "' … Finally, these properties will be managed by the firm of Luigi Catanzaro and Son until such time as Giacamo Del Forno or his heirs deem it appropriate to take ownership. Funds have been set aside from the field rentals to maintain the properties.' Wow, this Giacamo Del Forno is one lucky man," she said as she handed me back my copy. "I can make a verbatim translation for you if you'd like. This sounds very intriguing."

"Thanks," I answered in a semi-stunned voice. I chose not to say more because I was taken aback and my mind was racing. I was reluctant to think what this could mean, especially with regard to me. Interesting how one of the first thoughts I had was of the resolution that I'd made not more than forty-eight hours ago to try to make greater contact with people in my world—and here I was breaking that resolution at what appeared to be an excellent opportunity. I folded the copy and put it back into my bag. I then made matters a bit worse by offering to pay her, a decision made even worse when she declined. It must have shown on my face, because she tried to soften things by adding that this was the most excitement she'd had in a while. I replied, "It's just a paper that I found in the basement of the house that I'm living in. I suppose it doesn't mean much, but it's fun to imagine, isn't it?" She agreed and made her way down the hall. I made a mental note to catch up with her at some point in the future.

The language department was housed in a building near mine on the campus, so I walked back to my office and tried to figure out, yet again, what this implied for me. I decided to stop thinking about it and re-examine the document when I got home.

Feeding on the excitement that this latest clue afforded me, I skipped my dinner, turned on all of the lights in the kitchen, sat down at the table with a magnifying glass, and began poring over the will. It's a good thing that I was in the publishing business, as a decent magnifying glass is one of the tools of the trade, albeit an old one. I started on the letters, hoping to see anything that looked different—a different font, a lightly written note, anything. In the text, I couldn't find a single clue. I next examined the key at the top of the page: a raised gold embossed key, presumably an indication of the official document of the office that certified these types of papers. The key itself had the appearance of an old-fashioned ornamental single-barrel or spine key with a toothed flag at the end. This was reminiscent of those enormous keys that one is given when offered "the key to the city." There was a great deal of scrollwork around the cutouts in the handle of the key, positioned in a circular or diamond fashion of one at the top and two in the middle followed by one at the bottom, and although the areas in the cutouts were unmarked, one could discern some sort of imprint on them—perhaps something written on a paper on top of this so that a pressure mark was made, possibly unintended, but with no actual writing.

With the magnifying glass, I could make out some tiny lines, but they meant nothing. They appeared to be backward. Then it dawned on me. I turned the paper over to find where the four openings were, four corresponding markings, apparently pressed just hard enough to register on the reverse side. They could have been made with any pointed object, and in light of the fact that I found the document in the basement workshop, I would have guessed that the object of choice was a nail. I could clearly see that the first cutout was the letter *A*. Looking at the next cutout, I saw either a letter *D* or a letter *O*. The way it had been imprinted, it was hard to tell the difference. Next to that, in the third cutout section, was the letter *F*. And in the final section, on the bottom, were lines crisscrossed to look like the pound sign on a computer keyboard.

If I were to presume that the markings were made by Nonno (which would have explained the nail), then I would have to presume that he made them to remind himself of something. And by doing this in such a minute, almost secretive fashion, I would also presume that he didn't want anyone else to know. If, instead, these markings were made by whoever drew up the will, then I was going to have to do some more research to find out if this was a common practice in law offices, or a common practice in Italian law offices, or a common practice in Italian law offices in the 1920s, or just an impression made inadvertently that I was, in the heat of the moment, taking to an adventurous extreme. That seemed like a great deal of research.

Here at the table, without any means at hand to perform such research, I decided to pretend for the moment that the answer was the former and not the latter. If this decision led me to a dead end, then I could always go to one of the libraries at the university and look for more information.

I wrote down the three letters and the pound sign in both possibilities, "ADF#" and "AOF#." The first things that struck me was that *ADF* could stand for "Anna Del Forno." I was still unclear about the "#." Listing as many possibilities as I could, I came up with "American Document Form" or "American Deed Form" (as this could have been a standard form that was used in such cases) or "Anno Domini F#" (this might have been a manner in which these documents were dated or catalogued, an idea that I discounted as I could find no number or date following the "#" sign). I guessed that the O might stand for "origin" or "origination," but as I wrote down this word, I wondered if I had been mistaken in thinking of words in English. Unable to think of too many more, I remembered that my grandparents had kept an Italian-American dictionary somewhere in the house. In their generation, it was fairly common in immigrant households to have such a dictionary, as there was always some little-used word from either of the two languages that they wanted to communicate, and without this book it would have been just out of their grasp. Such a book was usually in a place of honor, say on a shelf near the family Bible and, if the family had money, a set of Funk and Wagnall's encyclopedias, usually purchased within five years of their arrival to America "so the children would do well in school."

I knew that such a book would not be found in any of the rooms that I had already cleaned or was using, so I started by looking in the third bedroom, the one I hadn't gone into more than two or three times since I'd come back to the house. The room itself was small, no more than eight feet by ten feet in area. It housed a single-width knotty-pine bureau in what I would have guessed to be a colonial farm style and a full-size bed with a salmon-colored tufted headboard, reminiscent of the 1950s. All in all, this was really more of a guest room. I continued my search.

Not having any more rooms on the main floor, I returned to the basement. Descending the stairs, I turned not to the left and the workshop, but to the right where there was an old table apparently set up to serve as a de facto desk. There were still a few papers strewn across it with farm-related receipts, and a chipped cup that housed pencils and a pen advertising the local supermarket. Scanning the desk further, I saw nothing ... but on a small shelf, just above the desk, between a Farmer's Almanac from 1977 and an old telephone book, was a dictionary. Just as I expected, it was an Italian-American dictionary. I brought it upstairs and began anew.

I found dozens of possibilities just for the letter *A*. After two hours and six pages of hand-copied words in Italian, I was almost finished with the letter *D*. The possibilities were daunting. I was beginning to wonder if this was the best method to use for deciphering the puzzle. I felt as if I'd been given a gift, a wrapped present, and upon opening it, found another, smaller wrapped present, and then a third and a fourth in like manner. Partially out of laziness, and partially because I wanted to give my eyes a rest, I decided to review the other alternative—that the letters stood for my name. If they did indeed stand for my name, then what would the # sign represent? It wouldn't be my age, because that changed every year. Neither would it be my address, as I have had three different addresses in my life—four, if you counted the farmhouse—and although this document was created long before I was born, I had no way of knowing when these letters were written. If this was pertaining to me, then there must be some numerical constant that I'm attached to. My social-security number? Possibly, but what would Nonno's purpose be? As I stared at the key and the letters, struggling to come up with a numerical possibility, I drummed my fingers on the table, first with all four fingers of my left hand and then my just the index finger of my right. Oddly enough, I arrived at the idea of assigning drumbeats to my initials, or rather assigning a numerical value to each of the three letters. If *A* equaled one, then *D* equaled four and *F* equaled six, and the pound sign was merely a clue telling me to assign numbers to the letters. If this was so, I now had the number "146" to play with. Seeing a new series of possibilities, I listed a first few. It could be 146 dollars, perhaps a small bank account somewhere. It might refer to a direction (146 degrees, but from where and to where?), but I dismissed this idea as just too vague. I looked around the room to see if there were any items that numbered one, four, and six, or even 146, but without success, both in that room and in the subsequent rooms in the house that I searched, the last room being the bedroom where the portrait of Gelsamina hung. Not finding any examples, I looked at her portrait. I sat in the wing-backed armchair in the room and stared at her face, asking her silently to point me in the next direction, or at least help to make some sense out of this confusion. She stared out at me as she always had, with the sad sentimental eyes and slightly pouted mouth that hinted at being forlorn. She always seemed to be looking at me, much in the same way that some paintings have a way of following the viewer around the room. I have no idea how such a thing is accomplished, but whoever drew her long ago seemed to capture this sense. It was almost as if there was something she wanted to say, some secret that she had and needed to yield. Finding nothing, I looked at my watch and only then realized that it was late. I rose from the chair, almost reverently, and after cleaning up the kitchen table, turned out the lights in the house and went to bed.

The next morning I awoke determined to have a calm day. I had spent far too much time on these imaginative wild-goose chases, hunting down clues that may have existed for people in my past but probably not for me, at least not anymore. I came out to the kitchen and prepared myself a genuine breakfast of sausage and eggs, some toast and coffee. I even sliced up a leftover potato and fried it in the sausage grease. I admit that this was probably not the best of choices for my waistline, but there is a magically restorative quality to eating some of the foods that most diets do not recommend.

My work at the college went well that day. I spoke with more people, taking a greater interest in the day-to-day simple things that made up their lives. I even called my on-the-spot translator, Natalie Genova, to thank her again for her help and offer to meet over a cup of coffee. Sadly, she wasn't in, so I left a message on her answering machine. As a supervisor, I made it a rule not to eat my lunch with the staff, primarily for the reason of never putting myself in a compromising position at work. The rule works for some supervisors; others have no problem drawing a line between work and social associations. But today, I felt differently. I spent my lunch in the smallish room that had been assigned as the lunchroom. The walls were fairly bare, painted in that industrial off-white that I'm sure universities and big companies must be offered at a discount. Why else would so many rooms be painted that color? The two tables in the room were clean but a little worse for wear, and they were surrounded by a number of non-matching yet eclectically interesting chairs. The five people in the room continued their chatter when I arrived. I thought this was a good sign, so I sat down at the first empty chair and opened a container of yogurt, listening to the conversation as I did so. Four of the five people were involved in a discussion on what they would be making or where they would be going for Thanksgiving. As is always the case, it wasn't until my mouth was full of yogurt that one them asked me what my plans were for the holiday. This being a college, we did get two days off, Thanksgiving and the Friday after. With Saturday and Sunday, one could enjoy a four-day holiday to either sit back and relax or, as one of the women in the group grumbled, "Yeah, I have five kids, three of them married and two of the three with children. And they're all coming home for Thanksgiving. With my husband and me, that makes fourteen at the table. And they're staying! I'm gonna need a holiday from my holiday."

To be frank, I had been so preoccupied with the house and its history that I had completely forgotten about Thanksgiving. I suppose that my answer reflected some of this when I told them that I really hadn't given it much thought, and I thought would call my sister in Texas to see what she was doing. As the words came out of my mouth, I had a feeling of relief, as if I was finally wading back into the present and away from the past.

Then it happened. The one person who was not part of the conversation, an older man who was sitting in one of the chairs apart from the tables of workers enjoying their lunch and each other's company, was doing a crossword puzzle. I recognized him as one of the veteran printers from the shop. He asked, quite innocently, "Hey, Miss Del Forno, you're Italian, right?"

I nodded, with yet another mouthful of yogurt.

"Who is the patron saint of Sicily? It looks like fourteen letters."

I gulped. I felt a little like something was pulling me back.

The group laughed as they chided him. One of the women must have noticed something in my expression, because she turned and said, "Jerry, the poor woman comes to the lunchroom for the first time in over two months, and you have to start quizzing her. Will you put that stupid crossword puzzle away?"

"Saint Andrew of Avellino, but sometimes he's called Saint Andrew Avellino," I answered, having regained some composure.

"Son of a gun, that works! Hey, thanks," Jerry replied. He turned to his coworker. "You see, Josephine? Finally, someone who understands and appreciates the smarts needed for a crossword puzzle. You need to come to the lunchroom more often, Miss Del Forno," he crowed as he filled in the fourteen spaces. With just a few minutes left, I picked up my empty container and tossed it into the trash can near the door. I straightened my skirt and left the room with the rest of them.

The remainder of the day went smoothly. I found no ribbons, heard no wolves baying, had no dreams, and was not visited by anything that could have been counted as a spirit of any relative alive or dead. This was the time of year when, as a result of a slower rate of production on the mass-distribution level, we sometimes printed five hundred to a thousand copies of various papers and monographs from professors who have had them recently accepted into their respective departmental journals. It was a fairly routine set-up, and I thought very little of it until I passed by the finished copies of one particular tract being collated at the main secretary's desk. The title was *The Transmigration of Souls*, and the thing that caught my attention was the symbol that was being used on the front page of the paper. It was a shield, encircled three times by a banner, and written on the banner were these words in Italian: "*Consentitemi di Vita e Morte Il Danza, Faccia a Faccia e Braccio in Braccio.*" Startled, I reached out and tore a copy from the stack. I imagine that, based on the ferocity of my actions, the secretary thought that she had done something wrong. I quickly changed my demeanor to one of more mundane concern, declaring, "I've seen that crest somewhere before. Isn't this on a sorority banner somewhere on campus? I wonder if the author did this on purpose. Helen, I'll be in my office for a while. I'm going to review this paper. I may need to speak to the professor who wrote it. Could you check and find out what his on-campus hours are? Thanks." And with that I turned and retreated into my office with the monograph in hand. As far as turning that incident around, I think I did pretty well.

The monograph itself was only forty-three pages long. On the first page was a reproduction of the crest from the front cover, but this copy had the banner words in English. Presuming that the words were an actual translation, I read the following line: "Let Life and Death Dance On, Face to Face and Arm in Arm." It sounded familiar. I was certain it was from my grandfather's story, although I couldn't remember the exact words, and I couldn't think of where I might find my answer.

I began to read the tract, hoping that it would tell me something, anything regarding the mystery that I was trying to unravel. It was written in that lengthy, dry, professional style that one would expect a professor to write in—or at least someone who wanted to give you the impression that they knew what they were talking about. It spoke about a series of beliefs that dated back to the early 1800s, primarily in Western Europe, and existed, although in a much reduced state, even today.

The basic theory holds that while all living things eventually perish, that which is the essence or core of an individual, the soul, lives on, sometimes in another living host. This belief runs along the lines of reincarnation but doesn't get into as great a set of details. It also speaks of the ability of a soul to reach out and communicate on a spiritual level—say, perhaps, through the medium of dreams or visions. Those would be under very specific circumstances, say for instance a knowing or willing recipient, or a direct bloodline. I was nonplussed. I fit all of the requirements. The visions and dreams had just moved one step closer into the realism column and one away from the column marked "I've been having some very unique dreams." I quickly thumbed to the back of the paper, into the footnotes, in the hopes that they would tell me where the crest had come from. I found, first among the footnotes, a description of the family crest of the baron D'Arcamo. The seventeenth baron and his wife had been rumored to be proponents of the soul transmigration theory. As they disappeared from their estate when the soon-to-be eighteenth baron was yet young, surviving family members were purported to believe that while they had vanished, they had not, in fact, died, but rather had their essences or souls migrate into someone or something else. A number of relatives mentioned hunting animals, for example, hawks or wolves. But over time these theories faded, as the number of relatives and their specific memories declined. I left thirty minutes early that afternoon, to get home and plot my next course of action.

It was five forty-five when I arrived home. I set down my bag in the kitchen and walked into the back bedroom where Gelsamina's chalk portrait hung. Monograph in hand, I stared into the eyes of the portrait, not thinking or saying anything, just staring. After some fifteen minutes, I spoke out loud. "I don't know what else to do. I feel as if you have taken me down a road only to leave me standing alone in the darkness. What do I do next? I am losing my mind." My voice wavered a bit as I spoke; the frustration was obvious.

"Little one," the voice began in my head, "your mind is sound and you have never been alone. I have been with you; we have been with you all along your journey, but there is still one thing more for you to do." The voice in my head was a quiet one, imploring me. It was not my voice. It was hers. "Find the legacy. It is yours, little one. Look at me, and you will find the legacy." And then it stopped.

I stood and yelled, my eyes moist with tears, "But how?"

I walked up to the portrait in its inexpensive plain wooden frame. "How? How can I find it?" I ranted and raised my fists to the picture. In doing this, between the movement of my arms and the strength of my voice, the frame shook, giving the impression that my great-aunt was trembling at the passion in my words. Only then did I hear the sound that I hadn't heard before—the sound of metal scraping against metal. Something was behind the portrait! I lifted it from the nail and placed it on the chair I had been sitting in.

The wallpaper around where the frame had been was faded. I would guess that the portrait of my great-aunt had not been removed since the day it had been first been hung there. In the area that the frame would have covered was a wall safe—silent, stolid, just waiting to be discovered.

I ran to the kitchen, where I had left the paperwork and translation of the will two days before. I found the letters and the corresponding numbers and tried them, first left, right, left and then right, left, right. On this second attempt, I heard the much-anticipated click of the tumblers. Grasping the small handle, I pulled to the right and opened the door to what felt like a miniature sarcophagus. Inside was another document and a small velvet pouch.

This document was in English. It had no letterhead but was typed double-space, signed by Giacamo Del Forno, and witnessed by an attorney from Binghamton named Blake. It was dated September

28, 1980, which was a short time before my grandfather's death. The contents read in a clean, matter-of-fact way, as many of these documents do: "Being of sound mind and body, I, Giacamo del Forno, hereby bequeath my property in the hamlet of Conklin Forks, NY, to my son, Anthony del Forno, for dispersal and distribution as he sees fit. This property includes the land and buildings and all contents therein, with the exception of the portrait of my sister, Gelsamina, her legacy and my holdings in the town of Arcamo, Sicily in Italy, as well as any properties attached thereof. This also includes the ring included herewith. These will be the sole property of my granddaughter Anna del Forno. They are hers to claim." I presumed this to be a last will and testament, signed by my grandfather and witnessed by Arthur Blake.

I felt around the velvet bag and produced the ring. It was an impressive gold ring with the Arcamo crest engraved as a bas-relief on a large oval face. The thrice-circled banner was evident, but one could not read the words that they carried. The ring alone would have been an honor to my grandparents and great-aunt, but the property in Arcamo was beyond my wildest dreams. This was indeed a legacy!

In the time that had passed between the death of my grandfather and now, there had always been speculation about his leaving a will, but one had never been found. We had all been in our own parts of the country when it happened. I remember being called by my father, who had been notified by an officer from the local police department. When the postman noticed that Nonno's mail had not been picked up after a number of days, he became suspicious and called the police. They answered and entered the house, finding him on the floor near the back door. He had been dead for maybe two or three days.

There were no more than a handful of our relatives left at that time, and when my Aunt Marie (really a distant second cousin to my father who had been referred to as Aunt Marie since I can remember) had decided that the house was too much for her, she left, along with any desire to ask for consideration. My father was reluctant to part with the house and property when he was broached the subject a year later. He just felt that it should stay in the family for a little while longer, not really having a good reason for his decision. I suppose he had too many good memories to let it go. He often mentioned that something would turn up if we just waited a little longer. I must admit that although I didn't think too much about the subject at the time, I was certainly glad that he decided to keep it.

I stored the will back in the wall safe, thinking that I might take a drive into town and celebrate at the one restaurant on Main Street. I slipped the ring onto my index finger and admired it. Not only was it a good fit, but I decided then and there that I would keep it on. I fetched my bag from the couch where I had thrown it and, closing the door behind me, made my way to the car.

As I drove, I can remember feeling famished. A thick juicy steak seemed like the perfect meal to celebrate my good fortune. I parked the car and strolled happily into the restaurant. This being a local eatery, there was nothing as fancy as a filet mignon, so I settled for a marinated skirt steak and a baked potato. It was delicious. I supposed that my idea of solving the mystery fueled this newfound appetite, and I must say I felt as if I'd earned it. I was ravenous.

The most bizarre circumstance occurred soon after. I can remember coming back to the car after my meal still feeling a little hungry. I started the car, turned onto Main Street, and began my journey home. Halfway there I saw, in the road, a squirrel that must have been recently hit by a car. It was alternately writhing in pain and lying there, presumably trying to muster enough strength to escape, not realizing that it had been mortally wounded. Under any other circumstances, I would have felt sad for it but kept on driving. Now, I brought the car to a very abrupt halt, pulled over, turned the engine off, got out, and looked down at it. Through twitching eyes, it saw me and vainly attempted to move. I don't know what came over me, but I put one of its paws over its head and the other over its arms and chest. Then, I bit it. It chirped the last ounce of life left within and died. I watched it momentarily, carried it to the side of the road in my mouth, and now, down on all four legs, ate its fleshiest parts. Only now was I satisfied. I licked my hands clean and then, with moistened hand, wiped my face.

I had no idea what overtook me, but I found myself, fully conscious, crouching over the carcass of a squirrel. I came to the realization that some overwhelming desire rose within me to perform this act. At first I thought that this realization would have caused me revulsion, but it did not. I stood, collected my thoughts as best I could, got into my car, and drove home. As I drove, I could only hope that there on that desolate road, no one had seen me. I took mental stock of my appearance. Clothes slightly disheveled, a trace of blood at the collar of my blouse but nowhere else. Shoes perhaps a little more scuffed than usual, but hardly the worse for wear. Hair practically untouched (funny how I thought about the absurdity of the word *practically*, as there was nothing truly practical about it or this incident). And I still wore the baron's ring.

I pulled into the driveway and walked up to the door, a bit surprised to find yet another red ribbon at the threshold. I picked it up and, placing it into my bag, entered the house. For some reason, I was now very tired. I could almost sense that feeling of fatigue that follows a satisfying meal. I dropped my bag onto its usual spot on the couch, disrobed as I walked to the bedroom, and got into bed, not bothering to wash, brush, or perform any of my usual nightly rituals. I just wanted to sleep. And sleep came quickly.

As I fell into sleep, I felt as if I was falling—as if the bed, and then the floor below me, had just vanished. All around me was dark until I landed with sort of a skip onto the ground. I was outside of the house, and from the looks of the trees it was still that mid-November, leafless time of year when the air is crisp and more than suggestive of the cutting cold to come. She was waiting for me; my great-aunt Gelsamina looked pleased as she watched me regain my composure and stand before her. "Welcome, little one," she smiled as she spoke. "I knew that you would find your legacy, your birthright. Your nonno and nana are so proud of you, as am I. And now we must talk, because your real life is soon to begin."

"But I have a job here, and the house. I'll certainly take care of the property in Sicily, but ..."

"Little one, stop and look down. Are your clothes neat from your fall? Are you wearing the ring?" I looked down at my hand and realized that I had none. The ring was gone as were my hands and clothing. I was looking at the body of a wolf. It was sleek and gray-brown with occasional flecks of black on my shoulders and chest. I was no longer a five-foot eight-inch woman. I was a wolf, a beautiful cunning wolf. I was startled. I awoke in a sweat.

I looked down at my hands. They were once again hands, albeit with sweat-covered palms; the baron's ring, now mine, was there on my left middle finger as if nothing had happened. But something had indeed happened. My senses had been heightened. My behavior became calmly inhuman, and again, I had dreamed of my great-aunt. Even when I was a young girl hearing the story for the first time, I never experienced the feelings that I felt now. But this was no longer the scintillating excitement that comes with a good story. This wasn't even the bittersweet romanticism that I'd felt when I first looked at the portrait. This was fear.

My life, in my thirty years, had covered many of the same things as any woman my age, but through most of it—almost all of it—I have to say that I was in control. Control was, *is* an important thing to me.

There are those who look at their lives as if they are victims. They believe that Destiny, or Fate, or whatever cosmic entity one chooses to give credit to has them in its sights and will relentlessly bombard them with misfortune. There are even some who attribute this power to the Almighty. Then there are others who see life as a test track, conferring no power at all to Fate, rather choosing to careen down the track, bumping into walls from time to time, hopefully correcting their steering at each instance of impact. Personally, I always viewed my life as a sort of adventure. I have always felt that somehow, in some way, there is an entity far deeper and greater than me, giving tips and hints and clues along my way to somehow get me to understand something that I'm supposed to know. I felt that way after leaving my grandparents' house following that extended weekend fifteen years ago. I felt that way when I applied for and got the job up here. Funny, but I never really worried about leaving my old job in New York before I actually lost it. It never dawned on me that I might be out of work for a long time. I rarely thought about the fact that I was thirty years old and without any long-term meaningful friends or relationships. However, when I needed to talk to someone, and it wasn't often, I just called on my family. I suppose I'd never really thought about it before, but in light of all that had happened to me, one might consider me to be a bit of a "lone wolf."

But now, with this, I was scared. Someone else was dropping breadcrumbs, and I was following along, picking up each crumb along the way, right up to this moment, here and now. The dreams, if that's what they were, were eerie at best, and downright scary at worst. I took stock of myself and then my surroundings. I was naked, lying in bed. The remains of a cold sweat could still be felt on my body, and a foul gamy taste was in my mouth. It was then that I remembered the events coming home from the restaurant. Fear was turning to terror. I got up and went to the kitchen, to the only telephone in the house. I called the office at work. When the secretary answered, I spoke in as calm and nonchalant a voice as I could muster. "Hi, Helen. Listen, I'm not going to be coming in today. I really feel terrible. Yeah, I'm going to stop by the medical center and see if they'll take a look at me. I'm hoping that this is just a twenty-four hour thing. Take care, and thanks." I hung up. Taking a day off was not really a big thing, but the last thing I needed was to have people think that I was losing it. Realistically speaking, this was all about control, and I was indeed losing it.

I made a pot of coffee and then picked up the phone. While the coffee brewed, I called information. I wanted to find the number of Arthur Blake from Binghamton, hoping that he was still practicing. Fifteen minutes later, I received my answer. Mr. Blake was no longer practicing. In fact, he had passed away a year ago. The attorney who had taken over Blake's practice had routed all calls to his number. He still had a copy of the will but had no other information. The receptionist, although very pleasant, informed me that a copy of the will was still kept as part of legal procedure, and that if I had the original copy, we could certainly compare them for authenticity, but without retaining him for further research, little else could be accomplished. I could contact Italian municipalities to get further information. One last thing she did leave me with was that, in some areas, certain titles to property revert, after a specified amount of time, to whomever is currently residing there—"sort of like squatter's rights," she said—but there are so many variations on the legal agreements and the states or countries that decree them, that I would be better off getting the facts from the local government that the property was connected to. I made a note of the telephone number, thanked the voice at the other end, and hung up.

I sat down. By now I was on my second cup of coffee, and I had no idea what to do next. I owned a ring, a heavy gold ring. I might or might not own property in Sicily that I heard about in a story years ago. I had fantasized and had delusions of probably the most bizarre things that I could imagine. If I were to tell someone of all this, there was a very good chance that I would be put under psychiatric observation. But it was time I spoke to someone. To say that the phone call from my parents at that moment was an uncanny stroke of fate would not be overstating. In fact, the ring of the phone jarred me out of my thoughts to the point where I actually let out a little shriek. Composing myself, I was relieved to hear my mother's voice at the other end of the line. Such a call in the face of what one would expect during a workday was not an unusual thing for my mother. Not that she had any paranormal abilities, but for some reason she could call and get through to a person when few others could. It had gotten to the point where she practically expected the person on the other end to answer regardless of what logic dictated.

"Hi, sweetie. I just had a feeling, so I thought I'd call you now and not wait until tonight. If you're not doing anything for Thanksgiving this year, why don't you come down and spend a few days with your father and me? Tina's going to be hosting her in-laws, so she can't make it, and I thought that it would be nice to have you all to ourselves. Watta you say?"

My mother, having been a teacher, made a point of speaking clearly and succinctly, with the one exception of that phrase. One of the family jokes was that we were going to have "Watta you say" engraved onto her headstone. "Mom, you couldn't have called at a better time. You know, I really needed to hear your voice."

At this, I heard the expected "oh" of being pleased, followed by the "oh" of *is something wrong?* that my mother issued, as if on cue.

"No, I hadn't made any plans yet. I've just been so busy at work. In fact, I was going to call Tina and you to see what was going on. I'd love to come."

We spoke for a few more minutes, both of us cheery, but secretly for different reasons. She, for getting her daughter home for a visit, and me, for getting a taste of sanity away from all of this, and hopefully some answers and advice in the bargain.

Thanksgiving was the following Thursday. That gave me six days to arrange for a flight to the Tampa airport and rent a car for myself for the three days that I'd be there. I looked at the clock on the wall. It was a few minutes after nine o'clock. For a moment, I stopped and stared at that old clock, an electric clock with stylized Arabic numbers that had been hanging on the kitchen wall for what seemed like forever to me. I wondered, as I stared blankly at it, what secrets, what events it had watched over and held in safekeeping since it was first hung there. If only objects could talk.

I snapped out of my mental meanderings and got up. I walked to the wall phone and called information for the number of the nearest travel agency, and after about thirty minutes of telephone conversation, I had reserved a seat on a morning flight to Tampa, via Philadelphia. The flight from Binghamton to Philadelphia would be on a twin-propeller twenty-nine-seat airplane (referred to as a "puddle jumper" by the travel agency), but the flight from Philadelphia to Tampa would be on a jet. Apparently, the airlines still used propeller-driven planes for short-distance flights—sort of a shuttle bus in the air to a larger airport. At any rate, my flight was confirmed, as well as the car rental. I was asked to stop by sometime that afternoon to pick up the tickets and rental confirmation.

I spent the next hour or so sprucing up the house, trying not to think of the ordeal that I'd been through. This was not easy, when in every room there was something to bring me back. When I got to the room with Gelsamina's portrait, I stopped. I waited for a few minutes, almost anticipating hearing that little voice in my head again, but this time there was no voice, only silence, an empty silence. I wondered if, in going away to visit my parents, I had offended her. What else could she have wanted? I'd found the ring, and eventually I'd find an attorney to deal with the legalities of actual property ownership with an Italian counterpart. It might even be worth something, or perhaps nothing at all. As far as my behavior and the dreams, I really didn't have an answer, at least not yet.

That afternoon, I drove to the travel agency, a little shop near the airport. The travel agent was friendly, very helpful. I took a card and made a point to keep it near the telephone, just in case I flew to see Tina in Texas, or my parents again.

At work, the week went by without event. There were a few remaining theses and papers to print, but our big projects were either already completed or not yet ready for production. I found myself, by Tuesday, actually looking forward to seeing my parents, although I was constantly rehearsing what I would say to them regarding Nonno and the documents. I resolved to bring them, and if the subject didn't come up, I would ask my father if he had ever heard or seen anything like them. I would bring the ring, but before I actually got to the house, I felt it best to take it off and tuck it away until the time was right to show it to them. As far as the squirrel incident, some things were better left unsaid.

That evening, I drove home a bit more lighthearted than usual. The calmness of the week and the past few nights of sleep all contributed to my mood. I decided to clean out whatever bits of leftover meals still remained in the refrigerator. There were still three pieces of chicken, also a small dish of peas and onions, some olives, and a few slices of eggplant. I felt like creating, so I stripped off as much of the chicken as I could, diced the eggplant slices into little cubes, and added the peas and onions to a cup of chicken broth. I then made a small bowl of pastina, and when both were done, I mixed them. I could almost hear my grandmother saying "Needs salt" as I tasted it. I found that, for my taste, the fewer the seasonings, the more I enjoyed the taste of the ingredients. All in all, it was pretty good. I poured a glass of red wine from the half bottle that was left in the refrigerator and waited a few minutes for it to warm to room temperature. Warmed, it went well with the meal. I turned on the radio, hoping to get the weather report for the next few days (specifically tomorrow and Saturday, when I'd be in the air) along with my dinner music. To my pleasant surprise, Thursday morning would be a crisp, clear, cold day—perfect for flying.

I finished my meal, and instead of throwing out any remains as I had intended to do, I found one of those disposable foil pie plates that supermarkets sell baked goods on. (I wasn't at all surprised to find at least one in Nana's pantry. She had always saved such items for future use. In fact, she must have had half a dozen stacked in her pantry.) I deposited the remainder of the meal into it and then walked outside to where the field met the woods and left it there. After all, it was nearly Thanksgiving, and I thought that my grandfather would have been pleased. I looked around into the woods as the dusky darkness deepened into night before my eyes. Finally, I turned and went back into the house. I picked up my goblet and the wine bottle, which now held perhaps one glass. Filling the goblet, I brought it with me as I went inside to pack.

That evening, when I finally got into bed, I slept well. I remember having some small fragment of a dream. I say "fragment" because this piece of a dream involved my grandfather, downstairs in the basement, standing at his workshop, turning to me and letting me know how glad he was that I remembered the wolves. "Did you see any of them, Anna?" he asked as he returned to his project at the bench.

"No ..." My voice was my voice as it is now, although I remember the image of Nonno from when he was much younger.

"Well, don't worry, they'll be around soon enough."

That was the sum amount of what I could remember from the dream, with the exception of one more thing, not so much an event or something spoken but rather a feeling. While this dream took place, I felt as if I was not the one speaking to Nonno, but rather I was removed. I was instead watching a conversation between Anna and Nonno. I was someone else, or perhaps something else.

I awoke the next morning, washed, dressed, made sure that all of the appropriate electrical plugs and devices were turned off or pulled, hauled my suitcase into the car, checked to make sure that I had my keys, locked the doors, and made my way to the airport. I have found that being single often requires a series of routines performed in checklist fashion in order to avoid spending the rest of one's vacation wondering whether a stove had been turned off, or the cold water faucet had been left running. Having assured myself through my little regimen, I arrived some twenty minutes later at the airport.

The municipal airport in Broome County wasn't exactly the size of the airports that I'd been used to in New York City, but it didn't need to be. A smaller airport had certain favorable points all to itself. There were fewer flights, and while one often had to make a connecting flight in another larger city, the people in a smaller airport are, by and large, very friendly and helpful. I parked the car and entered the terminal, where I was given my boarding pass with enough time to spare for a cup of coffee and a buttered roll. By the time I was finished, my flight was being called to board.

The flight from Binghamton to Philadelphia was relatively brief and mercifully uneventful. Propeller engine planes always seem a little "iffy" to jet passengers, especially to those who don't fly that often. I'm sure that they are equally safe, but I often find the image comparison of the two to be a little disconcerting. At any rate, in short order, I was on the connecting flight to Tampa. The flight was full, and I had been lucky enough to get a window seat in the rear of the jet. If it were possible to be considered hidden away on a flight, being situated where I was would probably be the closest thing to it. Far in front of me were enthusiastically loud children, lanky teenagers, and a varied assortment of adults ranging from young parents to older (and more sedentary) seniors, all being tended to by a small platoon of flight attendants hovering over them in a methodical manner, seeing to their needs much in the way certain worker bees tend to the needs of the locked-in, incubating larvae in a hive. It was fascinating and, in a way, comforting. With that thought and the drone of the engines, I soon found myself drifting off.

The sun shone brightly through enormous banks of whipped billowing clouds, illuminating them in a way that resembled the sunny cold day after a snowfall. I felt as if I were half walking, half drifting weightlessly among them. I felt as if I was not alone here, although I could see no one else. I could hear voices speaking softly but was unable to make out what was being said. From time to time, I could pick out a word or two, I suppose in English, but really nothing more than that. I tried to concentrate on the voices but with no success. I sensed that the sun shone most brightly high and to my left. When I looked in that direction I saw something that, for a moment, took my breath away. There, seated majestically on a precipice of one of the snowy cloudbanks, was what appeared to be the figure of a white wolf.

Three things happened almost simultaneously in my dream. I thought of those games that we, as children, have all played. We gaze up at the sky and try to recognize or form objects out of the shapes that clouds take. At the same time, I thought that with all of the twists and turns of events that had occurred to me in the last few weeks, it was no wonder that I was imagining some cloud formation to resemble a wolf. It was then that the third thing happened. The object that I, just a second ago, took for a shape, turned and stood, looking directly at me, and howled. It howled the howl that I heard back at the farmhouse, the howl that I heard with my mind's ear from Nonno's story: *l'anelito*.

When the attendant touched my shoulder, I awoke with a start. She apologized and reported to me that we had landed and I had been asleep for a while. I later ascertained that I had slept for over two hours. I was now the last passenger on the plane, and they were preparing for the next flight. I awkwardly thanked her, composed myself, and left. My suitcase was waiting for me in the baggage-claim area. By now, it was the sole remaining piece of luggage on a now-vacated luggage belt. I collected it and trudged off to the car-rental kiosk, still recovering from my dream-filled nap.

I was somewhat disappointed when told by the car-rental clerk that the sporty little number I'd planned on renting was unavailable. He tried to make up for it by offering, at no extra charge, a Ford Crown Victoria. I signed the papers and took the keys. I hoisted my suitcase into the cavernous trunk, slid into the driver's seat, and slowly, cautiously, maneuvered my way out of the car-rental lot. It had been years since I'd driven a car this big, and this was a giant of a sedan, but in the hour and a half that it took to get to my parents' house in Ocala, I pretty much got the hang of it. It was very comfortable, but I must admit, it wasn't exactly something that one expects to see a single female in. As I got to Ocala, I saw more and more cars like mine, and more than half of them were being driven by lone females, women who were older and apparently much shorter. I recalled that my mother had mentioned there were a lot of widows in Ocala. Apparently, they were all driving their late husbands' cars.

By the time I arrived, it was late afternoon. My parents were waiting at the door of their two-bedroom home as I pulled into the driveway. The house was a neat little stucco ranch, just different enough from the other houses on the street in their gated community to stand out, but not so much that the community board would harass them. My mother attributed this to my father's landscaping and he to her ability to cajole the board members into complacency with her baked treats.

Mom looked good. I hadn't seen her in almost a year. That was when Tina, her husband, Steve, and I helped our parents move from New York to Ocala. They had retired the previous June, and with the move down here, they were finally realizing a long thought-about dream. The year in Florida seemed to take some of the stress out of Mom's face. Her hair had always been blond, but it seemed brighter now. I remember wondering if it was highlights or a tanned complexion, or perhaps both. For a woman in her late fifties, she had a good figure, one that I wouldn't mind having now. I knew it still bothered her to avoid sweets. "It's easier now," I remember her saying to me later on at dinner, "because it's so hard to find a good Italian pastry down here."

My father beamed as I got out of the car. As I was the firstborn—and still, in his eyes, a bit unsettled in my life—I often felt that he quietly worried a little more about me, although I don't think he would have ever admitted it. He hadn't changed a bit in the year since I'd seen him, his gray-white hair as always a week or so past when he should have gotten a haircut, his wire-rim glasses guarding a careworn exterior. From the driveway, he still looked every inch the academic, but as I got closer, I could see that the remains of yard work had replaced the ink stains and chewed cuticles that I remembered from when he taught English.

We all hugged and went inside. Dad took my suitcase, and Mom sent me into the guest room to freshen up before dinner. It wasn't until she mentioned it to me that I realized I hadn't eaten all day and was about to sit down to Thanksgiving dinner. I cleaned up and performed what small makeup repairs I could before coming out to a lovely dining room table, set with the same china we'd been using all my life.

Even with only three of us at the table, I could see that my mother spared no expense in making this a festive meal. It was a miniature version of the afternoon-long extravaganzas I recalled growing up. A first course of soup, followed by macaroni ("It's been macaroni for my entire life," my father would say. "Now, the world wants to call it pasta and raise the price!" It often seemed that his half-mocking diatribes had a piece of truth in them). After the macaroni came the guest of honor, a golden-brown turkey crammed full of mushroom-and-onion stuffing. It was surrounded by bowls of side dishes—yams, eggplant, the perennial green-bean casserole, and the eternal mark of a special-occasion dinner at the Del Forno home, stuffed artichokes. The aromas and tastes brought back wonderful childhood memories; mixed in with the talk of how my parents were doing in their new home down here, they made the afternoon perfect. It was a symphony in which each aspect played a vital part but never overplayed, rather demonstrating its quality by sharing with the qualities of each of the other aspects. It was warm and memorable. Later, after we all helped wash and put away the dishes, we sat down for coffee and cordials. This was the time I chose to bring up the subject on my mind.

"Dad, did Nonno ever tell you stories about Sicily? You know, about when he was growing up?"

"Oh, plenty, especially when I was young," he answered, with a look on his face that made me think he'd gotten the wrong impression.

Growing up, we'd often had family stories told to us after a good meal. "Why do you ask?" he continued. "Would you like to hear a story?"

Avoiding his question, I pressed on. "Did Nonno ever talk about the chalk drawing in the back room, the one of his sister?"

"Zia Gelsamina? He probably spoke about her more than anything else, when he did talk about the old country. After your great-grandparents died, she was all he had. He was just a teenager when their parents died. And then there was the story of how she went missing. If you want an honest opinion from your old dad, I think that Gelsamina ran off with the artist," he concluded, half-smiling.

"What artist?" Obviously, the drawing had to have been done by an artist, but I'd never been told anything about an artist, and so that part of the story never even existed for me.

"What artist?" my father mocked my question. "Well, little girl, if you pour me another cup of coffee and another glass of Amaretto, I'll tell you all about the artist."

Dutifully, I got up and filled his cup and cordial glass, as he waited for my mother to sit and pour herself another cup of coffee. "It must have been when I was about eighteen years old. I had heard the stories about Zia Gelsamina and the baron for most of my life. Nonno told us all about how she disappeared and the two wolves took off, and how the baron blamed himself for it all. But it wasn't until I turned eighteen that I started asking about the portrait—or rather, that he started telling me about the portrait. Did Nonno ever tell you about the feast?"

I nodded in the affirmative.

"Good. Then you know that in Sicily and in Arcamo, the town would hold a feast in honor of Saint Andrew Avellino, and to this feast would come all of the local merchants and farmers selling their goods. Ladies who could crochet or knit would make fine tablecloths or bedspreads and bring them to sell. Over time, artisans from neighboring towns would ask if they could come and do something special for their homes—for a special fee, of course. This was also true for woodworkers and ironworkers (known then as blacksmiths), who would show their work in miniature, hoping that someone would commission them to make a gate or a piece of furniture, maybe even a chandelier.

"Such was the case for Marco Colisanto, an artist who traveled the region in and around Palermo. He would come to feasts and, for a small fee, would do a simple portrait with a piece of charcoal. For a larger fee, he would use many colors from a box of chalks that he kept. He would pose the person in a formal setting and draw the person with an elaborate background, similar to a Renaissance painting. He was very good. Nonno told me that he'd seen some of this artist's work at the feast once before.

"He had made a portrait of Vito Alessi, the local butcher. By the time Marco had finished, Vito looked like a wealthy nobleman, seated in a great chair at a desk with a long feathered quill pen in his hand. Now Vito Alessi was a nice man and a good butcher, but according to your grandfather, he could neither read nor write. So for Marco Colisanto to create this type of a picture and do it so beautifully could only have been at Vito's request, and only for a handsome fee. My point here is that Marco was a talented artist—and if I remember from your grandfather's stories, he was good looking to boot.

"By today's standards, he would be considered young (I think that he may have been in his mid-twenties), but by the standards of the time in Sicily, he would have been considered a man of the world. His looks were not Sicilian, or even of Southern Italy, for that matter. I think Nonno said he was from Florence in the north. His skin was more fair than ours, his hair lighter, and his nose was small and had a gentle slope to it. His eyes were a bluish gray. He was so handsome that he looked like a porcelain doll. In fact, between his talent and the foreign looks, many of the women of Arcamo were smitten with him, just as many of the men didn't trust him. It had even been said, over a glass of wine, that the men of Arcamo wondered if he was, in some way, demonic." At this last point, my father's eyebrows raised to exaggerate. "Well, after all, how could it be anything but the work of dark forces?" he continued playfully. "He was handsome, talented, 'not from 'round here' (Dad spoke in a false western drawl), and the ladies loved him. Yep, this must be the work of the devil. The talk was that he was some sort of witch or a necromancer.

"That having been said, there was one time at the feast when the baron hosted a grand dinner party; Nonno and Gelsamina didn't set up a booth during the day, but they did attend the feast, even if only for a little while. If I remember it right, Nonno had gone to the feast with Gelsamina, but he returned soon after to oversee the sale of some produce that merchants he'd visited had discussed with him. I remember that it was a big thing to him, both in terms of money and honor, but I also remember that Zia Gelsamina stayed at the feast a while longer. Nonno said that when she returned to the house with her pets, she was in high spirits.

"At first, he thought that it was merely in anticipation of the evening affair to come. But when he took a closer look at Fiero and La Notte, he noticed that they almost looked as if they'd been groomed, not exactly a natural look for wolves. His concern was confirmed two days later when a boy from town arrived with a package for Gelsamina.

"It was a large package, some two-and-a-half feet by three-and-a-half feet, and flat. When she opened it and showed it to him, it was a beautiful colored chalk portrait of Gelsamina, seated with Fiero and La Notte at her sides. She looked regal, as if she were meant to be pictured as nobility. And while one would get the impression that she held dominion over her pets, it was not difficult to see something deeper there, especially in her eyes. Nonno said that the wolves loved her, and the way they were drawn, one couldn't tell if they were her personal bodyguards or something more. The way that Nonno said it, you couldn't tell if they were guarding Gelsamina from you or they were guarding you from her. It was as if Marco the artist saw something in her that no one else in the town, including Nonno, could see.

"At any rate, this beautiful portrait came in a frame woven with red ribbons all around it. It was a treasure and probably worth a great deal of money. But I can remember your grandfather telling me with half a smile on his face that he never found out how she paid for that portrait, or if it was a gift, perhaps in the hopes of a kiss. Zia Gelsamina was a very attractive girl. That's why the baron was so taken with her. In fact, Nonno told me once, that was why she would never let the baron see the portrait, because she couldn't be sure of his reaction. She didn't know if he would grow angry with jealousy, or fearful.

"I have my own theory about the portrait. Nonno told me that when he was preparing to come to America, he couldn't bring the portrait, so one night, he delicately cut it so that just the face and the upper body could be framed and brought with him. And that's the portrait you see today at the farmhouse in New York. This is all well and good, but my theory is a little different. I remember one time when Nonno was dozing off in his chair, he muttered over and over again that the portrait was cursed and that the curse could only be lifted when the portrait was destroyed. I think that after Zia Gelsamina disappeared, Nonno thought she would return if he cut up the drawing. But he didn't want to lose the only picture he'd ever had of his sister, so he couldn't bring himself to destroy the smaller, central part of the original. In fact, I wouldn't be surprised if somewhere in the house, maybe in a trunk somewhere, is the rest of the chalk portrait." And with that, my father reached for the coffee and poured himself another cup, having been sipping at it all through the story.

I was fascinated. I'd come here hoping to get more of the story, not really knowing what to expect, and was given this. But if it was true, where exactly did it fit into all that I already had? I thought that I should put more of my cards on the table. I got up and went into the guest room, where from my cosmetic bag I took the little velvet bag I'd brought. Withdrawing its contents, I returned to the dining room and placed, into my father's hand, the baron's ring. "What can you tell me about this?" I began. "I found it in the house, and to be honest with you, I've been having some really interesting dreams."

My father took the ring and held it in his hand. He looked over at my mother and then turned back to me. My mother, who was normally a bit on the impassive side, looked serious, first at him and then at me. Finally, she spoke. "Don't wear this ring, Anna. It really has nothing to do with you. Your grandfather's stories are just that—stories. Whatever truths existed have been so heavily decorated that whatever you may think, it's probably not so, and to wear this ring would only lend strength to whatever he said to you." She added, with a hint of realistic dismissal, "Frankly, I'm surprised to hear that you still remember half of those damn stories."

Although always loving to her in-laws, my mother never fully bought into the Sicilian view of many things, especially when it came to stories of the past, and most especially when they involved Gelsamina. My mother's point of view was more grounded in the present. Her parents had been divorced before I was born, and she rarely saw her father—a man, I was told, who because of his job in sales spent a lot of time on the road. Her mother struggled to raise her and her sister, and the divorce, which came when they were in their late teens, was not a shock. After putting herself through college, she met my father, who represented a form of warmth and stability that she was unaccustomed to. When they married, her need for that encompassing emotional hug was finally fulfilled. They loved each other madly. At the risk of sounding like a cliché, they found in each other those aspects that they did not each possess. An added piece that she still dealt with uncomfortably was probably my dad's appreciation for the past. But what he brought from the past, she equaled with the here and now. In many cases, the future was a compromise of their two opinions.

"Mom, you're not going to believe it, but this ring was bequeathed to me. Along with the ring, I found a document that I think is a will … well, maybe some sort of a will. Anyway, it was signed by Nonno and witnessed by an attorney in Binghamton. I found it in a wall safe behind the picture of Gelsamina. On top of that, Nonno left the entire farmhouse to Dad."

The looks on their faces told a great deal. My father looked surprised at first and then smiled at me. "So, there really was a will after all. When your grandfather passed away, we had a feeling that he would have had something written up. But to be honest, with that generation, one doesn't talk about wills. It was considered bad luck. Did you bring the will with you?" My father was slowly regaining his composure, returning to the matters at hand.

I went back to the guestroom and retrieved the document. I thought that I caught a glimpse of concern in my mother's expression, as if something was about to be opened that she didn't want opened. She recovered enough to say, "I'm going to put on another pot of coffee. There's a lot to talk about."

My father read the single page two or three times over, then lifted his glasses to wipe away moisture from his eyes. "Well, it certainly looks like a will, but if you want, I'll have my attorney down here look at it. I'll have a copy made tomorrow and show it to him." Somehow, I didn't think that the moisture in his eyes was from the news that he'd just inherited a farmhouse from his parents. He was obviously reminiscing about something, but at this point, I couldn't tell what. I wondered why my father had never gotten an attorney and settled the estate of his father, especially in light of the fact that he was an only child. Perhaps whatever he was keeping from me had something to do with the answer.

As far as I knew, Nonno owned the farmhouse and property, but little else. There had to be a reason Dad never finalized the situation.

Mom brought out the coffee and a plate of fig cookies that she knew I was fond of. "I thought you might like some *cuccidara*," she said as she offered the plate to me. I nibbled at one as my father spoke, "I see that you have inherited something from my aunt along with the ring. How did my aunt come into possession of the baron's property?"

I went back again into the guest room, this time to produce the copy that I'd made of the document in Italian. "I made this copy of a document that I found in Nonno's workshop. I had no idea what it was until I had it translated. As near as I can figure, the baron felt remorse over Gelsamina, so he left everything to Nonno. And Nonno left it to me!" I stated this all as plainly as I could. I wondered how much of this my father had actually been aware of.

"Anna, keep in mind, we've never even seen this property that Nonno talked about. It might be something, or it could just as easily be nothing. And we don't know anything about Italian law. There may be a term limit on inherited property. This will take some real research. I'll try to find out what I can and let you know where you stand. Who knows? If you owe thousands in back taxes, and the property is nothing more than a few run-down buildings in the middle of nowhere, this may not be quite the legacy that Nonno described, but we'll see. Now, tell me what you remember about the ring." As my father spoke, I wondered what he was up to. It was clear that he was trying to keep me grounded by bringing in realistic and largely negative scenarios.

"I remember that Nonno said the ring belonged to the baron of Arcamo, and it was his family crest."

Dad looked up as if at some imaginary screen and said, "Let me see if I remember the words: 'Let life and death dance on … something, something, something …'"

"'… face to face and arm in arm,'" I added, completing the motto.

My father looked at me and said, "You've been doing some research of your own, haven't you? What do you think about all of this?"

"That's just it, Dad, I don't know what to make of it—a nice story, a fairy tale. But then, I find these things and I lean toward believing them. Then I hear your story tonight, and I lean the other way. That's why I brought this all here with me. And I haven't even told you about the dreams that I've been having." I'd gotten so deeply into the conversation that I thought I might as well tell them everything at this point.

"What dreams?" asked my mother.

"Dreams like I've never had before," I continued. "At first, they were just nice dreams. Sometimes Nonno and sometimes Gelsamina, or at least how I imagined her from the drawing. But then she started telling me to look for things, talking about the legacy. That's how I found the papers. She said that they were mine to find."

"Did she frighten you?" asked my mother.

"Oh no. In my dreams, Gelsamina always seemed loving. She was what I would expect from an aunt, or a great-aunt. Her voice was soothing. Neither she nor Nonno ever said or did anything that was harmful. That's why I was so confused by the last dream."

"What happened there?" my mother asked, in a way that made me feel as if she was almost holding her breath, a little fearfully.

"In the dream, I became a wolf. Nothing scary or creepy; I was just a wolf. I was sleek and warm, and I felt oddly free. I could run and leap. I even saw things differently, as if everything was in black and white, with occasional splotches of color, like one of those old, hand-tinted photographs. Then I woke up, and I was in a sweat." Sensing my mother's growing reaction to this conversation, I chose not to say anything about the episode with the squirrel.

"A wolf!" my mother exclaimed. Her voice rose as if this was the thing that she was afraid of hearing. She looked at dad angrily. "A wolf, Anthony! A wolf! Again, this happens!" My mother was angry and frantic and pointing at me as she looked at my father. "We come all the way here, where there are no wolves. 'Only a few,' you said. 'And they're red wolves, not gray,' you said. 'Things will be better,' you said. 'The girls will be safe; the red wolves are in the state park, all the way on the east side of Ocala.' Tell me, Anthony, are the girls safe now?" She got up quickly and stormed into her bedroom.

The discussion had obviously opened wounds for them. It also put me back again into a position where I had more questions than answers. My father sat there, alternating between rubbing his temples and smoothing his hair. He was obviously thinking about something, perhaps something to say to me, but would it be an explanation or just another dance around some truth that he was still withholding? It made me wonder how many times he'd danced around the truth as Tina and I were growing up. It also made me think again of the baron's motto, of the dance between life and death.

"Dad, I really need to know what's going on. Why you haven't said anything to us up until now is almost not important, but I really need to know."

He was reluctant to speak. It was not unlike the reluctance I'd seen in my grandfather all those years ago. "Anna, when Nonno told you girls the story of Gelsamina and the baron, he told you an actual story. And yes, sometimes a relationship fails. But there were parts that he left out or changed. Think back to the stories that he used to tell you. Did you ever wonder anything about those stories?" My father was trying to calmly explain, but I still got the impression that he wanted to explain only the parts that he thought I would need. Could it be that my mother's reaction to the mention of wolves was yet another part of the story that he was reluctant to speak of?

"Well, now that you mention it, I always wondered why this happened to our family. I mean, I understand that Gelsamina was attractive and that the baron, even with his hang-ups, was smitten with her, but the whole legend thing with the wolves, and her pets—why was it that only Gelsamina and Nonno were affected, out of the whole town?"

"Anna, the short answer would be that Gelsamina loved Fiero and La Notte, and when she took them in, you might say that they also took her in. To them, according to Nonno, she was a mother, a sister, a wolf. He always said that she would have laid down her life for them if it ever had come to that. A longer answer is one that I can't explain. To answer your question, we really don't know if the wolves in the woods and hills around Arcamo treated other people in town as they treated Gelsamina. We only know that she loved her pets, and at some point in time, she disappeared. The stories that Nonno told us about the red ribbons might have some truth in them because we have the ribbons. Wait …" he said and then stopped, rose, and went over to a drawer in the china closet a few steps away. He withdrew a box from it, and from the box he took a few red ribbons. "Do you remember Nonno telling you any stories about these?" he asked, holding them out in his hand. I said nothing. Instead I went back into the guest room and returned with my red ribbons. I held out my hand. They were identical. My father placed his ribbons back in the box. Then he rose and came over to me, bending over and hugging me. I felt something warm and wet on my neck and hair where Dad's head was resting. It was tears. Still silent, he turned and put the cordial and his coffee cup away. He came back and sat down.

"In the weeks and months before your grandmother passed away, she and I had been talking a lot. She was concerned about Nonno. He'd been having dreams about his sister. He started going to the library, returning home with all sorts of books on wolves. He even took out books about werewolves and legends that pertained to them. But he soon dismissed most of them as 'Hollywood,' as he would say. The books that he kept taking out could be divided into three groups: The first group consisted of any books on wolves in Western Europe and North America. The second group of books was much smaller. It dealt with a legend, largely in Italy and France, of the *figli del lupo*, 'the children of the wolf.' The third group was also small. These were books that studied a little-known spiritual concept from the nineteen hundreds known as the 'transmigration of souls.' Briefly put …"

"I know a little bit about the transmigration of souls," I interrupted, shocked that I had unknowingly followed the same path as my grandfather.

Dad looked at me, his eyes showing that he'd expected this was the case. He continued. "When Nana passed away, Nonno was understandably very sad. At the funeral home, he barely spoke. But at one point, when he and I were alone, he took me by the arm and said, 'She's with them now.' At first, I took it to mean that she was in heaven, that her soul had gone to heaven. A normal enough Christian presumption, wouldn't you say?" I nodded in agreement. "But, what if," he pressed on, "Nonno wasn't referring to heaven, but instead the transmigration of your grandmother's soul, say to that of a wolf? Now I know that on the face of it, this is just a theological hypothesis that poses one set of beliefs against another, but how do you explain the ribbons? Or the documents that you found? Or the ring? Coincidence? How about the dreams that he had, or for that matter, the ones you're having? Love? The missing of a loved one? Longing?" As if on cue, I heard something outside; an animal was baying at the moon. It sounded mournful, lovely—*l'anelito*. "Oh, and that's another thing. I'll bet that you read about the efforts to repopulate the gray wolf numbers in the Great Lakes–Western New York region. The population's always been strong in Canada. Did you know that there's been a push to do the same thing with the red wolf population here, in the South? Largely in the state and national Parks, like the one on the other side of Ocala. I think it's called Silver River, but it's one of quite a few that they're trying to use as sites to repopulate the wolves. Sometimes, we'll get a stray pack come into this area. Let's face it, there are still a lot of working farms down here with livestock. Taken separately, each of these is interesting, or even lucky, but all together?" He stopped, still looking at me with a sort of wide-eyed expression.

"Dad, you don't believe that any of this is coincidence, do you?"

He sighed and looked down at the table. "No."

"What do you think it is?"

"I think that since the time of the baron, the Del Fornos have been cursed—or blessed, depending on how you look at it. I think that in their time, every Del Forno has, in some way, become a wolf, or at least a child of the wolf. And I don't think that the baron left everything to Nonno because he felt bad about what had happened to Gelsamina. I think he left it to Nonno in gratitude because Gelsamina had taken care of his parents, Fiorello and Nicoletta, the previous baron and baroness D'Arcamo, or at least in memory of them."

"How did you come to that conclusion? Oh, you don't think that the two wolves ..."

"Well, if you subscribe to the idea of a transmigration of souls, the answer is yes, that is, them or some relative of his or theirs. There's no way of ever really knowing, but I'm tempted to say that, at the end, the baron may have thought along these lines, too. The previous baron, who by the way was the seventeenth baron D'Arcamo, and his wife were believers, in fact proponents of the idea that a soul could migrate from one living organism to another. If such was the case, then they came across a great champion in my aunt."

"Dad, this is all supposition."

"You're right. You are one hundred percent correct. Now, give me a better explanation."

We both sat there for a few minutes longer, not saying anything; not believing what we'd concluded, but not having any other explanation. Finally, my father got up, took the few remaining glasses with him to the kitchen, and, commenting on the lateness of the evening, bid me good night. I was stunned. My father (and indirectly, my mother) didn't want to say that they believed in what amounted to a family curse, but having no other way out, took this as their strongest option. I now had more information, but I was still stymied. And by now, I was afraid to go to sleep. Reluctantly, I lay in my bed until my eyelids grew heavy. Mercifully for me that night, I slept.

The next morning, I awoke to a sunny Florida day, not giving much thought to the events and information of the previous night. I performed my morning rituals and came out to a pleasant, if slightly reserved breakfast. My mother, pouring a little coffee for herself and then me, asked if I'd like to go shopping. "After all, what better time to find a Christmas present for you than when you're here to try it on?" At first, I made a face, but upon further thought, decided that some shopping might be a good solution for taking our minds off of everything.

Regardless of what one may hear or believe, shopping for clothes can be very therapeutic ... well, at the very least, it is for me. I was not blessed with my mother's trim little figure. I inherited yet another Del Forno curse: I had broad shoulders, broad hips, and unless I behaved myself on a regular basis, a waist that was very capable of becoming equally broad. Because of my breasts, I bore a resemblance to a typical Italian immigrant from the early twentieth century. On a kinder note, I have been called 'earthy' and 'voluptuous.' At any rate, having a second opinion when I try something on is a very good thing. And at the age of thirty, I am spared the usual motherly opinion, it having been replaced with the 'Let's find you something that a steady boyfriend might like to see you in' opinion. Two sweaters, two shirts, a really attractive dress, and a blouse that I had to be talked into filled the bags that we set down as we ate a light lunch, still saying nothing of yesterday's conversation. We were determined to shop our way into a temporary amnesia. We laughed at silly, mundane things, and sipped our iced teas until it was time to return home with the spoils of our day. This was the type of day I needed. And even on the day after Thanksgiving, with crowds at the stores unlike crowds on any other shopping day, I had consciously made an effort to think of nothing. With my mother's help, I succeeded.

My father was outside, tinkering with his flowers, as we pulled into the driveway. He set aside his garden tools, and kissing us hello, he asked if he could have the pleasure of taking us both out to dinner at a local restaurant. Apparently, he had joined in our efforts to "keep the wolf at bay." (There must be something embedded within the English language that has seen predicaments like this before. Why else would there be so many references to wolves?)

A few hours later, we were all clean, dressed, and getting into my father's car. "I hope you like this place, Anna. Your mother and I went here about a month ago and immediately thought of you. It's a little out of the way. But then again, this is Ocala; most of the good places are a little out of the way."

Dinner was lovely. The wine matched the meal, and our conversation matched the wine. We talked about Tina and her family. I hadn't seen the twins in over a year, largely because of the move and the change in jobs. Mom and Dad had visited about a month ago, and true to form, my mother pulled a sleeve of photos out of her bag. We talked about the changes that were starting to take place in Ocala; development was going on all around us. Ocala was growing by leaps and bounds from the quiet little city that my parents once knew to a sprawling suburban center. By the time the check came, we were genuinely tired, having spent the evening catching up. As a result, we all slept well that night.

The next morning was rainy and gray. Muted sunlight crept onto the breakfast table and sat there waiting for me as I sat down. My parents were already up, and my father was already dressed. I greeted them both and sat down as my mother poured my coffee. Dad spoke as I sipped my first cup of the morning. "I didn't get the chance to tell you yesterday, but I brought your paperwork to my attorney in town. They are both actual documents, and the farmhouse is mine, barring disputes from any distant remaining family members. Frankly, I don't see that happening. As far as the property in Arcamo, it will take him a few weeks to research Italian law and give us a full report. If he needs it, could you send me the actual document? Send it by registered mail, and I'll sign for it at my end."

I knew he'd purposely held off from speaking about this yesterday, and to be frank, I was grateful for a day of actual peace. It felt wonderful to have the respite of merely being a daughter for a day. But the day and the respite had ended. I listened to him intently, sipping my coffee, and agreed to send the baron's document to him.

"As far as Nana and Nonno's property goes, as long as you work up there, the place is yours to stay in and care for, so you might want to give that some thought," he said.

"I really don't want to make any changes, Dad. Maybe some paint and carpeting, but that's all for now," I replied.

"Sounds reasonable. How's the heat and electricity up there?"

"I haven't had any problems yet, but then again, I haven't spent a full winter there yet."

"Okay, just let me know how things go." He did not seem to want to go further with what we all knew were the remaining parts of the conversation. Then it took a turn I didn't expect. "Anna, I had a dream last night. I was sitting at the table at Nonno's house. I was sitting with your mother, Nonno, and Nana. He had his wine, and she was quietly knitting like she always did. In the dream, he looked at me and said, 'You know what is in your heart, because you know what is in my heart. My blood is in your veins and in hers.' Then he motioned for me to look out the window into the backyard. In the yard, you were bringing a tin plate of table scraps out to two wolves who were standing at the edge of the woods. You put the plate down and caressed them both before they bowed their heads and ate. I turned back to Nonno, who said, 'You know ... ' and then I turned to look out the window again, but this time you were gone. Anna, there were three wolves standing there. And when I told your mother about my dream this morning, she looked at me wide-eyed. She had the same dream."

I found it difficult to hold my coffee cup, as I began to tremble. At first, I wondered if I had brought them into my nightmare, if it was indeed a nightmare. Then, I began to wonder if my being with them had merely strengthened the chances of what was becoming an inevitability. I chose not to speak. I drank what was left of my coffee, got up, and hugged them both. I vaguely remember saying something to reassure them, something that we all only believed half-heartedly. Then, I went into the guest room to pack. My flight wasn't for another four hours, but it would take me at least two to get to the airport, and I hated waiting until the last minute. Besides, I felt that it was time.

It had been almost eight years since I'd lived with my parents, but I still found that our parting embraces brought tears to my eyes. My mother kissed me on the cheek, and my father made me promise to call when I got to the airport and then again when I arrived home. This was a routine that I'd performed since I first left home.

Although there were a number of cars on the road, traffic moved at a good pace, and within two hours I found myself at the airport, seated and waiting to board my flight. Letting my mind wander as I gazed out the plate-glass window onto the runway, I thought about what it would be like to live here, in Florida. Then, as if jumping from one mental railway car to another, I thought about the red wolf that they were trying to repopulate down here. I made a mental note to look up the subject when I got back to work. The sun felt warm on my face, and I must have dozed for a few minutes, lost in my thoughts. I was brought back by the announcement that my flight would be boarding momentarily. Without giving it any thought, I reached into my handbag and slipped on the baron's ring, my ring, my legacy. The action felt right, as if it was something that I'd done before. And it fit so well on the middle finger of my left hand that I decided, there and then, that I would keep it on.

I produced my boarding ticket, walked in that sort of passenger-line lockstep that one does on an airline on-ramp, and found my seat, again next to a window. The plane soon filled up, and as the passengers all settled into their seats, I reached for a magazine. Flipping through it, I found an article on the latest colors that fashion designers were choosing for the coming season. It seemed light enough, and between it and the warm sun, I was again dozing, this time through the takeoff. I must have awakened as the flight attendant asked the woman next to me if she wanted something to drink. I returned to my magazine article. I must have been in a half sleep, because the words that discussed fashion began discussing something else.

As I read them, the words were addressing hemlines and then, as if it was merely the next paragraph, I read the following: "The ring and the property are indeed yours, little one. But your legacy is deeper. It means so much more. It is yours to embrace. You will be the next generation, the next of the *figli del lupo*. Look, little one, look out the window." I turned, and in the sun-filled puffy clouds in the sky, I saw it again, the white wolf, seated majestically, looking out royally over the distance, and then turning to focus on me, returning my gaze. Now the words that had been on the page were being spoken by the great white wolf. "You will be my next bambina, little one. This is your legacy."

I didn't shudder this time. I didn't wake with a start. I kept staring out the window, and as the clouds passed and blocked my view, I saw less of the white wolf and more of my own reflection in the glass. My reflection was not the face of Anna Del Forno, but instead it was the face of Anna, the gray wolf. This time I continued to stare, exploring each aspect of the face. The brown, highly reflective eyes; the soft grey fur; the smoke and black tufts near my ears. I was beautiful. I fell off to sleep for the remainder of the trip and awoke surprisingly refreshed. I felt invigorated, as if I had finally been given answers to both sides of my questions. I had come closer to the truth.

It took another two hours for the connecting flight from Philadelphia and the drive back from the airport before I reached the farmhouse and was in the kitchen calling my parents to let them know I'd arrived safely. Next on my agenda was to unpack and get some food for the week. Not having had anything to eat since breakfast, I decided that I would treat myself to dinner as well. The house was pretty much the same as I had left it, with the exception of a small pile of mail from the past few days. Still, I looked around before I left to shop for food.

Something seemed out of place, something that I couldn't describe. I couldn't even describe how I sensed that something was amiss. The rooms? Each one of them seemed greyer … no, more monochromatic than before. I sensed a stillness, although it seemed that sounds outside the house were more intense: an ax chopping some wood, the bark of a dog, the chatter of a squirrel, these all seemed vibrant to me. And I had a growing hunger. I decided not to wait and went into the kitchen to see if there was anything that I could snack on. Walking toward the kitchen, I tripped. My clothes had become too large for me. My shoes and pantyhose already off, I easily slipped out of my skirt and panties. It was merely a matter of backing out of my blouse and bra before I was completely naked. I trotted to the bedroom and leapt onto the bed to see my reflection in the mirror over the bureau. I only half expected to see the soft pink-skinned body I was accustomed to examining after a shower. The other half of my expectation was not disappointed. I was the wolf. The same reflection that I saw on the plane, I saw now. I had transformed into something wild, something different.

Gelsamina entered the room and admired me from the doorway. She wore the dress that she'd always worn, the one from the chalk drawing in the other room. Her hair and eyes seemed to be bathed in a glow I'd not seen before—but again, it was monochromatic, shades of gray ranging from black to white. I watched her intently, still sitting on the bed. My softer gray ears pricked up as she began to speak. "So, my little one, you have finally realized your legacy. Come, it's time to join your family. But first …" She stopped, stepped forward, and reached down for something on the floor, near the bed. It was the Baron's ring, which must have slipped off as I changed into my current state. "You will need your ring. Here, let me help. May you keep this with you always." She withdrew a red ribbon from a pocket at the side of her dress and tied the ring to it. Then she wrapped it around my neck, tying it not so snugly that I would feel it, but enough that it would not easily slip off.

I looked at her as she stepped away, having completed her task. My mind was flooded with questions, as it seemed the one thing that I retained from the transformation was my intellect. She looked at me but didn't speak, yet I could hear her voice as clearly as if she spoke. "All will be explained in time. But first, it's time to leave," the words came into my head. I leapt off of the bed and tore down the hallway into the kitchen, still hoping to find something to eat. I nosed and pawed at one of the lower pantry cabinets until I finally clawed it open. I tore at a cardboard box of cookies, gnawing at it until the contents burst out onto the floor. I hopped back from the explosion of cookies, licking first and then devouring quite a few of them before stopping and looking around.

This was exactly how the house would be found, I thought: clothes strewn about, but no body to be found. It was possible that an animal had wandered in and caught my scent on the clothing. Scratch marks could be seen on the pantry door, with food found and eaten, presumably by a wild animal that somehow got in. By the looks of the claw marks, it would be traced to a wolf. My keys were still in the door. Police finding this scene would assume that I'd left them there since before Thanksgiving. And the door was still ajar, so I could now leave undetected. Perhaps Gelsamina was right after all. This was my legacy, what I had in store.

Gelsamina had silently appeared from the hall. She observed me as I deduced what I could thus far, and she smiled. "With each passing day, more will be revealed to you, both about the world around you and about yourself. Go now. Hunt. Find your food and feed, little one. I will be with you, here" as she pointed to her head "and here" as she pointed to her heart. "Go." I nosed the front door open and trotted out into the backyard, past the trees and into the woods, to my new life.

Chapter VI
Anna, the Little One

Imagine a really well-made black-and-white movie in which each shade of gray is crisp, even in the shadows. Blacks are blacker, whites are whiter, and everything has a visual electricity to it, almost totally in monochrome. I say *almost* because you must now imagine that the brightest and most intense colors bleed through, not unlike a black-and-white photograph that has been hand-tinted. This is what I saw as I walked through the woods on the first day of my new life. Branches that never stood out against the sky, or each other for that matter, now did so easily before me. Rocks that I might have tripped over, even small ones that blended into the forest floor, appeared before me as objects to see and appraise. My sight, to a large extent, had been enhanced.

My hearing, too, was more acute. On top of everything else that I've mentioned, I heard a stream. My human experience told me that there was no stream for at least a half-mile in any direction, the nearest being deeper in the woods, on state land. But I could hear it. I could hear the rippling trickle of water as if it were no more than a hundred yards ahead of me.

And scents—I had no idea that trees had a scent. I am not referring to the Christmas-y pine smell that one remembers after brushing up against an evergreen. I mean oak, and maple, and birch. I don't know how to describe it, but they each have a scent, an aroma that is unmistakably their own. Some are musty, some dusty, or rather spoor-filled; some, well, there was one tree in the woods that I can only describe as smelling like cardboard. I realize that the things I'm relating sound ridiculous, but at the moment, I was a bit delirious with the headiness of my new senses.

Then I caught the spoor of another wolf … no, two wolves, a male and a female. They were upwind of me, near some pines. I approached cautiously, wondering if I should. Then I stopped, deciding to avoid others for now. What if they wanted to fight? Or I was trespassing in their hunting ground? I knew nothing of what I should do. Better for me to remain alone. Besides, I was still hungry.

I sniffed at the air. Near the stream was a doe, drinking. She was skittish, and I could actually smell that in the air. Some distance, a short walk away from the sun, was a road. A family of quail had crossed. Two didn't make it, an adult male and a chick. The chick had hesitated as a car sped down the road. The adult stopped to gather it. Both were hit and now lay bleeding. The other adult and the remaining chicks in the brood stopped at the other side of the road and then moved on. I took in this new way of dealing with life and death as I made my way to the freshly killed birds. I mouthed them both and brought them to the side of the road. Holding the adult beneath my paw, I devoured the chick. The adult would not be as easy a meal. Sensing that others had caught the sent, I removed the quail to a quiet spot between some rocks and an old fallen log. As a hawk circled above, searching for what she hoped would be her next meal, I ate. It had meat; not much, but enough for now. At least I could explore without the gnawing hunger. And if I caught the scent of more food, I would feed.

I sniffed the air again. I still had a while before sunset, as I followed my nose. It brought me to that stream I'd heard before. The water was cold and clear but not very deep. It was deep enough to drink, but not enough for fish, maybe frogs and turtles but little else—at least, not at this point in the stream. I tried to remember where the stream led. I tried to envision any local maps I'd seen. This had become difficult. I had come up against my first obstacle: I had lost my ability for abstract thought. I knew what a map was. I just found it very difficult to conceptualize. It was as if I were being exposed to whole paragraphs of *War and Peace* written in longhand, in the original Russian. I could not make any sense of it, let alone keep it in my mind long enough to analyze it.

Using the tools that I had, I decided to follow the stream in the direction that it was flowing. This required little thought. The stream must be heading somewhere, and I caught no scent of any larger animals. Except for the occasional bird in flight or squirrel on a branch above, I encountered no one. Stopping to take a lap of water from time to time, I walked in and along the stream. The water tasted cool, and it washed away any remaining quail blood that I hadn't already licked off.

I heard noises up ahead, human noises and splashing water, human children noises. They were coming this way. I retraced my path back to where I had eaten the quail. It was easy, as even I gave off a spoor. I merely followed it. Stopping there for a short while, I realized that I needed shelter. Even though hunting at night would hopefully produce better results, I needed to find a place to sleep undisturbed. The children's voices died away as the splashing moved upstream and away from me. I found a thicket that was sheltered by rocks on two sides and some type of thorny bush at the front. For now, it would serve as a den. I sniffed at this smallish space for any signs that it had been recently occupied. It hadn't. I curled up and closed my eyes, burying my nose into my own fur for warmth. I found it impressive that I could sleep a good, sound sleep for what seemed like about two hours, and all the while, I could register and experience sounds and even scents. It was fascinating. And it was one more thing I'd learned about my new life.

When I awoke, it was dark. The moon was still rising. I was hungry. I looked around. Surprisingly, I could see. I've never had the experience of seeing through night-vision goggles, but I have to assume that this was something very much like it. I could see pretty much everything. I sniffed at the air. An owl was nearby, perched on a relatively low branch. I had to imagine that he was just as hungry as I was. Now, I had competition. At the stream, a family of raccoons washed their take of the contents of a local garbage pail. Their spoor and that of the garbage was repulsive. It made me snort in disgust. Redirecting my attention to the owl, I saw him swoop and disrupt a squirrels' nest. In the disruption, two young squirrels fell out, plummeted to the ground, and lay there, stunned. The owl swooped in and snatched up one of them, rising to a lofty perch to dine quickly. In the moments that it took him to gulp down the young squirrel, I made my move. He flew in for the second victim, only to find that it was gone. I discovered that I enjoyed freshly killed meat more than old roadkill. My next test was to kill something on my own.

It was then that I caught the spoor again. The two wolves from earlier in the day were back. My fur began to bristle as I sensed their approach. They both came from one direction. This led me to believe that they were not hunting, therefore I was not to be considered prey. And they did not approach stealthily; cautiously, but not stealthily. They seemed to want their presence known. I saw them both a short distance away. They walked with heads upright, not bent or cowed in any way. They looked similar to me—that is to say, they too were gray wolves, with colorings similar to mine. But they seemed a little older, more mature. I knew nothing about how a wolf ages, and even less about whatever it was that I'd become. Then, I heard the voices.

"Welcome, Little One. It is good to see you this way. Gelsamina told us you'd be here. We saw you before, but you were not ready." I looked at them both, first one face and then the other. They weren't speaking, but as they looked at me, I heard voices in my head, voices like the ones I'd heard back at the farmhouse. Could these be the wolves from my dreams? It was difficult to tell. They acted as if they knew me. They could sense my hesitation. The larger of the two walked up to me. He sniffed at the air around my face. I froze, not sure of what to do. "Anna, look into my eyes. Do you know who I am?" I peered deeply into his face, searching for some inkling of recognition. The night gave an eerie reddish glow to his eyes, and if it weren't for the warm expression and sincere words that I was hearing, I'd have been far more frightened. It was as if he had a hard-looking face. Then the other wolf, a wolf more slight and a little smaller in size, approached. She came up on my side and nuzzled me behind the ear. It felt oddly familiar—although, I must admit, I'd never been nuzzled behind the ear before. They acted like a couple, as if they'd been together for a long time. And they both seemed to know me. Then I saw it. Something in his eyes made me think of the farmhouse, and my grandfather.

"Nonno?"

"Yes, Little One, it's me." He came up and nuzzled the right side of his face against the left side of mine, as the other wolf began licking me.

"Nana?" I asked.

"I'm here, Anna. We're both here. Come, we'll take you back to our den."

I was caught up in emotion. If these truly were my grandparents, then the transmigration of souls was true, but I felt as if I understood it less now than I did before. I knew the words, but not what they meant. If these were my grandparents, and I felt the happiness that I expected to feel, then why were there no tears of joy? Then I remembered that wolves don't weep; they are incapable of crying. I was glad, but unsure. I felt safer, but still very cautious.

I followed then for some distance in the night, past fallen trees and rock outcroppings, to an area where the land seemed a bit more hilly, and the tree growth was thicker. Finally, we arrived at a small cave, big enough for perhaps five or six of us. It was set up at the midway point of a hill, so that once inside, one could look out and see danger coming but remain unseen. It afforded a modicum of safety.

Once inside, Nana turned to me. "Your mind must be full of questions. I know ours were. You know, your Nonno talked all the time about the *figli*, but when he finally turned, he was just as intimidated as you are. Your great-aunt helped me when I turned, but I, too, was confused. Now rest here, Little One. Tonight, we will hunt for you. Tomorrow, we can begin to help you with your learning. Now, sleep." She turned away from me and headed toward the mouth of the den, where Nonno was waiting. In an odd way, I felt as I had those many years ago when Tina and I stayed at our grandparents' house during the storm. I felt quietly excited. The adventure had begun. I curled up toward the back of the den, closed my eyes, and slept a deep restful sleep. Outside, the weather was cold. I heard a breeze kicking up. It would probably deepen the chill, but here inside, I was not affected at all.

When Nonno and Nana returned, it was almost sunup. They brought with them part of a fawn, having eaten some of it before arriving. Nonno's snout was still a little wet from the now congealed blood on it. He sat at the mouth of the den, licking himself and grooming, while Nana brought the meat closer to me. I knew of their arrival, having sniffed their spoor and the scent of the fresh kill as they approached. I fed hungrily, as Nana watched. Alternating between tearing off bits and grunting as I chewed, I caught glimpses of the two of them grooming each other in turns, licking and smoothing with their paws. In the early morning light, and now with a full stomach, I saw them both. They were handsome, Nana having more gray and tan in her coat than Nonno, who still had black around the face and ears. If it were possible to call them noble, I would. With fur tufted at the chest and jowls, they gave a stoically beautiful appearance. And these were my grandparents. Were I still in human form, I think that I would have felt pride. Sensing that I had finished feeding and was watching him, Nonno rose and came over to me. As he looked at me, I heard words in my head again.

"So, my little one is awake and has eaten. Can you talk to me?" I had to assume that he was asking me this question.

I opened my mouth and tried to speak, coming out with a guttural "oerrrr" and not much else. The sound that I heard in my head was something akin to what you would expect from a wolf trying to laugh.

"No, no, Little One. Speak with your mind. Make words to me with your mind."

"But how?" I asked, without realizing I'd done just that.

"You see? It's just a matter of focusing on me and speaking with your mind. You'll soon get used to it. You did it last night without realizing it. Wolf-born wolves can't speak this way, but we can. And more. Tell me, what can you see when you look out there?" He pointed, with a motioning of his nose, toward the woods beyond the mouth of the den. We spent some time thereafter discussing my heightened senses. To put it more accurately, I did very little talking but a great deal of listening. Then he and Nana talked to me about hunting—where and when to hunt, what was good to eat and what was not. Finally, when the sun was high in the sky, they took me out to explore. I was a wolf, but a brand-new wolf, sort of a fully grown baby. For the next few days, we explored the stream, a nearby lake, hills, highways, ravines, and each other. Concepts had grown to become more difficult with each day, so the idea of parents or grandparents was almost alien to me, but with Nana and Nonno, I was safe, and I learned to survive. After a while, the concept of marking calendar time became difficult as well.

We returned to the den. Nonno looked up and sniffed as we approached. He turned to Nana and said, "She is here."

"Who?" I asked, sniffing the air for a scent of someone or some animal.

"Gelsamina," said Nonno. "But she doesn't look like her picture, Anna. She looks like us." I was confused, partially because of my lessening ability to think abstractly and partially because I had a memory of seeing her before I entered the woods. To me, she always looked like the picture. I wondered if she looked differently to each of us.

"No, she doesn't," said Nonno, who had heard me, apparently, speaking out loud. I needed to practice speaking to myself and speaking to others.

When we got to the mouth of the den, there sat a wolf with fur that was almost entirely white. Although the same size or even a bit larger than Nonno, this wolf was more trim, more sleek in the body and legs. The expression on her face, though, was similar to Nonno's in the way the eyes were set and the impression that they gave.

"Anna, this is Gelsamina, the White Wolf," said Nonno.

Again, I sensed something in his voice, something like pride but not exactly. I was, however, focused on her. Her eyes met mine as I came into the den. She rose and nuzzled me. We exchanged this display of affection as the words came into my head: "So Little One, I see that you are learning the ways. You hunt, you eat, and I see that you are getting comfortable with the world as you now see it."

I lowered my head in acknowledgement. I sensed that she was Gelsamina, but she seemed to be something more, something that I should defer to. Her bearing lent stature to her appearance, making this feeling I had even stronger.

"Come with me, Little One. There is more for you to learn," she said as she left the den and trotted down the hill. I looked at Nana, then Nonno, and then back to Nana, who said, "Go now," and nothing more. I followed Gelsamina down the hill and into the woods. We traveled some distance silently, coming finally to the point where the woods ended. The clearing after the woods was where the farmhouse land began. The White Wolf and I moved single file toward the back of the house and then into the shed that once housed farm tools.

When we were both inside, she turned and stood before me. The words that came into my head explained that we were unlike wolf-born wolves. We had the ability to change back, when and as we needed to. She knelt down with her forelegs and bent her head. Slowly she rose, and as she did, she assumed the form of the twenty-year-old woman I'd seen in the chalk drawing.

To my surprise, she was naked! It startled me. Her body struck me as flawless. Barefoot, she padded over to a shed locker that held some clothing and, turning away from me, quickly dressed, as it was very cold. Completing her task, she turned back to me and, now speaking aloud, cleared her throat and said, "You try. Bend down and have your spirit well up inside, to the point where you feel yourself as a woman."

I was hesitant. "Do not have fear. You have learned so much so far. You can do this, too." I bent down and began to breathe deeply. Wisps of steam curled out of my flared black nostrils. I find it still difficult to describe, but somehow I felt a small self welling up inside of me and growing within me until eventually we became one and I became me, Anna Del Forno, once again. I too was naked, and very cold. After all, this was the first week of December in western New York.

Gelsamina reached into the shed closet and covered my shivering body with an overcoat. I didn't need my senses to tell me that this coat was old and foul-smelling, but inside it, I found some warmth.

"Now comes the most difficult part for us, little one. Anna del Forno has been away for almost a week, without a word to anyone. A postal delivery person must have noticed that your front door was open and your mail piling up. The authorities have probably been notified. Now we are going to have to get in and somehow concoct a story that will satisfy everyone as to your absence. And remember, you have been away from your work for a week. We will have to address that concern also." There was a serious tone in her voice, one that replaced the calm reassurance that she'd had when we spoke of things *figli*.

The cold in my legs and feet was now making me shiver all over. Through chattering teeth, I stuttered, "C-c-can we go inside first?"

"Certainly, but the door is locked."

Still shivering, I smiled and gingerly walked over to the door of the shed, where I reached above the wood that framed the doorway. "I always k-keep a s-s-spare car key here, just in c-c-case of emergencies. And a s-spare house key in a bag in the t-trunk of my c-car." As I reached up and felt around for the key, the coat fell off of my shoulders and onto the ground. In the sunlight that peered through the doorway I could see that I'd lost weight. I was trim, and my shoulders, arms, and legs were more defined. I looked downright athletic. In fact, I looked really very attractive. Gelsamina noticed my taking stock of this change in my appearance and said, "In your new form, you did not eat very much, only what you needed. And your body has relied exclusively on its muscles for everything. When you turn back, this is your new form, little one."

I was still very cold, new discovery or not, so I quickly retrieved the key and put the coat back on. I picked my way to the driveway with now-numb toes and unlocked the car, which looked as if it had been tampered with—presumably by the police when they had been notified of my disappearance. Opening the trunk, I found the little leather bag that I'd tucked up behind the spare tire, and the key inside got us both into the house. After dressing and warming up, I joined Gelsamina in the kitchen. She was sitting in the chair that Nonno always sat in, waiting for me. She looked at me and began, "Now, for your story …"

"Well, I could tell them that a relative from Italy had unexpectedly arrived for a visit, and together we decided to take an impromptu trip out of town." As I spoke, I realized that everything that I'd just said to her was true. "As far as leaving things in disarray, in the excitement of seeing you, I left my keys in the door and left the door open. An animal could have gotten in and foraged. As long as nothing was stolen or damaged, and I'm alive, I can't see how this would make much of a problem."

Gelsamina smiled at first, then upon further consideration asked, "What kind of relative am I? If they want to speak to me, I can't be your great-aunt."

"You could be my cousin," I answered. She seemed pleased with the answer.

"And where did we go?" This was becoming a game to her.

"We went to a cabin in Canada. And we had to leave quickly because we needed to get there before sunset. I was driving the car that you rented because mine couldn't make the trip." I was pleased with myself for coming up with such plausible answers off the top of my head. Gelsamina smiled too, although not as strongly as she had at first.

She said, "Or I could simply 'go back,'" referring to our ability.

"Please don't," I interrupted. "There is so much I want to ask you about, so much I want to say."

She smiled reassuringly again. It was only then that I realized that she was now playing a game with me. "As you wish, little one. But I must admit, I have been observing you for some time now, and I'm not yet comfortable in these ways. Perhaps we can learn from each other."

Coming up with answers at my job was more difficult. I offered the same explanation of the cabin in Canada with my cousin from Italy and apologized profusely to Mr. Howard, my supervisor. Mr. Howard was a large man—large in girth but not so much in stature. He had the general appearance of a weasel, with a balding head and a face drawn forward with an extended nose, an overbite, and not much of a chin. And there was an aspect of his demeanor that went along with his facial expression. He was opportunistic. He looked at every event at work as his personal chance to either better his standing or convert it to a situation where someone owed him a debt. His secretary, Lucille Mason, an equally porcine individual, had worked for him since his assumption to supervisor some two years ago. Her prime responsibility, at least as she saw it, was to keep people away from him. The only person who had easy access to Mr. Howard was his supervisor, the Director of Ancillary Services, Mr. Baker. I'd heard from the clerical pool that when Mr. Howard got the job, there had been talk of Cuban cigars, gambling junkets to Atlantic City, and even a golf weekend in Bermuda. After such an investment into Mr. Baker's good graces, it would have been difficult for Mr. Howard not to get the job. And according to my sources in the clerical pool, the department moved gradually downhill from there. Oh, projects were completed, but only if they were done without his hand. He treated the department like he was its feudal lord. And my week out and excuse were viewed as my getting something from him for free. He looked at me oddly and then sternly. He then told me that I'd be docked one week's wages, and if I ever did this again, he'd have to let me go. With what I knew about him, his reprimand and penalty were to be expected. What I didn't expect was the attitude that began creeping into the office from that time on. Workers and secretaries alike treated me with a respectful but icy distance, as if it were only a matter of time before I'd either quit or be asked to leave. Apparently, this was how he employed Lucille. In short order, word had gotten out that I was unhappy and was looking for more money and benefits in the private sector. Such rumor and insinuation did not sit well with the rank and file, who viewed this opinion as coming from someone who considered herself above them. Although this attitude prevailed, I couldn't allow it to get to me. There would soon be a Christmas break, and after it ended, the schedule called for a lot of work to be done in short order. Even thinking about it made me a little nervous.

At home, we adopted a routine where Gelsamina would sit on a kitchen chair and keep me company while I prepared dinner, interspersing cooking hints with her stories. It's not that she couldn't cook. It's just that when she had learned to cook, it had been on a wood-burning stove. In the days and weeks to come, I told her, we'd prepare the food together, and eventually I'd teach her how to use the stove. Although she seemed pleased with this offer, the look on her face wondered something.

The first thing I remember asking her had to do with her ability to "turn back." I wanted to know how it was done. Why was it that only we could turn back, and then turn back again? Her answer to my question was really very simple. "I don't know," she said, looking plainly at me. I then asked her about the first time she turned. "That was such a long time ago," she began as if she was reluctant to remember. Then, as if opening a door to a room she hadn't entered in a while, her eyes looked into a far-off direction, and she spoke.

"When it seemed to me that Leonardo was determined to destroy the wolves of Arcamo, I had no choice but to leave him and protect them. I had done all that I could, but they needed more of me. I had begun hearing voices from the time of the hunting competition, and it was then that I learned that my two pets, my Fiero and La Notte, were in fact, the cubs of Leonardo's parents. They told me so themselves. And his stubbornness in refusing to even consider the possibility that the transmigration of souls could actually be real stood a good chance of having them both killed. I had no alternative but to join them."

"Zia Gelsamina," I said while stirring sausages, peppers, and onions in a frying pan (I used the title *Zia* for "Aunt" only when I wanted to be emphatic). "In his defense, for someone in that area and time when Arcamo—in fact, all of Sicily—was largely Roman Catholic, how else could you expect him to react?"

Gelsamina looked at me in the way that an adult looks at a child with a naive question. She spoke in a tone that made me feel that she wanted to explain, and it would be hard not to sound as if she was chastising me. "There are many who believe that when a person dies, their souls leave them and move on to face judgment in heaven. Would you believe me if I told you that in the east, there were probably five times the number of people in all of Italy who believed that when a person dies, their soul enters into another living being? I cannot tell you a great deal about reincarnation, but I can tell you that many people believe in it. Neither can I be the one to tell you what is right and what is wrong. In fact, many times I don't know. I only know that at one moment I feared for the lives of my pets, and the next, I was with them, running wildly through the woods away from Arcamo and the man who would have overseen their destruction. Did my brother ever tell you about the ribbon I left for Leonardo? That was truly the only way I could communicate with him. He could never have heard my voice. Something inside of him would never listen."

"Did you love him?" I blurted out.

"Yes, once," she said quietly, "but hatred makes all things blind to love. And in time, all he had left was hatred. Careful, the peppers will burn." I looked down at the pan of food and stirred a bit more.

We set the table, and as Gelsamina served the food, I opened a bottle of red wine. Pouring her some, I waited to get her reaction. She tasted it and looked at me. Wincing a little, she said, "It tastes a little bitter, as if someone added something to it."

"They did," I replied. "Wine today has preservatives in it, so that it can be sent all over the country or the world without going sour. Sadly, all wine has it."

"This is a crime," she announced. "Doesn't anyone make their own wine anymore? Oh, what I wouldn't give for some of Signor Castigliola's wine. It was thick and a deep red, not too dry but not too sweet. And if you had more than one glass, your head would swim."

"Was Signor Castigliola from Arcamo?" I asked.

"Oh yes," she answered, "If you ever tasted that wine, you would understand the difference. That, my little one, was *wine*," she mused. "Tell me, what else do they poison with 'preservatives'?"

"Pretty much everything," I answered, tasting my dinner.

"Eating and drinking this type of food will be helpful, I think," she said.

"How so?" I asked.

"When you turned, I saw the look on your face, the way that you admired the changes your body had gone through. You were pleased. I think that the more often you change, the more often you will detect these 'preservatives,' and you will like what becomes of your body."

Although her opinion seemed a bit harsh, I had to admit that in losing some of my weight, my body looked quite a bit different. Even my face was more lean. Overall, I was pleased with the change. Reading my mind from the expression on my face, Gelsamina volunteered to take in the seams on some of my clothes while I was away at work. I thanked her. I also thought it would be a good idea if the two of us went shopping for clothes on Saturday. If she was going to spend time with me, then some current-looking clothes would be useful. "Little one," she said, "when we have each learned all that we need to, I wonder how much we will need them." I was puzzled by her statement. It made me wonder about the future. I had so much time in the past, and the present was merely an instant in the midst of it all, but the future held even more questions than I'd had before. I was so enamored with Gelsamina, so wrapped up in her stories and the piecing together of the information, that I didn't give a thought as to where this path was leading me. Would I meet Fiero and La Notte? Would I see Nana and Nonno again? Now that Gelsamina had shown me what my legacy was, would she stay with me or go away? And the villa D'Arcamo, would we ever see it? And in what form? It seemed that the more I learned, the more I needed to.

I looked at her as we finished our meal. "How did you get from Sicily to here?"

She smiled a small smile, not unlike the one depicted in chalk so many years before. "You may find, little one, that when you need to travel somewhere, you can become enveloped in your spirit, and spiritually join with another to travel some distances. It may take a while, sometimes weeks or months, but you can eventually reach your destination. For me, it was Arcamo to Palermo. Then I soared, country to country, until I found my Giacamo. I sensed him, where he was. The love of my brother has always been strong. I suppose you could say that I rode on the strength of his love. It took some months to travel such a distance, but I joined with people where it was populated and with wolves where it wasn't."

I discovered later on that she had traveled from Italy to France and England. Then north to Iceland, then Greenland and the Canadian Maritimes, finally on to Ontario and then here. This concept of "spiritually hitchhiking" intrigued me, and although I really didn't understand it, the idea of traveling around the world in this fashion held a certain appeal. It was with these thoughts in my mind that I bid her goodnight and went to my room. She cleaned up the remaining dishes and pans from dinner and returned to her own room.

The next morning, we shared some coffee and drove to some of the larger department stores in the suburbs of Binghamton. I discovered that I'd shrunk two complete sizes. Gelsamina was a size six. I was already impressed with the sleekness of her figure. With the exception of her chest, she had a very athletic frame. Her chest size was larger than most athletes. I chuckled as I realized that it would be difficult for her to fend off attention.

We spent most of the day trying on skirts and blouses. Gelsamina felt uncomfortable in pants, and any shirts that proved to be too revealing were quickly discarded. She was not used to heels of any height, and it was amusing to see her attempts to walk in them. We both laughed like young girls as we completed our purchases and I drove us home.

As the laughter died away, I asked a question that had occurred to me only recently. "Gelsamina, are there any more like us? I don't mean those who died and were reborn, like Nonno and Nana, or those who were converted, like in the old stories. I mean like us."

"That is a question that I have never been able to answer, little one. I sometimes hear voices that I think are the voices of the *figli*, but as I listen, even straining to listen, the voices die away. As the *lupo* died out when I still lived in Arcamo, I heard voices less and less. But now, as they seem to be finding places to live, I hear them more. Perhaps in the future, we will know. But for now, our family is what our family is." She spoke with an air of sadness in her voice, all the while looking out the car window.

We arrived home and went inside with our newly acquired treasures. The sun was starting to set as we both came into the living room. "You know," I said, "we should take some of our old clothes and put them into the shed closet for any future changes." Gelsamina agreed and went to perform the task. When she returned, she came bearing an armload of firewood.

"I would like to have a fire for after dinner—and some of your bitter wine. I am growing fond of the time that we share stories," she said. I enjoyed our time together probably more than she, but relating to her was a confusing thing. For all intents and purposes, she was a beauty in her early twenties, but in reality (if I dare even use the word) she was my eighty-year-old great-aunt. There were times that I felt myself wanting to treat her like my sister, Tina, but something eventually stopped me. I suppose I could envision her as something like a distant cousin, one who I had only heard about but never actually met until recently. And then I discovered that we had some things in common, like the ability to transform into higher-intellect wolves that could travel great distances through the manipulation of our spirits. Other than that, the relationship was completely normal, practically run-of-the-mill.

We had stopped on the way home to pick up some chicken and vegetables to prepare for dinner. I thought I'd impress her with some fried eggplant and chicken with lemon and basil. I succeeded. As I was taking the chicken out of the oven, she asked me from her place on the kitchen chair, "Do you ever feel confined?" I asked her what she meant. "I mean, you drive your car to a place where you work. You are paid for your work. You spend your pay on food and provisions so that you can do it all over again, over and over. Do you not ever run free or fly? Do you not ever feel the wind bristling at your fur?" I didn't know how to answer her. Gelsamina had come from a time when life was lived more fully. A time when life had to be grasped with both hands, if one could survive it. My time was, by comparison, practically sterile. She sensed my difficulty and changed the subject. "Someday, I would like to take you to see the villa D'Arcamo. Did you know that since Leonardo, the baron, had no heirs, and he left everything to my brother, who then left it to you, I suppose you might be able to consider yourself the baroness D'Arcamo. I wonder how you would be received if we visited."

I hadn't given a lot of thought to the villa in the past few weeks, but as she spoke, the thought of it did intrigue me. Coupled with her comment about living a confined life, it appealed to me even more. But as I thought of it, another thought came to mind. "Gelsamina, how could you go there? Wouldn't you be afraid that there would be at least someone who could make a connection? I'm sure that stories were told, just as they were told to me."

"I think, little one, that I would change my name. As much as I love the name that my parents gave me, I would probably choose an American name, perhaps a version of it, so as to appear to be my own granddaughter. Now, what name shall I take?"

"Mina? That would be a nickname of Gelsamina," I suggested.

After a minute of thought, she said, "I remember a story about a man who couldn't die. He lived by night, drinking the blood of his victims. In the story, the name of a girl that he sought was Mina. I don't think I would like a name that one might associate with the victim of such a ghoulish person."

"Well, how about Chelsea? It is another feminine derivation of Charles, just as your name is. And Chelsea is a more modern name," I volunteered. "What do you think?"

"Hmmmm, Chelsea." She repeated the name a few times. "I like it!" she announced contentedly. "And I will keep my last name. Chelsea Del Forno! I like it!"

The chicken was delicious. I never considered myself as having too many special dishes, but this had to be one of them. And I wasn't sure, but it seemed to me that "Chelsea" was learning to appreciate the taste of modern wine. When the meal was finished, we had enough for a glass each to take to the fireplace. We pulled up two wingback chairs to face the fire that we'd set, and as she looked into it, she began, "You know, over the years, I never turned, not until now, not until you grew up, and even then not until I felt that you were ready. I suppose that's why I never pursued the idea of finding more of our kind. What we have is a gift, something to be shared. Perhaps now, we should think about sharing it."

"Are there any male *figli*? You know, males who can turn," I asked.

"I don't know, but I don't think so. What we have can only flow through the women. Men can eventually join us when they pass, but only that way, and only once. When they choose, they cannot turn back. I suppose that's why I waited for you, little one." I finished my wine and moved from the chair to the floor at her feet, where I could rest my head against her leg. There, staring into the fire, she continued talking.

"When I first turned, the baron was furious at my disappearance. He blamed the wolves, especially my pets. He grew angry and antagonistic to his own men. Those who could, left him, until eventually his staff dwindled down to a few, perhaps a half dozen men, mostly house staff. His income from renting land and property, and water rights from the well, insured that money would always be available. But his was a sadness that could be expressed in the only way he knew how, through violence.

"I asked Fiero many times over the years what had could have turned the baron to such a dark place. I remember once, on a rainy night, both Fiero and La Notte were sitting deep in the lair, their voices pouring into my head, telling me that he wouldn't understand, he couldn't understand. His ignorance bordered on arrogance. The only way in life was his. Everything else was dismissed as unimportant. I was there when he died, and it would have been a cruel irony to turn him into one of the *figli*. I was so saddened that I left; I went off on my own. I remember many of my clan, perhaps all of them, biting and tearing at him. I can't say what happened after that. It would have been hard to convince the others, the wolf-born, to accept one who devoted much of his adult life to their deaths, even with the knowledge that his own family was here among us."

"Will I ever meet Fiero and La Notte?" I asked, not moving my head, just staring into the fire.

"Their lives will be long, but spent entirely in Sicily. They cannot turn and turn back the way we do. I suppose that you would meet them if you were to visit Arcamo. You know, Arcamo is much warmer in December then it is here. I mean, even as one of the *figli*, we can feel the cold here. But there, the sun is warm and the blossoms from the lemon trees have bloomed. Not only are they beautiful, but they have a soft sweet fragrance. I remember once, as a little girl, falling asleep under a lemon tree, just breathing in that scent …" Gelsamina had a way of painting a mental picture that proved awfully inviting. She made unspoken invitations to join the rapture that she was a part of. It made me wonder how much a part of it she really was, or rather, how much a controlling part of it she really was. And how much she wanted me to be a part of it.

"Let's say, just for argument's sake, that I were to come with you to Arcamo. I have my life here, my work. I have to make a living. When could I go that wouldn't disrupt it all?" I felt that this was the right time to pose these questions. I loved to hear the stories, but there was always a part of me that was tethered to my life and work here. I had spent my life, up until now, doing all of the things that one must do for a career and the financial well-being that comes with it. As I pulled my head away from her leg, she sensed that I had doubts, doubts brought on by the realities of a career.

"Little one, you will be the *baronessa* D'Arcamo. You will have the wealth that has been building steadily for decades. If you choose to, you need never have to work at your university, printing again. I don't presume to know all the needs and requirements of your modern 'jobs and careers,' but I tell you this seriously and with the love of one whose blood courses through your veins as completely as if I were your mother. And in the way of the *figli*, I am your mother, and your sister and your cousin and your aunt. We are bound together not as friends but as family. You have finally been given that which you were born into. Your heritage is to be a matriarch of a grand family. I was of one—the Del Forno clan of the *figli del lupo*. You will be of two—the Del Forno clan in America and the D'Arcamo in Sicily. If you choose it, your life will be of considerably more luxury than you are living now."

At this point, I had climbed back into my chair and was staring intently at her face. She wasn't telling me a romantic story of the past. She was offering me a future that went far beyond my imagination. And she was saying, in no uncertain terms, that I had been born into this. It was one thing to look at this from the safety of a farmhouse in America, to fantasize about something ancient and mysterious. But to abandon a large part of my life to completely enter into a new world? This was a decision I could not make in haste. She saw this in my face.

"Anna, you are already part of us. If you do not learn the ways with me, you will lack the control that you need to change and turn back. Imagine being at the place where you work and getting angry, so angry that you turn, right there. How would you explain your life then? And who would believe you? And in your anger and frustration, how would you turn back? Nonno couldn't help you. What would you do? If you were cornered, would you attack? Do you know what happens to a victim of the *figli*? And I mean an actual victim, not someone who wished to join and be one with us."

I lashed out at her. "You knew that this moment would come eventually. You knew that I would have to decide, but the decision wouldn't really be mine to make. You knew all along!" I spat out the words, feeling as if I'd been played.

"I'd hoped that you'd make the decision by yourself, that you'd see the beauty, the majesty of the place where you alone are and can be. Eventually, you could come and go as you pleased, leading your pack here and coming back to the farmhouse, and leading your pack in Arcamo and living at the villa. And you would never be without wealth." She spoke in a manner that made me feel as if she was doing this only for me.

"Hold it," I stopped her. "You just said that I'd be leading a clan of wolves in Arcamo. Where would you be?"

"Little one, I am the White Wolf, *la Regina dei figli del lupo*. I have been called to watch over us all. But I could not do this until you came into your legacy. Now, say no more about this. I have angered you enough this day. Please know that I could never hurt you, just as I would see to it that no one else would ever hurt you. Come and rest your head by me again. Look at the fire. Let the flames warm you as you rest. Come." She raised her hand, and as I rose to sit by her leg once again, she raised her glass and finished her wine. "To Anna," she toasted, "my little one."

I awoke the next morning to a bitterly cold mid-December Sunday. It was bright and sunny, but the temperature hovered in the single digits, and with the wind that whistled into the trees, it felt like a few degrees below zero. Our day was spent entirely indoors, save the single instance where Gelsamina went outside to distribute food scraps. She had filled an aluminum pie plate with table scraps from the morning's breakfast and last evening's dinner and set it out at the edge of the field just before the woods began. In this weather, all life would be hunkered down, and at the very least, she was determined for Nana and Nonno to avoid going hungry. When she returned to the house, she came into my room. I was lying on the bed reading. We had not spoken more than a word or two all morning, but as she came in, I began again. "Did you realize, when you first turned, how much thought you'd lose?" I spoke acidly, as I still felt that I'd been tricked into this position.

"At the turn of the century," she answered, "there was far less reading, and one didn't give a great deal of consideration to thought. Then, in most cases, one would merely respond." She was trying to be helpful, to give information that would explain her actions. "And besides, when I turned back, my thoughts and abilities returned to me, as they did with you." I sat silently, blankly staring at the room that had not been redecorated since the days of my grandparents.

"Why didn't you just ask me?" I spoke with hurt indignation. My feelings had gone from the thrill of an exciting adventure to the predestined, preordained double life that I now knew of. "And another thing—how long will this go on? Will I lead a pack until I die? Until another wolf attacks me? If you're choosing me to replace you, who are you replacing? And will you choose another to replace me eventually?" Again, one of my questions rushed into many more. I continued in my anger, "How long would I live? I have heard about alpha males. It sounds as if you and I are alpha females."

"Little one, stop. Your head is filled with questions. Whether you realize it or not, I have been 'hearing' your questions all morning. It was not fair of me to come right out and tell you of that which is your birthright, but let us be honest. Wouldn't you have been frightened if, after hearing Nonno's story, you learned all that you now know? And what would you have done at the age of fifteen? You needed the wisdom and maturity that you now possess to fully comprehend all of this. And even now, you base your questions on what you know. Anna, you are not merely wolf, at least not wolf born of wolf. You are of the *figli del lupo*. Although I can't say for certain, I have every reason to believe that you and I will live on, long after others die. That is why we have the ability to offer the turning to those that we care for. And even then, only if they accept it, will they turn."

I remained silent, taking in every word that she said.

"As for alpha males," she continued, "I am glad that you have learned something of your brethren. But you must know now that any pack that you are a part of is not an ordinary pack. An ordinary pack would have an alpha male and his mate as leaders. All members would follow them and work together on behalf of the pack. My pack, and eventually your pack, has no alpha male. Your abilities are far stronger than an ordinary alpha. You would not only beat an ordinary alpha, you would kill him. And that is something that we must avoid, even in self defense."

"Are you saying that I'm immortal and invulnerable?" I asked.

"I am saying that your strength and wisdom create cunning and abilities that you will use for the safety and preservation of your pack, and perhaps others in addition. And I'm saying that as far as I know, our spirits will never die. I can only speak for the eighty or so years of my life, but I feel as vibrant and youthful now as I have ever felt. And I know of nothing that can harm me, except perhaps your unkind words."

This hurt a little, but I was angry. I still wasn't ready to relinquish my life as it was. Granted, I didn't have the house, husband, and family that my sister had, or the thirty-odd years of fruitful toil that I could proudly look back on with my husband, as my mother could. I was thirty years old, living in a relative's house, looking at a job that I might not even have at the end of next semester. And outside of my family, I was alone. Looking at it this way made me wonder if my whole life had been set up to accept this destiny. Perhaps it was best that Gelsamina, and even Nonno, eased me into this. I probably would have never accepted this fate earlier in my life. Although I had to admit, I was conceding a lot of trust to Gelsamina.

She broke my contemplation by saying, "Little one, I know that you have much to think about. Please let us say no more for now. Let me cook today's dinner for you, for a change. It will be my way of showing you my sincerity. This time, you sit in the chair. You can help me with that complicated stove. Watch me, and I will make you a feast to remember."

I followed her into the kitchen and sat in the chair she pulled out for me. I watched as she took a package of ladyfingers—a light absorbent cookie in a rounded, oblong shape—and laid each one neatly in a baking dish. Then, into a cup, she poured rum and the juice from a jar of maraschino cherries. The combination smelled sweet with a hint of alcohol. She poured this over the cookies and set the dish into the refrigerator.

She looked at me and asked if I would mind going into town to buy some cream for whipping. She said that she, too, had a job to do. I shrugged and consented. By the time I returned, I found her in the kitchen holding a freshly killed rabbit over a cutting board, skinning it. Keeping the carcass, she took the head, skin and entrails and placed them in the aluminum pie plate that she had apparently retrieved. "For Nana and Nonno," she said.

She cut up the carcass into pieces, similar to the way that one might cut up a chicken, dredging each piece in flour and then placing it in a thick iron pot, in the bottom of which she had browned garlic in olive oil. I showed her which dials to use for the stove, as she turned the pieces of rabbit over and over, browning them lightly. Then she added red wine (a good amount of it), onions, carrots, and potatoes, all cut up into inch-thick chunks. Seasoning it all with a little salt and pepper, she turned the burner dial to a low heat and covered the pot.

"Now," she said, "I need the cream." Pouring it into a bowl, she took a whisk from the drawer and began beating the cream, every few minutes adding a teaspoon of powdered sugar or vanilla extract until she had a bowl of sweet, fluffy whipped cream that hinted of vanilla. Setting the bowl alongside the cookies in the refrigerator, she returned to the pot on the stove, removing the lid to inspect and stir once or twice. The inspection and stirring continued sporadically for over an hour; the aroma of the rabbit simmering in the wine was intoxicating. I eventually set the table, poured two glasses of wine, and set out a small loaf of bread that we'd purchased the day before. Soon after, we sat down and ate.

Although Gelsamina told me that this was Nonno's recipe, I don't ever remember having it. Frankly, I didn't think that a child would have appreciated it the way that I was doing now. The concept of eating something that was once cute and furry aside, the combination of flavors, the wine and onions mixed with the rustic character of the rabbit meat, would have been totally missed by a child's palate. But here and now, this stuff was ambrosia! The blending of the tastes was extraordinary, and I thoroughly enjoyed it. Gelsamina could see that I was eating with gusto and she smiled, pleased that she could present something as appealing as this to our table.

I opened my mouth to ask a question and only came out with, "Did you ..." before she interrupted me, all the while smiling. "You didn't think that I'd sent you out for cream out of laziness, did you? I work fastest alone. After turning, it did not take me long to find a rabbit suitable for us. After all, it is late fall. This is a good time to hunt for rabbit," she said as she cut into her entrée.

"For us, or for wolves?" I asked.

"For us, silly. As wolves we couldn't afford to be so particular, but then again, as wolves we would digest things differently," she answered blithely.

I was still getting used to the matter-of-fact quality in which she spoke of physically, mystically changing from a human being to a wolf-like being. Neither of us understood it, and while I was still in awe, Gelsamina reveled in it. After the rabbit and wine, I cleared the plates and made coffee. I set out the dessert plates while Gelsamina added the sweet whipped cream to the rum-soaked cookies. By the time she had made two plates of the confection, the coffee was ready. It was a dessert worthy of the meal. We were preparing to go into the living room, careful not to speak about the subject that caused concern from the night before. Gelsamina asked if I'd like a fire, but before I could answer, the phone rang. It was my father.

"Hello, sweetie, how are you?" he began.

"Hi, Dad. I'm good. ... You and Mom?"

"Fine, fine. Listen, I just wanted to call to let you know that yesterday I got a letter back from my attorney friend. Are you sitting down, little one? Congratulations! You are worth a lot of money. My friend spoke to someone at the Association of Estate Attorneys in Palermo, who reviewed the wording on the document that you left with me. He asked me to get a Xeroxed copy to him, but I think that you should make copies of it first and keep two or three with the actual document before you send it to me. Remember, send it by registered mail. Anyway, the guy in Palermo says that the wording is genuine, and if he could see the document, he's pretty sure that it's the real thing. You would have to pay some fees and taxes to transfer ownership, but that's to make everything legal." My father paused, sensing the silence at my end. "Anna, are you there? Did you hear me?" he asked.

"I'm here, Dad," I answered. "I'm just taking this all in. Did he say that there was actual money in all of this, or is it the villa and the property?"

"Anna, it's everything!" he responded ecstatically. "I didn't call you yesterday because I've been on the phone with him and the attorney from Luigi Catanzaro and Son, the firm that's been managing the estate for the past fifty-eight years."

"Fifty-eight years?" I exclaimed.

"Yeah. This was a good thing for them. They were getting fifteen percent off of the top on the rentals, the water rights, and the property all that time. All they had to do was manage it, collect the rent, and bank it. They didn't even have the right to invest it. So there's a lot of money in an account that probably has your name on it. Granted, it's a flat savings account, but with interest, it's worth somewhere between nine hundred thousand and one point four million American dollars. The farmland has been rented out for lemon trees and blood oranges, and the villa itself has been rented out from time to time, short term, by dignitaries and rock stars."

"Rock stars?" I quipped.

"Yup. It seems that the acoustics are great for recording, and they've been willing to pay a lot for the place. They've been doing this since the early seventies," he added.

"Wow," was really all I could say at that point. After another moment of silence, I said, "Do they need me to sign something? Anything? Can it be done by registered mail, or do I have to go there in person?" I wanted to make sure that I was really the one who was going to get all of this.

"'Do I have to go in person?'" he repeated my words in a mocking voice. "Are you kidding? You may be a millionaire, and you probably own a villa in Sicily. I'm surprised that you're still talking to me on the phone." To say that my father's level of excitement was increasing with each added bit of information that he offered would have been an understatement. "You know, sweetie, now that your mother and I are retired, we could keep you company on your trip to Sicily." My father's ability to hint was as subtle as a bulldozer. "I might even buy you dinner." At this point, he laughed a little. "Oh, and are you ready for one more piece? He's not sure as to the legal ramifications, but if you were to apply for and establish a dual residency between Italy and America, the title of *baronessa* might be transferred to you. What do you think about that?" He stopped, waiting for a reply.

The phone call had brought to fruition a big part of all that Gelsamina had talked about. In fact, a lot of what my grandfather had talked about. And it was now all mine. Oddly enough, I was looking at this enormous package not through the eyes of desire or fantasy, but rather through the eyes of responsibility. I'd never managed enormous sums of money before, much less an entire estate, and at the same time been part of a transformation that was nothing short of supernatural. "Anna, sweetie, are you still there?" my dad asked again.

"I'm here, Dad. This is a lot to digest. Let me call you back in a little while. Oh, and does Tina know? Let me call her. Oh my. Oh, and Dad?"

"Yes, little one?"

"Thank you, thank you, thank you. You're the best."

I put down the receiver and looked at Gelsamina. She could have gloated, seeing the reaction I had to my father's validation of all of her contentions. Instead, all she said, as she turned her slightly outstretched arms palms up toward me, was, "Now it begins." She lit the fire. Then she rose, walked over to her chair, and sat, smiling and staring at the slowly growing flames. "So, *Baronessa*, where will we go from here?"

For the first time I could remember, I responded with enthusiasm. Normally, I would have been quiet and still, my mind swimming with questions, but this moment was different. Perhaps my mind had been affected by my turning, but I felt as if I actually had a plan in mind. It seemed rather linear, now that I think of it, with one goal followed by another and so on, but for me, this felt very different. "Tina. I haven't spoken to my sister since before Thanksgiving. She should hear about this from me," I began.

"And what will you tell her, little one?" came the voice from the Cheshire cat grinning in the chair.

"I'll tell her about the will and the villa in Sicily. I'll tell her about the money, and that I'm going to Sicily for Christmas, and hopefully I'll see her when I return. By then, maybe we'll come up with a plan to have you come along." The Cheshire-cat smile grew even wider. I believe that Gelsamina liked what she'd heard. We stared at the fire for a few more minutes in silence. I wondered what a million-dollar investment, made judiciously, could provide as an annual return. That, with the fees that would still come in on a regular basis, might prove to be ample enough for my needs. And if the law firm that managed the money for all of these years proved to be reputable, I felt that they should be rewarded, maybe by upping the percentage on their management fees. "Would you be my translator in these matters?" I asked Gelsamina, forgetting that she could hear my every thought. We were inexorably linked. She looked at me and, without speaking, put the words, "I thought you'd never ask. Of course," into my head. Now it was my turn to smile. I wanted the legalities to be completely aboveboard, but I spoke no Italian. No matter what happened, I would always feel at a disadvantage.

But with Gelsamina, "You will never have a worry as long as I'm here, little one," she finished my thoughts. "Now, go and call Concettina and tell her the good news." Gelsamina could see that I was too excited to continue with my plans until I spoke with Tina. It was at that moment, though, that I stopped from rising out of the chair.

"I probably already know the answer, but how did you know …?"

"That Concettina is her christened name? Little one, am I not your great-aunt? Are we not all one? What else would your parents have named her? And true to her nature, what else would she have avoided using since her childhood? Hers is not a shame for her past, but a passion to be a part of what lives now. She never really understood the richness of her history in the way that you do. To her, we were just one more interesting story, far less important than her work at the hotel, or her husband's job, or her daughter's trip to a dental surgeon in the hopes of having her teeth made to look straighter. Even then, she tries to break her ties with the past by removing the way teeth have looked in our family for generations."

"I never mentioned any of that to you, Gelsamina," I interrupted. "How did you know this?"

"As long as you know me, and think of and care for me, I live. This was the way with my brother, and to a smaller degree, with your father. But with you, I come fully alive, in all of the glory of the *figli del lupo*. That is why you were the one to hear me, to join us. The joys and sadnesses of your life are the joys and sadnesses of mine. And soon, mine, yours. I love you, Little One, and will always protect you." And with that, she returned to her room.

As the flames in the fire died down, I rose to get to the telephone in the kitchen. I dialed the number and waited to hear that pert professional voice say, "Austin Hotel, San Antonio. Tina Corcoran speaking."

"Are you sitting down?" I began, deciding at the last minute to be a little dramatic.

"Anna, is that you?" she asked, suddenly changing in tone from businesslike Mrs. Corcoran to Tina, my sister. "Figures, on the one day I have to work late, my sister calls."

"Well, Tina, if I had to choose one place to try and reach you, you know I'm going to call the hotel first." Actually, Anna had forgotten that it was well after five o'clock and normally Tina would be home with the kids. But the joke did seem like a good way to break the ice with her sister.

"So, what's going on?"

"Well, a couple of weeks ago I found some papers in Nonno's basement," I began. "I brought them to Dad during Thanksgiving, and he gave them to his attorney. Dad called me a few minutes ago. Are you ready for this? Nonno left the farmhouse in Binghamton to Dad! It's official!

"That is great news, Anna."

"But wait, there's more," I said, sounding like an advertisement for steak knives. "Included in these papers was a document that transferred ownership of a villa in Sicily to Nonno, and he, in turn, left it to me!" I could barely contain my excitement in repeating the words to her. At first there was silence. Then Tina said, "You don't mean that old story about the baron and the wolves, with Nonno's sister. I thought that he just made up that old chestnut. Well, I'll be damned. So tell me, Anna. What are you *gonna'* do with a villa in Sicily? Arcamo, right?" she said, starting to remember a bit more of the story.

"Well, the first thing I'm *"gonna'"* do is visit and see what it's all about. Then, when I come to your house some time after Christmas, I'll give you a full report. Oh, and there's some money attached to it." I thought it best to keep the money part of the story light, for now, as I was getting a sense that the unspoken words in this conversation included the phrase, *What about me?* I addressed this by saying, "You know, Dad will probably leave this place to you in his will. That is, if you want it." Tina was quiet again. She wasn't angry, but this was a lot to digest.

"And where would you live? I already have my house here," she said.

"Maybe I'll rent the farmhouse from you, what with me having a villa in Sicily and all," I quipped. At this, the tone of the conversation brightened considerably. Tina realized that a lot of what I'd just said to her was speculation, and I was just calling to tell her of my good fortune. She was a good-hearted person, after all, and was genuinely happy for me, having felt that I was a bit of a late bloomer when it came to a career, love, and life in general.

"Well, congratulations, my wealthy, landed big sister, and I hope that we can at least expect a call from you at Christmas, just like you did at Thanksgiving. Oh wait, you didn't call at Thanksgiving." Now it sounded more like Tina.

"Tina, you told me that you were having your in-laws for Thanksgiving. I didn't want to intrude, and I got so caught up with Mom and Dad that I guess I just forgot. I'm sorry." Now it sounded more like me.

"I'm gonna hold this one over your head," she said in mock anger, "to make sure that you call at Christmas. And when do you think you can come for a visit? I have some days left that I have to take before March first, and honestly, spending them with you will be a welcome change from school field trips and dental appointments for braces."

"Oh come on, you love those kids," I interrupted.

"The twins are wonderful," she continued, "but sometimes I get a little tired of kids, kids, kids, Dan, Dan, Dan, work, work, work, and then the whole thing all over again. Sometimes I need to do something for *me*. And you being here would be just what I need—a little time with my sister, the university printer. And if she's a wealthy landowner, maybe I could talk her into buying me lunch." The atmosphere had become playful.

"I'll call as soon as I get more information. You know, now that I think of it, I hope that there is some money attached to this. Who knows how much a phone call from Italy is going to cost?" We both laughed as I said good-bye. I felt that the conversation went well. I told Tina enough without saying anything that would cause unnecessary concern.

Gelsamina came back into the kitchen from down the hall. "You love her, don't you?" she asked.

"Of course I love her. She's my sister. We're not as close as we used to be, but then again, it's hard to be close emotionally when someone's life is eighteen hundred miles away."

"I didn't listen to your words with her, but I sensed that you were guarded. Little one, there will be parts of your life that she will learn of, and she will probably not understand."

"Will she turn? Is she one of us?" I asked, having never thought of it before.

"I don't think so, but I'm not certain," Gelsamina replied. "I hear voices when I think of her, but I don't understand them. I cannot answer your question." When she asked me if I loved Tina, she almost wore an expression of envy on her face, but now, she said this with a look of desire to help but an inability to do so. It puzzled me. I extended my arms to her and we embraced, an embrace that felt comforting and familial, as we both knew that the next part of our adventure would soon take place and we could never really be fully prepared for it.

Chapter VII
Preparation

The next morning, I rose a little earlier than usual. I made a pot of coffee and, pouring a cup for myself, sat down to plan what I would say to my supervisor at work. This would be an awkward time to ask for a leave of absence. But I felt that it would be wise, at least for the time being, to be able to return to the job if things in Sicily proved to be less than advertised. With a rough idea of a plan in my head, I returned to my room and made my bed. Thirty minutes later, I was cleaned, dressed, and made-up. I even wore one of my new outfits, one of those that fit my new figure. Gelsamina was just stirring as I opened the front door, called out "Wish me luck," and left. The drive was brisk and of little note except for the presence of two wolves at the side of the road a mile or so from the house. They looked familiar, but I couldn't be certain if it was Nana and Nonno. I was driving and most of my attention was on the road. I merely saw two animals that looked roughly like wolves. I do recall, however, as I drove by, that their gaze followed me all the way down the road.

I pulled into the parking lot and made my way into the building. I received a cordial but slightly distant "Good morning" from my secretary as I passed her and went into my office. This being the week before Christmas break, I didn't have a lot of unfinished work to do, so I called Mr. Howard's office. His secretary answered in a put-upon voice, and the tone didn't change when she recognized my voice.

"He won't be available 'til noon, and even then I could only squeeze you in for fifteen minutes," she said, giving me the impression that he really didn't want to see me, and she was doing me a great favor. I thanked her as if this meant the world to me, playing the game that she had called the rules to, and hung up. I then went out to my secretary and asked her to come in. I positioned myself behind my desk as she came in and sat down.

"Clara, I'm afraid that I have some bad news," I began.

"I knew it," she said. "First the week off 'camping,' followed by the weight loss and then the new clothes. I'll bet you found a better job. I knew it was just a matter of time before some commercial company found you. We always lose the good ones."

I waited until she had finished ranting. "Well," I started again, "you're only a little bit correct. I need to ask for a leave of absence to take care of some family matters."

"You mean the cousin from Italy? I heard all about it from the secretary upstairs," she added, not waiting for me to finish.

"As a matter of fact, yes. But I really can't say anymore. Hopefully, I can be back at work within the next few months—one semester, at most."

"Howard isn't going to like this," she answered. "He's gonna think exactly what I thought. And he always reacts badly. Tell him about the family stuff first. Is it medical? He can't say no if it's medical. Is it drugs? You can tell me. And that's why you lost the weight. Because your cousin needs money for drugs."

"Clara, where do you come up with these things? None of that is true. Saying things like that would only make matters worse. Now stop and tell me if we have any projects that need to be finished before Christmas." I spoke with a firm authoritative voice. She stopped, went to her desk, and retrieved the one project that still needed my attention. Thanking her as she left, I proofread the piece and made the necessary changes and notes on it. I then instructed her to bring it to the print shop with my directions. It would be completed by tomorrow, a statement I asked her to make to the professor whose work it was. The proofreading had taken up most of the morning, and by the time I got back to my office, it was eleven forty-five. I had just enough time to get to my supervisor's office.

As I entered, it appeared to me that he had not left the office all morning. There was a half-finished cup of coffee and a plate of various pastries that he'd been working on, similar to the platter that was outside, where his secretary sat. From what I could gather, I was being squeezed in after a morning office holiday party. His demeanor was far different from the one that I experienced when I was spoken to the previous week. This was downright jovial. It pained me a bit to be there for the reason that I had. I spoke about my "family situation" that I felt duty-bound to address, hoping that I'd need only a one-semester leave of absence. I trusted that my work record thus far would give the indication that, not only was I dedicated to the job, but that I was making a serious contribution here at the university—so much so that I would make every effort to make the leave shorter than one semester. I felt that my performance now, in his office, was very realistic. This was the most information, false as it was, that I could give without being committed for psychiatric evaluation. I touched the baron's ring, which was again on my finger. It gave me a sense of strength. Based on my experience with the businesses I'd worked for previously, I thought that he would believe my story, ask for some kind of documentation, and let me go for at least a month. That would give me the opening I needed. I knew this was shameless, but I had to try. Too much had happened for me not to.

He sat, listening to me, with his eyebrows arched and his fingers knit together, forefingers tapping as if they were letting off spurts of steam at measured intervals. Finally he spoke, looking at me and then looking at his fingers before finding some fixed point on the ceiling beyond my head. "I am truly sorry to hear that there is a family emergency that needs your attention. Your work has been good here, but as you have worked for the university for less than one year, you aren't eligible to be granted a leave of absence under any circumstances. In your situation, you'd have to resign, and upon your return, if there were any openings, I'd put in a good word for you." He shrugged his shoulders as he said, "That's about all I can do for you at this time." I got the feeling that he was exacting revenge for my week away and expected me to dangle on a string until he chose to rehire me at a lower position in the department. When I said nothing in reply, I think he felt I wasn't taking his bait. "Have Lucille give you a resignation form on the way out, and be sure to give an accurate description as to your reasons for leaving. Oh, and don't forget to put down when you think you'd be able to return. Better yet, don't fill it out now. Just send it to this office."

My eyes grew moist as I rose to leave. He did not rise. Instead, he picked up some papers that had been piled on one side of his desk—to make room the pastries—and pretended to be returning to work on them. I would not give him the satisfaction of showing my emotions, but by the time I left his office, I needed desperately to go to my car and cry. My mother had always said not to leave one position until you found another, so as never to leave yourself without resources. Italy was an ocean away, and all that it held was still, at this point in time, conjecture. Right now, I was without funds, save whatever I'd put aside since coming here to Binghamton. It's not that this wasn't just one more incident of my feeling that I was heading for a very specific destiny, it was that for some reason that I couldn't fathom, my supervisor seemed to be getting some calculated pleasure from letting me go.

Soon, surprised sadness was replaced by anger. I needed to find out if there was more to his agenda, and I only had the afternoon to do it. If I was being asked to resign, I certainly wasn't staying for the remaining four days until the holiday break. Using tissues and whatever makeup I had in my bag, I blotted my tears, patched myself up, and re-entered the building, determined to go down swinging. The combination of tears, the slightly caked powder, and the December cold stung my cheeks in a way that gave me a sense of purpose.

I returned to my desk followed closely by Clara. "So, what did he say?" she asked, sitting down as I did. I sighed and told her that I'd be resigning my position effective immediately, and that when I was able to return he'd try to find something for me. Giving her an abbreviated version seemed best for my purposes, especially when I asked if she'd heard anything about him. She seemed to be a font of information lately.

"Listen," she began, "you were his ace in the hole. He had gotten into some trouble with the last woman who sat in your chair. There were accusations of sexual harassment, but she left before anything could actually be pinned on him. By hiring you and promising Baker that he'd behave himself, all was well again. The amount of work and the quality that you turned out was really the icing on the cake. Sadly, it just made Howard look better in Baker's eyes. So now that the golden goose is asking for a leave, Howard's back to square one. And Lucille has a twenty-two-year-old son that she thinks is the greatest thing since sliced bread, so you just know she'll be pushing him. On top of that, there's the new secretary over in maintenance. If you've seen her once, you'll know who I'm talking about: short skirt, stiletto heels, lots of cleavage, big hair and red lips, and she can type all of fifteen words a minute. Well, it's hard to type with those long red nails." I nodded and smiled, having a pretty good idea where her report was going. "So now, he has a choice," she continued, "between a bimbo and his secretary's kid. And the two of 'em together aren't half of you and what you've done. Knowing Howard, the only thing he'll try to angle for is to hire both of 'em. This way, he'll be happy, and his secretary will be happy. Only problem is, nothing will get done around here. For your sake, Miss Del Forno, I almost wish you *were* leaving to take a big job in private industry."

I assured her again that I wasn't and, with a reluctant smile, asked her to hold all calls for the rest of the afternoon. This was a polite way of letting her know that I would need some time to collect my things. She understood and, in getting up, came over to give me a hug. As sad a moment as this was for the two of us, our sadness came from two different directions. Mine was from being dismissed in such a curt fashion. Hers was for the problems in the workplace that she feared would lie ahead.

It took less than an hour to collect the contents of my office and box them. I then set about the task of filling out the resignation form. I stated that under the circumstances, I was needed by my family, and based upon the work that I'd done during my employment, I would hope that when I was again available to return, a position suitable to my abilities would be available. I asked Clara to make a copy of it, and signing both, I kept one and had the other hand-delivered to Mr. Howard's office. I then bid the people on the printing floor good-bye. Clara had already told them of the day's events. I hugged her again, picked up my box, and left.

It was an odd feeling. I was moving into the next phase of what might prove to be a life-altering adventure, but I was still sad at the way that this aspect of it had been handled. I suppose that, all things considered, I was hoping for more than I should have. Still in all, Bart Howard was a man not to be trusted. I remember thinking how interesting it would be to see how Gelsamina would react to these events when I related them at dinner.

The sky had grown dark by the time I arrived home that evening. Gelsamina was in the kitchen, hovering over a pot of soup. The savory aroma welcomed me as soon as I entered the house. "Hellooo ..." I called out. "Chicken?"

"And carrots, and onions, a little potato, garlic, and a tomato for character," came the reply. "It is good to cook again. It has been a long time, and I missed it." Gelsamina's voice sounded pleased. It was like having a roommate, something I hadn't had since college. Only something more than a roommate—Gelsamina was, after all, part of my family. For a moment, it made me forget the day I'd had. I suppose that's something family is supposed to do.

We sat down to steaming bowls of the soup, perfect for warming up such a cold day. "So, how did the day at your work go?" she began.

"Well," I said, drawing in a breath, "I applied for a leave of absence and was denied."

Her eyebrows rose. "I do not understand this work of yours. You said that such a thing is allowed. That people can ask for a leave of absence to help their family."

"Yes, but," I interrupted, "I've been there for less than one year. Apparently, I must be working there for at least one year before I can apply. Personally, I think that more could have been done, but my supervisor ... well, I found out some things about him today, and he is ... not a nice person. By the time I left his office, I could have done bad things to him. I think that he was trying to manipulate me," I said in exasperation.

Gelsamina sensed my hurt pride. She was silently weighing the emotions hidden in the words I'd spoken. We each ate a little more soup. Finally, she spoke. "Well, this may be a blessing in disguise. You still have some money here, and it will give us more time to plan our trip. There is still a lot for us to talk about." She poured a glass of wine for each of us. "One chapter has closed and another is soon to open. Let us not look back at the last chapter. Mr. Bart Howard has done you a great service, although he will never know how good a worker he has offended. Let us never think of him again." And with that, she took a long, healthy drink.

"Gelsamina, I never mentioned his name. How did you know it?" This was an odd point that I had just picked up on as she spoke.

"Little one, part of what we are is that we can hear each other, even when we don't speak. I suppose I just heard you thinking about him. Here, let me show you. Imagine what this man looks like. Picture him in your mind. There, now, do you have him?" As I tried this experiment, she began to giggle. "Either I am not very good at hearing you, or Mr. Howard is a fat man with a ratty face."

Now I giggled. "No, you're right. That's him."

"See," she answered, "I made you smile. Now let's talk about the future. We still have some time before we leave, and we must talk about how we are going to get there."

"What is there to talk about?" I asked. "We get on a plane to Palermo. From there, we drive to Arcamo."

"You flatter me, little one. You think of me as a relative, a friend. Think of me now. How did I come here?" She pointed to herself with her spoon, and although it was a simple enough gesture, I blushed because I realized that I'd mistakenly considered her as a person who could merely purchase an airline ticket, board a plane, and fly to another country. This was America, 1980. She would need a passport, government-issued identification, even money of her own; hard to get for an eighty-two-year-old supernatural being, capable of transforming herself from the outside appearance of a twenty-year-old girl into that of a wolf at any given moment. She was invulnerable and, for all we knew, immortal—a chosen member of the *figli del lupo*. And she was my great-aunt. Clearly, we needed a different plan to get to Sicily.

"What if I brought you as my pet?" I wondered out loud.

"I believe that this country has a law regarding wild animals, and at any rate, a pet would be quarantined before being allowed to travel, so as to make sure that you're not illegally transporting some sort of virus into another country," she answered, almost matter-of-factly. She seemed a little perturbed that I would offer that idea as one of the first ones, thinking perhaps that she was valued less than she should be. Quite the contrary was true, but I admittedly was still very new at this type of problem-solving.

"Oh my," I said, impressed at her answer. "Someone has been doing research."

"I paid a visit to your library this morning. I wanted to review my options. And yours," she continued. "Apparently, one can apply for a passport at any time, but I believe the one that you used when you and your family took a cruise to the Caribbean is still valid."

I now put my spoon down. I had completely forgotten the cruise that Mom and Dad took us on. It can't have been too many years ago. Tina had been working for the hotel for a few years already. In fact, I don't even think that the twins were in elementary school yet. It had been the last family vacation we all went on. Tina and I were old enough to enjoy the independence of a cruise, but still young enough to be our parents' daughters. And we looked the part. It was great—tanning ourselves on the beaches in Saint Maarten and Saint Thomas, drinking fruity and unashamedly girly drinks, getting dressed up to go dancing. It was all absolutely silly and fun. And I think I still had that passport somewhere in one of the drawers of clothing I'd brought. I remember my mother sending it to me some years ago, advising me to keep it in a safe place. I even remembered renewing it, because it had been close to expiring. Yet another time that Gelsamina had unearthed some fact I'd long forgotten.

"And you may as well start calling me Chelsea, so that we will both get used to it when we do arrive," she offered, again almost matter-of-factly. I couldn't tell if she was mocking me with hurt feelings, or if I'd really offended her. I decided to try to "listen" to her, as she did so easily with me, but my attempt was clumsy. "If you keep 'listening' that intently, you'll give us both a headache," she said, smiling. "I need for you to understand that I won't be able to fly to Sicily with you, because it would bring about too many questions. I think that for this trip, the best thing for us to do is arrive separately. You could fly to Palermo and stay in a hotel there. I will arrive a day or two later and from there, we could go to Arcamo."

To me, this sounded like a feasible plan. I presumed that Gelsamina would travel much in the way that she did to come to Binghamton, so it would not be a problem. "Will you be all right, I mean, traveling in your way, 'Chelsea'?" Saying this new name would take some getting used to.

"I will be fine, little one," she said as she finished her soup. "Perhaps we can visit the travel agent that you had success with when you traveled to Ocala. You could arrange for your flight and ask for the name of a good hotel in Palermo."

"I should call my father, too, and let him know that I'll be spending

Christmas in Palermo," I added. "I'll get his attorney's name and have him let the people in Sicily know that I'll be there."

"Very good," she responded. "Our plans are moving forward, and to be honest, I look forward to seeing my Arcamo again. I know that it will have changed from when I was there, but I hope that there are at least a few things that I can show you. And when we turn, ahhh, Little One, when we turn ..." Her eyes glistened as she looked through me to something far in the distance. "We will be with my pets, my Fiero and my La Notte. Of all the things I left in Arcamo, I think that I have missed them most of all."

A moment later, she returned from that far-off place that held her, and she rose to clean up our dishes. After washing and putting them away, we went down the hall. I had asked her what she thought I should bring for clothing. "I think that the clothing you bought this weekend would be very suitable at first, but you will need more things when you get to Palermo. Keep in mind, for as cold as it is here, it will be that warm there, Anna." She took great pains to pronounce my name a little differently. I realized why she had done this. In front of the rest of the world, I could not be known by the name that she and Nonno had used for me. It was a nickname bestowed years ago and in love, but hardly appropriate for use by a "cousin" who would always appear some eight years younger than me. I will be thirty years old forever, apparently one more aspect of "turning." And "Chelsea" would be eternally twenty-two. We would be comfortable in front of Tina and my parents for probably the next few years, and then we'd have to figure something out. Anna and Chelsea would be our names, at least for the time being. Who knew what needs we would have by tomorrow?

"I have another question," I said to Gelsamina. "If you travel the way that you did before, you'll have to turn from time to time. Yes? And if you do, you will need clothing. You'll cause quite a scene if you appear naked in front of some northern airport, although I'm sure more than one airline employee will be pleased."

We both laughed. Then Gelsamina spoke. "Fortunately, my host will be clothed, so I needn't worry. But you might be surprised if you meet someone in Palermo who doesn't look like me at first. My goal is to join you in Palermo. Everything else will be taken care of as it arises."

I wasn't clear as to how she was going to accomplish her task. After all, she looked like the Gelsamina that I knew. Did transmigration only affect the personality and not the appearance? Or did the appearance change afterward? Or did Gelsamina/Chelsea appear as she did only to me? Yet again, the answer to one question merely led to the asking of a handful of others. I retrieved my passport and set it out on the bureau. Tomorrow, I would withdraw most of the money from my accounts. Then, it would be on to the travel agency to book a flight and find a hotel. She could also help me arrange for things like a car. I was getting excited. I'd almost forgotten the incident with Mr. Howard and my resignation. As Chelsea said, this was the start of a new chapter.

The next morning, I arose a little later than usual, not having a job to go to. Chelsea was already up and dressed, and was sipping coffee at the kitchen table. She was wearing a smart little sweater and tights outfit that made me think she'd really taken to this "Chelsea, the younger cousin" scenario. I greeted her with my usual semi-pleasant morning grunt and poured myself a cup. It smelled good. I had always enjoyed the aroma of coffee brewed in a pot on a stove, and for someone who'd just learned how to do this, Chelsea made a good pot of coffee. After hearing my sigh of contentment, she looked at me and said, "You're welcome." We spoke a bit more about the day's itinerary and agreed that the first thing I should do was call my father. A few minutes after nine, I called. He picked up the receiver immediately. Mom was already out at the hairdresser, and he was just finishing the breakfast dishes, only too happy to stop and talk to me.

"Anna!" he said with pleasant surprise. "How is my little heiress this morning?" We talked for a few minutes, and after registering his disappointment that I wouldn't be around for the Christmas holidays, he made me promise to call from Sicily and reverse the charges. "Oh, and bring back something nice for your mother," he added before giving me the name and phone number of the attorney. He promised to call the man as soon as our conversation ended. Dad was sure that his attorney would contact the firm in Palermo to let them know I'd be coming. Armed with this knowledge, they could prepare a folder outlining the assets and accounts, all with the necessary financial documents. I thanked him and, after hearing the always expected kissing sounds at the other end of the phone, gave my love and said good-bye. I then got washed and dressed to take care of business.

It was nearly ten-thirty in the morning before Gelsamina—Chelsea, as she would be known in public—and I got into the car and drove to the travel agent. Not having done this before, I thought it best to bring along my passport. On our trip there, we agreed that our story for the travel agent would be that I had to go to Palermo for business reasons and was unsure as to when I'd be returning. The trip would take as little as two weeks or as long as two months, so I'd get the return ticket in Palermo. We both knew that our time in Sicily would take us considerably longer than two weeks, but for our story, this little untruth would suffice. Chelsea, for now, would play the part of my younger cousin who's just keeping me company, and who wished she could come along. She admitted to me that she was never really very good at making up stories. "It is better to leave out parts of a story than to make up a whole new one," she said, "so unless I must speak, it would be more realistic for me to remain quiet." I agreed.

I was pleased to see the same woman who I'd worked with for my flight in November. She recognized me immediately, and offered us both chairs.

"What a nice surprise to see you again," she began. "So, where will we be visiting? For Christmas, maybe?" I remembered mentioning to her that I'd probably be traveling for Christmas, but at the time, I was thinking about Tina and her family in San Antonio. I never thought I'd be here now, talking about Sicily.

"Well, actually," the words came out, "this is a business trip. I have to go to Palermo in Sicily." I was tempted to say more but decided that giving less information would probably serve me better in the long run.

"Well, nice place for business. I'd guess that it's probably sixty degrees warmer there right now," she added before asking me when I'd be leaving.

"Anytime within the next three or four days, and preferably before Christmas," I responded.

"That's good, because the closer you get to a holiday, the harder it is to get a flight, and the more expensive."

She found a flight for me out of Binghamton to Kennedy International in New York, that Friday evening. From there, I'd take a flight to Rome and then transfer to Palermo. The trip in all would take twenty hours in the air. The price was pretty much what I had expected, so I had her reserve the flights. As far as a hotel, she found a number of possibilities in Palermo that had rooms available for the week before Christmas. I explained to her that I'd stay in the hotel for about a week and then make other arrangements if I needed to stay longer. If she had any concerns about the scenario I'd presented, she seemed to care less about them when I asked if I could take her card and told her that if I couldn't get what I needed there, would she mind if I called and booked an additional stay and return flight through her. She then smiled and said that she'd work up some alternatives for me, keeping them in my folder, just in case I called. I decided to pay the entire amount in cash so as to make this one less bill that would be coming to my address at the farmhouse. I wasn't sure where this would all end, but I figured that in the event that I stayed for a month or two, the fewer items that I'd have to have forwarded to me the better. She probably looked at my paying cash a little oddly, because she started to suggest using my credit card for the purchase. I told her that I was saving my credit card for any purchases in Italy. Sadly, this was another lie. My credit card had a balance of zero, a habit I'd picked up years ago. I bought very little that I couldn't pay for within thirty days. It just made things neater, as far as I was concerned.

"And who is this?" the agent asked, looking at Chelsea. "Where would you like to go today?" Although she was trying to appear genuine, her tone came out a bit on the condescending side. Before my great-aunt could open her mouth, I jumped in with, "This is my cousin Chelsea," who picked up on my words and merely smiled at the travel agent. "She has to stay with her family for the holidays, but I've promised her that on my next trip, she can come with me."

"And I'm the witness, so your cousin can't get out of it," exclaimed the agent, apparently eager to make yet another sale.

Chelsea merely looked at me and then smiled at the travel agent. "So it's official. You have to take me," she said finally, playing her part beautifully. Our work here was done. I collected my papers and reservations, and after showing the travel agent my passport just to make sure that everything was in order, we left.

Once in the car and away from the building, Gelsamina leaned over and kissed me on the cheek. "You were brilliant," she said. "That was masterful. From what I could sense, she suspected nothing." I smiled as we drove on.

Wednesday and Thursday flew by. Gelsamina and I had nonstop conversations ranging from things as mundane as what to wear in Italy in December to more serious topics. I should arrive in Palermo sometime late at night on Saturday. I would wait for her in my hotel. By her guess, it could take as long as a week for her to get to me, this being an age of much faster travel than when she came to America. I would pack some clothes for her, but until she got to the hotel, she would be on her own. Apparently, this was a more daunting concept to me than to her. She explained to me that, for as long as I still had my passport and many of the attachments to my life as Anna Del Forno, I should use them. In time, I would have to resort to her means of travel, what I started referring to as "spiritual hitchhiking." She seemed amused at my analogy. "When the time comes, Anna, I will teach you the ways," she said.

As I was finishing my packing, Gelsamina, who was sitting on the floor with her back against the wall, watching me, said, "Why did losing your job make you so sad, Little One? A new life is opening before you."

I paused for a moment as I buckled the last buckle on the suitcase. I sat down on the bed next to the suitcase and said to her, "It's not so much what Howard did, but the way in which he did it. I have spent pretty much the last ten years of my life working in printing and advertising, and I think I do a pretty creditable job. Now, to be honest, my life over the last few months has been turned upside down, and each time I try to rationalize an explanation for it, I'm drawn to the conclusion that something is in my future. I'm still trying to come to terms with that. But to have this petty, manipulative excuse for a human being treat me that way ... I mean, yes, I was asking for a leave of absence, and I had the weirdest reason in the world to ask for one, so I had to create a better reason. But that wasn't why he said no. He said no because I would no longer be around to make him look good, and he had plans for my spot that would make his life easier—not the department's, not the university's, his. Squeezing me in between bites of a pastry, just to tell me to resign, well, I ... I ..." I began to stammer in anger. Gelsamina sensed the affront that I was feeling. She said nothing, choosing instead to get up and look at the collection of red ribbons that I'd kept in a small dish on the bureau.

"Did I ever tell you about my red ribbons?" she asked, not waiting for a response. "I was a little girl, and my mother and father had taken me to the feast in the town. I think that my brother was only two or three years old at the time, so I suppose I was just old enough to remember. My parents were having a wonderful time, laughing and looking at all of the sights.

"The feast itself was a blur of brightly decorated booths and tables, filled with enchanting smells and happy music. And when the statue of Saint Andrew Avellino was being presented in the square, people would offer money to pin on a sort of cloth cape that was draped around the statue's shoulders. I was sitting on my father's shoulders, watching a man standing on a platform, accepting money donated by the people of the town to attach to Saint Andrew's cape. As my father neared the platform, I reached out to touch it. My arms were too short to reach the statue, but at least I could touch the *giglio* that it stood on. In Italian, a *giglio* is a lily, but at the feasts the special stand that was used to carry the statue was called a *giglio*, probably because it stood up straight, like a lily.

"There must have been something sharp on it, something that I couldn't see, because as I reached, I felt a sharp stab of pain on my wrist. I withdrew my arm quickly to see a thin line of blood from the wrist to the tip of my finger. I said nothing but winced a little. My father didn't notice, but the man on the *giglio* saw it. When my father offered his donation, the man reached down and gave me a red ribbon, the color of the blood that was on my hand and long enough to put in my hair. He looked at me and said with a smile, 'For you, *gioia*. May this always remind you of the ribbon of life. It runs from Saint Andrew to your father, to you and on and on forever.' As a little girl, this made no sense to me. I just loved the ribbon. In fact, it was the first one I'd ever seen. But as I grew, my father, who had been touched by the man's words, remembered them, and reminded me of them whenever I wore the ribbon. "It got to the point where I would put a red ribbon on just to hear my father tell me of the ribbon of life, a ribbon that runs through lives, connecting them even into death, and in our case, the dance that goes round and round, with both life and death. It's a symbol for us, as much as the ring that you are wearing around your neck."

I had decided that from time to time, I would wear the ring around my neck instead of on my finger, especially when I finally got to Arcamo, as I didn't want to bring about any additional unwanted questions. "And I do like the red ribbon that holds it there," she added. Since turning, I had replaced the short red ribbon that she had originally given me with a longer, stronger cloth ribbon, keeping the ring safe under my clothes.

I eased off of the bed and reached out to lift my packed suitcase. As if on cue, a wire on the edge of the luggage snagged at my finger, causing a few drops of blood to appear. I raised my hand to suck the blood and stop the bleeding, but Gelsamina stopped me. She held the hand and studied my bleeding finger, holding it first toward the red ribbon and then, appearing pleased at the match of colors, raising it to her mouth and sucking it, not in an erotic way, but rather to symbolize that we were joined by our blood, the ribbon that connected us both. I stood there watching her. She finished and helped me lift the suitcase. Together we brought it into the living room, near the front door.

Gelsamina looked at me as I rose from setting down the luggage. She said, almost prophetically, "You will return here from time to time, and you will see those who you love, although less and less over the years, but as time goes on, you will understand. This is what you were meant for, Little One; this is your legacy. Your appearance will never change, but your life already has."

As she spoke, I saw not Chelsea the twenty something-year-old, but Gelsamina, the family matriarch. *But which family?* I thought to myself. I soon realized that she was matriarch of all of the families. She was the White Wolf of the *figli del lupo*, and whether I believed it or not, she was my mentor, my guide, related by blood, by skin and fur, by blessing or curse, forever.

We embraced, only to hear a knock on the front door. An airport taxi service had been called that morning, and true to their word, they had arrived to take me to the airport. I rechecked my bags to make sure that all my documents were there, especially the ones pertaining to the inheritance. I kissed Gelsamina on the cheek and left. Anna Del Forno had said good-bye to her former life and now embarked on her new one.

Part II

Chapter VIII
A Visit

Friday evening was clear and cold. Not the bitter single-digit cold that had prevailed over the previous days, but still cold enough to make one long for the days of spring. The winter solstice had yet to come, but it was apparent to all who thought about it that here in Binghamton, people would be hunkering down to a long, gray, snow-covered winter.

This being the Friday before the holiday vacation—which for most colleges is a week or two before the actual holiday—most employees of the university looked forward to five o'clock, when they would bid one another "Happy Holidays" for the last time and return to their homes to begin a three-week-long vacation. Bart Howard had left work early that day. He'd invited his boss, Lee Baker, to a late lunch, and between that multi-cocktail meal and the morning's holiday party, he was in no shape to stay at the office. With his appetite and size, it didn't take long for indigestion and a rather interesting hangover to develop. Uneasy in his easy chair in a futile attempt to sleep it off, Howard realized that he'd left his briefcase at the office. Normally, this would mean nothing, but in that briefcase was a box of Cuban cigars, two plane tickets, and hotel accommodations in Hilton Head, South Carolina, for a golf weekend, and he still had to get them to Baker before Christmas. Howard figured that if the Cubans didn't seal the deal for his getting approval for the two workers to fill the Del Forno spot, then the golf weekend would. He couldn't leave that briefcase there. What if it was stolen? He'd be out over a thousand dollars. And then he'd have to decide between Lucille's son, who was either lazy or stupid but had Mommy as a cheerleader, or Ramona, the secretary whom Baker had dubbed "the woman must likely to accede." Howard smiled at the joke, but then cursed as he realized he'd have to get up and go back to the office.

He grunted some lie to his wife, a diminutive little woman with the personality of a victim, and told her not to hold dinner for him, a directive that she had grown used to. He put on his coat and shoes and headed for the car, hoping that the cold would help with the pounding in his head and stomach. As he started the car and headed down the street, he came to the conclusion that it did not. The glare of headlights from oncoming cars over the six-mile trip was enough to stoke the hangover to the point where his eyes now hurt as well.

He pulled into the now desolate parking lot and walked quickly into the building. The custodians who were normally busy in his part of the building were themselves celebrating, although far less spectacularly than he had. His offices were silent. He picked up his briefcase and left the darkened office, hoping to get out without even having to say a single "Merry Christmas." Successfully exiting the building, he approached the car, only to see that three dogs were between him and the driver's side door. He yelled something gruff at them, expecting them to scare easily. They did not. They raised their heads to face him. In the dark, they appeared to be German shepherds. They looked at him and growled, one of them snarling through bared teeth. Howard panicked, first swinging the briefcase wildly at them, and failing that, throwing it at the leader of the three, missing by a great distance.

The three approached—not surrounding, but now only a foot or two away from him, snapping and snarling. He turned to run. One of the three remained at his heels while the other two fanned out at either side. With his feet pounding toward the end of the parking lot, they followed. He ran as he had not run in twenty years, indigestion and hangover still very present but suppressed by fear. He headed out of the parking lot and down a service road toward a security guard's kiosk. As one of the flanking beasts turned on him, he realized that he wouldn't be able to reach the kiosk. He wheeled and ran into a thicket of trees that led to what would in another circumstance be considered a secluded "make-out spot" for university students in warmer weather. Hoping to lose the snapping, snarling animals in the woody underbrush, he ran on, heart pounding, girth rolling, coat and pants torn by low-hanging branches and thorny brush. As the growling continued further behind him, he pushed on, feeling a blackness at the edges of his sight, his heart now thumping to the point where he could hear nothing else. They had stopped nipping at his heels, having successfully run him into a very isolated area with thick trees and a fence. He knew he could go no further. He turned to see the three of them approaching slowly, still yapping and snapping their bared teeth. He could hardly hear anything. He fell to his knees. He was losing consciousness. He clutched at his chest and, breathing heavily, collapsed. They stood around him silently. Within the hour, his breathing stopped. He was dead. They had run him as they would have done a weaker member of the herd, waiting until he could no longer escape.

At another time, they would have fed, but this was not for them to do. It was important that Howard's death not be associated with anyone in particular, and equally important that no one connect his death to wolves. His body was found thirty-six hours later, frozen stiff, by a security guard on his normal rounds. When Howard's license-plate number was checked and identified as his, the search began. It wasn't difficult to find a man this large, as he had broken quite a few branches in his crashing through the woods. His death was attributed to a heart attack, brought on by a life that was indicated by the contents of his stomach and liver.

In the den, miles away from the scene where Bart Howard's body was discovered, the White Wolf licked and nuzzled the other two wolves in her presence. She communicated to Nonno and Nana that she would return, although she could not say when. They looked at her with eyes that expressed their care as she left.

Chapter IX
Chelsea Goes to the City

After Anna left, Gelsamina ate a meal at the house. The following morning she called the bus station in Binghamton and found that there would be a bus leaving for New York City at six o'clock that evening. She called for a cab to bring her to the bus station. She gave her address and was told they'd be there at five. After putting down the receiver, she mentally reviewed her plans. She would use the money they'd put aside to take the bus to New York. The trip should take about five hours. From there, she could take a cab to JFK International, and from JFK she would deal with matters in her own way. Comfortable with the plan as far as it went, she went off into the room with her portrait and rested, curling up in the big chair until late in the afternoon.

It was a quarter to five when Gelsamina was awakened by the sound of someone walking up the steps to the front door. She opened the door just as the cabdriver was about to knock, taking him a little by surprise. She said that she'd be ready in just a few minutes and went into the bathroom to wash her face and freshen up. He called out to her, asking if she had any luggage for him to load into the car. She said, in between rinsing her face and toweling off, "No thanks, I'm traveling light." She smiled as she realized just how lightly she actually would be traveling. She came back into the living room and together they left the house, Gelsamina locking the door and running around to the shed in the back to hide the key as the cabdriver got back into his car.

Once seated in the car, she took stock of her surroundings. The cab itself was careworn but warm. The driver said next to nothing, perhaps a bit annoyed at having to go all the way out to the country for a fare. Fifteen minutes passed, and with a "thank you" and an exchange of money, she found herself standing at the entrance of a smallish bus terminal. It was a brick building with dark-green painted wood sash windows permanently sealed with some steel mesh, so that air and some light could get in but nothing else. "Not unlike a cage," she thought to herself. In the large parking lot there stood three buses—one idling, two not. Their size and the newness of this experience kept her on her guard. She pushed on the heavy dark-green wood door of the terminal and entered.

Inside the building, wooden benches lined two of the walls. A third wall offered two doors, one with a "MEN" sign and the other with a "WOMEN." The final wall had two openings, waist high and four feet tall, also protected by bars similar to the ones on the windows. Behind one of them was a small man with gray hair. He was looking down at something on the workspace in front of him, writing numbers into some sort of book. She approached him, and as she did he raised his head.

"Excuse me, I'd like to go to New York City."

"One way or round trip?" he asked in a monotone that sounded as if he'd asked it many times before.

Caught off guard, she stammered, "Uhhm, one way please."

He told her the price, which she paid, and gave her a ticket. As she turned, he said, "Bus fourteen, lane four. It leaves in about twenty minutes." She thanked him and went outside to find the bus. It was not hard to find it, one of the great lumbering metal boxes that sat, apparently asleep, in the lot. She returned to the warmth and light of the terminal. Holding her ticket, she looked at her surroundings. On one of the benches sat an old woman, dark-skinned and tired, two shopping bags at her feet. She was eating a sandwich and chewing in measured intervals, as if she wanted to make sure that she enjoyed every morsel of the food.

Some six feet down the bench was a young couple, dressed shabbily but with brighter, younger faces than the old woman. They held hands and looked into each other's eyes, feeding off of the hope that they saw there. They seemed immune to the empty utilitarian pall that hung in the terminal like so much resignation. To them, this was merely a prelude to something better, something brighter. She watched them for a while, musing on their future and thinking sentimentally of her own past—but soon, her reverie was broken by an announcement from the gray-haired man behind the ticket window.

"Bus fourteen to New York City Port Authority Terminal, leaving from lane four, is now boarding." Gelsamina rose, as did the couple. They stood for a moment, collecting their belongings, and then exited the building and boarded the bus. Gelsamina handed the driver her ticket and took a seat at the back of the bus. She reasoned that, in her state of mind, she was still unsure of her surroundings. If she sat at the back, then all she would have to do is watch those in front of her. A short time later, the bus, half-filled, started off on its nightly journey to New York. Although she was unaware of the difference, this was not an express bus. It stopped at Scranton, Pennsylvania; Fort Lee, New Jersey; and three or four other smaller terminals along the route, picking up a few passengers with each stop, all presumably heading for New York. Gelsamina alternated between watching the passengers in the now filling bus and looking out her window at the sometimes lit, sometimes not, small-town rural scenery.

Somewhere in New Jersey, she nodded off for what would be her only rest for a while, and it wasn't until the glare of the lights in the Lincoln Tunnel summoned her attention that she awakened. The uneventful trip came to an end at one-thirty in the morning, after some five and a half hours of travel. As she stepped off the bus, Gelsamina looked around, trying to get her bearings. Even at that early hour, the Port Authority Bus Terminal was bustling with people. She looked for a place to step back from the coming and going crowds, and found herself exiting the building onto a side street. It was still cold, and although lit by store and streetlights, to her perception it held dark corners. That is to say, it seemed to her that there were far too many shadowed and uncertain places along the street where something dangerous could be lurking.

She remembered from one of her conversations with Anna that, upon leaving the Port Authority, she should take a cab to Kennedy Airport. She naively expected there to be something that immediately would put her right on the path to do so, and in fact had she come out from the main entrance, her chances of success would have been far greater. The hairs on the back of her neck were bristling at her unsure feelings about this place. It looked ominous—especially to someone who was not familiar with the surroundings.

Before she could even see him, she heard and sensed someone walking up the street toward her. She tried to look as if she was there with a purpose as he approached her and asked if she needed a cab. He had a swarthy appearance and a faint smell of alcohol on his breath. Uncomfortably, she nodded yes to him, and he raised the arm of his dark, hooded sweatshirt. To her surprise, a car appeared. It was not yellow or black and white, as Anna had described to her in their conversations. In fact, it was dark. In the light of the street at one-thirty, it could have been any number of dark colors. She got into the back seat of the car and began to say "Kennedy Airport," but the man who hailed the cab jumped in beside her and the car lurched forward. Gelsamina grew fearful as the car sped west toward what she surmised from the random glints of reflected light to be a river. Then, without so much as slowing down, the car turned right, pulling into a very dark riverside parking area that was surrounded to the left and right by construction sites. The men looked ahead silently until the car came to an abrupt stop near some large heavy machinery. The man next to her got out and ran briskly to her door, opened it, and pulled her out. The driver exited the car and pulled out a knife.

"Just do what I say, and nobody gets hurt. You might even like it." The driver took her wrists as the swarthy man unbuckled his pants, exposing himself to her.

"Now, we'll just bend you over the hood like a nice little girl, and we'll all have a good time," he said in a macho sneer. What occurred next could not be, by any stretch of the imagination, considered a good time.

Gelsamina was terrified. She had never experienced any terror like this. In seconds, from within her welled up a howl that made the two men stop and stare. Before their eyes, she shrank, only to transform into the White Wolf. They had actually seen her turn. Sadly for them, no one would ever hear of their experience. Snarling, she bit into the leg of her captor, severing something that caused an immediate gush of blood. The pain made him drop the knife. While the swarthy man attempted to raise and re-buckle his pants, she was on him, biting into his face and throat. He was down, gurgling blood and writhing in pain.

She returned to the driver. He shifted his focus from the gash on his leg to her as she approached, shoulders arched, eyes red with rage. He tried to run, but stumbled and fell. The White Wolf now flecked with the blood of her would-be attackers, leapt into him, tearing at his throat and finally clamping down onto it, refusing to let go until she was sure that he had been killed. As her rage subsided, she could think of only one thing—that these two men would never do this again.

The car door was still open, so she hopped into the still-warm car and slowly cleaned herself as best as she could. Turning back, Gelsamina felt spent. This was not something she had anticipated. She felt as if she was guilty of not being more vigilant. Considering the event, she decided that these two did not ultimately intend to kill her, but she was sure that they each intended rape. She gathered up the clothes that had fallen from her transformed body, dressed, and walked quickly away from the scene, wishing that, as Gelsamina, she could see as well in the dark as the White Wolf.

She walked some few blocks east of the parked car, having seen lights in the distance. Hearing noises of cars amid the lights, she crossed Eighth Avenue and continued heading east. At Broadway, she walked into a coffee shop and sat down to what passed for coffee at two o'clock in the morning. She was still dazed from her ordeal. She needed to collect herself. Neither fear nor rage had ever been the motives for her turning before, and certainly not a reason to kill. She felt horror at her realization. And yet, deep inside, she was yielding to the exhilaration of having taken control of her surroundings. The conflict was startling. She struggled to put it out of her mind, to escape from the moment.

She took in the sights and sounds of the people in the booths around her table. The aroma of newly arrived pastries offered a sweet scent as she sipped the burnt brown last-of-the-pot liquid in her cup. The man behind the counter was whistling softly to himself as he put the pastries on display. In the booth next to her were two older women, one dark-skinned and one lighter, but both haggard and worn. Their clothes looked slept in. They were discussing a friend of theirs who had been diagnosed with cancer. They referred to a nearby hospital and how it "didn't cure nothing, but at least she got no pain no more." As Gelsamina listened, she hatched a plan. If she was lucky, this information might help her.

She stayed with the burnt coffee until the ladies got up to leave. As they did, she touched one of them on the arm and said, "I'm sorry. I couldn't help overhearing you talking about your friend in the hospital. Is it nearby? I need to go myself."

"Aww, honey, I'm sorry. Yeah, the hospital is close. Can you walk? Yeah? Okay. Now listen—you go up about eight, nine blocks right up here on Broadway; then look to your left. It'll be one, maybe two blocks over, but you can't miss it." As the well-meaning woman gave her directions in her thick New York accent, Gelsamina realized that she'd been close to it before and probably missed it by two or three streets (as is often the case for people not used to the tightly packed grid that is New York City). She thanked the woman, who replied with a "God bless" as they both left, ambling off in different directions. Gelsamina watched the curious bedraggled characters shuffling away, one uptown and one downtown, and found herself wondering for the moment on the lives they led, so completely foreign to everything that she knew. And yet, they had shown her kindness. If nothing else, this encounter helped return her to the state of calm that she would need to continue on her mission. She began her walk up the street in the direction that she was given, past the brightly lit garish signs and advertisements, past coffee shops and restaurants, theatre marquees and hotels, stores and even a few seedy-looking shops offering pictures of young women posed provocatively. She found it all largely confusing. Undaunted, she pressed on, looking to her left, street after street, until at last she saw some banners hanging above a large entrance. Without the banners, the entrance would have looked pretty much like any of the other entrances in the area. The banners announced a hospital, and so she entered, sat in the waiting room, and listened.

The waiting room, a large lobby filled with chairs, was even at this time of the morning heavily populated. It seemed easy to sit here, amid the wounded and ill, and listen, so as to accomplish her task. In her human form, her senses were not nearly as sharp as when she turned, but her ability to "listen"—that is, to catch the unspoken words of people around her—proved to be still intact and quite useful to her purpose. The original plan of taking a cab to the airport ended with the attack on her, and more so, her response. She needed to remain as much in the background as possible. So Gelsamina decided to find someone who was visiting the city and had gotten sick. After they received treatment, they would be released and would return to wherever they came from. It might take her some time, but she would travel with them, spiritually of course, moving ever closer to her destination.

She concentrated. In different Spanish dialects, she heard of towns in Nicaragua and Ecuador, Colombia and the Dominican Republic, all towns and places she was unfamiliar with. Then she heard of Atlanta and Cincinnati. These were in English, but were still unfamiliar to her. Finally, almost an hour later, she heard it. From somewhere on a floor above came the thoughts. They were fevered and in Italian. Although it was a dialect different from her native Sicilian, she knew the words. The voice was male, and in the tormented anguish of a medicated sleep, the voice spoke of giving up. In bits and pieces, it talked about going home, as there was nothing more to do. Through sighs and snippets, it reflected on the flight over to New York from Rome, and how he would at least feel better knowing that he could see home once more.

She put the messages together as best she could, but Gelsamina needed more. The words gave her hope. This could be what she was looking for, but to be sure, she needed to get closer. She focused, waiting patiently, not unlike a lioness when she senses prey and remains very still so as to gather as much information as possible before the attack. But hers would not be an attack; no, quite the contrary. Her plans, at this point, were very different. Again, her patience paid off. In his semiconscious musings, the patient thought of his nurse, the big Latino woman with the mole, and how she had mispronounced his name. *How could anyone confuse "Prizzi" with "Pree-zee"?* he thought. Normally, he wouldn't have been annoyed with this, but now, after today, it bothered him.

Gelsamina smiled. She now had a name and a description of his nurse. She got up and walked over to the front desk where a volunteer sat.

"Excuse me," she began. "I just got into town. I'm here to see Mr. Prizzi. I forgot what room he's in, but I remember that he's on the floor with the Latino nurse."

The volunteer smiled. "Miss, we have many Latino nurses." He then looked in his book for the name "Prizzi."

Trying to look as innocent and in need of his help as she could, Gelsamina added, "She's very nice, and she has a mole …"

"All of our nurses are very nice, miss," he interrupted. He stopped with his comment. "We have a Bruno Prizzi on the fifth floor, and the nurse in charge is Mrs. Lopez. He's in room five fifty-two, but it's two-thirty in the morning. You can't go up there now."

"I know," she answered, "but I'm not from New York, and well, that's my Uncle Bruno from Italy, and he's supposed to be going home soon, but I don't know when, and …" Tears began to well up in Gelsamina's eyes, primarily because she saw her chance to get to Italy slipping away. She continued, sniffling a bit, "I promise I won't bother him. I only want to see him, just once before he leaves." She spoke with a measured anxiety, making up the parts of the story that she didn't know. All in all, it was a very convincing performance. The volunteer said nothing, but she could see that he had been touched by her display of "familial affection," as he began to write something on a slip of paper. "This is really against the rules, but seeing as how he's on the fifth floor. And he's leaving tomorrow. As long as you're quick and you don't wake him …" His voice trailed off as he handed her the slip and allowed her to pass to the elevators. She thanked him and followed two orderlies into a nearby elevator.

Not knowing what to do, she stood there next to them, silently, looking up at the ceiling of this metal box. "What floor?" said one of the orderlies.

"Hmm?" she responded.

"What floor are you goin' to?" he elaborated.

"Oh, the fifth floor." He pressed the button for the fifth floor and then stood there silently for the next thirty seconds as the doors closed and slowly, finally, opened at the fifth floor. The orderlies exchanged a look as Gelsamina exited the elevator. From the way she spoke, they both got the impression that she had no idea that this was the floor that held the cancer patients, and they surmised that if she was being allowed to come up and visit at this time in the morning, things must be pretty serious. Gelsamina had other things on her mind and so seemed respectfully oblivious to their glances. She looked at them both, smiled a slight smile, and walked from the elevator onto the floor. The doors closed as she scanned the hallway. She found room 552, and then, more importantly, two doors past it, a door that had no number on it. She walked up to the darkened room and saw a man in his late fifties tossing and turning beneath a sheet and a blanket. Although asleep, he appeared to be in a discomfiting dream. At this close proximity, it was as if his sedated ramblings were being spoken out loud to her. This was Bruno Prizzi, and it said so on the chart on the wall opposite his bed. Turning her attention to the door with no number, she reached for the handle. It turned easily. It was a utility closet. In it were shelves of medical and sanitary supplies. Less than five minutes later, in the corner of the closet, inconspicuous amongst the stacked boxes of pads and bandages, was a small pile of clothing—a top, a pair of pants, and some underwear, along with a coat and a pair of casual shoes. If you weren't looking for them, you would never have noticed them. Neither would you have noticed that Gelsamina was no longer in them.

Chapter X
Conversations

Bruno Prizzi slept uncomfortably. The monitors showed slightly elevated vital signs. He couldn't seem to lie in any one position for an extended period of time. The subdued lighting only added to the problem. Even sedated, he had difficulty sleeping. He'd gotten the word one, maybe two days ago, and he was still coming to terms with it, mentally reviewing the conversation over and over again.

After seeing the doctors in Rome and meeting no success, he'd still held out hope as they recommended New York. Now he remembered the first hospital here and the doctors' consultation. The good news was that it wasn't cancer, as the doctors in Rome had thought. The bad news was that it was something more rare and just as incurable. Although acting more slowly, the polysyllabic disease would eventually put its victim into a coma, leading to death. Bruno had been apprised of this at the first hospital here and given the option of starting treatments—the purpose of which would be to extend his life by six months to a year, but with continuous pain—or be put on the list to receive a new kidney, free from the disease. This was a risky operation that would hopefully allow for a greater extension to his life. With weekly visits to the hospital, he could live for ten, maybe fifteen more years. Bruno Prizzi chose a third option. He stated, in a calm and collected fashion, first in his native Italian and then in the textbook English that he'd learned in college, that it was his wish to cease all medication and return to his home.

The medical staff at the hospital he had been sent to in New York tried to persuade him, over the next forty-eight hours, to reconsider.

They invited members of his extended family, those few members who remained and were living in New York, to visit and encourage him to change his mind. They brought in a staff psychiatrist to meet with him. It was all to no avail. Bruno Prizzi's mind was made up. If he could not have a full life, he did not want a life at all.

Finally, he was sent here, to St. Claire's Hospital, a little medical center in the heart of midtown, to one of the few beds available anywhere in the city, to the fifth floor, the oncology floor, to await a flight back to Rome. Perhaps this transfer was done as a last-ditch attempt to get him to reconsider his decision. His paperwork was all in order, but there was only one flight a day that had the medical accommodations appropriate for his problem. His turn on that flight would not come until tomorrow, at eleven in the morning, and as of that moment, his decision had been made.

His sleep, intermittent as it was, represented the final battleground. In tormented dreams, he was visited by a myriad of characters, some from the past few days, some from years gone by. It was as if he was mentally looking for validity in his decision—or lacking that, closure.

In one piece of a dream, he was in his childhood home, a modest two-bedroom apartment. His mother, a frail brown-haired little sparrow of a woman who had passed away some twenty years ago, was sitting with him at the family table. He had been away at university and had returned. They had finished a meal, and she had just put out coffee. He loved the aroma of the strong, black coffee, especially today when, as a treat, she asked him if he'd like it with a little anisette. To his mind, the sweetness of the licorice-tasting anisette mixed with the coffee into a palpable contentment. Mama poured the anisette and then sat in the chair next to his. She sipped from her cup before asking him where he would go after his time at university had ended. He answered her, "Probably take a job in Rome. I think that the insurance company where I interned likes me enough to hire me."

"Will you live here?" she asked.

"Only until I can get a place of my own," he answered. He was young and wanted to spread his wings. Living here wouldn't be conducive to the lifestyle that he hoped for. She seemed a bit saddened at his decision but said nothing. The silence urged him to qualify his answer. "Mama, I need to live my life. If I stay here, I would be living your life." Although disappointed, she understood. Her husband, Bruno's father, had been killed in an automobile accident when Bruno was young, and mother and son had lived their lives together since then. She knew that this day would come eventually. She had hoped that it would have come much later. Her eyes spoke volumes to this feeling, and in his dream, Bruno relived it. "You know that I love you, Mama. I just have to live my life. I'll visit, I promise."

The scene in his dreams shifted to some years later when he uttered those same words to her. This time she was sitting in an easy chair in the front room of a much smaller place in the country. She had grown far more frail and was being cared for by a matronly cousin. Surrounded by what few mementos she brought with her, her life was quiet, secluded, and lonely. "But when will you come to visit, Bruno?" she asked him.

"Soon, Mama, soon," he replied. He felt as if he was watching the scene, as if it was a movie. He repeated the words to himself. "Soon, Mama, soon."

Another voice crept into his head. "She seems so sad. You were her life." He heard the voice but couldn't recognize where it came from. It was as if this disembodied voice was his conscience. He turned in his bed for what seemed like the hundredth time. And tried to return to sleep.

Another snippet of a dream came from the conversation he'd heard, perhaps yesterday, in the first hospital, between two nurses. In between the clatter of dinner trays in the hall outside, the first one said to the other that if she had to go for weekly dialysis, she didn't know what she'd do. For her, it would be like slow torture. "It's not forever," said the other, "eventually, you have to go every day," and then she laughed a little. The sarcasm was easily understood. The first one shushed the second, considering aloud that they might have been overheard. "Relax," said voice number two, "he only speaks Italian." Their ignorance proved to be hurtful, but ultimately validated in his decision.

"An insensitive nurse is like constipation. They're both a pain in the ass," said the voice he'd heard but couldn't place before, but this time, it spoke in Italian. And this time, the words seemed less like they were coming from within his mind.

In a church in Rome, the Church of San Francesco di Paola, stood a teenage boy. It was a Saturday afternoon, and as the sun was setting, it cast an intricate multicolored glow on his face as Bruno stood in line for confession. The setting sun, the brilliant stained-glass windows, the marble all around him, all added to the grand stillness he felt in the moment. There wasn't much that he felt he needed to confess, but *rules are rules, and if I want to receive communion with Mama, I have to do this,* he thought to himself. He saw his mother exit the confessional booth, her eyes moist. She deposited herself into the nearest pew and knelt to pray her penance. It was now Bruno's turn. He entered the confessional booth, settled onto the kneeler, and blessed himself, explaining to the unseen priest on the other side of the screen that it had been two weeks since his last confession. Bruno strained to see through the heavy screen, hoping to make out at least some aspect of the face that belonged to his confessor. Normally this was not a difficult process. He felt more at ease knowing who he was talking to, especially if he had something important to talk about. But this time, it seemed darker behind the screen. And the voice seemed less like that of an old priest and more like that of a young girl. And she called him by his name. The dream was growing more absurd. He felt that he was himself, not the teenage boy of a moment ago. He turned to part the curtains and leave, but the curtains felt odd to his touch, as if they were sewn shut. He felt as if he couldn't leave. The voice spoke to him again.

"Bruno?"

"Yes."

"Why do you choose to give away even one extra minute of life?"

"Who are you?"

"I am curious."

"But who are you?"

"When your father died, you felt that your mother needed you. But then you went away."

"I needed to live."

"Did you?"

"I tried. I couldn't."

"Did you know how?"

"Don't chastise me."

"I'm not. I'm wondering how one can live, fully live a life, without knowing how. Of course, mistakes will be made, but that is part of it. Who was there to teach you?"

"My mother."

"As much as she loved you, she couldn't teach you because she didn't know how to live herself. She was trained to cook and care for, but she never evolved past that. When your father died, so did her evolution. And when she transferred all of her feelings to care for you, and was eventually denied, she came to that realization all the more. She gave up so that you could live life."

"Father, how do you know so much about me? My mother is right outside, doing the penance that you gave her. Did she say all this?"

"Bruno, look outside." Bruno now parted the curtains. The cathedral was empty. Neither his mother nor anyone else was present in the now-darkened church. The sun had set long ago, and with the exception of a few small lights at the back of the church and a single altar candle, Bruno felt the dark tomb-like quality of being very alone. He returned to the confessional.

"Father?"

"I am not your priest. Neither am I your confessor. I have just been here, listening and watching. And I find it sad that you have a bit of time left and still haven't lived your life." Her words hurt a little as pieces of truth often do.

"What can you tell me about life?"

"When you return to Rome, will you go back to your job? You have a month or two, maybe more, to learn what most people learn over a lifetime. Will you spend it counting and making sure that one person has not mistakenly cheated another out of a few lire?"

"I don't know. I haven't given it much thought. I have been busy thinking about the past."

"The past is important, but largely as a guide to what we can do in the present and the future. You couldn't live because you had very little to base life on."

"Will you teach me?"

"No, but I will speak with you. Together we might both learn."

The dosage of intravenous sedative administered to Bruno Prizzi had been increased, and for the last four hours of his hospital stay in New York, he slept.

Chapter XI
Life Lessons

The attending nurse came into room 552, followed by a discharge representative and an intern. The attending nurse began waking Bruno as the intern took and recorded the vital statistics from the monitors he had been attached to. Having entered the numbers into a chart, the intern made a few notes, wished a fully awake Bruno a safe trip, and left. The nurse prepped him for a final dialysis treatment and began the process. As the dialysis machine hummed and did its job, the discharge representative spoke. In a slow, steady tempo, she asked him how he was feeling, a ridiculous question to ask a patient under these circumstances, something that she realized only seconds after asking it. Understandably, he didn't know how to answer without sounding sad or angry. She read the perfunctory script to him and then gave him specific information regarding the medical flight to Rome. "Because you are receiving a dialysis treatment here and now, you won't need one for seven days, but in the event that you have a reaction to anything that you drink or eat during the flight, there will be a portable dialysis machine on board, along with a nurse and medication. All your prescriptions will be in her bag, along with some medicine to help you sleep. It says on your chart that you've been having some problems sleeping this past week. Hopefully, this medicine will help."

Although he would have normally asked for the names and dosages of the medications, Bruno, even awake, seemed to care little about all of this, apparently happy that someone else was thinking about it and only too happy to relinquish responsibility for it over to them.

By eight-thirty, the treatment was complete, and Bruno, dressed and finishing his sterile-tasting hospital breakfast, was about to begin his trip. He spent a few minutes in the bathroom and, after washing and brushing his teeth, came out to a hospital gurney and two attendants. They helped him onto it, strapped him in, and took him down to the main floor where an ambulance was waiting to carry him to the airport and his flight home. The nurse who would accompany him met them in the lobby and sat with him in the ambulance.

The ride was bumpy and uncomfortable, and the nurse bumped her head more than once, softly cursing in what sounded like an Americanized version of Italian. He smiled when he heard it, wondering if he'd be able to understand whatever she said, as she spoke what she thought was Italian.

JFK International Airport was a city unto itself, and for such an enormous bustling place, the people were remarkably nice to him, from handlers to attendants right on to the liaison people whose job, he presumed, was to make this a smooth transition. He was led up elevators, down corridors, and eventually to a special waiting room where he was transferred to a wheelchair that the nurse would push. A door was opened at the end of the room and a flight attendant approached. He was a young man with a simple smile and blue eyes that struck Bruno as hopeful but tired. The young man greeted them both and escorted them to the open door and down a connecting ramp to Bruno's seat at the rear of the plane.

The attendant, helping both of them strap in, announced that if there was anything he could do to help make the flight more enjoyable, all they needed to do was ask. "Now relax," he said "and by tomorrow, you'll be seeing the sun shining over Rome." He then turned and went about helping the other attendants who were beginning to welcome the other passengers on board.

Bruno watched as the plane filled with people. The attending nurse, seated next to him, began thumbing through one of the magazines offered by the airline, finally settling on an article about priceless artifacts being returned to their native countries. When the plane was finally full, the attendants began their safety and security scripts, concluding, as screens slid down from the ceilings above every fourth seat, with a short instructional video, describing in three different languages what to do in case of an emergency. Although Bruno was glad to be returning to Rome, he felt tired, worn out.

Before long, the flight was underway. The first thirty to forty minutes were fairly quiet, as Bruno, eyelids already heavy, reluctantly gave in to an exhausted sleep. As the layers of sleep were plumbed, he soon found himself dreaming. He was once again in complete darkness.

"Are you here again? Are you with me again?" he spoke in his native Italian.

"I am here," came the reply, although in a Sicilian dialect. He understood it, but was surprised to hear Sicilian. By and large, Romans did not think highly of their Sicilian brethren.

"Why do you speak like the Sicilians?"

"Do you not understand me?"

"Of course I do. I'm just surprised that you're not speaking to me with my language. After all, you are my conscience, aren't you?"

"I never said I was."

"Then, the voice of my soul …"

"Your soul is your own. I am no part of it."

"Is this the voice of God?"

There was a silent moment. Then in the richest dialect that she could muster, the voice replied, "While I am flattered that you believe the Almighty to be Sicilian, I must tell you that mine is not the voice of God. Neither am I the voice of any devil."

"Am I going mad?"

"Of course not. Don't be ridiculous."

"Show yourself." Bruno Prizzi's heart began to race. As he tossed and turned in his chair, still fully asleep, the nurse took his pulse. Noting the increase in heart rate, she mistook the situation as flight anxiety and promptly administered a sedative that, within minutes, deepened the level of sleep and slowed the heart rate.

Back in the darkness, the voice spoke again. "I told you already, I'm here to listen to you. Sometimes I'll ask a question about what I hear. Why is your biggest concern who I am, when what you might consider to be more helpful is to examine who *you* are? You sound as if you are a lonely man. You escape your loneliness by working. You pay your bills, but your life goes on unlived. When you bite into an orange and savor the juice that it yields, do you question whether it came from Taormina or Palermo, or do you enjoy the orange?" Bruno said nothing, partly because of the medication, but partly because he was considering the relevance of the question.

The voice continued. "There are souls, countless souls out in the world, who look at the moon on a cloudless night and think of those who they once loved or cared for. And they weep and howl and gnash their teeth, longing to see them again and wondering if they ever will. And there are others who live in rage or anger or even fear and look up at the moon and instead see a light by which they can continue their work, fully illuminated, but in the dark nonetheless."

Bruno listened. At first he felt as if he were being chastised, but as he reflected further, the words seemed more to be imploring him to take stock of his life.

"I wonder if you can imagine what it would feel like to run through a forest and breathe in all the scents it has to offer you? Or lie down in a field of wildflowers, all yellow and white, at the level of your eyes, smelling a sweetness unlike anything you've ever sensed before? These are simple things in life, but to you, they may as well be words on a page in a book—a book that tells about someone else's life. But it's not too late. The life that the words talk about could be yours. You still have time. This, I know."

Bruno was calm again. In his mind, he had no reply, no more questions. He reveled in the silence of the darkness. He rested.

Some few hours later, he awoke. Gelsamina stayed within him, dormant, herself resting. She never expected to carry on conversations with him, let alone get him to think about improving whatever time remained in his life. But oddly enough, she felt guilty. When she first came to America, her mode was one of survival. Her travel was through various hosts, and in an age when life was far more hard-fought. This host represented something very different. While he was certainly not one to be told about the *figli*, she saw no reason why she couldn't get him to explore himself. And in the process, she could tell him as little or as much as she cared to regarding herself. She thought of this as her way of saying "thank you for the ride." She lingered there, deep in the recesses of his self, ethereal and disembodied yet alert. She waited, mentally ready.

Her moment came some two hours later. Bruno had eaten a small meal and, having visited the men's room, found himself in discomfort. His nurse checked his renal levels and, finding them only slightly elevated, offered a heated pad to place upon his abdomen. The heat usually helped alleviate the pain to the point where Bruno could sit in comfort. Within twenty minutes of the heated-pad application, he was dozing off again.

The cabin was dimly lit, and aside from the hum of the jet engines, it was relatively quiet. From time to time, a child could be heard from a seat toward the front. In an odd sort of way, Bruno was hoping to return to his dream. It had been a very long time, certainly long before the kidney problems became evident, since he'd had interesting conversations with someone. He sat in his reclined seat, giving reasons for and against whether he was actually having these conversations with himself. He wasn't sure where the voice, if it was not his, was coming from. Perhaps he was hallucinating, but it asked him interesting questions. He supposed the questions had been there all along. He'd just never heard them put to him this way. He had to admit that there was much to life that he hadn't experienced.

And while he'd told his mother those many years ago (and himself ever since) that he'd wanted a life, the goal he'd actually been working toward was financial. He was a marvel at finding ways to make money work for his clients. He kept track of their investments, plotting and re-plotting courses of action that often brought in sizable returns with minimal risk. He was very, very good. But such effort required diligence. Bruno worked tirelessly. His supervisors loved his determination. They had every reason to. He made them successful and wealthy.

And although he was monetarily repaid, his reward came from their praise—which, sadly, often came with a greater workload. He relished the increase. His workspace went from a two-desk office to a one-desk office to a corner office. For Bruno, it was his world. It was not unusual for Bruno to go home only to shower and change his clothes. His social life was nonexistent. The only friends or acquaintances he had, outside of business, were those people who delivered the food he ordered from nearby eateries. His work was his life. And although his disease was hereditary, its timeline was continuously being shortened by his day-to-day stress.

As his thoughts and the images that they carried flashed by,

Gelsamina silently observed both Bruno's thoughts and his reactions to them. She watched as he came to revelations. It occurred to her that such action was not uncommon in those with limited time left. If it were possible to smile in her current state, it could be said that she did.

In his mind, Bruno spoke. "Do you have a name?" Apparently, he sensed her there.

She felt that he'd earned at least this. "Gelsamina."

"Are you here with me?"

"For now; for a while."

"Will you talk with me? I've been giving what you said some thought."

"I know."

"I don't know what to do."

"You don't have to."

"What do you mean?"

"The money that you have made over your career has been watched over and managed very carefully. Some would say that you are wealthy. The doctors have told you how much time you may have left. Stop your work and start your life. The money you have will carry you. If you were to die tomorrow, to whom would you leave it?"

Bruno immediately thought of a cousin from his father's side. He remembered him as a young boy who he'd seen at his mother's funeral, and sadly, not since. Outside of a greeting card at Christmas, he'd never kept in touch with him. That was one of his only living relations.

"So, whatever is left after you're done with it, you could leave to him. And if not him, then a maybe a charity."

"But how will I live?" asked Bruno, primarily of himself. What he meant had so little to do with the financial aspect that so many people attach to that question. What he meant was that he did not know how to live life.

In his mind, he was taken back to the darkness that he first felt in the confessional booth. The voice, Gelsamina, told him to part the curtains again. He did so and saw, in the pews of the church, people—mothers with babies, families with multiple brothers and sisters, fathers with sons, each interacting in different ways, little boys annoying little girls, babies being comforted, daughters watching quietly as their mothers read quietly to them, even a young couple holding hands as they looked toward the altar at the front. This was just one infinitesimal aspect of life, a glimpse of the infinite. It did not offer an explanation to Bruno. Rather, it whetted his appetite, leaving him wanting more. Again, if such a thing could actually occur, Gelsamina smiled to herself.

Bruno awoke with a start. He was still in his seat next to the nurse, but a light had been turned on overhead. An attendant was speaking to the nurse. A meal was about to be served, followed by a movie. Although Bruno wasn't really interested in the movie, he did feel a bit hungry. The nurse had reviewed the menu, searching for any foods that might adversely affect him, and thankfully found none. In fact, the airline meal, as Bruno expected, was bland. But it did fill the spot that his hunger had created.

He looked forward from his seat to see his fellow passengers stirring, more cabin lights being turned on, and an increase in movement as the attendants took orders from the menu. He had to pass on all offerings of wine or liquor, but gratefully accepted a fruit juice, having been resting in his seat for some time now. Within a few minutes the meal was served, perhaps a perk of being the medical patient on the flight, and Bruno decided that this was a good time to get acquainted with his "handler."

The nurse was a broad but not heavy woman. In fact, even in a sitting position, she appeared to be rectangular in shape. As he observed her, he noticed that her shoulders were even with her chest, waist and hips, giving the impression of girth. He considered what shape she'd have if she lost some weight in the waist and was pleased with his imagined modifications. She had a sweet face, dark hair framing dark eyes, a small nose, and pouty lips. All in all, under the right circumstances, he decided that she would be an attractive individual. His observation did not go unnoticed.

"So, you're awake."

"Yes."

"Mr. Prizzi?"

"Err, 'Pritzi'—it's pronounced 'Pritzi.'"

"Thank you. How are you feeling?"

"Well enough, I suppose. Have you ever traveled as an accompanying nurse before?"

"Oh yes, but you are my first kidney patient. You're a little bit different, having refused treatment and all …"

The pain that comes with most kidney ailments is often felt in waves, and Bruno's waves were ebbing. He continued. "I'm curious, Miss …?"

"Schulteis—Teresa Schulteis, but please, call me Terry."

"All right, Terry," he said cordially. "I'm curious. How does one become involved in traveling as a nurse?"

"Well," she began, "the pay is good, and I'm only responsible for one person so that I can give him my full attention. Also, I like traveling. I don't have a steady boyfriend or a husband, and no kids, so I can take advantage of this. If I had a family, I don't think I could even consider doing this. It wouldn't be fair to them. And like I said, only one patient, and frankly, they should all be as nice as you." She leaned forward to put down her book, and Bruno caught a glimpse of flesh over the top of her bra as it peeked out through an unbuttoned part of her blouse. Upon realizing what he was looking at, he averted his eyes. Terry did too, and yet she did nothing to address the situation. Harmless as it was, she'd noticed that he averted his eyes. Some women would press the matter; others would have covered up. She did neither. She considered it to be a natural fact, and just continued on, eventually re-buttoning her blouse.

Thinking about how he'd reacted, Bruno stopped himself. He wondered, in the guise of looking out of the cabin window, if this was yet another aspect of what the voice meant by living life. He felt no pressing desire to be with her, but a conversation now, and perhaps a meal when they weren't "professionally" connected, would do no harm. He turned back to her and asked, "So, what are you reading?"

Terry reached down for the book, and this time he didn't avert his eyes. She had certain attributes that caused him to think of her not as his nurse but as something else.

"This? Oh, it's a biography of Giovanni Fattori. He was an Italian artist from the eighteen hundreds. He was a big proponent of Impressionism, only in Italy they called it 'the Macchiaoli Movement,' she said as she handed it to him. Bruno knew very little about art, and if he'd heard of Giovanni Fattori before, he didn't remember.

"Hmm," he said as he took the book and looked at the cover. "I've never heard of him." Inwardly, he was a little embarrassed that an American was telling him about an Italian artist.

"The Macchiaoli School was a forerunner of the impressionist school in France. As unification was taking place in Italy, some of the more well-known artists of this school spoke out against the politics of the time, and the impression I've gotten so far is that, as a result, some of his work wasn't well received. I guess, like a lot of artists, he would remain aloof and sometimes even avoid people for months at a time. His friends would say that he needed the time to work on his paintings, but after he came out of hiding, he'd only have one work done." As she spoke, Bruno leafed through the book. Toward the middle, on a series of glossy pages, were photographic plates of some of the artist's works. They called to mind the impressionist works of Monet, an artist Bruno was only slightly more familiar with, in their manipulation of splotches of color and light. Although there were portraits and historical scenes, the most vibrant renderings were of landscapes—simple pastoral and countryside paintings.

"He seemed to like to paint these types of scenes the most," said Bruno as he handed the book back. "Is it me, or did he do a lot of his working from a sitting position?"

"What an interesting observation. Why do you ask?" said Terry.

"I don't know," he replied. "I suppose that when I think of a painting, I often get the feeling that the person is looking down a little at the subject, as if he was standing and the subject was lower than the line of sight."

"Okay ..." Terry answered, giving a rise at the end of the word, in the manner that was meant to say that she wanted to hear more of his idea.

"Now, in these paintings, he's almost looking up at the subjects. See? Here," as Bruno pointed to a picture of two oxen in a field, "and here," of a house in a meadow. Terry had never noticed it before and said as much. In response, Bruno answered, "I really don't look at much art. It's just that this idea came into my head. Perhaps it's my medication making me see things that aren't really there." She smiled at him.

The conversation continued, although it drifted away from the subject of the book and more toward Terry Schulteis. Art appreciation was sort of a hobby of hers. And although she enjoyed viewing the art, she had no aspiration to become an artist. "I've been a nurse for seven years," she said, "and I like it. But going to art museums and seeing the masters helps keep me calm."

Bruno found that he was enjoying their talk. It was taking his mind off of his troubles. "If you have time, I can accompany you to the Modern National Gallery in Rome. I understand that it is a storehouse of great art."

Terry smiled again, and in her smile he knew that she'd like that. Then, looking down at her watch, she said, "I almost missed it. It's time for your medication." With that, she went into her case and took out a vial, a syringe, and a blister pack containing two tablets. She offered him the tablets along with a cup of water. As he drank, she prepared the syringe and injected its contents into his arm. "The pills will help keep your kidneys working, and the shot will help break down a lot of things into water waste, which the kidneys will pass with no extra exertion," she said as she removed the now-empty hypodermic.

All Bruno could say was, "Thank you." He wondered at first if he had made himself clear as to his wish to cease all medications outside of dialysis. Then he considered the possibility that the plane trip counted as a sort of wheelchair ride to the exit doors of the hospital, where they were still responsible for his well-being until he actually left their care. At any rate, his mind was focused elsewhere, so he dismissed the whole incident.

Terry smiled the smile of a nurse this time—a reassuring but careworn sort of smile. "You seem quite a bit calmer now. That's a good sign, because often this medication makes a person sleepy. In fact, you may want to close your eyes for a little while. We still have a long time before we reach Rome." Bruno felt comfortable—in fact, more comfortable than he had felt in a while. He leaned back and closed his eyes, and soon, he was asleep.

It was fully an hour before Bruno's sleep brought him into that state where he dreamed. The darkness of the confessional booth did not seem so ominous as it had before. He looked toward the screen, still dark, still impenetrable save for the voice that came from the other side, the voice of Gelsamina. "Are you still there?" he asked.

"Do you need me to be?" she asked in reply.

"I suppose I do. Why do we speak here? I mean, why have you chosen to speak to me in a confessional booth at San Francesco di Paola?" Bruno's question was genuine. He was trying to make some sense of it all.

"I haven't chosen a church confessional; you have. I speak to you in your mind. I walk the floors that you create, sit on the chairs of your making. This is where you wanted to talk to me," Gelsamina answered.

"Do you mean that if I concentrate on somewhere else, that is where we will meet?" Bruno was now figuring. He immediately imagined a public space he'd seen on Sixth Avenue in New York City, one that had a reflecting pool and large geometric shapes. On nice days, even in winter, he'd seen people congregating around it, eating a bag lunch or just standing, trying to get a little fresh air and sunlight.

Gelsamina interrupted his thought. "You still won't be able to see me. We can speak, but you have no control over me."

In his mind, Bruno sat in the public space on Sixth Avenue. He felt a shiver of cold, but what he saw was brightly lit with sunlight. People milled around him, each with his or her own business and focus. He was alone in a small sea of humanity. "Is this what you mean by life?" he asked.

"This is only a small part of it," was her reply. "Speaking and listening are the start."

"So, what I said to Terry …" he began to ask.

"Of course, but keep in mind that you are standing at the entrance to a hallway with many doors. How many doors you open and how many doors you enter is up to you. It is, after all, your life. Oh, and she enjoyed sharing her book with you."

Bruno smiled. "You're not referring to her book right now, are you?"

"Of course not," Gelsamina said with a laugh. The laugh melted away into the gurgling ripples of the water in the reflecting pool. The sound grew as Bruno looked into the water. The ripples distorted the faces of the reflections of the people standing nearby. The gurgling sound grew into a gentle splashing, as if the flow of the water had been increased. As he raised his head toward the sound, Bruno was no longer in New York at the public space. He was sitting at the Trevi Fountain in Rome. Where great muscular horses rose out of the sea, water flowed, creating turbulence as it bubbled and seeped down the steps and into the fountain basin. The statuary, noticeably from a far different time than the great geometric shapes back on Sixth Avenue in New York, bespoke a grander message. The fountain didn't evoke an emotion, per se, it told a story. And it made Bruno feel more comfortable. As he looked into the basin, he saw it littered with various coins, thrown in by passersby with the hope that the legend of the fountain would come true. Bruno knew that soon he would return home, just as the fountain legend predicted. As he looked into the water, again he saw distorted faces. These were the people around the fountain. This was life. Gazing up from the water, he saw people interacting—children with children, an old couple walking with a youngster, one or two families, and even a few hand-holding lovers. The sun shone just as brightly as in New York, but Bruno felt warmth on his face.

"The warmth is not from the sun, you know," came the voice. "It is the warmth of life. You have opened your first door."

"*Bene, molto bene,*" he said quietly as he reflected on the scene. And for the third time, Gelsamina smiled.

Bruno Prizzi slept for another hour or so before waking. He was hungry. There were still a few hours before they landed in Rome, and the other passengers had already been fed. He asked Terry if they could bring him something. The nurse got the attention of one of the attendants and spoke quietly to him. As he turned toward the front of the plane, she looked at Bruno and said, "I thought that you might get a little hungry, so I asked them to set something aside for the two of us. Now remember, this is airline food, and it's not part of your special diet, but it will do for now."

The attendant brought two trays, each containing a dish of salmon sprinkled with dill, some steamed vegetables, and two baby red potatoes. On a side dish was a roll and some type of butter spread. Finally, next to a small cup of coffee, was what looked like a slice of pound cake with two strawberries on it. As Bruno watched, the attendant set the trays before each of them and left. He smiled, and as the attendant left, Bruno turned to Terry and said, "When we are settled in Rome, would you care to let me show you what a real meal looks like in Italy?"

She smiled as she picked at the blanched piece of salmon and said, "Only if you promise not to have blanched fish." They laughed politely, and he agreed to her request. Bruno decided that it was time he spoke in Italian. Up until now, whatever he said was in his most carefully thought out English. He was feeling more relaxed now, and she did, after all, profess to speak the language. In a casual yet metered pace, he asked her if she had any family that came from Italy. He'd surmised that the dark eyes and hair might have at least some part of Italian descent, "and," he continued in Italian, "not everyone reads a biography of an Italian artist like Fattori. Most Americans don't even know about him."

Terry smiled, pleased that he spoke to her in his native tongue and that she could reply in kind. "My mother's family is from Naples, and my father's family is from Germany. As for Fattori, I look at his work and I wonder if sometimes he saw things differently from the way we see them. In fact, many of the artists in the Macchiaoli movement painted outdoors, in a sort of pre-impressionist way, you know, using color and light, the way that Monet did. It's as if he could see things deeper and more vibrantly than you or I could. That part of him intrigues me."

"We will have to look for his work in Rome, and maybe you can show me what you mean. You have piqued my interest," he answered, finishing the airline supper.

Now it was her turn to say, "*Bene. Molto bene.*"

Gelsamina rested. It took a certain amount of energy to communicate with a host and maintain the veil of anonymity that she kept. But hearing about Fattori aroused her curiosity. She remembered hearing his name mentioned so many years ago as she was tutored at her mother's knee. Fattori, Abbati, and Gioli were among the proponents of the Italian movement that, while in vogue around the time of Italian unification, never really gained the popularity of its French counterpart. The Italian artists became involved in the politics of the day, and as is often the case of those who back the losing side, the light that was the Macchiaoli Movement dimmed all too soon as public opinion turned against them. Gelsamina remembered, however, that she liked one painting in particular. A painting that she had seen at the baron's villa, a farm scene of two oxen in a field. She decided then and there that when she reunited with Anna, she would introduce her to Fattori's works and that painting in particular. Perhaps her interest, too, had been piqued.

As she lay there now, in a fairly dormant state, she reflected on the trip. She had done something she'd never done before. She had meddled in another's life. And what's more, she felt as if she had needed to. What surprised her was the ease with which she mastered the viewing and use of his thoughts. She could actually see and be part of his memories. In this capacity, she felt an excitement she hadn't felt before. She also felt a sense of guilt, wondering if she'd pushed him too far in a direction he didn't want to go. Her thoughts, weighing the pros and cons, argued that she was protecting a life, encouraging him not to give up. Wasn't his conversation with the nurse a good indication that she'd done the right thing? If he had to walk out of this life at the end of a few months, how sad it would have been to do so alone. And this was a good way to repay him for her "trip to Italy."

She gave little thought, if any, to the ordeal of the attackers back in New York City. She had been caught off-guard, threatened with bodily harm. She had reacted in the only way she knew how, in the most visceral and self-preserving manner. She had taken no pleasure in killing them. It was simply something that she needed to do in order to protect herself from being raped or, worse, killed. Now, spent from her interaction with Bruno Prizzi, Gelsamina Del Forno closed her soul's eyes and let her host begin his life.

Part III

Chapter XII
Palermo: There and Back Again

Getting off the plane in Palermo, Anna was filled with emotions. Back at the farmhouse outside of Binghamton, she'd never really felt alone, not the way she did now. Here she was, in the land of her ancestors, hopefully on the verge of the type of event that one only imagines, an enormous inheritance. But with it, the type of trepidation that imagination fears—her legacy, the *figli del lupo*. She fingered the ring that she wore, hoping it would connect her to something here. The baron's crest felt warm to her touch, shining a bit in the artificial glow of the lights on the plane. She reached for her bag and carry-on and worked her way down the aisle toward the last flight attendant, who was bidding each passenger a pleasant stay.

Without thinking, Anna asked the attendant if there were people who spoke English there. The attendant looked at her with a hint of surprise, trying not to reveal her thought that this question really should have been researched by now. "Signorina, many people in Italy speak two and three languages. When you get your luggage, just go to the information desk, and I'm sure they will help you," she said with all the care she could muster. Anna thanked her and moved on, into the connecting ramp to the terminal.

The attendant returned to bidding her passengers good-bye and then straightened up her assigned area of the plane, reflecting as she did so on the arrogance of Americans in this respect. Most Americans of this generation never had the need to learn a language other than their own. For all intents and purposes, the natural isolation of the country kept most Americans insulated. Reflecting further, she considered herself to be a little envious of the situation. Most European countries relied so heavily upon each other that it was far more of a necessity to learn the language of the people that one would probably be dealing with for the rest of one's life. Brits learned French, French learned German, Portuguese learned Spanish, Italians learned the language of whatever country bordered theirs—Greek, Albanian, French, German, even Swiss. All of them learned at least a little English. It wasn't merely a quest for knowledge; it was good business. "It always comes down to that," she thought as she gathered her belongings and exited the plane.

Anna followed the line of passengers as they made their way to the baggage area. The signs marked *"BAGAGLI"* clearly pointed the direction, with the English translation neatly printed beneath. She gathered her suitcase and looked for a valet to help her. Seeing none, she lifted it and made her way to the information desk. The woman sitting there was very helpful, telling her where she could exchange her dollars for lire and where she could get a cab. She offered Anna a map to the hotel where Anna had booked a room, and all in perfect English. Anna was impressed and reassured.

The streets were more narrow than she'd expected as the cab pulled up to the Hotel Grand Vittorio. It was morning and, although light out, a bit more gray than Anna had anticipated. There were some people out, going about the business of the day. All in all, it was less than the spectacular "sunny Italy" scene that she'd imagined. Palermo was a city, and although it was not a large city, it was certainly one of untold business and innumerable daily transactions.

She emerged from the cab and paid the driver, who handed her suitcase to the doorman while she fumbled for what she thought would be a good tip. Apparently, the cabdriver agreed, as he blessed her. Acting for a moment like a tourist, she took in the sight of the hotel, a large building with wrought-iron work on each of the dozen or so balconies that began on the second floor and continued up to the fourth. The windows were large on the second floor and were replaced by what looked like French doors on the third and fourth floors, each surrounded by ornate architectural framework, scrolls, domed arches, garlands, and shields—all very impressive.

At each side of the canopied entrance was a small potted pine tree, festooned with white lights in honor of the Christmas season. In fact, upon further inspection, she noticed that each of the balconies held the unlit wiring for what appeared to be a baroque half-circle ornament the length of each individual railing. Anna mused that it must look like a fantasy at night.

The doorman allowed her those few minutes to soak it all in before respectfully calling, "Signorina, se ir piace?" which translated to, "Miss, if you please?" Fortunately, there were no cars in the street, as they would not have been nearly as polite. Anna followed him into the lobby, a smallish room as lobbies go, perhaps the size of a large living room, with a marble counter at one end and toward the other, two sets of gold-flecked baroque-style furniture, arranged so that someone sitting on a couch could converse with someone sitting in one of the large stuffed chairs that faced it. The tables, all marble-topped, each held some arrangement of red and white flowers, presumably in honor of the season, in a crystal vase or urn. In the far corners, near the lobby furniture, stood two enormous vases, each holding a vast array of longer-stemmed flowers, their beauty reflected in the various gold gilt-framed mirrors that had been hung in strategic locations throughout the room, making it appear even larger and more ornate. The marble floor was divided into two parts. The more trafficked area was bare and glossy, with gray and black veins throughout the milky whiteness of the floor. The other part, the part that was designated for guests to sit, was covered by a large burgundy-and-navy Oriental carpet. The floral pattern, a design heavily studded with white and gold flowers over the burgundy background, paired perfectly with the furniture, and gave one the impression of either genuine wealth or a gaudy copy thereof. Anna looked and immediately thought the former.

The desk clerk welcomed her and, with a few pleasantries, informed her that her reservation was in order and they had been expecting her. She offered Anna the key to the room and reminded her that if she should require anything, she had merely to call the desk. Anna thanked her and followed the bellboy up to the room.

The stairs leading up to the next floor were also made of marble, but were far less ornate than the lobby. The railing was of marble posts, with wrought-iron railings and sides. At the second-floor landing, the floors were again carpeted, again in burgundy and navy similar to the lobby décor. Anna followed the bellboy down the left corridor, past dark wood doors that contrasted the off-white walls. They stopped at a door marked 25. He opened it to an anteroom that held a console and a desk. The console was not large or as decorative as the furniture Anna had seen thus far. It was of a dark wood and a simpler style. Atop it was a silken runner, again of burgundy, and twin Capodimonte porcelain vases, each decorated with delicately painted roses. The desk and its accompanying chair were of a similar style. On the desk was a lamp and some stationery.

The bellboy continued into the next room, a bedroom not more than the size of her grandparents' bedroom back in Binghamton. Here she saw yet another style of furniture. A queen-size bed with nightstands on either side, against one wall, with a wardrobe and chest of drawers adjacent. The style of the headboard was heavily gilded baroque, replete with various scrolls and fans, the patterns of which were repeated on the nightstands, armoire, and chest of drawers. The bedspread was rose-colored, embroidered with a metallic gold thread to compliment the headboard. It had two rose bolster pillows tied at each end to look like two large wrapped candies. Although lovely in a fairy-tale sort of way, this was not what Anna had expected. It was far more. She decided then and there, after tipping the bellboy and opening her suitcase, that this opulence would be her Christmas present to herself. As she began to take out her things, she thought of Gelsamina and wondered how long it would take before she would see her great-aunt again.

The water for the bath did not take long to heat up. Anna looked forward to a soak in a tub that, unlike the rest of the accommodations, seemed opulent but worn over the years. She eased herself into the oversized claw-foot tub and just let her body relax in the soapy water. She closed her eyes and tried to imagine what it would have been like in Palermo during the time that Gelsamina was first there. For Anna, this was difficult. To look at the furniture and surroundings of the hotel was easy, but these surroundings would not have been there. They would not have been Gelsamina's. They would have belonged to someone with more, someone with bearing.

With her eyes closed, she could imagine someone like the baron in a place like this. She could see him sitting in the chair, leaning forward, cane at his side. The ring that now adorned her finger, gleaming on his hand. She romantically imagined him as dark and handsome, although she had never gotten a complete description of him from Gelsamina. She imagined his clothes, well-tailored and creating a fine silhouette of a man for him. She imagined the coach that he took when he accompanied Gelsamina for a ride. The heat and moist air that she breathed in helped with her daydreaming, and soon she was nodding off in the deep old bath.

She caught herself as her head slipped back into the water, and she stopped to reposition herself. Taking a towel and rolling it, she tucked it under her head and, tilting back, slipped once again into the water, its warmth now covering her up to the shoulders. She closed her eyes again, half dreaming. This time, she imagined this furniture mixed in with the thick dark furniture that she'd been told of in the baron's villa. She imagined being in the villa, walking in the rooms she'd been told about in the old stories, looking out the windows into the garden replete with flowers. She let her mind wander through the rooms until, in her mind, she heard it, the sound that she would eventually hear, the baying, *l'anelito*. The sound no longer caused worry or tension. In fact, in her dreams, the howls were coming from her own throat. She was calling out.

She looked through the window in the upstairs parlor of the villa, the private room kept only for the owner of the estate, and looked out over the garden and into the fields, hoping to see the one thing that would give her comfort at this point—wolves. In her mind, she howled again, calling out to them, telling them that she was here, that she longed to see them. And there, at the edge of the field, they appeared: two beautiful black and tan wolves, eyes gleaming in the sunset, ears pricked up to catch the sound that they'd been waiting so long for, a call from one of their own. She watched as they sniffed the air and trotted to the base of the stairs outside the villa. She opened the doors that led to the landing at the top of the stairs, as they crept stealthily up the stairs, the sun now fully set. As she came out to receive them, she was no longer Anna Del Forno. She was herself, the wolf that she'd seen before.

They approached her, sniffing at the air to reassure themselves that she was, in fact, the one they had been waiting for. She approached too, and as she leaned her dark, sleek muzzle toward them, they both in turn nuzzled her, silently at first, and then with the thoughts that formed in her mind. She knew who they were and why they had come. They knew that Anna was the "Little One," the one that the White Wolf would have brought. And they were there for her, the former owners of the villa, Fiorello and Nicoletta, the parents of the baron himself, the former baron and baroness D'Arcamo. They assured her that when she came, they would be there waiting for her, to welcome and help her. As she leaned forward again, she found herself face down in the hot water, its warmth now evaporating into the tiles and marble of the room.

She raised her head with a start, and realizing where she actually was, she rose and wrapped herself in one of the thick, soft bath towels folded neatly on a tufted stool across the room from the tub. As she dried herself off, she wondered just how much of her dream was imagined, and how much of it was, in fact, another part of the legacy that was unfolding before her with each step. Only time would tell. She finished drying herself, hung the towel, and went into the bedroom, where she pulled back the covers and crawled into bed. And there, Anna slept.

When she awoke the next morning, Anna looked at her watch. Coming to the realization that she'd slept for eleven hours, Anna also realized that she was hungry. It was early afternoon, sunny and fairly warm, a few days before Christmas, and Anna, dressed in black capris and a simple blouse, went downstairs and outside for a walk. Hoping to find a bistro, she strolled along the street, taking in the holiday decorations, until her sense of smell told her what her eyes would soon confirm. There, a block from the hotel and around the corner, was a little sidewalk bistro. A few people sat at tables, some in animated conversation. The happy mixture of sounds included, among other things, the clinking of goblets, spoons stirring in coffee cups, and the soft crunching of focaccia bread. The aromas convinced her that this was the place she was looking for. Her body clock still coming to terms with the difference in time, Anna couldn't rationalize having a glass of wine, but a steamy cup of latte and a piece of focaccia bread looked wonderful.

The focaccia was a rectangular slice of a thick-crusted dough that had been baked in an oven so that the bottom was crusty while the dough on top had a fleshy moisture, drizzled in this case with a pecorino cheese and some olive oil. *This is a meal in and of itself* thought Anna as she nibbled hungrily at it, alternating sips of the steaming milk-and-coffee blend. It wasn't a dinner, but it would certainly do until evening.

This was more like what Anna had envisioned her time in Palermo to be—sitting there, watching people walk by, enjoying a light meal while the world went about its business.

But as she watched the world, Anna didn't realize that she herself was being watched. She was an attractive, unaccompanied woman. She looked Italian, maybe even Sicilian, but her mannerisms gave her away as something else, possibly an American. Her relaxed demeanor suggested that she was a tourist. Tourists were ripe tomatoes just waiting to be picked. These were some of the thoughts that ran through the head of Francisco Amendola.

Francisco Amendola was a thirty-two-year-old, ruggedly handsome, and arrogantly charming out-of-work tour guide, salesman, escort, and out-and-out rogue. He viewed Anna, thoroughly enjoying her moment, as an opportunity for a meal at the very least, and at the most, well, crimes of passion sometimes involve the heart, and sometimes other body parts as well. But this would not be a simple bump-and-run purse snatching.

He caught the eye of the waiter and asked about Anna.

"The American?" replied the waiter. He added that, other than her abuse of the language, he knew nothing.

"Well then, it's up to me," answered Francisco, and he rose. He ordered two proseccos to be brought to her table as he slowly approached her.

"They say that the best way to watch the world go by is through a glass of prosecco, signorina," he said as he stood by her table. His English was passable, made better by a warm, smooth voice. "I see that you are enjoying the city, and I thought that you might enjoy it more, in the manner that we do."

Anna was slightly taken aback. In spite of all that had occurred to her in the last few months, she was still caught unawares by this simple, yet slightly questionable introduction. She gave him a hesitant smile.

"Please, signorina, let me offer you this token to celebrate Palermo."

She continued to smile, but still said nothing.

"My name is Francisco. I am a guide here. Is this the signorina's first time in Palermo?" he asked. He was good.

As the two proseccos were delivered, Anna spoke. "Anna, and I'm just staying here for a few days …" then she stopped.

"Ahhh. Well, if the signorina is looking to see the sights of Palermo, I would be happy to show her." He paused, searching her face to find a clue, all the while smiling. "My fee is very reasonable," he added, having found his clue. This woman was Sicilian, or at least had been told enough about the old country to withhold trust. As an American, she would feel safer if this were a pure business venture. He pressed on. "Is this the signorina's first time in Palermo?"

"Yes, it is," she replied. "I've heard a lot about the city, but I've never been here before. What is this prosecco?"

"A light sweet bubbly wine, perfect for the daytime. Sometimes one adds fruit to it or just drinks it as we are."

"It's very nice," she responded, "like a light champagne."

"*Si*, like a light champagne." He smiled as he agreed with her.

Over the next few minutes, she talked. While not offering any information about herself or her purpose, Anna flirted with Francisco. Perhaps flirting isn't the best way to describe the nature of the discussion. Smiling all the while, both Anna and Francisco sparred, attempting to establish a position of security while finding out more about the other. Neither was entirely successful, although Anna did decide to hire him to tour the city for an hour.

Price was negotiated, the bill was paid, and a short time later, Anna was riding on the back of a black-and-tan Vespa scooter, crisscrossing the city of Palermo with her guide. His first stop, always a safe choice, was the Duomo, a cathedral that housed the tombs of two hundred years of Sicilian kings inside its collection of architectural styles. Between the bell towers and the north and south transepts, one could see architecture in the Gothic, Catalan, Norman, and even Islamic styles. It was impressive even to someone who knew little about churches. He parked and told her a little about it as they walked up to the entrance. Once inside, he let her stroll and observe for herself, choosing to sit in a pew in the back.

After some twenty minutes of letting her absorb the richness of her surroundings, he gently touched her on the shoulder, saying, "Signorina, your chariot is waiting." She smiled and allowed herself to be led out of the church. The next stop was the Fontana Pretoria. Set in the Piazza Pretoria, a square that touches two other separate and beautiful churches, the fountain is a cornucopia of smaller sculptures, animals, mythical creatures, even the gods and goddesses from Mount Olympus. However, it earned itself the nickname *La Fontana Vergogna* or "the Fountain of Shame" because many of the figures were nude, causing a public outcry when it was built in the 1500s. "You should see it lit up at night," suggested Francisco in a mock lascivious tone.

She smiled at the juxtaposition of Sicilian logic—that this would be looked upon as questionable when here, even in December, girls walked by wearing surprisingly short shorts and blouses revealing ample décolletage. Francisco noticed the smile and asked her what she was thinking. When she told him of her observations, he merely replied, "Here in Sicily, suggestion is one thing, but revelation crosses the line."

"Aren't there nude beaches in Sicily? In fact, just outside of Palermo?" she asked. Apparently, the jousting was to continue.

"Signorina, it is illegal to be on the beach without a bathing suit," he began, trying to sound offended. "What you are referring to are the topless beaches, and even then most of the women who visit them aren't Sicilian, they are vacationers from the north," he said with an air of smugness. Anna gave him a knowing, smirking smile—the type of smile that a woman gives when she is both flirting and arguing at the same time. Francisco looked at her and knew that somewhere in that smile was someone who was at least partly Sicilian. He decided that his chances for greater things were improving.

After riding around the city and pointing out various churches and statues, Francisco decided that it was time to make his move. "And now, Signorina Anna, I have one more place to show you. It is, as you say, just outside the city, and I think that it is the most beautiful sight of all," he began as he started off west of Palermo. "In between Palermo and Mondello are the prettiest beaches that I have ever seen. And you may notice something interesting: unlike the beaches in Palermo or in Mondello, these beaches are smaller, and give a closer view of the *Golfo Palermo*, er, the gulf." He drove northwest to a stretch along the *Lungomare Cristoforo Colombo*, a spot where the gulf was particularly close to the road, really too narrow for a beach but lovely nonetheless—and isolated. He slowed the scooter down at this spot, some ten or eleven miles from where they'd first met, and then parked the Vespa off to the side of the road. As she was looking at the gulf, he chose his moment.

He tried to get close to her and, speaking in a low, romantic voice, told her that it was destiny that brought her to Sicily.

"You have no idea," she answered, smiling. Confused by her answer, he continued. He attempted to embrace her, but she turned to him and said that she was flattered by his attention, but really wasn't interested.

"But Anna, mi amore, how could you lead me on like this?" he asked with a hurt look that actually gave her pause for a moment. Collecting herself, she realized that his words and actions were a bit too rehearsed.

"Listen," she began, "the tour has been lovely, and this has been fun, but I really must get back to the hotel now."

"Signorina, look around. If I leave you here, who will take you back to your hotel? I could kill you here and now, and no one would know for days."

Anna's eyes grew wide. She wasn't sure what Francisco was going to do. If she tried to walk away, he might attack her. Surely he wouldn't rape her, she thought; maybe rough her up and rob her. As she considered this, her nerves got the better of her. She started to walk quickly, then run, away from him. He bolted after her, cursing in Sicilian. Tackling her, he turned her on her back and, straddling her middle, tried to rip open the pullover top that she was wearing. Then, it happened.

From deep inside her, in the pit of her stomach, she felt the tingle. It became a burning sensation in seconds, so much so that, even with the weight of a man on her, she doubled over. He jumped off of her and stepped back as she writhed on the ground in what looked like the pain of severe stomach cramps. Before his eyes, she transformed. Her body, hunched over from the sensation, sprouted hair, and as she changed, she actually wriggled out of her clothing. Her face elongated into the graceful muzzle of the wolf, made less so only because of the howl that she was emitting. Francisco stood transfixed in shock. For the fifty or sixty seconds that it took for Anna to change, her would be attacker found himself unable to move, watching something he'd never seen before. By then, it was too late.

The transformation was complete. Anna turned on him, and in one step lunged at him snarling and snapping. Francisco raised his hands to his face as he fell back. They tumbled over onto the road, and as they did, Anna lost her footing, forcing both front paws into a painfully awkward angle. She yelped and scrambled back a step, but not before leaving Francisco with a series of cuts and scratches on his face and arms. Terrified, he leaped to his feet. With blood now streaking from his wounds, he limped to his scooter and bumped it to a start. To his eternal and undeserved good fortune, it turned over, and in seconds he was gone down the road.

The good news for Anna was that for now, she was safe. The bad news was that she was now stranded some ten miles outside of a city she knew very little about and would probably have to walk back. She looked around and took stock of her situation. She was on a quiet piece of road overlooking the Gulf of Palermo on a sunny afternoon in December, and she was a wolf. Even in her new form, she was trembling. She needed to lie down and rest. She spent the few minutes carrying items of clothing and her bag to the sand. It was there, in the warm solitude of the Sicilian sun, that Anna curled up near her belongings and slept.

Some time later Anna awoke, feeling a change in temperature as a late afternoon breeze brought in cooler air to the unprotected sand that she lay in. She stretched out of her curled shape to realize that she had changed back. She was still without clothing and, as she reached for the items she'd been sleeping next to, she also realized that she'd gotten a bit of a sunburn. Anna gingerly re-dressed, amused at the thought that she'd just broken her first law in Sicily by lying naked on a beach. She put on her shoes, picked up her bag, and began to walk down the road toward Palermo.

As she walked and gradually calmed down, she had time to think about what had happened. She'd been stupid, trusting some good-looking jerk and leaving herself open to all kinds of danger. She was the victim of an attempted rape but couldn't even think of reporting it. What would she say when she was asked how she fended him off? "Well, you see, I just turned into a wolf and tried to rip his throat out, and I would have, too, if you people took better care of your roads." The ludicrous nature of this thought made her laugh, but not the laugh of mirth. Not even the laugh of irony. It was the nervous laugh of fear. She was afraid, really afraid. Not at the possibility of rape. Not even at the possibility of physical violence. Anna was afraid of her inability to control her ability to change. She had been lucky, if one could call it that, to have been accosted on a desolate stretch of road. *What if this had happened in the city?* she asked herself. As she walked, she meditated on this new development in her "legacy."

With each step came questions and feelings. With her fear came anger—anger at Gelsamina forever cursing her with this, anger at believing that this was her destiny, and anger at herself for accepting it. Then another thought crept into her mind. What if Gelsamina was not aware of this? Gelsamina had told her, earnestly, she thought, that until Anna came into her legacy, the only changing that had been done was by her, decades ago. Could it be possible that there was more to this legacy than either of them knew? Anna decided, as she walked on, sunburned and with feet becoming more and more sore, that she needed to talk to her great-aunt, and soon. Anna needed answers, and she needed them before this could happen again.

Between stopping when her feet became too sore to walk and stopping to ask for someone, anyone who spoke enough English to give directions, it wasn't until nine o'clock that night that Anna finally returned to her hotel room. She arrived tired, having found a garage just outside of the city where she could call someone and arrange for a cab.

Once she got the cab, it took only twenty more minutes for the driver to find the hotel. She literally walked out of her clothing, threw her shoes away, and turned on the shower. The next twenty minutes were spent standing under the hot water scrubbing and rinsing. After toweling off, she dressed for bed, climbed under the covers, and slept an uncomfortable sleep.

The experience of the day tumbled over and over in her mind. Would she ever get control of her emotions? Would this thing she'd become take her over? Would she cease to be Anna? Would she only be the "Little One? What if she had killed him? Throughout the snippets of dreams she had, these problems arose again and again. In one piece of a dream she was the wolf, tearing at Francisco's throat. What was frightening to her was that she enjoyed it. In another, he was attacking her. Beaten and bleeding, she couldn't change into her lupine self, and the frustration maddened her.

This went on until about two o'clock in the morning, when the phone rang. It had to have rung some eight times before Anna could rouse herself out of that dazed stupor enough to answer it. Sleepily, she said, "Hullo?"

A voice she was not familiar with was on the other end. "Palermo Airport, ten o'clock. Ladies' room near the baggage carousel." The voice was that of a female, but unfamiliar to her. It wasn't until Anna heard the phone click at the other end that she realized she'd just been given the signal from Gelsamina, or rather from whomever Gelsamina was currently inhabiting. She would meet Gelsamina in the ladies' room near the baggage area at the Palermo Airport.

From their previous conversations, Anna knew that it would be very important to bring clothing, as when Gelsamina concludes her "hitchhike," the host leaves, unaware of the experience, and Gelsamina is left behind, completely naked. Hence the ladies' room stalls, with their lockable privacy doors, would serve an excellent purpose until Anna and Gelsamina actually met.

These thoughts soon mingled with Anna's now subsiding rage at Gelsamina for omitting yet another aspect of the legacy from their discussion. Granted, Anna would never have allowed any type of rape or attack, but it was an isolated area and even with her fairly strong physique she wouldn't have been able to hold him off for long. And to change, right there without any thought … Again, she realized that she could have killed a man. The fluctuating feelings circled her mind until, at last, she drifted off into sleep.

Part IV

Chapter XIII
O Canada

After separating herself from Bruno, on the New York to Rome flight, Gelsamina did not have to wait long before she saw her next opportunity. As the wheelchair carried Bruno Prizzi through the terminal toward a waiting ambulette, she merely leapt into a flight attendant standing nearby. The flight attendant, a perky young female with expressive eyes and jet-black hair, was standing by a shop, waiting for her partner from a recently concluded flight. For them it was the last leg of their shift, and they were both intending to go straight to the hotel. Now, Gelsamina would go home with her.

Seeing through the eyes of her host, she followed the wheelchair-bound figure and the female form walking beside it until they were both out of sight. The attendant, not knowing why, merely finding interest in the couple, wondered if it was a business relationship or something more.

The attendant, Joan Richardson, returned her thoughts to the next day's flights, which started at seven in the morning on Christmas Eve. The first leg of the run would be the Rome to Palermo flight, followed by Palermo to Athens, then Athens to Bern, Switzerland. Today had been a tiring day, and she expected tomorrow to be no better. "A good night's sleep would mean the world to me," she thought. Deep in the recesses of her mind, Gelsamina agreed. But she had to get word to Anna, so she waited until two o'clock in the morning, when she was certain that Joan would be in a deep sleep.

Joan Richardson always took a room in the Hotel Gladiatori

because it had the most spectacular view of the Roman Coliseum. She loved to look at it before she turned in for the evening. She felt that it relaxed her to be in the presence of such grandeur and history. As Gelsamina watched through her host's eyes, she observed a number of things. She was awed by the imagined splendor of what was once one of the wonders of the world—and puzzled by her host. Joan was sitting in a comfortable chair, relaxing and admiring the view from her window for what, from the information Gelsamina could gather, was just one of numerous times doing the same thing over the past three years. Yet Joan Richardson had never actually visited the Coliseum, never stood inside of it, never touched the walls or breathed in the air or the scents of the actual place where ancient Roman citizens actually stood. Why, Gelsamina wondered, would someone allow herself to watch something so many times and yet never come any closer? Was it a question of time? She doubted it. Fear? Hardly likely. Gelsamina searched her host. Could it be respect? This was something that one observed from a distance, not feeling worthy of approaching or coming any closer to.

Joan Richardson was a Canadian who had worked for a small airline out of Toronto. When the company was bought out by a larger European airline, Joan stayed on. With her European looks and her ability to pick up languages, she was well-received on flights that took her to the interiors of Western Europe. At first, she enjoyed the layovers in certain European cities, but gradually, she developed a feeling for some of the older, more historic places. She watched tourists—Asian, European, American—walk around those venues that had stood over centuries, acting, for the most part, bored, and in many cases, in manner far closer to that of a buffoon than of one who has had the privilege of viewing historic beauty. In her own way, she was atoning for their "sins" by offering a respectful worship from afar. *Like the Israelites not approaching the sacred tent, half out of fear and half out of a feeling of unworthiness*, thought Gelsamina as she read the mind of her host, who was now finishing her gin and tonic and had risen to change for bed. Gelsamina was both fascinated and pleased, having found yet another soul of interest. She decided that she had so much to learn by observing this era of people. Together, yet apart, they rested.

At two o'clock in the morning, Joan awoke, and half in a dream, reached for the hotel phone. She pressed some numbers and waited for the ring on the receiver. "Operator."

"Hello. I'd like to place a call to the Hotel Grand Vittorio in Palermo." Joan waited the few seconds until the Hotel Grand Victor's desk clerk, sounding a bit roused, answered.

"Hotel Grand Vittorio," he said as emotionlessly as possible.

"Hello. I'd like to speak to Ms. Anna Del Forno."

Without speaking, the clerk put her through. At that moment, Gelsamina actually used Joan's voice to communicate her message. She was unsure that she could do such a thing, so when it happened she was pleasantly surprised. The short informative sentence served all the purpose that she needed. Joan hung up and returned to her sleep. To her, at best, this would be an unusual dream, and a question to the desk clerk at the Hotel Gladiatori when she saw the call on her bill. By tomorrow, Gelsamina would be reunited with her Little One."

Chapter XIV
Merry Christmas to Us All

The ladies' room in the baggage area of the Palermo airport had three stalls, each made private by a handle with a sliding bar.

Joan Richardson ended her flight at seven minutes after nine in the morning. She finished the policing of her assigned area of the plane and told one of the other attendants that she had to run an errand, and she'd be back in a few minutes.

"We board at nine forty-five," he called out as she walked down the stairs to the tarmac and into the building. She quickened her pace, knowing that the baggage area for all flights inside the country was on the other side of the terminal. For some reason, Joan had to get to a ladies' room—in fact, *that* ladies' room. She didn't know why. She simply had to go there.

A few minutes later, she pushed open the door and entered. One lone woman had finished washing her hands and passed her, leaving the room. Joan looked into all three stalls and, satisfied that they were empty, entered the last one. She felt as if she was about to black out, so she exited the stall and leaned over the sink. In a few seconds, she regained her color and composure. She checked herself in the mirror, primped her hair, and then washed her hands. She left the ladies' room, never realizing that the stall door she'd just left had closed and quietly locked behind her.

In the last stall of the ladies' room was a naked young girl who appeared to be in about her early twenties. She was crouching on the seat of the toilet, her arms folded around her, attempting whatever modesty they could afford her. Gelsamina waited.

Some few minutes later, at ten minutes to ten, a young woman walked in. She was dressed in a one-button cardigan sweater over a top, Capri pants, and slip-on shoes. She entered the first stall and used it, much to the dismay of Gelsamina, who remained crouched and silent as well as she could. She was beginning to get cold.

Finally, the young woman left. Gelsamina listened as the door closed. The door opened again. She heard someone rushing into the room. There were steps, first in one direction and then another. Finally, Gelsamina "heard" the sentence in her mind, "Oh no, she's not here. Either I'm too early or too late."

Gelsamina spoke out loud. "Lock the door if you can."

"Gelsamina?" Anna called out softly.

"I'm here, Little One. You are right on time, but lock the door first."

"I can't. It doesn't lock."

"Then say nothing," answered Gelsamina. She communicated silently to Anna, asking, "Did you bring the clothes?"

"Yes," Anna answered silently in her thoughts as she opened the unlocked stall door and lifted a paper bag with clothing in it. Gelsamina could hear the rustling of the bag as Anna reached into the stall and handed it to her. She dressed as quickly as she could. Slipping on the tennis sneakers that Anna had packed, she opened the door fully to see her great-niece.

The expression on Anna's face was not exactly one of joy. She'd seen that face before. Anna wore that expression when she was upset. That face contained many feelings—sadness, confusion, anger, uncertainty. Anna felt all this and more. But she was silent, as at that moment two older women walked in and trudged into the first two stalls, almost knocking the girls over in the process.

Gelsamina followed Anna out of the ladies' room and into the terminal, to the nearest exit, and over to the end of the sidewalk, where Anna had a cab waiting. As they entered the cab, Anna looked at her great-aunt. This time, Anna did not speak, but rather communicated to Gelsamina in such a manner that mere words could not have conveyed. Buried in the clouds of feelings were the words that Anna wanted to have her hear. "When were you going to tell me that at any moment, if I got upset, I could change? I almost killed a man. Not that he didn't deserve it, but that's beside the point. And don't give me that soothing 'little one' stuff. I feel like a time bomb, and I don't know when I'm going to go off. *I ALMOST KILLED A MAN!*" she reiterated. She now realized that, even when silently communicating, she could yell.

"I did kill a man," Gelsamina replied, looking directly into Anna's eyes. Then she looked away, as if she were looking at the sights on the road between the airport and the hotel. "In fact, three men: one intentionally, and two out of self-defense. The first one wasn't important, but the other two were out of my control. I had no idea that when I'm threatened, I too could change." Gelsamina continued staring out of the window of the cab, trying to appear as aloof as possible, all the while yelling at roughly the same pitch as Anna. To the driver, the argument was in total silence, but to the two recipients, the feelings that Anna had were being shared and returned.

"Threatened?" asked Anna.

"Yes, threatened—I mean really threatened. Like in danger of being beaten or raped. It was horrible." They both sat there in true total silence. Then Gelsamina broke the moment. "Did someone try to rape you?"

"He tried, but I changed and attacked him. If I hadn't lost my footing, I would have killed him. As it was, he took off on his scooter with bites and gashes."

"Oh, Anna," Gelsamina began, and then stopped, remembering what Anna had "said." She looked back at Anna and then spoke out loud. "I had no idea that such a thing could happen. Sometimes I think that I'm as new at this as you are. Please believe me, I had no idea." The look in her eyes made Anna feel as if she really was sincere.

"If you really didn't know, then where do we go from here? I mean, this could happen again." Here the anger subsided from Anna's eyes, which grew moist as she said, "I'm afraid." Gelsamina reached out and took her hand. They sat there in the backseat of the cab for the remainder of the ride in silence.

When the driver pulled up to the hotel, the doorman took the door and opened it. Anna got out, followed by Gelsamina. Together, they went up to Anna's room, not really noticing anything or anyone. As they both got into the room, Anna locked the door. She turned to her mentor, translator, relative, and said with disdain, "Oh yeah, and it's Christmas Eve. *Buon Natale.*"

As arriving and meeting in Palermo was the focus of their goal, the two of them had completely forgotten the approaching holiday. Anna, under the strain of the past forty-eight hours, was fairly oblivious to the lights and ornaments that adorned shops and terraces throughout the city. The Christmas trees, both traditional and contemporary, seemed like just so much landscape to her. This cloud lasted for the remainder of the afternoon until, true to her fashion, Gelsamina smiled and said, "Let me shower and change, and we'll go out for a good dinner. At dinner, I will tell you how I came to arrive here, and what I have learned. Together, we will share what we know, and hopefully we will be stronger for it." And with that, she turned and went into the bathroom. Some twenty minutes later, she emerged, wrapped in a towel and looking a bit more refreshed. Anna had changed and was now wearing a skirt and blouse with a small jacket. Not formal, but nice enough for a good restaurant. Gelsamina dressed in a similar fashion and within the hour, the two of them, lightly made up and in low heels, went downstairs to the restaurant that was attached to the hotel.

In the restaurant, the walls were stucco, painted the color of parchment, with black-framed windows that stretched from the tops of the tables to the ceiling. There were probably only twelve to fourteen tables in the room, each table a small rectangle with two chairs facing each other. The tablecloths were of white linen, with white plates and simple silverware. There were six tables filled, scattered throughout—not surprising, as Christmas Eve was traditionally a big day for a family meal at home. The two of them were escorted to a table near one of the windows, where they could look out at the city, but of greater importance in terms of the restaurant, the city could look in on them—two attractive young ladies, dining here in the afternoon on Christmas Eve. This was good advertising.

A waiter, in his best attempt at English, welcomed them and asked if he could bring them a glass of wine. Gelsamina looked at Anna and said, "Do you trust me?" At this, Anna burst out laughing—not the funny, happy sort of laughing, but rather the incredulous sort of laughing that means to say *After everything that has happened so far, you've got to be kidding me.* Looking rather sheepish after she realized how the question was taken, Gelsamina turned to the waiter—who was a little surprised at the discourse of the two women—and speaking in Sicilian, advised him that this was her cousin's first trip to Sicily, and she wanted to show her a traditional Christmas Eve meal, requesting that they be served family style. He answered that it would be a pleasure. She asked him what the freshest catches of the day were. He rattled off two or three types of fish. She asked about clams and mussels. He looked back, smiled, and said "*Certamente!*" which translates to "Certainly!" Finally, she told him about a family favorite that she'd remembered for years. She spoke almost wistfully as she described scungilli fra diavolo, which is conch sliced thin and prepared in a peppery hot tomato sauce. He smiled again and asked if she had family in Palermo. She said that her grandparents came from Arcamo. He bowed his head, proud that he had picked up the clue that she might have had local roots, and exited, returning a moment later to apologize for not taking their order for wine. "Signor, what would you suggest?" Gelsamina asked.

"Perhaps the signorina would like a nice pinot grigio?"

To this, Gelsamina wrinkled her nose.

"Something stronger, more dry?" he offered. At this she smiled. "Ahhh, we have a dry wine from Sardinia, very good, Vermintino di Gallua. Permit me to offer you both a glass, a 'Christmas present.'"

"*Grazie,*" replied Gelsamina as the waiter vanished, returning with two stemmed glasses and a bottle. He poured the pale yellow wine into each glass. Anna raised the glass to her lips. Stopping, she waited until Gelsamina did the same. They bid each other and the waiter "*salut*" and tasted. It was cool, not cold as one might drink white wine in America, and dry, with almost a sharpness to it. One would expect it to go well with a sharp cheese or fish, or even chicken. The women smiled, and the waiter bowed slightly again, saying '*Buon Natale*' as he left. Alone and sipping their wine, they could finally talk.

Anna began the conversation. "We must make a list of what we know. Will these things happen to both of us?"

"I don't know. You are only a little newer at changing than I am. Remember, I was somewhere else for so long."

"Where were you?"

"I don't have the words to say where I was. I can tell you that when you or my brother, or even your grandmother, looked at my portrait, I knew that I existed. I *was*. I suppose that whenever I was thought of, I was. And when no one thought of me, I wasn't. Here and now, with you and I so close, I am just as real as you, and with that comes my abilities, which are yours, too."

"So, what do we do?"

"Well, we talk without talking. We know that we can 'change.'"

" … and 'change back.'"

"Yes, and that."

"And when we changed back at the farmhouse, we could talk to Nana and Nonno."

"Soon, there will be at least two more for you to speak to. At least, I hope that they will be there. It has been so long."

"Who are you talking about? Fiero? La Notte?"

Gelsamina nodded. "And their family as well. I felt in my heart that we would all live forever. We will see if my heart told me the truth when we get to Arcamo."

"What else do we know?"

"Rage and fear bring about the change, I think even faster than if we try to will it."

"Was it me, or does the change make us very tired?"

"Now that I think of it, you are right. It did make me weary." Gelsamina stopped as the waiter approached. In Sicilian, he explained to her that the soup he was presenting was a house specialty—a fish stock with little morsels of cod, tubettini, and finely chopped carrots, seasoned with garlic and fresh parsley. It was delicious and yet not overpowering. He refilled their glasses. As he turned, Anna gave out a sigh of contentment. "The signorina likes?" he asked, turning back to them.

"Oh, this is delicious!" she replied.

"*Bene*. Enjoy."

Between polite sips and nibbles of tubettini and fish, the conversation continued. "What happened after I left?" asked Anna.

"I took the bus into New York City. New York City is very big. What do they call it? The Big Apple? More like an onion, it has so many layers. And some of the layers are bad, rotten. Just as I thought I was getting into a cab to go to the airport, these men took me to a secluded part of the city, where there was a lot of big machinery, all shut down for the night, dark and empty and near a river."

"Oh no," said Anna, as she realized that Gelsamina had been taken to the West Side, by the river, where it seemed like construction or repairs were always going on. At night, it was seedy at best; at worst, dangerous.

"They forced me out of the car, and one held me while the other …" she paused. "The other one …" she paused again. Emotion was getting the best of her. Eyes moist, she dabbed at them with a napkin and gulped down the refilled glass of wine, its dryness fortifying her to continue.

Anna interrupted, "When they attacked you, you changed, didn't you?"

"Without even thinking," Gelsamina added. "I killed them both. I don't remember what I did exactly, but I remember that it was savage. And I did not stop until they no longer moved, until I knew they were no longer a threat to me. Anna, I love changing. It is beautiful and freeing and so deeply passionate, but this was ugly. I had no control over this. It was as if something deeper and darker took over inside of me. As one of the *figli*, I always felt more heightened, more in tune with all of life around me, but in these moments when I had changed, I was no longer defending myself, I was attacking, I was killing, and I needed to. When I changed back, I was exhausted. I remember walking, sort of in a fog, like I really didn't know where I was going. It took some time before I had my self-control back."

Anna was silent, listening, half to learn from her and half to hear of her ordeal. "How did you get here?"

"Do you remember how I told you that I can, what did we call it? 'Spiritually hitchhike'? I could leave my clothes and 'get into' the mind of a chosen host. I did that years ago to leave here and come to America, although then it took me much longer. Doing this also takes great will and effort. This also makes me weary. When things are settled here, we must see if you can do it."

"So you 'hitchhiked' to Sicily?"

"Well, first I went to Rome. Once there, I found a suitable host who was traveling to Sicily. I won't tell you all about it, but I can say that when I found someone who was going from New York City to Italy, even though it was Rome, I jumped at the chance. I can also tell you that while I was taking the spiritual piggyback ride, I could speak with my host. I even interacted with him."

"Him? Does that mean what it sounds like?" Anna asked with a warm smile, seeing that the sadness of the previous moment had subsided.

"Don't be silly. A host is a host, and this was never an opportunity for anything base or physical."

"So we now know that we can 'get a ride,' talk, and interact with a host," concluded Anna.

"Yes, but this too takes its toll," said Gelsamina. "Often, I had to rest. And just keep in mind, one cannot eat while one takes a ride. As you say, 'hunger plays a part, too.'"

As she spoke, the second course arrived. As a second waiter cleared away the first-course plates, a fresh set was laid out. In the center of the table was placed a bowl of spaghetti, fairly covered with mussels steamed in olive oil and garlic, the juices of the three making for an intoxicating aroma. The waiter, after setting out the bowl, offered to serve, and after completing his task, offered to grate cheese over each bowl of spaghetti. Once again, the sharpness of the cheese and the salty hint of the mussels complemented the wine that they sipped. After the waiter vanished, Anna restarted the conversation.

"What did you do with the bodies?"

"I left them there. I think I turned off the ignition to the car, but I left there as quickly and quietly as I could. What else would you expect of me? The *polizia* would think that I was insane if I were to tell them this story. These two men were attacking me. They were trying to …" Gelsamina struggled with the word.

"Rape you?" volunteered Anna.

"Yes, they were trying to rape me. They deserved to be left there. When they are found, the *polizia* will see the marks of some type of animal. It will probably take them a day or two until they decide that the bite marks are from a wolf."

"You said before that you killed three men. You only mentioned two. When was the third one killed? And where?"

Gelsamina began eating her spaghetti with gusto, attempting to make it look as if she hadn't heard the question.

"Gelsamina, what about the third one?"

"The third one was not important. He also did bad things."

"Did he attack you?"

"Let's stop all this talk of attacking. I see that you are wearing the ring. Listen, I want to give you a Christmas present, but I need you to lend me the ring," she said as she extended her hand. Anna knew that she was trying to shift the conversation away from the distasteful subject that they'd gotten to. She decided to humor Gelsamina and go along with her.

"What are you thinking of?"

"I've been giving it some thought, and I think that the red ribbon that held the ring around your neck is not safe. You could easily lose it when you change, so if you'd like, we could cut the back and open the curved ring part so that the crest is in the front, but on each side there could be a loop, made from the ring. Then we could string a leather thong through the loops and around your neck. It would never come off; no matter where you were, you would never be in danger of losing it."

"Could we do that? I mean, today? After all, it's Christmas Eve," Anna asked.

The conversation having been successfully steered away from the unpleasantness of the past few days, the two enjoyed the good food and each other's company. As the waiter cleared away the pasta course, Gelsamina asked him in their language if he knew of a jeweler who could perform such a task as she had described. He replied that she was in luck. His cousin was a jeweler, with a shop around the corner. The shop was probably closed by now, but the waiter agreed to call his cousin and ask if such a special order could be done. He lingered for a moment, just long enough for Gelsamina to grasp the requirement of the situation, and she added, "Of course, I would be glad to pay for the short notice of the special order." The waiter smiled, pleased that his gesture was clearly understood, and disappeared again.

Throughout the next two courses, Anna, while enjoying her meal, felt stuffed. The scungilli fra diavolo was spicy but not "over the top" hot, in the manner that some meals are. And by the time it was served, they were on their second bottle of di Gallura. The meal was incredible. Even though she had small portions of each course, Anna felt as if she wouldn't need to eat again for days. And by the time the fruits and nuts were brought out, she had to defer.

"Would signorina like a small glass of Cynar? Maybe a small *aperitivo* to help with *digestione*," asked the waiter, seeing that his goal of culinary contentment was more than accomplished.

"Could I have an espresso?" Anna asked, looking across the table.

"I'd like one, too," added Gelsamina.

"Very good, and my cousin said that he would be happy to help the signorina with her request," he said, speaking once again in Sicilian. "He suggested that you meet him in his shop at five o'clock. The door will be locked. You must press the buzzer, and he will let you in."

"Thank you so much," replied Gelsamina, taking the espresso that he had just poured. "Anna, we still have a little time to enjoy our meal." She poured the espresso for Anna and they sipped, its strong warm flavor helping their digestion after the sumptuous feast. They thanked the waiter, tipping him generously over the bill, and left.

Although it was December in Sicily, the sun shone. A brisk wind chilled the sunshine in the lateness of the day. But it was still nice enough to stroll happily to the jeweler's shop around the corner. Pressing the buzzer once, they were immediately let in. Gelsamina thanked the jeweler for his generosity in seeing them at such a time and explained what she needed him to do.

After agreeing on a price, he took the ring from Anna and went to his workbench at the back of the shop. Some twenty minutes later, it was finished. The crest itself was left intact, but the arms of the ring had been cut, straightened out, and split, making for an upper and lower loop on each side. Sensing what she was trying to achieve, the jeweler took a tightly woven black cord and looped it through the upper loop, with another one through the lower loop, repeating the process for the other side. He then fit them into a gold lobster-claw fastener, which connected the black cords at the back. The contrast between the newly polished gold and the black cords was striking and well worth the fifty thousand lire they were charged. He attached the completed piece around Anna's neck and admired it as Gelsamina said, "Merry Christmas, Little One" quietly to her. They paid the jeweler, wished him a *Buon Natale*, thanked him again and left.

Outside the shop, Anna took Gelsamina by the arm and said, "We've had a wonderful meal, and you've given me a lovely present. Let's take a walk." The sun was still fairly high in the sky, but it wasn't quite as warm as it had been, so the two enjoyed linking arms, if for nothing more than warmth. Gelsamina smiled at the "little one" as they strolled, arm in arm, down the street.

"You know, I think that I will always treasure this—I mean, what you did for me today," said Anna. She wanted to tell Gelsamina that she didn't have anything to give in return, especially in light of the fact that, up until yesterday, her emotions had cast her great-aunt in a very different light.

Zia Gelsamina heard her thoughts and smiled a melancholy smile. "Your gift to me is to forgive me for not having more to tell you. Sadly, the one book that even talked about what we are only speaks of it in basic rudimentary terms."

"What book?" asked Anna. "Oh, wait, you don't mean *The Transmigration of Souls?*"

"Exactly, the book that mentioned the baron's parents," Gelsamina replied.

"It's hard to believe that they created Fiero and La Notte," said Anna.

"Not hard at all, Little One. They saw logic in what we are and soon after, believed. The rest, supernatural as it seems, followed naturally. It was Leonardo who, in his blind stubbornness, saw nothing." Gelsamina looked downward as they walked on, fighting back a sad moment of recollection.

"What do you think became of his soul?" asked Anna.

"I don't know. I cannot really say," replied her mentor. "There are so few of us that I know of, one could only guess. I would like to think that his is out there somewhere, hopefully learning."

"Learning what?"

"To love; to accept life, all life."

They walked on for a few more minutes. As they turned a corner, Gelsamina asked Anna what they needed to do next.

"Well, tomorrow being Christmas, I thought we'd spend the day relaxing, maybe taking another walk through the city. And then on Monday, we have an eleven o'clock appointment with the attorneys. If all goes well, by Tuesday or Wednesday, at the latest, we'll be in Arcamo."

As if perfectly timed, they turned the final corner of the square block that they had walked and found themselves not more than a few dozen steps from the doors of the hotel. Lingering a few moments in the lobby while Anna arranged for the additional guest with the front desk, Gelsamina found herself smelling the flowers and admiring the décor. Anna returned and suggested that they have a drink in the restaurant while an additional bed was moved into the room.

This pleased Gelsamina, who immediately agreed. "Something sweet, to celebrate the holiday," she recommended.

Together, they went into the restaurant and were escorted to a table. Their waiter from before saw them and rushed over to greet them. "Ahh, the signorinas missed me. Alberto is touched," he joked. "Did my cousin meet with your satisfaction?" he asked. At which, as if on cue, Gelsamina raised her hand, palm up, a finger pointing at Anna's neck. "*Oh, que beddu*," commented the waiter in the Sicilian vernacular. "May I offer you something?" he said, smiling.

This time, Anna answered. "We would like something sweet, something for after dinner. Something to give pleasant dreams."

"I have just the thing," Alberto remarked as he walked quickly to the bar. A minute later, he returned with two tulip-style glasses of a thick white liquid. It looked like a cordial and smelled sweet. "This is marsala, grown in vineyards just outside of Palermo," he said as he offered the glasses to them. "I promise you that after a glass of marsala, you will dream of gardens and happiness. Salut."

They sipped at the wine and, finding it to their liking, sipped some more. Seeing their approval, Alberto brought a second round to them and, wishing them a *Buon Natale*, said that this round was with the compliments of the hotel. They enjoyed their after-dinner drink and, after settling the bill, generously tipping their newfound friend Alberto, made their way up to the newly made-up room.

While they relaxed, Anna placed a transatlantic call, as promised, to her parents.

"Hello?"

"Hello, Dad?"

"Anna? Well, you remembered!" he said with a bit of sarcasm in his voice.

"Hi, Dad."

"Merry Christmas."

"Merry Christmas to you, sweetie."

dreamed about since leaving Sicily those many years ago. In her
...am, she walked though the rooms at the villa D'Arcamo.
Coming in through the main-floor doors, she stood in the entrance
...l. She called out "hallo," as if in anticipation of hearing someone's
...ce return her call. To her disappointment, no one answered. Yet she
... as if she was not alone. She crossed over into the dining room, with
... crest hung mightily at one end and the statue of Diana, the huntress,
...he other. Still seeing no one, she left. Climbing the interior stairway,
... entered the sitting room and expansive parlor with dark massive
...niture, all neatly polished and beautiful. She called out again, and
...in heard no one. Yet the sense of someone else being there remained.
...e entered a room that she had never been in before, the master
...droom, a suite of two rooms. The smaller anteroom held a settee and
... ingle armchair at one end and a dressing armoire at the other, very
...sculine in appearance, although regal in its dark woods. Her sense
... anticipation grew as she entered this room, looking at each piece
... if expecting to see someone there. She walked into the connecting
...droom and there, beside the bed, dressed in burgundy and regarding
... as if her presence had been requested, stood the baron, Leonardo,
...oking as if he had not changed a moment since she left him that day
... the carriage. His haughty expression masked a devilish grin, which
...on melted into an expression of what she could only describe as, well,
...ging.

"You see, my Gelsamina, you are not the only one who hears the
...wls of *l'anelito*." He spoke as if he had been there waiting for all this
...ne. But something was wrong. He seemed taller than she remembered,
...d more vibrant. Then she realized what had taken place. She looked
...wn at the richly carpeted floor. There, standing on the carpet, she saw
...o white paws. She had once again become the White Wolf. She was
...nding before him in her changed state.

She awoke with a start. Her hands and face were damp with
...rspiration. Was this just a dream, she wondered, or was it the next
...rt of the journey that she would embark on? And what of her Anna?
...uld it be that she had brought Anna to this point for something
...ore selfish than the legacy? She became tense. Her mind raced. She
...tually began the process of turning, right there at that moment, in
...e bed. Then she heard a muffled sound from outside the window. It

"How are things in sunny Florida?"

"Not too sunny, in fact a little rainy, but it's nice. without you and your sister and her family, but that's n How's Palermo?"

"It's interesting in an old way. The people here at the nice, and the food is unbelievable. The wine, too. I have lot tell you about when I get home. And who knows what San bring you?"

"Just come home safely, little girl. We'll talk when you Wait, here's your mother."

"Hello, honey, Merry Christmas. So how are you doi in a big foreign city?"

"Believe it or not, Mom, it's not as big as you might Christmas. But it is the type of place that you could spend exploring. You know, cathedrals and churches and statues a I was telling Dad, the food is wonderful, and the wine ..."

"Don't get crazy with the wine, you. Don't forget, you'r and pretty. I bet they'd love to get to meet you over the without your mother (hint, hint). I bet some Sicilian man take you out for a drink and help you 'celebrate Christmas

"Oh, Ma," said Anna. She knew that her mother w could tell that both of them wished she wasn't alone for If only they knew. But then, they would never know. She conversation with them and then made a similar call to Tir happily to her sister, brother-in-law, and the kids before wis a happy holiday and hanging up. For a moment, she felt a bi thinking of how they would go on with their lives, growin eventually dying, but if Gelsamina was right, she would out Even if it wasn't forever, it would be a very long time. Funny tend to make one think of sad things, she thought. Anna at Gelsamina, who was reclining on her bed. If she had I thoughts, she wasn't responding to them, perhaps because agreed with them. At any rate, they turned out the lights a asleep.

Perhaps it was the wine or the feeling of calm with whi to sleep, but that night they did both indeed dream, as promised. Gelsamina dreamed of being at the villa, sometl was midnight, and church bells throughout the city were ringing in the start of Christmas Day. This seemed to give her solace. In that calm, she returned to herself. She rose and went to the bathroom. She washed and changed into a dry nightshirt and returned to bed, lying there for some time before finally drifting off to sleep.

As for Anna, her dreams took her down a different road. In her dream, she had returned to Binghamton, to the farmhouse. She was straightening up the rooms, one at a time. Pausing to look out the window, she saw that the fields had been tilled and planted and crops were growing. The breeze that wafted in through the window was warm, making her think that this was sometime in the summer. As she straightened the beds and dusted one room after another, she felt very comfortable. She got to the room with Gelsamina's portrait in it, only to find that the portrait was no longer there. It had been removed and replaced with another portrait in a different frame. This was a painting, possibly oils or acrylic, she really wasn't versed enough to tell. But the face of the main figure looked a great deal like her, and this figure was flanked by two good-sized gray and black wolves. At this revelation, Anna felt a little surprised but not startled by any means. She felt a sense of calm, as if her portrait should be there. The dream faded, and Anna turned over to sleep soundly for the rest of the night.

There was an Italian legend, over a century ago, of the power that Christmas Eve held over creatures with wandering souls. Over the years, it has taken on many different faces, but one of them is of particular interest. Before the turn of the nineteenth into the twentieth century, when wolves were far more prevalent in Italy and Sicily, people believed in the ringing of church bells as the absolute herald of an event. And in the event that Christmas Eve ends and gives over to Christmas Day, the heralding bells would have performed their task that night. It was said, and generally believed at the time, that in the peace of that starry night over two thousand years ago, all souls were granted the blessing of calm. Upon hearing the peal of the bells, their souls would wander no more. They would be what they were, no longer tormented to wander from host to host.

But in the lives of the two souls asleep in their room at the Hotel Grand Victor in Palermo, Sicily, the blessing of the bells took on a very different meaning. As they slept, they both again dreamed, this time sharing the dream. They had both entered the villa D'Arcamo and were in the entrance hall on the first floor. They both wore red empire-style gowns, fitted in a formal fashion. Gelsamina ascended the curved grand staircase to the landing at the second floor where two large chairs were set out. When she reached the chairs, Gelsamina sat and, reaching out an opera-gloved hand, beckoned Anna to do the same. Anna followed her and, reaching the chairs, also sat. As she looked out from her "throne," as it were, Anna saw wolves, mostly in pairs, on the first landing. Not many, mind you, but at least twenty of them. They neither spoke nor howled nor even whined in the sympathetic sound that wolves have been known to make. They all, to a soul, merely stood and looked, focusing on the two figures who were seated regally at the top of the stairs. It was, for all intents and purposes, a silent acknowledgment of matriarchal fealty. They stood there, frozen, for what seemed like long stately moments until slowly, the great front doors on the first floor opened. There, in the doorway, stood a man, resplendent in a rich dark-brown tailored suit. It clearly marked him as a person of refined tastes and perhaps wealth.

The wolves all turned their attention to him. As they did, he looked to the two seated women and removed his coat, leaving it on the floor. He grasped his shirt, a simple white collarless blouse, and ripped it open, bursting the top four or five buttons, baring the upper part of his chest, a mess of dark curly hair covering it.

The wolves turned on him, first slowly and then, as the first few reached him, with more rapidity. At first, it seemed as if they were attacking him, biting and pawing at the figure. Anna's eyes grew wide as she felt a sense of terror at the sight, but Gelsamina said nothing. In fact, she raised her hand to stay Anna from even rising from the chair. *Is this a sacrifice?* Anna thought. *Is this yet another facet of what it means to turn?* Anna writhed in her bed as the dream tormented her.

But upon closer observation, the wolves were not attacking the sole intruder. They were welcoming him, giving something of themselves to him, almost feeding him, not unlike some wild mother hawk feeding her young. From the entangled pile of moving paws and fangs there was still no sound, save the rustling of so many lupine bodies performing some barely discernable task. Then they started to recede, to return to where they were standing at the start of the dream—leaving there, among the torn and ripped clothes that once adorned the solitary figure, not a man unclad and bleeding, but a young male wolf, fur the same rich dark brown of the tailored suit. Anna and Gelsamina had witnessed the formal transmigration of a soul. What's more, they had presided over it.

"And so," thought Anna, "there is another way to become one of us." She looked over at Gelsamina, thinking, "Did you know?"

"No," came the reply, "but there have been times in my past when I had hoped." Anna wasn't sure what that meant until she heard Gelsamina, looking at the new wolf, say, "Leonardo."

The wolf, who had been standing nearer to two older wolves, looked up at her. Perhaps out of the moment, perhaps out of some other very different reason, he said nothing, but looked down and away. Tears of happiness appearing from her eyes, Gelsamina looked at him, in perhaps the loving manner that she did as a young girl so many decades ago. "I have longed for this moment," she said, fighting back the desire to shed more tears. Anna looked first at Gelsamina, then at the object of her affection. She too said nothing, largely because she sensed something other than love.

Chapter XV
A Visit to Yesterday

As the sun rose the next morning, it made all things on the street outside the hotel stand in a crisp brightness, giving a feeling of renewed spirit and strength to all who noticed it. Slowly the refreshing power of the Mediterranean sun worked its magic on the two sleeping figures buried beneath blankets in their respective beds at the Hotel Grand Victor. As they slowly awakened, one of them could still taste the saltiness of tears, left to dry on her face from sometime before.

It was rare that Anna got up this late in the day, and under the circumstances, a very good reason to relax and, perhaps, take the day in a more luxurious manner. As she went into the bathroom to prepare for the day, she thought about the Christmases in her past, especially when she was a teen. Her family would wake early to exchange presents, and then, still dressed in their nightclothes and a bit scruffy from sleep, they would all come to the table for eggs, bacon, and a coarse heavy bread with fried bits of pork in it that her mother made from a generations-old recipe. The gifts were always nice, but what she remembered most was the familial warmth.

A hint of melancholy came over her as she stepped into the shower. She told herself that while these memories were wonderful, they could not be recaptured—at least not in the way that one would hope. The people in those memories were younger. She and Tina were younger; Mom and Dad were younger. The only parts that stay the same are the feelings and the food.

I suppose that's why food is so important to me, she thought to herself. *It reminds me of where I came from.*

"You know, if you take any more time in that shower," she heard Gelsamina call out, "you won't be able to find any food to let you know where you're going. Hurry up in there, I'm hungry!"

"Well, *Buon Natale* to you too!" said Anna out loud, realizing that her silent musings had been clearly heard by Gelsamina.

They dressed in nicer clothes that day, skirts and tops, and bidding whoever they happened to bump into a *Buon Natale*, they walked out and into a sunshine-laden day, warmer than they expected. Crossing the street and walking down about two blocks, they came to a little bistro. The bistro stood adjacent to a small park with a statue of some larger-than-life mythical Roman figure. People were walking across the square toward a church at what appeared to be the other end and across the street. In front of some of the doorways that lined the square on either side were older women, some with hair whiter than others and some with hunched backs more pronounced, sweeping their entranceways. Here and there were Christmas decorations festooned around a window or doorway, with more formal reminders of the season lining the semicircular walkway around the statue. The reverie of the scene that they were taking in was broken when the waitress came to their table.

She was pleasant enough, but gave the impression that she would have preferred being home for the Christmas holiday. When Gelsamina spoke to her in Sicilian, her appearance softened, but it was still evident that she didn't want to be waiting tables that morning. They ordered cappuccinos and rolls, and while munching and sipping, they took in the sights from their table.

"Where is the attorney that we have to meet?" Gelsamina asked, picking at the doughy center of her roll.

"Mister, err, *Signor* Sagrigento left a message that he'd meet us tomorrow in the hotel lobby at nine o'clock. He said that he wanted to apprise us of our current standing before we met again at the villa," answered Anna.

"*Our* current standing, or *your* current standing? Remember, I'm Chelsea. In fact, from now on, I'm Chelsea. You know, I went back to the desk after you asked for the rollaway bed, and I had them change my name. I explained that you were trying to make me more Italian than I actually was. I think that they believed me, especially when I played the role of the silly little girl."

"Thanks, I have to remind myself," said Anna as she tasted a little of the cappuccino and got foam on her upper lip. They both laughed a bit and enjoyed the beauty of the moment. "From this point on, you are Chelsea, my cousin. Where do you live again?"

"My family came from here, but I was born and raised by relatives in America when my parents passed away," Chelsea answered in a slightly exasperated, know-it-all twenty-year-old girl voice.

"Oooh, sounds a little sad. Should we know how your parents died?"

"Mmm, let's see. I know, they died in a car accident. They swerved and hit a tree to avoid hitting an animal that they saw in the road," came the answer.

"Chelsea, you have an unusual sense of humor. Would the animal be a wolf, by any chance?"

"Why yes," Chelsea responded incredulously, "how did you guess?" They laughed again, but this time, there was a hint of the nervous laughter that is often evident when there is trepidation about everything turning out all right.

The next morning came more quickly than they expected. It was a bit cloudy and cooler than the previous day. They both washed and dressed in clothes similar to those they wore on Christmas, neat and attractive yet fairly informal. Anna made sure to wear a top that buttoned up to the neck, hiding her crest for the time being.

They went downstairs to the restaurant and ordered coffee and rolls from the waiter they had come to know as their own. Anna had brought down with her the papers that she felt might be necessary to show to the attorney. While they were still eating, Gelsamina (now Chelsea) excused herself and went to the front desk. She explained that they would be expecting a visitor soon. If he came to the desk enquiring after Signorina Del Forno, she asked that he be shown to their table in the restaurant. The clerk assured her that he would do so.

Within fifteen minutes, a short balding man in a dark gray suit was brought to the entrance of the restaurant, where he was greeted by Alberto. After a few short words passed between them, the waiter escorted him to the table, where the man introduced himself as Carlo Sagrigento of the law firm of L. Catanzaro and Son.

They welcomed him and introduced themselves, being careful to introduce Gelsamina as Chelsea Del Forno, a younger cousin who was traveling with Anna. As her relative, Anna assured him, it was perfectly all right to speak freely in front of her. His English was fairly good, but from time to time he came across a word that he couldn't translate to an appropriate meaning. At this juncture, he would turn to Chelsea who would offer one or two possible solutions. The conversation, all in all, went well.

Signor Sagrigento asked to see the papers that Anna had brought. She first showed him her grandfather's will, bequeathing the property and possessions of the villa D'Arcamo to her. At receiving it, he had no expression, but rather asked to see the baron's document. His eyebrows arched at the sight of the seal. Having been an attorney for the past twenty years, Sagrigento had seen this seal before. It appeared to be the real thing. He would take a copy of it and verify the names and signatures. This would probably take some time, possibly a week, but as the firm served as custodians of the account, he was authorized to invite them to the villa as guests of the practice.

If the document from the baron was authentic, then Anna would be the sole heir to the estate, along with the monetary account that it brought in over the years, minus the fees, of course. When Anna asked Sagrigento how much was in the account, he hesitated in answering. "Please understand, signorina, but it would be, errr, umm ..." at this, he looked to Chelsea, who volunteered the word "inappropriate."

"*Si, grazi,*" he said and continued. "It would be inappropriate for me to discuss money and possessions with you, if there should be questions regarding the documents."

"Do you mean to say that we can visit, as your guests, but we can't know anything about the estate until it can be proven that the will is real?"

"*Si,* exactly, and also that you are who you say you are. Please forgive me, but this estate has been in my office's care for almost seventy-five years, and it is sizable. Hopefully, you will see that we look after the properties of all of our clients as thoroughly and completely as we can. I would like to think that when all of our work is done, if you are pleased with the outcome, you would retain us to represent you, for exactly that reason. I will try to finish my work as soon as possible. In the meantime, please, go and see the villa. I understand that this your first visit to Sicily," he said. Anna nodded. "Well, I hope," Sagrigento added as he held the papers at eye level, "that this will be the first of many visits. Signorina," he said, as he rose and turned, nodding to Chelsea. Moments after he left, Chelsea reached across the table and poured them both another cup of coffee from the carafe Alberto had kept refilling.

"As you spoke, I was listening to him. He believes that this is the real thing. He just wants to check to make sure. I could hear in your voice that you were getting annoyed with his questions. I don't think that we need to be overly concerned. Did you notice that he never asked you for your passport? He didn't even ask to see it. I got the sense that has already had you, er, emmm … what is the word for when one looks at something over and over, in may different ways? In my language we say *scrutare*," said Chelsea.

"I think that you're trying to say that he's already checked me out," replied Anna.

"Yes, as you say. But I also think that you could have listened to him here," Chelsea said, pointing to her head. "In your anger, you didn't. You must try to keep your feelings from getting in the way of your abilities." And then, thinking of her dream last night and the transformation that it almost brought about, Chelsea added, "I suppose we both should."

Inviting Anna and Chelsea to the villa was not only a courtesy, it was good business. If Anna was indeed, as Sagrigento suspected, the sole heir to the baron's estate, then she would be entitled to the estate and its funds. Although he wasn't sure of the amount, he knew that it was worth more than a few lire. In fact, his conservative guess was somewhere in the vicinity of four million American dollars. To invite them to stay as guests might encourage them to keep the account with his firm, thus ensuring custodial fees for years to come. Especially if, from time to time, she returned to America, and in her absence, allowed them to represent her interests in leasing the property out to celebrities, a practice that had been privately lucrative for the firm in the past. Of course, the estate made money on each deal, but as the original documents never stipulated things like rental fees for filming, the law firm's partners had a greater hand in creating the contracts, allowing for a more profitable deal for themselves. It wasn't really stealing; it was a creative manipulation of payments, all of which could very well be left intact if Anna was pleased. To this end, Sagrigento would see that she was treated like aristocracy. As far as her cousin, the fact that she could speak the Sicilian dialect was impressive, but she still just seemed like a silly young girl.

As they were leaving the restaurant to return to their room, Anna said, "You go up. I'll be there in a little while. I want to take care of something down here. And don't look into my head," she added silently to Chelsea, in a mock order. Waiting until Chelsea climbed the stairs and was well out of sight, Anna went over to the station where Alberto, their waiter, was standing and polishing silverware. His professional attentiveness ever visible, he listened for a few moments as she spoke and then took the envelope that she handed him and left the building. She then returned upstairs.

Entering the room, she saw Chelsea talking on the telephone.

"Yes, well, I, oh wait, she has just come back. Here," said Chelsea, handing her the phone. "It's Signor Sagrigento."

Anna took the phone. "Hello."

"Signorina," came the voice at the other end. "This is Carlo Sagrigento. I was wondering if you and your cousin would be available this afternoon to come out to stay at the villa. I can have a car at the hotel at, hmmm, say two-thirty. You could be at the villa by three forty-five."

"Signor Sagrigento, that would be wonderful. Thank you so much for your offer," Anna said, smiling and looking over at Chelsea, whose eyebrows had arched and head was nodding. It was not difficult to discern what actual words were being spoken.

"*Bene*," said Sagrigento. "I will have the car there at two thirty. Signorina, leave everything to me. I will call you this afternoon at the villa. Ciao."

Anna put down the receiver and looked at her "cousin." In mock disappointment, she said, "Well, I suppose our walking tour of the Quattro Canti will have to wait." Chelsea smiled at her, knowing that the next step of their journey was about to be realized. Filled with ideas and things to say, neither of them spoke as they began to pack their clothes.

They finished their packing within the next ten minutes and left their bags in the room as they went downstairs to the front desk. Anna spoke to the clerk, explaining the new arrangements that had been made. She settled the bill and asked to have the bags taken down and stored. After completing the transaction, the desk clerk graciously complied with her request. Anna then asked where they could go to spend a little time shopping. The clerk listened and pondered for a moment. Giving directions for some shops a few blocks away, he named some stores that she could look for, adding that this might be a good start. She thanked him, turned, and left the hotel, taking Chelsea with her. Arm in arm, they walked the three blocks down and one block over to a series of four shops in a row. The first shop sold shoes, and although they were stylish and the two of them lingered at the window for a moment, Anna said, "Let's shop here last, depending upon what we find at the other three."

The first shop of the remaining three was a lovely little store that sold women's separates—blouses and shells that could be matched with skirts. It offered slacks, but they seemed a bit more stylized, and more for evening wear than the skirts and tops. "This would probably serve the most purpose," thought Chelsea. Over the next hour, she tried on a number of skirts, settling on two respectable knee-length items, one in black and one in brown, and a third longer, more dressy number that, by its length alone, accentuated her slim waist. Anna was a little envious and said so. Chelsea responded by declaring her envy for Anna's chest, which, in comparison was larger, and with the right blouse could be considered very attractive.

They actually laughed amid their repartee, causing the saleswoman, an older lady who spoke no English, to smile. She wasn't sure of what they were saying, but it was always nice to hear that sort of chitchat with clothing and figures. In addition, it was always a sure sign of a sale. All told, just from this shop, they bought three skirts and four tops—the skirts that Chelsea chose plus two matching shells and a formal blouse in burgundy, in addition to the aforementioned "right" blouse for Anna.

They stopped in the remaining two shops, finding a sweater and a jacket that went with all three of Chelsea's skirts. Chelsea was now a bit closer to being complete, for as one will always say, one is never fully complete. By this time, the shoe store would have to wait until another day.

They arrived back at the hotel, packages in hand, and after finding their luggage, repacked. As it was only one o'clock, they decided to stop into the restaurant for one last time, as all that shopping had made them a little hungry, and they still didn't know what to expect at the villa. Alberto was waiting and offered them a dry red Nero d'Avola that was gratefully accepted. He mentioned that the chef had just made a *focaccio* with olives and onions. This also sounded good to them, and it was. The focaccio bread was still warm, and the tangy taste of the olives complimented the slightly oily crunch pf the bread itself. Along with the dryness of the Nero d'Avola, it made for a memorable good-bye meal at the Hotel Grand Vittorio. Before long, Alberto came to their table and announced that the car that had been sent for them had arrived. They thanked him and gave him a warm hug, settled their bill, and left. The bags had already been put into the car, and in no time at all, they were on their way.

The driver, a local man, had been an employee of the law firm for close to twenty years now. His sole job was to pick passengers up and deliver them to the villa. He had done so for all visitors, celebrated or private, who had availed themselves of the now quiet sanctity of the villa D'Arcamo.

The car, a sedan, was black with the sleek lines and chrome of a late-seventies luxury car—perhaps a Lincoln or a Cadillac—but they hardly paid any attention to it. Anna noticed that the backseat was large enough and far enough away from the front seat that she could speak privately to Chelsea.

"I need to tell you about a dream I had last night," she began. "Two dreams, in fact. The first one took place at the farmhouse. I was there alone, cleaning up, and when I got to your room, the room with your portrait, it was gone. Instead, I saw a portrait of me, with a wolf at my right and my left, as if they were protecting me."

"Little One, err, *Anna*," replied Chelsea, who first misspoke and then corrected herself. "Wolves will protect you for the rest of their lives, and yours. That was a nice dream, certainly not one for concern. You will be the matriarch of your clan when you return to Binghamton. Now let me tell you …" Chelsea had intended to tell Anna of her own dreams when she was cut off.

"No, let me finish with my second dream. The first one made me feel as if it was supposed to happen. But the second one was very different. You were in it, and we were in what I could only guess was a house or something like the baron's villa …" As Anna went on to describe the dream in detail, Chelsea sat and looked on silent and motionless. She tried mightily not to show the astonished feeling she was experiencing at hearing that the exact dream she had last night had also been dreamed by Anna. Her shock and amazement was broken only by Anna's question, "So, what do you think?"

"If I told you that I had the exact same dream, would you believe me?" she asked Anna, careful not to divulge her first dream. This opened up a new line of questions that, at this point in time, could generate no answers.

Anna answered, "Well, we were both in it, but who was the man? Did another member of your family just die? Please tell me it's no one in my family." There was a tension in Anna's voice as a stray thought crossed her mind. She had never thought of her father as being a part of the *figli del lupo*, but as she spoke, the idea seemed more possible now than before. And the thought of losing her father in this manner was a concept that frightened her, more because it took her unaware.

"No, Anna, I don't think that your father has anything to do with this. My nephew's destiny does not lie with the *figli*, at least I have never sensed his soul in that way."

"Then is this some kind of ceremony?" Anna's questions came quickly.

"I don't know what it means. And I don't know of anyone else in *our* family, going all the way back to when I was young, that this would have been. As for a ceremony, you know as much as I do," Chelsea said. What she said was not completely true. Although the man involved in the dream they shared was not a relative to either of them, Chelsea knew in her heart who it was. But she said nothing of it. Was the dream an event yet to come? Had it already happened? Or was this merely a desire newly revisited? Chelsea was at a loss, and so, until she could be more certain, the secret would remain hers to keep.

The time passed quickly as they traveled down one and two lane roads, passing an occasional small village or lemon grove. Eventually, the car slowed as they entered the town of Arcamo. Driving slowly through the main road, they passed the square where the church of

Saint Andrew Avellino still stood. It had been almost sixty years since Chelsea had seen it, but it seemed almost as if it hadn't been touched by time. The stores that lined the street had changed. Cars replaced the horse-drawn carts and carriages of her memories, and of course, the way that people dressed and interacted seemed, to her, far more immodest than when she was young.

She wondered, as she peered out of the car window, if this was how the old feel when they revisit a place where they lived and grew up. Her memories were mixed—happy to see some buildings with similar views ("You know, Anna, if I close my eyes just a little and I look at that old building over there, I can almost see the butcher shop from when I was growing up") to sad ("You see, by these houses and that gas station? That used to be all olive trees"). She was still adjusting to her surroundings, not expecting to react in this manner, when, leaving the town, they approached the iron gates of the low stone walls that surrounded the villa D'Arcamo.

The car stopped and the driver got out and unlocked the gates, first walking back the one side and then the other. Then he returned to the car and drove though, stopping after some twenty feet to close the gates up again. Re-entering the car, he drove up to the villa itself. The driveway, now more defined by stones and gravel, opened at the house itself—which, recently painted, appeared to meet the expectations of everything that Anna imagined it to be. Chelsea smiled contentedly, seeing this to be the only other building so far that seemed unfazed by the years.

As the car stopped the second time, the driver came around to each side to open the doors for Chelsea and Anna. He then accompanied them to the doors at the main floor, the doors between the grand sweeping stone staircases that stood curving at either side. There were flowers in the vases on the stairs as well as at their base, but they were unlike any flowers that Chelsea remembered. In fact, for as attractive as they were, she felt oddly nauseated as she walked by them. She passed them without saying a word, remembering that she was twenty-year-old Chelsea, the American cousin who had never been to the villa before. Anna, on the other hand, was making no secret of the fact that she was taking in as much of this as she could. She hardly noticed the flowers other than the fact that something yellow and attractive had been planted there.

The entrance had a quiet old stateliness about it—mixed, Anna felt, with a hint of sadness, partly because she knew something of its history, but also because it seemed to have no life in it, no laughter, no aromas of lovingly prepared meals, no telltale signs that people, young or old, loved life here. Anna and Chelsea stood in the entrance hall, now laid with a highly polished marble floor, and peered at their surroundings.

The stucco walls looked clean and white, as if preparations for guests had been going on for some time. The chandelier, a great wrought-iron monstrosity that once held who knows how many candles in its great curves, had been re-invented. It no longer cupped candles, but had been wired in such a way that where once a candle burned, now a flame-shaped lightbulb took its place. Light switches had been mounted on nearby walls in as unobtrusive a fashion as possible, and every attempt at modernity seemed to be hidden away in like manner.

The driver returned from the car a moment later, carrying the bags that they had brought. He then called out in a singsong voice, "Hal-lo." The call achieved its goal when three people emerged from different doorways in the home. The first to appear was an older woman wearing a darker dress and flat-heeled black shoes. Over the dress was a full-length cook's apron. She was wiping her hands on what appeared to be a dish towel. Looking at the two guests, she smiled cordially and said, "Ciao."

From somewhere upstairs, a door closed, and after the padded soles of sensible shoes approaching made their presence known, another woman, this one appearing to be in her thirties, came down the stairs and smiled a more formal smile, tipping her head a little in an informal version of a curtsey. Over a similar dark dress, she wore a smaller apron tied around the waist, suggesting that she was responsible for something other than cooking.

Finally, from yet another door, possibly one from outside, came a man. He was older than the other two staff members. His movements suggested that he had been doing this a long time. They were paced a bit slower than the ladies', but regular and purposeful. He was holding a part to something, perhaps something from a car engine.

In Sicilian, the driver looked at Chelsea and said, "I was told that you speak Sicilian."

"Yes," answered Chelsea, careful to offer no more and no less.

"Good. This is Francesca Paola," he said, leading an open hand of introduction to the woman holding the dish towel. "She cooks for all of our guests."

Chelsea said hello and introduced Anna and herself. Francesca Paola asked her if she'd "like a little something to eat now." Chelsea thanked her but said that they'd eaten before coming. She then asked Chelsea when they'd like to have their evening meal. Chelsea in turn translated the request and asked Anna. Grateful that Chelsea was there and doing this, Anna asked if six o'clock was all right.

"Absolutely," said Francesca Paola. She retreated back through the doorway, returning a second or two later to ask, "Oh, is there anything that you don't like?"

"No, we really enjoy pretty much everything," Chelsea replied.

"Very good," answered the salt-and-pepper-haired cook as she left.

"Next, I'd like you both to meet Elena," the driver continued. "She takes care of the rooms in the house, and if there's anything you need or if you're curious about the house, just ask Elena." She nodded again to both of them, choosing not to say anything at this point. "Now, before Elena shows you the rest of the house, I'd like you to meet Antonino. He has worked with us the longest. I am told that Antonino did odd jobs for the estate as far back as when he was a little boy. And he's been with us ever since. I think that is why he is still called 'Antonino.' He is a sort of, emm, what you call a 'handyman.' He does all kinds of things here. He takes care of the property outside and repairs things inside."

Antonino had a gruff appearance. He looked as if he would have been much more glad if there were never any guests at all, so it struck them as odd when he, under hooded eyes, smiled a little and said, "Welcome to you both." Then he stood there in anticipation. Finally, it dawned on Chelsea what he was waiting for. He was waiting for her to translate his welcome to the *Americana* who couldn't speak his language. When she did so, and Anna finally smiled and nodded, he returned the smile and left, saying "Ciao" before doing so.

Finally, Elena took them on the grand tour. As she showed them the two large rooms adjoining the entrance hallway, Chelsea maintained as naive an expression as she could muster, trying desperately not to let on that she'd seen these rooms before. In the dining room, the crest still hung. Before she walked up to it and translated the words aloud, she looked over to Anna. Her great-niece's neck was covered; nothing was revealed. She read the words in an elementary fashion, not really putting them together, similar to the way one not thoroughly proficient in a language might do. This obviously was done for the purpose of convincing Elena. She then asked her what it meant.

"Just before the turn of the century, the baron and his wife believed that the soul could leave one body and enter another. The local legend at the time was that they practiced it, too. When they disappeared and their son became the heir to the title, all the legends stopped," stated the housekeeper, as if she'd said this all before.

"Why?" asked Chelsea.

"The people in the town said that he held his parents responsible for leaving him alone, so as he grew into adulthood, he denounced all that they believed in—except, of course, the villa and all of the actual properties. Because, let's face it, if one has a choice between being angry and being angry and wealthy, angry and wealthy will always win." Elena smiled at her remark; Chelsea smiled back at her and translated the conversation to Anna, who now became even more aware of the game that Chelsea was playing—and then Anna, too, smiled.

They crossed over to the room on the opposite side of the entrance hall. What Chelsea remembered as a great room with an oak floor on which stood freestanding bookcases and shields mounted on stuccoed walls was now bare with light gauzy curtain panels allowing late-day sunlight into the room.

"This is the room that musicians use when they record."

"Do a lot of musicians come here to record?"

"Not so many in the past few years, but during the seventies, we had a stream of musicians, all rock and roll with big hair and clothes that made them look a little like women. I remember that there was one who liked a vest that I was wearing one day, and he asked me right there, on the spot, if he could buy it from me. He paid me thirty thousand lire for it—just an everyday cheap vest that I wore so I wouldn't get cleaning fluid on my uniform. Could you imagine?" said Elena, still smiling. This time, Chelsea's smile was more perfunctory, and so she when translated to Anna, the words came out in a melancholy manner. Anna sensed this, so she repressed her desire to ask which rock stars specifically rented the villa.

"Beyond this room is the kitchen, but we should just poke our heads in. Francesca Paola doesn't like it when we go in if she is cooking. And she's probably already started making some kind of dessert for tonight." Elena held the swinging door, a heavy wooden affair that seemed to swing effortlessly on its silent hinges. As Anna and Chelsea poked their heads in, Chelsea called out, not seeing anyone, "Ciao," making it a singsong two-syllable greeting. From behind a large black stove came Francesca Paola, wiping her hands on her apron.

"Signorina, have you ever tasted *cassata?*" she asked. At this question, the expressions on the faces of both Chelsea and Anna gave them away. Anna understood the word and knew very well what pleasure the creamy sweet filling would add to a dessert. Their eyes grew wide and a chorus of "ooh" came from the doorway. Knowing that she had just won the hearts (or at least the tastebuds) of her two guests, Francesca Paola shooed them out of the kitchen and, in mock warning, called out in Sicilian, "Dinner is not until six o'clock! Go away!"

Elena took them back into the entrance hallway, where they ascended the curved staircase up to the next floor. Viewing the scene from atop the stairs, it struck Anna as sparse—recalling a grandeur that might have existed years before, yet was no longer. It made her a little sad. Chelsea was still unsure what to make of all this. She understood that they were being treated as guests, but when the time came that the representative, Sagrigento, returned, would she stay here, or would she take a small place elsewhere? She presumed that Anna would offer her the villa to stay in, but she wasn't sure that she should. Some inner voice was speaking to her. So many thoughts were coming into her head, she could hardly focus on Elena, who had been speaking all the while they were climbing the stairs.

She had been describing the bedrooms, six in all—two guest rooms on either side of the parlor here, near the landing, and two more down the hall. She motioned in the direction of the hallway over the recording room and the kitchen. "There's a bath at each end of the hall," she directed.

"Elena," Chelsea interrupted, finally returning her attention to the housekeeper. "You mentioned six bedrooms."

"Yes, two rooms downstairs are used by Francesca Paola and me. Antonino lives in a room in the garage.

"But what rooms are down there?" Chelsea pointed to the hallway that ran over the dining room.

"At one time, that was the master bedroom. I suppose one could still call it the master bedroom, but we use it for storage now. It hasn't been used as a bedroom since the last baron passed away in the twenties. When the estate was created, a part of the agreement was that the room not be used."

"Oh," replied Chelsea, as she translated the conversation and pointed to specific rooms for Anna.

"Are you okay?" asked Anna. "So far, you seem to be holding up pretty well, but this all must be affecting you at least a little."

Chelsea smiled a wan smile and, in English, replied, "Maybe later on, we'll talk," trying to disguise the inflection in her voice to mask her feelings, more for Elena than anything else.

"Please feel free to choose either of the two rooms down the hallway," said the dark-haired thirty-year-old housekeeper as she walked toward the doors, opening them as she did so. Choosing the rooms that were nearest the bathroom, Anna and Chelsea entered. Seeing that there was nothing else to do, Elena offered to have their bags brought up in a moment, and nodding, left them.

Each on her own looked first at her own room and then at her companion's. Each of the rooms was similarly furnished in a simple manner. Chelsea immediately thought to herself, "This is not what was here while the baron lived, but then these were probably not guest rooms." She looked at the dimensions of the rooms and tried to guess at what they once might have held. She remembered the taste with which the home was furnished before and saw little of it here. Anna saw the look of mixed emotion on Chelsea's face and asked her if she noticed anything about the staff. Chelsea, too, had a feeling about that, but said nothing. Instead she thought, communicating wordlessly to Anna, "Tell me what you're thinking."

"I'm thinking," replied Anna, "that they consider us to be nothing more than curious guests from America. Do you think they've even been told?"

"I don't know yet. By the look of these rooms, I would say that they are friendly and formal but not very receptive—unless of course, they haven't been told the whole story. I wonder what parts of it they know."

At this, there was a knock at the door. When Anna opened it, there stood Antonino holding two sets of luggage. He looked at both of them in a mildly perplexed manner and then asked Chelsea in Sicilian if they would be staying in the same room. Chelsea replied that this would be her room, and Anna's room was next door. He nodded and set the luggage down in the appropriate places, but not before stopping and looking once again at Chelsea.

"*Pardon*, signorina," he began, "but there is something about you that looks very familiar." Anna froze a little, while Chelsea played at mock surprise. "Did you ever have family that lived here in this part of Sicily?" he continued.

"Why yes," she replied, keeping up the pretense. "My great-uncle Giacamo, her grandfather, lived here back in the early nineteen twenties, but he was the last one in our family to live in the area." She stopped there, not wanting to offer more information. If they hadn't been told, she did not want to add more fuel to the fire, not knowing which way the flames would spread. She smiled simply. He returned the smile. His older, wizened gray visage seeming to hide more than one truth, let alone a whole story. He left them and went down the hallway and stairs to a door that they hadn't been made aware of.

Chelsea and Anna continued their silent conversation. "Let us say nothing of why we are here," began Chelsea. "At least until we can find out if these people will be friendly to us." Anna agreed.

Chapter XVI
Local Lore

Dinner came soon enough. Elena found Anna upstairs in the parlor. This sitting room was replete with a marquetry style of furniture reminiscent of the 1920s. It was well-kept and had a distinguished fascination to it, yet Anna's attentions lay elsewhere. She was standing at the window admiring the view beyond the house. She looked out over gardens and groves, varying shades of green, with splashes of yellow from the lemons growing in the neatly planted rows of trees. In fact, she seemed so engrossed with the view that she hardly noticed the housekeeper's presence at first. Repeating her polite cough and her "Signorina? Dinner is presented in the dining room," Elena finally caught Anna's attention, and having done so, exited. Elena seemed a bit more no-nonsense than her fellow workers. Anna felt that there was probably a story there but wouldn't be surprised if it took place somewhere other than the villa. Elena seemed good at her job, but it appeared that her love lay elsewhere. Elena went down the hall to the room occupied by Chelsea. She knocked twice and softly called out, "Signorina?" When Chelsea responded, Elena said "Dinner" and left.

Behind the door, Chelsea, having already emptied her bags, had gone back to studying the room. She felt a need to deduce what this room once was, having convinced herself that it was not a bedroom. She saw no breaks in the walls that might have suggested something removed or covered over, no alcove or niche to reveal or even suggest a secret. The room was painted white, and the moldings that defined the walls, windows, and doorways were stately but simple in comparison to the more public rooms downstairs. But something told her, over and over, that this room was not a room for sleeping, as Elena had suggested. Anna felt it too, but not to the extent that Chelsea did. It seemed to bother her in the way a nagging headache does; it crept up on her, slowly but consistently making its presence known. Chelsea decided to leave it for a while and go downstairs for dinner. Perhaps a meal would help, or at least yield to her some information.

The two descended the stairs, having already washed and changed for dinner. They were invited into the dining room where they were seated, both at one end of the long banquet table richly laid out with linen, china, and silver. For a moment, Chelsea felt a memory of the evening long ago. Letting it linger, she savored it, but then let it pass. She looked across the table to Anna, who seemed to be taking it all in.

Silently, Anna asked if she was remembering. Chelsea replied wordlessly that she was. Then she spoke, making sure that Francesca Paola and Elena, who were both in the room serving, heard her conversation. "This is just beautiful! I wonder what kind of fancy dinners or parties must have gone on here." Then feigning to catch herself, she repeated her comment in Sicilian.

Francesca Paola smiled and began to talk of regional royalty visiting the villa. "One hundred years ago, the duke of Palermo graced this table. Since then, bishops and military heroes, even rock-and-roll boys came. But the rock-and-roll boys, their parties were different. The rock-and-roll boys ate like children, and they drank and took drugs." "The duke brought honor. All the rock-and-roll boys brought was money," added Elena as she set out the antipasto. The antipasto was a selection of pickled or spiced vegetables, meats, and cheese, all served chilled. Pepperoncini, roasted peppers, a sliced and rolled spiced meat called mortadella, and fresh mozzerella—a creamy, mild, semi-soft cheese made of buffalo milk that is a common favorite among many Italians. Served together, they achieved their goal, to whet the appetite for things to come.

As Anna and Chelsea sighed with contentment, Elena poured wine and Francesca Paola, hearing them as she returned from the kitchen and pleased with the reception her food was getting, continued with the story. "For generations and generations, this villa was owned by the same family. From father to son, the title of baron D'Arcamo was passed, and accordingly, the wife of the baron was his baroness. I have only heard of one or two times when, in a generation, there was no male heir to the title, and at that time, in each of those cases, a daughter would become the baroness D'Arcamo, retaining the title even into marriage. And in both of those two cases, the baroness gave birth to son, bringing back the title to the household.

"Only in the past three or four generations was the rule changed to where the owner of the property itself became the owner of the title. The parents of the last baron lived here in the 1800s, up until the turn of the century, when they vanished. I don't know all of the details to that story, but I do know that they left a son, the last baron, who died without ever marrying. Now, the estate is privately managed. It's used mostly for guests like yourselves, and anyone who wants to lease it."

Chelsea translated all of this to Anna, who smiled and said, "You see, when you want to know the truth, you ask the people who work here." Chelsea translated this back to Francesca Paola, who smiled at the flattery. Chelsea thought to herself and Anna, "It's working."

"But Francesca Paola, the baron lived in this big house all by himself?" she asked.

Francesca Paola, who was now clearing the dishes, replied, "They say he was lonely because he lost his parents at an early age. Whatever family came to look after him weren't very good at raising children. In fact, he became obsessed with hunting. He loved to hunt. When he was alive, he even kept the hides of the animals that he killed, mostly wolves. I was told when I first came here that he used to hang them from the walls, like trophies."

Chelsea was aghast. She fought any outward signs of revealing this but translated it all to Anna—who, having a bit more experience, played along. "Ewwww," she said, and picked up her napkin. Feeling that she had achieved the desired affect, Francesca Paola smiled again. She had been successful at what is known as making Anna *schifoso*, that is to say, disgusted, using local lore to play on the sensibilities of the American girls.

"Here? In this room?" continued Chelsea with a completely believable incredulous tone.

"Oh, no," answered the matronly cook. "One of the rooms upstairs, the one directly over the kitchen." Chelsea's eyes betrayed her. This was the sensation that was reaching out to her, the horror and sadness that she had felt up in the room. Francesca Paola saw this and asked if that bothered her. Seeing that something was wrong, Anna held up her glass and asked, in what proved to be ice-breakingly poor Italian, for more wine. Both Francesca Paola and Chelsea laughed at the attempt, as Elena returned with the next course, a little annoyed at the fact that she alone was serving while her colleague was laughing with the guests.

The next course was seafood—calamari and *polpo* brought in fresh from Palermo that day. While Chelsea hadn't tasted these delicacies in a long time, Anna couldn't remember ever having had them at all. *Polpo* is sometimes presented in its entirety and then cut at the table. Whether sautéed in a broth that includes garlic and oil, or cooked in a tomato-based sauce, to the uninitiated, *polpo* can make a dramatic entrance. And this time was no exception. *Polpo* is the Italian word for octopus, and to many who live in and around the Mediterranean Sea, it is quite an enjoyable entrée. As soon as the introductory effect wore off, even Anna enjoyed it. The calamari, a dish where squid (a smaller relative of the octopus) is prepared in a sauce that includes its own ink and ladled over a long, thin pasta called linguine, was surprisingly mild and enthusiastically received. Looking for a continued expression of revulsion—or, lacking that, at least negative surprise—and seeing none, Elena thought to herself, *There may genuinely be some Sicilian in these two after all.*

After the seafood and linguine had been enjoyed, a dish of fruit was laid out. The girls, by this time, were busy digesting their meals and politely declined. Waiting a few minutes, Francesca Paola asked Chelsea if they'd care for some coffee "to help with their digestion." Chelsea looked at Anna and said yes. It was then that Francesca Paola went into the kitchen and returned with the treat of the evening. With Elena trailing behind, holding a china carafe of strong black coffee, Francesca Paola re-entered the room holding a twelve-inch cake covered in a thick, dark icing with jellied fruit, decorated across the top. In spite of feelings of fullness, Chelsea recognized this immediately and actually squealed in excitement, exclaiming "*Cassata* cake!" This is the triumph of desserts, a light cake with a filling of sweetened cream made from ricotta cheese and powdered sugar. The icing was almost a shell of sweet ingredients whipped into perfection. The sweetness of the dessert married very well with the black coffee. This was not something one ate regularly, but rather a "once in a great while" treat.

When they had finished their meal thoroughly satisfied, they thanked both Elena and Francesca Paola. Elena asked them if they'd like to finish their coffee upstairs in the parlor, where Antonino had built a small fire in the stove. Lulled into a sense of contentment by the talk and the meal, they agreed. They climbed the stairs to find Antonino tending to a beautiful stove set into what was once a smallish fireplace. The fireplace itself was decorated with brightly colored ceramic tiles, which upon further inspection were each painted with different scenes. The colors and scenes fit very nicely with the style of furniture and fabric in the room, and the warmth of the fire added to their comfort. As they settled in, they were served additional cups of the black coffee, this time with anisette, a thick sweet cordial that tasted like licorice. Anna looked over at Chelsea, who had taken a nearby wingback chair, and thought to her, "Is this what you remembered?"

Chelsea responded, "No, these were Leonardo's private chambers. It would have been impolite or, worse, scandalous to enter here. I only remember the rooms on the main floor, and even then, things have greatly changed."

Aloud, Anna asked, "Do you know anything about the tiles on the stove? I mean, they look like they have similar figures on them, as if they tell a story."

"I don't know. I'll ask," came the reply. "Signor ..." she said to Antonino, who was just finishing the arrangement of wood in the stove. He closed the door but opened a panel in the front so as to let the fire peer though safely. His thinning gray hair and the wrinkles on his face took the light and shadows from the fire in such a way as to appear a little mysterious, even with his plain work clothes. "Signor," she repeated as he turned to her, "Could you tell us about the tiles in the fireplace? They look beautiful."

He looked at her and then at Anna, and sensing the opportunity, he spoke. "Signorina, the story of these tiles is a costly one, and for the price of a glass of anisette, I will tell it to you." There was a sparkle in his eyes as he smiled, seeing that the desired effect was achieved. Chelsea poured a glass of the liqueur for him from the decanter that had been left on the side table near the couch. He took it, saying *"grazie,"* and sat in a chair near the hearth. "Signorina, for the benefit of your cousin, I will tell you a little bit of the story and then let you tell it to her. I mean no disrespect, but I, ahhh, well ..."

"I understand," said Chelsea.

"Well, you've heard of the story of Romulus and Remus, the two babies who were found by a wolf and taken in by her, nourished by her? And you know how the legend goes? That they founded Rome?"

"Yes."

"Ahhh, but did you ever notice that no one ever really talks about what happened to the wolf? Eventually, as more and more people came to live in Rome, she was driven out. She fled, fearing for her life, and in time crossed over at Calabria, finally coming to Sicily. But she didn't stop there. No, it would have been too easy for man and the sons of man to find her at Messina, where it's the closest to the mainland, so she continued on, all the way to Arcamo, here in the hills. And, having spent her life raising Romulus and Remus, with no brood of her own it was here that she intended to raise a family." He paused and sipped from his glass. As Chelsea translated, Anna listened, thinking all the while of how this moment reminded her of her grandfather, sipping his wine and telling his stories about Gelsamina. It may have been the moment of familial contentment or simply the anisette, but Anna felt so right just sitting there.

"The wolf lived for many, many years here in Arcamo, but sensing that she was growing old, she decided to appeal to the Roman gods to intercede on her behalf." As he spoke, he pointed to the pictures that had been painted and set in order on the tiles. "Her appeals were met, as the gods of Rome rewarded her for caring for Romulus and Remus. But as was the case with many gifts from the Roman gods, the blessing was mixed. For giving nourishment to Romulus and Remus, she was granted eternal life. But to ensure that she would never give birth to a possible rival to Romulus and Remus, she was made barren.

"Now, many years later, probably centuries, Saint Andreas d'Avellino was walking through the hills of Arcamo, praying and meditating as saints often do, when he came upon the wolf. As wolves cannot cry, she looked away, howling in a mournfully sad way." He pointed to the tile that depicted a robed man coming upon a wolf howling at the moon, as

Chelsea translated this next part, referring to the saint by his English name, Saint Andrew of Avellino.

Sipping again from the anisette, Antonino continued. "Saint Andreas asked her why she was so sad, and she replied with her story, saying that she would give anything for the ability to have cubs. Saint Andreas was moved by the plight of the old wolf and prayed to God to have mercy upon her. He fed her with what little food he had and took a cord from his cloak, a red cord, and tied it around her neck, telling her that it was a gift of God's love.

"Days later, the wolf realized that a change had occurred. She was pregnant and, in time, gave birth to two healthy cubs, a male and a female. She loved them and cared for them and, from time to time, would see Saint Andreas during his meditative walks through the hills of Arcamo. But over the years, it became more and more difficult for her, because, you see, another gift that was given to her from the praying of Saint Andreas was mortality. And as she lay dying, she asked Saint Andreas to find someone to care for her cubs. He promised this to her and to this day, wolves are cared for in Arcamo to honor the promise that Saint Andreas made. No one knows if the story continues or how it does. But a story that ends in kindness is always a good thing, don't you think?" he said with a smile as he finished his drink.

Not waiting to translate, Chelsea asked, "But Francesca Paola said that the baron hated wolves."

"He hated wolves because he believed that his parents were taken by wolves. He lived his life in revenge. This I know, because I was here. As a little boy I worked here in the fields and the stable, before it was changed to a garage." The claim made by Antonino, especially as his voice raised in volume, said many things—first and foremost, that he believed the stories and legends that he told.

He continued, "His parents, the baron and baroness before him, believed this story. They are the ones who commissioned this fireplace to be created. They believed in things that went beyond life and death, just as the motto on the family crest says—the crest that hangs in the dining room." He seemed agitated at saying this, as if there was even more that he knew but was withholding, and this took Chelsea by surprise; Anna, too, when the translated retelling of the story was complete. Chelsea still couldn't tell if he was merely loyal to the memory of what he'd lived with for all those years or if he saw something in her.

Anna noticed something different. At the mention of the red cord, she looked at Chelsea, who had stopped sipping her coffee and put it down. On the tiles that Antonino pointed to, they saw a wolf and a figure they assumed represented someone holy, a saint perhaps, and although it may have been there, no red cord was seen. Anna put her coffee down, wondering if this was the origin of the red ribbons. She couldn't let her thoughts stray too far. Antonino had finished his story and was waiting for her to hear the translated version, waiting for a reaction at strategic points in the story. He watched the expressions on each of their faces. His story had achieved its purpose. When Chelsea had ended her translation, he rose, nodding first to Anna and then to Chelsea, saying, "signorina" to each of them. Bidding them goodnight, he left, descending the stairs and exiting out of the doors beneath them.

The two women sat silently for a moment, the coffee having been finished. They had come here hoping to keep secret their stories, but sat there feeling that the three servants not only knew of their stories but had stories of their own to keep. Silently, Anna spoke to Chelsea. "Do you think that he suspects?"

"Yes," came the reply, "but I think that he only knows the legend, what people in the town have said over the years, maybe even embellished by time and wine."

"But the red cord, and the two wolf cubs, and the looking after the wolves …"

"I admit that I was not aware of the care for the wolves by others here, but I'm not surprised. In fact, I'm pleased. In the future, this will be helpful. Regarding the cubs, having a litter of two doesn't happen often but is not unusual. I think that it adds to the story. The chance of him knowing about two specific wolves is highly unlikely. And please refrain from thinking about my two pets, because they wouldn't have been yet."

"Been what?"

"Been! Been born. Fiero and La Notte were the pups of the wolf that had been killed by Leonardo, but that was when I was, oh, I don't know, nineteen years old. So for him to refer to them wouldn't make sense."

"Do you think that there were wolves before the baron's parents were changed?"

"Wolves? Of course, there were wolves."

"You know what I mean, *figli*.."

"*Figli del lupo?* I see no reason why such a thing couldn't be. You and I are only one part of what may well be a much greater story."

"And the red cord?"

"Red cord, red ribbon. If Antonino has even a piece of another story to add to ours, then this might be the red thread that ties them both together." Amid the silent conversation between the two, a clock struck somewhere in the house, announcing the hour. Without words spoken or thought, Anna and Chelsea got up and went into their respective rooms.

While Anna slept soundly that night, Chelsea did not fare as well. She had washed and changed, crawling into the single bed. It was clean and comfortable enough, but she couldn't help feeling that somewhere, voices were speaking. At first, she thought that perhaps the house had been constructed in a manner more flimsy that one expected, and the voices seemed to be coming from the kitchen below. She steadied herself, trying to remain as still and silent as possible in order to hear. It was only then that she realized that the voices weren't coming from downstairs. They were coming from within her.   Reaching her silently, they talked, they pleaded, calling her *madre*—"mother." Some spoke to her telling of something to come, some asking, beseeching her to return and lead. And one—one voice asking her to forgive. The voices were growing, becoming more tangled and confused in an apparent need for each to be heard. She turned over, trying to shut them out, trying to get some sleep. Her eyes closed tightly, she experienced darkness, but the voices, although muffled, still continued.

From the darkness, she began to dream. Dim light cast strong shadows that fought to direct her attention on the figures she saw before her. There stood her family of wolves, some twenty or thirty of them, all beautiful, sleek, and strong, all looking to her with questioning or needful expressions. She knew that she had changed. She was once again the White Wolf, and her clan had grown considerably. The thought of such a large clan made her proud but a little frightened. She wondered if she would be wise enough to lead them all. She stood before them, meeting their gazes one by one, until all of the voices were quieted.

And then silently, she spoke. "My loves," she began, gazing out at them all. "Your devotion gives me strength, and my heart leaps to see you. Soon, we will meet, and when we do, we will talk. And you will see who I have brought to you, my Anna, my Little One. But for now, I need to rest. I feel that one part of my journey is coming to an end, just as another is soon to begin." And in small groups, the wolves turned to leave, back into the darkness, until the entire pack had gone, save one. Finally the lone wolf, looking long and hard at her, not seeing what he had hoped to see, lowered his head, turned, and left. And Chelsea slept.

The next day was cold by Sicilian standards. Chelsea and Anna in turn showered and dressed for the day and went downstairs into the dining room for breakfast, where they were met by the aroma of coffee laced with boiled milk. On the server next to the table sat a platter of rolls and two small dishes, one of butter and one of a fruit jam. As they sat, Francesca Paola entered the room and, bidding them *"Bon giorno,"* served them each a steaming mug of the coffee and a dish on which she had placed a roll. As they began to sip and nibble, she asked if they would be interested in seeing the gardens and lemon grove on the property. As this appealed to them both, she told them that Antonino would be over in a little while to give them a tour.

Some twenty minutes later, Elena came into the dining room to announce that Signor Sagrigento had arrived and asked if he could meet with them. Elena seemed a bit flustered by the announcement, certainly far different from the more distant attitude that she displayed the evening before. As they finished their coffee, Signor Sagrigento was announced. He entered carrying flowers, a large bouquet for Anna and a smaller one for Chelsea. The former, hopefully, as a token of congratulations, and the latter so as not to have the girl feel left out.

"Signorina, or should I say, *baronessa*," he began as he offered the bouquet to Anna. "Please accept these flowers as a token of celebration from our firm. The formality of reviewing the documents took less time than I anticipated, and as you know, you are the heir to all of this," he said as he stretched out his arm, palm raised to accentuate the motion. "As the title of baron is a transferable title—that is to say, it is no longer originated by the monarchy—you have every right to that honor here in Sicily. I could be wrong, but I do not think that the USA honors such titles, sad to say." This final step of validation pleased Anna greatly.

The title, while very nice, was to her merely a perk. She wondered what that fat pastry-stuffing director of hers back in Binghamton would say now. Would he consider it a coup to rehire a Sicilian baroness? What was she thinking? If the rest of the estate was accurate, she would not have to work anymore at all, especially not for him.

This entire line of thought raced through her mind as Sagrigento spoke, referring to water rights and managerial responsibilities when she wasn't staying at the villa. She shook her head, just a little, in an effort to refocus her concentration. This wasn't difficult, as he paused and asked her if she would like to speak about the financial aspects in private. Anna replied that he could feel free to speak about any money matters in front of her cousin.

With an expression that registered discomfort at her statement, Sagrigento informed her that when one totaled the value of the property and all its furnishings, the accompanying water leases to the town of Arcamo, investments made and overseen over the past sixty odd years, and the subtracted salaries for staff and annual fees for all monies managed by the firm, Anna would be inheriting over 7.66 billion lire, which when converted to U.S. dollars totaled roughly 8.2 million.

Once again, Anna started to drift into thought at the mention of this figure. She barely heard the additional statement Sagrigento made, hoping that she could continue to use the firm to manage her affairs, as they had been so faithful in maintaining them in the past. She did, however, snap back when he broached another subject, one that neither she nor Chelsea had considered.

"Under the present tax structure, it would probably not be in your best interest to apply for Italian citizenship or even dual citizenship. Even if you are an American citizen who inherited property here, you would still be required to pay according to Italian law. But there would be certain applications needed in order for you to stay in the country for an extended period of time. I will get all the necessary paperwork ready, as well as a list of what documents you will need to provide. We will proceed one step at a time. In the meantime, relax and celebrate your good fortune here, *la Baronessa D'Arcamo*, and once again, *benvenuto*! I will stop by in a few days with the legal transfer documents for you to sign. At that time, I will also provide you with a complete accounting of your assets and investments. But for now, the day and the night and all that you see, is yours to enjoy."

And with that, he took his folder and bid them good day. He felt that by offering this information to her, whether she'd thought of any of these things or not, he'd be helping to cement his firm's place in her mind as the people she'd choose to manage things in the future. It probably didn't amount to much with regard to her decision, but he felt that it was at least worth a try. By the end of his comments, even he felt as if he had been prattling on.

Anna looked at the twenty-year-old version of her eighty-year-old mentor as Sagrigento was escorted to the door. The journey that began with a story heard by a fifteen-year-old back in 1965 was coming to fruition. Anna Del Forno had indeed inherited the estate bequeathed to her grandfather from a man who, at one time, loved her great-aunt—a man who had inherited the estate from his parents, who he'd lost at an early age because of what they believed in, and who spent his life never forgiving them for it. The journey had taken twists and turns throughout, her discoveries finally yielding to her that which her great-aunt once promised.

But this wasn't the end of her story. Rather, it was merely the next step on a path that the two of them had yet to travel. They sat and smiled at each other, saying nothing, not even communicating in the silent way they had grown so accustomed to.

Finally, Chelsea looked at her thirty-year-old protégé and said, "Come, there is still so much for us to learn." They walked outside to the garden at the base of the staircase and, seeing Antonino, called out to him. He had been dressing some plants in a flower bed. The plants had already flowered, and he was building up mulch around each plant so as to feed them and let them rest until late spring. This was all part of a well-planned schedule that had plants and flowers blooming approximately every four to six weeks throughout the year. By maintaining and feeding the local flowering perennials, Antonino managed to keep an attractive estate garden on surprisingly less than one would have expected. Both Anna and Chelsea marveled at his diligence. Wiping his hands on his workpants, the aging handyman straightened up from the crouched position that he had been in and walked over to them.

"*Bon giorno*, signorine. And how are the two of you today?" Although his face bore a gruff exterior, his eyes twinkled, as if he had reserved a bit of kindness just for them. In Sicilian, Chelsea said that she didn't want to bother him, but they were wondering if he could show them around the grounds. He looked momentarily at the row of plants that he'd been dressing and answered, "If you give me twenty minutes, I'll come for you and show you the property. In the meantime, go to the back of the house, and I'll meet you there." He pointed to the other side of the house, the side that they had seen only through the windows of the upstairs sitting room.

They walked along a stone path that, in a winding way, paralleled the wall of the house, until they turned the corner to find that it opened to a broad curved patio complete with wrought-iron furniture. A table and some chairs, a few benches, all arranged near or around a two-tiered fountain made of what looked like the same materials as the railings of the stairway at the entrance of the house. It was breathtaking.

While Anna sat on a bench, Chelsea chose to sit on one of the chairs near the table, looking very much like someone who felt at home here. She looked at Anna and, feeling that she was well enough out of the range of everyone else, said, "Well, my Little One, what do you think we should do next?" When Anna tried to answer, Chelsea interrupted, "I don't mean here and now, I mean with your legacy, your birthright."

Anna hadn't forgotten. She just wasn't sure how the next part should play out. Should she stay for a while and let Chelsea re-establish her place here? Should she stay while Chelsea resumed her place as the White Wolf? If Chelsea changed, would she return? Would she find Fiero and La Notte? Were they still alive after all this time? Even at her age, the barrage of questions she juggled in her mind was taking its toll on her. Amid this quiet, rustic loveliness, Anna found that she was beginning to miss being home. The villa D'Arcamo was, even in this short stay, a beautiful place to visit, and she understood that she was its owner, at least legally.

But Anna was developing a feeling that she couldn't be the mistress of this place. There was an odd, isolating discomfort that she felt here. Something that she found hard to express, but didn't see in Chelsea.

For all intents and purposes, Chelsea—that is to say, Gelsamina—had come home. Home is where Anna felt she should be going, not now, of course, but in time.

"And so you will," came the thought from Chelsea, who had read Anna's mind as she raced from question to question. "And you are also right in presuming that I must visit my family here, to see them and let them know that I've returned. While I do that, you might want to sign the papers that Sagrigento talked about. Is that all right with you?" Anna was in agreement with the conversation. For now, it meant that she would spend some time here in Sicily, at the villa, and hopefully with Chelsea.

By the time Antonino came around to see them, they were laughing and chatting in a carefree manner that completely disguised their previous discussion. He started by walking them around the flower beds nearest the house, then beyond. The further away from the house they walked, the more pastoral and wildflower-laden the gardens grew, until they came to the lemon grove—eight rows of lemon trees, each of a certain height and approximate size so as to accommodate the picking of fruit. Antonino talked about the flowers, describing each with a name and describing color and size, but when he got to the lemon grove, his tone grew with pride. He discussed, in great detail, the importance of keeping the trees at just the right size, and of how feeding and fertilizing them with just the right ingredients grew the fruit "not too big, because that would mean that they had filled with water; and not too small, because then they would be too tart." Antonino was describing his passion, or perhaps one of them, and both women could sense it.

Finally, beyond the trees in the grove, was a stretch of woods, mostly scrub trees and brush. As Antonino showed this to them, he explained that the barrier ran anywhere from a quarter to a half kilometer and surrounded the property on three sides. They realized that for the first time since they'd taken the tour, they were indeed surrounded on three sides by a small Sicilian forest, with the fourth side as an entrance. "The whole estate is fenced, even here," he said, motioning to the woods before them, "but I'm sure there are places in the fence where animals can get through."

Although they both looked, Chelsea seemed to sense where she should focus her gaze more closely. Sure enough, she saw movement among the lower branches and brush in one particular direction. She raised her hand and pointed to where the rustling was taking place. Antonino spoke. "Ever since I started working at the estate, it's been my job to put out food for the wolves. I remember being a little boy, and being told by a man who was running the villa at the time, after the baron died, that every day, I was to take scraps out to the woods and feed the wolves. I don't think I've seen them more than a few times, but only from a distance. And yet, every day that I return with new food, the old food is gone."

"How do you know that it's wolves?" asked Anna after Chelsea translated.

"I don't," said Antonino, "not for sure. There are usually a number of tracks near the food. Some are wolf, some squirrel, and some, well, who knows what else," he said, not giving it any more thought. "But I can tell you that it was part of the wording in the management of the estate that always, food should be put out, and it was there that it was written 'for the wolves.' So I always presumed …"

Anna listened to Chelsea's translation, and the two of them nodded, accepting his explanation, not letting on anything other than satisfaction at an interesting story. They strolled at a leisurely pace back to the house, with Antonino talking to Chelsea about the herbs and vegetables that they grow from time to time in a small garden near the kitchen, Chelsea listening with the interest level appropriate for a twenty-year-old tourist. But soon this was all to change.

When they returned to the house, they found that a package had been delivered from Palermo to Anna. Seeing no markings on the outside of the package, she checked the return address, confident that this package was something that she'd had hoped to receive by today. She opened the paper wrapping and the cardboard box that held two smaller packages. As Chelsea stood by and watched, Anna withdrew from the package her crest and cord, but instead of putting it on, she put it around Chelsea's neck. Right there, in the entrance hall of the villa, in plain sight of any of the three staff members who might be there to see. This confused Chelsea. "Why do you give the crest back to me?" she asked. Saying nothing, Anna removed the second package from the box, revealing an identical crest and cord, and replaced it around her own neck. This was, in fact, the original that had been created from the ring.

"Before we left the hotel, I asked our waiter to bring the crest back to his cousin to make a copy of it and return both to me, here, as soon as possible. Did you notice that I haven't been wearing it?" she asked, with a slyness in her voice, proud that she had accomplished her task successfully and in secret.

"I hadn't seen it because you were wearing high-collared shirts for the past few days, but thank you, lit…" Chelsea stopped as Elena entered the hallway. Noticing the crests that they now wore around their necks, she excused herself and left the room by way of the kitchen.

"Oh well, there goes the secret," thought Anna. Between the three of them, they'll guess that one of us is related in some way, or at least an heir. At any rate, they'll know that we're not really just curious guests."

Surprisingly, nothing was said. The two spent the rest of the day relaxing and sunning themselves without incident. It wasn't until dinner that Francesca Paola commented on the gold replicas of the crest that hung on the wall in front of them. The plates for the main course had been cleared away and the coffee was being served when Anna decided to take the initiative and call the three staff members into the dining room. Antonino was in the kitchen eating his meal, so it was merely a matter of wiping his mouth and washing his hands before entering. They all seemed to expect something but in actuality only half-knew the details of the announcement that Anna would make. Having discussed her plans with Chelsea that afternoon, she assembled the three in the room as Francesca Paola served the coffee. As they stood, Anna began.

"You may have noticed the crests that my cousin and I wear around our necks," she said. Chelsea translated dutifully, still playing her role to a tee. "You may also have seen Signor Sagrigento, the attorney, come to visit us earlier today. I have called you all here because I feel that it is important that you all know what is happening. As you know, my name is Anna Del Forno. My grandfather lived here in Arcamo some sixty years ago and knew the baron. I suppose the baron valued my grandfather's friendship, because he left him his title and estate. My grandfather, upon his passing, left the estate to me. And to be honest, there really isn't much more that I can tell you." As Chelsea translated all of this, Anna thought of something to add. When Chelsea finished,

Anna said, "While I'm not sure of all the details yet, I would like very much if you all could stay on, doing what you do here." She smiled but tried to look hopeful, though she wasn't completely sure why.

"Will Signorina be moving to Arcamo to stay?" asked Elena.

"I really can't say, at this point, what my permanent plans are, but I will be here to the extent that both Italy and the U.S. allow me, ummm, us to." This took a bit more time, as Chelsea's translations to and from each person were listened and visually responded to.

The next day was cool and gray. It began when Anna and Chelsea, both clean and neat, came downstairs for breakfast. It was there, after serving their coffee, that Francesca Paola offered Chelsea a letter. It had been written by Elena, explaining that her position had always been sort of an "extra" job, a part-time job of housecleaning whenever the firm had rented the estate out. Because of family responsibilities and her job in town, she would have to resign from her position here at the villa. She offered her services if they should ever need extra help for a large party and thanked Anna for the opportunity of working for her full time, but as she mentioned, she could not accept the offer.

After Chelsea read the letter and translated it to Anna, Francesca Paola spoke. "To be honest, signorina, you're better off without her. The woman only came here to make a few lire and steal whatever small things she could. She knew that if someone lived here permanently, it would only be a matter of time before she was caught. And to be caught by an *Americana*, well ..." and Francesca Paola said no more. This too, was translated by Chelsea. Anna chuckled a bit as Chelsea spoke but didn't pursue it. Instead, she asked Chelsea to ask Francesca Paola if she knew anyone locally who might be interested in applying for the job.

As soon as Chelsea asked this of the cook, she replied, "I have a niece who lives nearby. She's only twenty-four, but she has cleaned houses in the past. I could ask her if she'd come. I will show her what to do."

Then Chelsea said something that showed Anna that she was coming into her own. Chelsea asked her without hesitation, "Francesca Paola, do you vouch for her? We will reward you if your niece does a good job, but what if she doesn't?"

"Then I will personally let her go," answered the cook, a little taken aback at the young girl's administrative attitude.

"All right, we'll try her for a week and see," said Chelsea. This decision-making coming from the young cousin instead of the newly declared baroness took Francesca Paola by surprise. She wondered if this was the way that things were going to be. "Francesca Paola, what is your niece's name?"

"Carmela," she replied.

"And when can she come here?"

"Tomorrow, if you'd like, signorina."

"That would be excellent, and thank you, Francesca Paola," Chelsea said, returning to her more recognizable younger cousin identity. Anna looked at the faces of the two as they spoke, realizing that sooner or later, she'd have to learn Sicilian.

When Chelsea translated their conversation as the cook left the room, Anna commented, "I'm glad that you said what you said, but do you think that you gave the wrong impression?"

"On the contrary, I think that it gave just the right impression. The people here, in this house, seemed to have an opinion of us that worked in our favor at first. Even though I could speak the language, they took us for naive Americans. They expected us to be receptive to everything and uncouth to local custom. They even tried to put us off with the *polpo* and the calamari. Bit by bit, they must be made to realize that we can't be taken advantage of, however nicely they do it. Little One, I need you to trust me with this." Chelsea had slipped again in referring to Anna as "Little One", something she hadn't wanted to do while they were playing the role of guests. But now, things were changing. Anna said nothing, choosing instead to give over her trust to her great-aunt. Yet she did wonder just how much Chelsea would revert back to Gelsamina. And how quickly? And at what cost? This transformation had an unsettling affect on her. In fact, the gray coolness of the day had turned out to mirror Chelsea's personality at the moment.

Anna went out to the gardens, hoping that the chill in the air would break her mood. It didn't. She returned to the house, grabbed a sweater, and went back out, deciding to take a walk past the gardens and into the lemon grove.

As she walked along the dirt path that separated the grove from the surrounding woods, she wondered if she had been used. Could it be that this was all an elaborate scheme to get her to come to Arcamo and take ownership of something that Gelsamina wanted? If this was so, she wondered, would Gelsamina stay? The discomfort she'd felt as she wondered these things yesterday returned to her.

As she strolled on, deep in thought, she happened upon an empty basket at the fringe of the woods. As she approached, she heard a rustling sound beyond the basket. Presuming this to be the spot where the wolves were fed, she decided to explore. Going into the woods some distance, Anna came across a tree that had fallen over, half-uprooted. The angle that it created made for a useful shelter in which she could safely hide her clothes. She decided to change.

Disrobing, she folded the clothing into a neat pile safe within the crook of the uprooted tree. Finally she changed, her transformation having a strangely liberating effect on her. She felt more free at that moment than she had for some time. Stopping to acclimate herself to the sights and sounds that now entertained her senses, Anna sniffed at the air. There were two, no, three others nearby—one male and two females. She wasn't sure how they would react but hoped that a lot of the things Gelsamina had said about what she remembered of Arcamo was true. Most of all, she hoped that they wouldn't attack her, thinking her to be a threat.

It took some time for her to finally approach them. They had taken the food that had been left and were now moving on, trying to eat on the run. While an efficient way to feed and remain safe, it rarely puts a wolf in a good humor. They were nearly finished feeding and were moving to a hillside when she saw them. Behind them was the hillside; to their right was an outcropping of rocks that they could use as an escape if they needed to. It was not accessible to her. To their left was an open area encircled by brush and low-branched trees. She entered their presence cautiously. Using her mind, she spoke to them, telling them that she meant them no harm. She wondered if she was communicating in English or Sicilian, or if it even mattered.

They seemed surprised, at first, to find that she could communicate with them, but this did not affect their resistance. Then the male caught the spoor, and that made a great deal of difference. He took a step forward toward Anna and sniffed again, this time in a more focused manner. As the two females stood motionless and watched, he spoke in the silent manner of the clan, in what she perceived as her own language. She wondered for a moment if their speech was universal.

"You are not from our clan. You are from no clan I know."

"My clan is from far away."

"We watched you change."

Anna lowered her head. "Yes."

"We have heard stories of man-born wolves. Can you change back?"

Anna was surprised by this question but nodded her head as if to say yes. "Are there any here who are man-born?"

"No. Fiorello and Nicoletta were man-born, but they went away. They told us of one other. One who could change and change again. Are you she?" As the male spoke, his eyes stared intently, looking to find something buried deep within Anna.

"I don't think so. I don't think that I am the one they told you about. I have heard stories about Fiero and La Notte. Do you know them?"

"They were the leaders of our clan. But one day, they too went away. They said to wait, for someone, a man-born would come. If you are not she, then do you know of her? They told us that she is the 'White Wolf.'"

Anna looked deeply into his eyes. She was unsure what to say. Feeling more and more as if she had stumbled into a prophecy, her mind stammered an answer. "I know the White Wolf. She is here."

"The White Wolf has come? Then you are the one who will prepare the way for her. The story has finally come to be," he said with the tone of accomplishment. Anna merely nodded, not knowing what to say at this. Her head was swimming. Could it be that even her presence here had been foretold? Again she wondered if she had been duped or if this had all been meant to happen. She decided that her only option was to move forward both physically and in her conversation.

"My name is Anna, but some call me the 'Little One.' I do not know a lot about the story that you speak of, but I know that the White Wolf is here. Where did Fiero and La Notte go?" asked Anna. She remembered that there was a loss of certain concepts that humans think nothing of—concepts like time and, in certain abstract respects, place.

"One of the old sisters lay down to sleep. When she lay down, she did not wake. La Notte saw this and stayed by her side. The old sister lay still. Her color was not bright and warm. She looked cold. She looked small. La Notte sang *l'anelito* for her."

"So this is death in the eyes of a wolf," thought Anna aloud.

"What is death?" asked the male.

"I will tell you, err, what are you called?"

"Il Sole," he answered. It was easy to see why. His fur was blond and tan, and in the light of day appeared almost yellow.

"And what of Fiero?" Anna asked.

"He waited for his mate. When she sang no more, they went out into the land, past us here in the wood. They are not back with us yet. They told us that they must look for the White Wolf. They knew she would come. And they told us that you would come before her, because you loved her and you would protect her. They said one last thing to us before leaving.

"What else did they say?"

"They said that the White Wolf was in danger from an old enemy, and to warn you on her behalf."

"Warn me? To protect her? You can't be serious. She has forgotten more than I have learned. I am her friend and I care for her, but I don't know how much protection I can offer to her. At any rate, I should go and tell her of our meeting here today. I'm sure that she'll want to meet with you all. Now Il Sole, what are they names of your two sisters?"

"This is Mattina and that is Sera," he said, nodding to wolves on either of his two sides. Unlike her gray and black coloring, they were both shades of caramel and tan. Anna was intrigued by their names, and she mentioned this. She realized that she would need to be careful with her thoughts, as they could be easily read. However, she couldn't help but think it appropriate that the offspring of Fiero and La Notte would be named Morning, Evening, and the Sun. She then asked Il Sole if they had been given other names.

"No, we are wolf-born, so our names are what we are."

As she listened to him, she still harbored mixed feelings. Anger and annoyance at Gelsamina, further compounded by the idea that they thought she was Gelsamina's herald or messenger. And still there lingered the question of fate. She had changed hoping to clear her mind, to get, perhaps, a better insight as to what was happening and what she should do about it all. And yet, as had happened before, she found herself more confused and at odds with her emotions.

"I must go," was the only reply she could give to Il Sole. She couldn't even find the words to tell him that Gelsamina would soon meet with them. She couldn't say, because she didn't know. She went off into the direction where she had left her clothing. Changing back to her human form, Anna got dressed. As she put on her pants, she heard the rustling sound of someone handling the pail that had been used to put food out for the wolves. It was Antonino. To her relief, he had just arrived and had set out the bucket for them.

She watched him as he walked away. Whether he was aware of her presence, she couldn't tell. Perhaps he was aware but felt it wasn't the right time to talk to her, or perhaps he just didn't care.

Chapter XVII
Meditation and Revelation

When Anna returned to the house, she found Chelsea sitting in a chair in the upstairs sitting room. She expected that Chelsea would apologize, as she had done before, but this time, no apology was offered. In fact, she barely spoke to Anna. The furniture in the room, arranged so as to encourage conversation, was disrupted by the chair that Chelsea had pulled out of alignment so that she could face the large twelve-paned glass doors that opened onto a private balcony. On a nicer day, one could sit out on that balcony and take in the grand view of the gardens and the grove and anyone who had recently walked down in that direction. Depending upon how unobstructed the view was, one might have even been able to see Anna transform her appearance into that of a wolf, and then after a while, transform back again. That is, if one sat out on the balcony and took in the view, as Chelsea had.

Anna saw this and decided then and there to play innocent. "Wait till you hear what I discovered!" she exclaimed in an excited voice. This received no response from Chelsea, who, even with her back turned, had focused her attention elsewhere. "Did you know that there are wolves here, now, on the grounds? And not just wolves but wolves that know of you. They spoke to me."

"You could have been attacked," came a dry voice from the chair facing the door. "They don't know you, and you don't know enough to react safely. I barely know enough to react safely in front of *figli* that I have never met. If any of them perceived you as a threat, they could have stood up against you. Why, even if my Fiero didn't know who you were, you would be seen as a threat."

"Your Fiero is out there somewhere, looking for you. He sensed that that you were coming, so he and La Notte left their clan to find you. I thought you'd be glad to hear the news," Anna replied, partly offended, and walked down the hall to her room.

Some twenty minutes later, a more composed Chelsea knocked on the door.

"It's open," said Anna, still hurt but using as nonchalant a voice as she could muster. Chelsea entered, looking at the figure that was lying across the bed. She crossed over to sit in a chair next to a small writing desk by the window.

"I need you to listen to me," she began. "Things have been happening quickly here, for the past forty-eight hours. It has almost been a game of chess with you and I on one side and the staff and the attorney on the other. We get the document confirmed and the attitude of the staff changes, to the point where one of them leaves. Another one quickly offers to replace her with a relative, and I react hastily to it all. I promise you that it was never my intent to offend you. It is just that the translation of everything that they say to you and you say to them slows things down, and I spoke in a way that made it seem like I was taking control of the situation. That was never part of the plan. It was never my idea to hurt you.

"And Antonino—I still haven't figured him out yet. It's hard for me to tell what he knows and what he doesn't know. How much does he know? Enough to be for us, enough to be easily dissuaded?"

"What do you think of Francesca Paola?" Anna asked, turning her head in Chelsea's direction.

"Anyone who can cook what she does with such passion is open. What happens to the world around is largely unimportant, as long as it doesn't affect her kitchen. When I was growing up, I knew of such people. They lived to cook. They were only truly happy when they were preparing food—playing, experimenting, creating. To them, a new adventure began each time a pan was set to the flame. No, I feel that Francesca Paola is safe."

"Then what about your feelings when she mentioned her niece … what was her name?"

"Carmela. Chances are she will do fine, but we'll see. I wouldn't be surprised if I just overreacted at the moment. But again, I am sorry."

"Stop. Let's do more things."

"All right, would you like to explore?"

"Explore what?"

"Well, for one thing, we haven't seen the master bedroom suite. We both know that eventually you'll be going back to America, at least for a while, and I will be here. I still don't know if I will stay in this house, but if I do, I must say that sleeping in Leonardo's trophy room is not a pleasant experience."

Anna called down for Francesca Paola to come up and show them the master bedroom. The cook was in the middle of preparing the evening meal, so she called for Antonino, who had been working in the closet nearest the dining room, to serve as guide. He grunted faintly, wiped his hands clean, and ascended the stairs.

"The signorina would like to see the room?"

"Yes, Antonino," said Chelsea. "My cousin is curious as to the size and view, and well, I suppose we're both curious." With that, she giggled. The twenty-year-old had returned. Antonino was impassive as he unlocked the door to the room.

It was large, easily thirty by forty feet in size. There were odd chairs and side tables, and a cabinet that may, at one time, have held books or bric-a-brac of some sentimental value, each piece covered by a white cloth and now one by one unveiled. Anna noticed that Antonino was uncovering the pieces that didn't seem to belong in the room first, possibly because they were closest to the door, or was there another reason? Finally, Antonino removed the cloth that covered a dark wooden dresser, some twelve feet long. Atop this many-drawered enormity was an additional set of drawers attached to a mirror. This was clearly the first piece of the bedroom set that they'd been shown.

Although neither Anna nor Chelsea spoke, as Antonino unveiled the final four of five pieces, Chelsea seemed to take a greater interest in each piece. She ran her hand along the side of the six-drawered armoire and stood at the footboard of a heavily carved four-poster bed, looking, just looking. Antonino noticed this and asked, "Signorina likes the furniture?"

"Yes, very much," answered Chelsea.

As she turned to translate the question and answer, Anna interrupted. "Please don't tell me that you've seen this stuff before."

"Oh Anna, don't be silly. It's just that as I look at this, I think of the time, the whole time in general. Oh Litt ... *Anna*, you would have loved my time. It was so much simpler. Work was more difficult, but the happiness was more ..." and at this, she hesitated, searching for the right word "... fulfilling." Finishing her thought, she turned back to Antonino, who was removing the cover from a heavy wooden washstand. The basin and pitcher in it were of a simple pattern, more indicative of use by a man than by a woman of the same era.

As Chelsea looked at the washstand, another piece from a long-ago time, Anna watched Antonino. He had started timing his unveilings to Chelsea's movements, so that he could better observe her reactions. In reading his eyes, Anna tried to find any indication of malice. She still felt that he was hiding something, but she was at a loss as to what it might be. He noticed her gaze and shifted his. Antonino then moved toward the windows to open the drapery.

Chelsea asked as he did so, "Why was this room chosen to store furniture and boxes? Why not the smaller ones? One would think that the celebrities who visited here would have liked to see how the master of the villa lived."

"From the time that he passed away," Antonino began, "until now, the baron's room has remained empty. In life, the baron shared his bed with no one. In death, it is no different." Chelsea listened and translated.

"Antonino, the baron has been gone for over sixty years, and now I am the mistress of the estate," said Anna. "In time, I would like very much to open this room up again, and use one of the two rooms down the hall as storage." As Chelsea translated, Anna thought, "Now, it's my turn to be in charge." Chelsea was secretly pleased, knowing that eventually the room and its stately wooden reminders of the past would be for her own use. At her translation, Antonino listened, first with arched eyebrows and then in compliance. He said, "As you wish, signorina," to Anna.

It was the next day, December twenty-eighth, when at breakfast Francesca Paola announced to Anna and Chelsea that her niece Carmela had arrived. Dressed in a blue poplin housekeeping uniform, Carmela was presented to them. Although she was only twenty-four, she had an expression in her eyes that suggested a life of work from an early age. There is an expression, "an old soul," that is used to refer to such a person—a person who has not known leisure but rather responsibility throughout her life. The phrase came to mind when one looked at Carmela.

As she made her introduction, Anna spoke in the silent manner, giving her thoughts to Chelsea. "Let me ask the first few questions while you watch. Then you can either build off of mine or ask a question based on what you observe."

"Good!" thought Chelsea. "I like it when we work together."

"*Bon giorno*, Carmela. Your aunt tells us that you have cleaned houses before."

"*Si*, I have cleaned houses and taken care of children. Also, I have helped in the kitchen, cooking and serving, but to be honest, I'm not as good as Zia Francesca Paola."

"No one is," muttered Francesca Paola under her breath, but loud enough to be heard. Both Anna and Chelsea smiled and nodded as Francesca Paola left the room.

"Have you ever been in charge of a house this size?" asked Anna.

"No, but I am young, and I will work hard until the house is cleaned to your satisfaction," answered Carmela.

After Anna had asked a few more questions regarding Carmela's choices of cleaning utensils and methods, Chelsea began. There really wasn't a great deal to quiz the girl on, so after handing it back to Anna, they closed the interview by discussing pay and reminding Carmela that they would try her out for one week. As all parties were satisfied, Carmela began her responsibilities by being taken upstairs by her aunt and shown the rooms.

Chelsea and Anna left the house in search of Antonino, who they found returning from the lemon grove, pushing a cart of gardening tools. He greeted them and mentioned that he'd enjoyed their time together the day before. Commenting that his chores for the morning were nearly complete, he wondered aloud to Chelsea if she and her cousin would be interested in visiting Arcamo in the afternoon, as he had to go into town for Francesca Paola and pick up some supplies for the villa.

The two immediately said yes—Anna to fill in yet another gap in her story, and Chelsea to see what bits of the past still existed for her, although obviously, their facial expressions bespoke none of this. Yet in the harsh, weather-beaten face of Antonino, one could almost guess that he saw something else in both of them. He said that he would bring the car around to the entrance of the house at noon.

The car was older than what one would have expected. Apparently, it had first been owned by one of the partners of the law firm, and then, seeing an opportunity to shift it to the estate, claim some obscure deduction, and earn some lire in remuneration, the partner sold it "at a loss" to the estate. At the time, Antonino had been using an old 1966 Fiat that had been on its last legs.

The car he'd gotten from the partner was an American car, a big one, very expensive-looking, although not too much newer than the Fiat. It was a 1970 Lincoln Continental, quite a car at that time, but here it was, ten years later, and although Antonino cared for it as if it was his child, it was still showing signs of a graceful aging. The odometer showed 120,000 kilometers, and the leather seats were worn in a way that makes a leather jacket look comfortable but a leather car seat look shabby. Still, Antonino cared for the engine and repaired the car to the best of his abilities, polishing it and cleaning the interior in a way that some men do, half dreaming of it as they work, possessed by the mechanical beauty of the thing.

Anna and Chelsea got into the backseat. It smelled of whatever leather polish Antonino had most recently used on it. He had put on a small brimmed cap to give himself more of a look of a driver. He was now on display for them, and he was taking the opportunity to put on a show.

He talked about the various inhabitants of houses and cottages along the roads and in the countryside, who lived where and for how many years. Chelsea, at hearing certain names, tried stoically to remain in character, never letting on to any recognition of the names she'd heard.

In short order, they arrived in the town of Arcamo—a small few blocks of shops that made up a U shape, capped by the church, "*la Chieza d'Andreas d'Avellino*, long the centerpiece of the town," announced Antonino.

"Longer than even you know," Chelsea thought, as she translated his words for Anna. As she looked at the church, she was reminded of the

Anna and the Tale of the Wolf

stories that her mother told her a lifetime ago, stories of Saint Andrew and how the church came to be.

While he had to deal with the grocers and the nursery merchants, he suggested that they do a little sightseeing and meet him later in the afternoon at the café just off of the square. The sight of the two foreigners in this small town in Sicily, at the end of 1980, must have seemed quite a spectacle. The two were not dressed inappropriately, but the fact that they were different, not from the area, was noticed by all they came across. And the fact that Chelsea translated Sicilian into English for the *Americana* made them even more exotic. These two weren't really tourists, especially since Chelsea could speak the language. And when she mentioned that their name was Del Forno, and that they were related to Giacamo Del Forno, even though there were no Del Fornos remaining in Arcamo, there seemed to be a kindred feeling among the locals. Sort of a "your people were our people" kind of attitude, especially with the older ones they met. And when one particularly senior parent of a shopkeeper suggested that they visit the church to see the register and look up Giacamo's name, Anna grew excited. At first Chelsea balked, giving the excuse that she didn't want to bother the priest who resided there.

"Nonsense," cackled the old woman. "You two are probably the first piece of excitement he's had all week, after Christmas Mass, of course. And seeing the two of you might remind him of what he gave up when he became a priest," she added, almost expiring into a fit of coughing amid the cackling laugh.

Chelsea politely laughed and then translated for Anna, who also laughed as they both blushed a little, mostly to be polite. Anna silently spoke as they exited the shop.

"Why don't you want to go in there?"

"You are young, since turning. You won't have these feelings for a long time to come. To be reminded of who you were, of when you were. To be reminded that everything you knew doesn't exist any longer …" came the silent answer from a now solemn Chelsea. "I cannot take a step without seeing a face from the past or hearing a voice that sounds like one I once knew. This too, my Little One is part of *l'anelito*."

"But what is it that you long for?" Anna asked aloud, now that they were alone and standing nearer the fountain at the face of the church.

"To be once more surrounded by those I love and who, in turn, have loved me," Chelsea answered.

"I don't understand. Nonno and Nana are back in Binghamton, and they love you now as they always have."

"Yes, but my pets, my loves, Fiero and La Notte, I haven't sensed their presence since we returned. I sense many others. I hear many voices, but not of Fiero or La Notte. And something else is here. I can feel it. I felt it when Elena announced that she was going to leave. I could see it in her eyes. There was another reason that she didn't want to stay when she found out that you would be the owner."

"Maybe she just didn't want to get caught stealing," Anna offered. "Maybe she just held this reason back and decided to leave while she was still thought well of."

"Everyone holds things back. Never forget that. But if you have someone and you truly care for them, in time, you will tell them."

There was silence after Chelsea said this. Anna hoped that she wouldn't continue, hoped that she wouldn't ask her if she was holding back something, but felt that if she asked, she'd have to offer what she knew. She should tell her. Probably not now, but soon.

Instead, Anna said, "Let's go into the church and look around. We don't have to see anyone. I can't imagine what it would be like to read my own name in a register dated from the twenties. And it's better that we don't tempt fate by letting someone else see your expression if you did. I don't think that either of us is ready for that yet." Chelsea agreed, and slowly, arm in arm, they entered.

La Chieza d'Andreas d'Avellino was, like most of the structures in this region of Sicily, old. Built in the early 1800s, the stone building with marble columns had stood through two world wars, serving as a transit hospital for the Allies in the last one. Here, soldiers who had been severely wounded would be taken to recuperate prior to being shipped over to Great Britain and eventually back home. The church miraculously escaped damage throughout all that time—its marble interiors and columns offering a solemn calmness amid the heat and uncertainty of battle. The church itself was designed in an old style— that is, with chairs instead of benches. And unless the situation called for it, the chairs remained in their places. Ninety-eight chairs, set in seven rows of seven on both the left and right, with a center aisle, and two additional chairs set on the altar for the celebrating priest or priests during the Mass.

The altar was made of white marble—a huge artifact some eighteen feet tall, carved from separate pieces of marble and fitted together to appear as one piece. Its shell-like shape housed three naves, the center nave displaying an ornately carved and gold-covered wooden crucifix. In the nave to the left, a statue of the Virgin Mary, and in the right nave, a statue of Saint Andreas of Avellino, the town's patron saint. Directly in front of this elaborately carved altar was an equally elaborately carved marble railing, with cloth cushions used for kneeling at Communion. And to the left and right of this railing were heavy metal votive candleholders.

As had long been a tradition in the Catholic Church, for the price of a donation, a candle could be lit and subsequent prayers could be offered on behalf of the donor. Roman Catholics have, for many years, held the belief in the intercession of the saints to deliver prayers to the Almighty. While it is not against any rule to offer prayers directly to God, more often than not, a patron saint, the sacred go-between, is beseeched to deliver either a request or a prayer of thanks. As patron of the town of Arcamo and the one whose name the church bore, it was not unusual to have a statue of Saint Andrew up on the altar with the statues of the Christ crucified and His mother.

As she took in the quiet grandeur of the town's religious centerpiece, Chelsea thought to herself, "It really hasn't changed much since the last time I was here." She recalled the moment when she, as a young girl, made her first Communion, a sacramental rite of passage among Catholics; she even remembered the exact spot where she was sitting—girls on one side of the center aisle, boys on the other, not unlike the seating at a wedding.

She looked up at the statue of Saint Andrew, letting her mind wander over the dozens of times she'd prayed to him for different things—her parents' health, and failing that, her parents' reception into heaven, her brother struggling to become a farmer, her pets (smiling as she remembered asking him to take care of this for her, acknowledging that she should have gone to Saint Francis of Assisi for prayers regarding wolves, and hoping that he wouldn't mind). She even prayed to him for the baron, that someday Leonardo's heart might be turned.

Her mental meandering came to an abrupt halt when Anna whispered to her, "This place is beautiful. I can't get over how so much wealth could be poured into a church. I mean, the town doesn't really seem to be that wealthy, so where did all of the money come from to build such beauty? This must have been long before the baron's parents."

"Oh, long before," answered Chelsea, "but one must keep in mind, in the eighteen hundreds and even before, whole towns revolved around the church. The calendar, feasts, even when to plant and when to harvest all were in some way related to the church calendar. Regardless of how poor they were, something was always found to offer to the church."

Satisfied with the logic, Anna went up and sat in a chair in the second row. Chelsea soon followed. After a short time, Anna went up to the votive candles nearest the statue of Saint Andrew, made a donation, and lit a candle. Again, Chelsea followed suit. As they walked back down the aisle to leave, Chelsea turned around once, eyes looking up at the altar seemingly for something. Not finding it, she turned back and followed Anna out through the heavy wooden doors.

"So did you ask for something?" began Anna as they descended the few steps to the square.

"You first," answered Chelsea.

"Okay. I asked for answers to my questions," said Anna.

"Questions like what?"

"Do you really want to know?"

"Of course."

"Well, questions like what happens next for us. Like, is the sense of family that I thought we shared disappearing now that we're here? Now that you've returned, and the villa is legally in my name, do you want me to leave?" The words weren't meant to sting, but Anna had come halfway across the world, largely to fulfill the legacy that she had been told about, the legacy that had been dangled in her path at her every step, the legacy that even her father agreed should come to her.

Chelsea looked at her great-niece. She had been quiet, and her personality had changed a bit since they'd arrived, but she hadn't thought that it showed to this extent. The pace had quickened now, far more than even she had anticipated. And for all of the goals that they had accomplished together, there still seemed something yet to do.

"Little One, in the days to come you may see just how much I truly care for my family—all of my family. Please believe me, I may have been distant or authoritative because I need to be. I can say no more about this now."

Annoyed at still being kept in the dark, Anna demanded, "Then at least tell me what is that you asked for?"

"Strength," came the reply.

Antonino met up with them both, and before long, they were all returning to the villa.

"So, what did you think of the town?" he asked Chelsea. Answering in a perfunctory manner, she replied, "Well, the shops were small, but the church was beautiful." She was determined to keep the young-girl persona on for him. She then dutifully translated, using the time that it took to translate to put space between his question and any further discussion. After she translated and Anna smiled, he spoke. Looking straight ahead in his drive, he said, matter of factly, "You don't fool me at all. I know who you are, and why you have come back. My master told me all about you. And you don't have to translate this to her. My guess is that she's pretty removed from this, and if you don't mind, I'd like to keep it that way."

Chelsea said nothing. Antonino had smiled as he spoke, so Anna really hadn't picked up on anything regarding the conversation. And Chelsea tried desperately to suppress any thoughts that Anna might pick up. Looking into the mirror and making eye contact with him, she replied to Antonino. "When we return, why don't you take me for a walk? Then, we can talk," was all she could think of saying.

In Italy, as in many places around the world that celebrate Christmas and the New Year, the festive mood in the public arena carries though from one holiday to the other. And in certain Mediterranean locales where Christianity is prevalent, it goes on into the beginning of January. Such was the case in Arcamo—in fact, all of Sicily and Italy. Decoration and merriment, ranging from abstract symbols created in white lights to reenactments of religious episodes in period costume, complete with choir-sung hymns, filled the eyes and ears of all who ventured through the streets of Arcamo. It was through this atmosphere that Antonino drove, smiling at passersby in the town, as if he were but a few steps away from joining in with the festivities himself. And it was through this same atmosphere that Chelsea looked calmly out the window of the car, in the backseat with Anna, trying to silently devise a plan, depending upon what information she could gather from the handyman. *What did he know?* she wondered. *And how had he learned it? And from whom?*

She was pleased at the composure she was maintaining. Anna continued looking out into the milling groups of people, through the holiday decorations festooned all around, so enraptured with the sights that it wasn't until they were out of the town that she even turned to Chelsea, who seemed to be focused on some point outside of the car.

"If they do the place up like this now, then what does New Year's Eve look like?" she asked, trying to break the spell of the unseen outside focus.

Thinking quickly, Chelsea turned to Antonino and said in a slightly smug manner, "My 'cousin' wants to know how people celebrate New Year's Eve here. I think that it would help things if you told her."

At first, Antonino said nothing. Then he grunted and began speaking rapidly. Chelsea struggled to keep up with him, translating for Anna. Finally she gave up, waiting for him to finish and then, consolidating his answer, she explained, "The people of Arcamo are not like the people who live in a city like Palermo. In Palermo, like many cities, the young single people get together and celebrate at a club, getting dressed to dance and drink." This was a greatly cleaned-up version of what Antonino actually said. He made references to lewd behavior condoned by an all too soft and weak family system; of whorishly dressed females and perverted men, neither of which had any morals or sense of shame. Chelsea's editing skills were impressive. She continued, "The people who live in Arcamo, however, more often have their celebrations in the homes of parents or grandparents. The parties consist mainly of relatives and close friends, usually with wine that someone in attendance had a hand in making, and traditional foods. After the ringing of the bells at midnight, everyone goes outside with pots and pans, making noise to frighten away the evil spirits.

"While they do this, the mother of the house, the matriarch, takes her broom and, opening the back door of the house, sweeps strongly, and declares '*Uscire diavolo,*' just in case there were any evil spirits still in the house, left over from the old year." This little story satisfied Anna, who listened to it intently as Chelsea spoke and joined in with the devil-shooing chant. Chelsea, too, seemed satisfied at her reconstruction of

Antonino's words, and that Anna suspected nothing of the now revealed animosity between her and the driver.

"Now it is your turn, signorina," said Antonino. "Make something up, so that you and I can talk."

"The best time to talk would be right after dinner this evening," she began. "I'll take a walk over by the grove where you feed the wolves. If you really want to talk to me, then you can meet me there." The lilting tone to her accent gave no indication as to what she was really saying.

"Ha, ha," he chortled. "Do you think I'm a fool? If you are truly who the master says you are, I'd be walking into my own grave."

"The master?" she asked. "Who is the master?

"Signorina, do you really want me to mention his name in front of your 'cousin'? If she hasn't caught on by now, that will surely give it away."

As a silent pause lingered between the two of them, Chelsea giggled, in further hopes of throwing Anna off, and then asked, "Where?"

"Go down the path from the kitchen to the garage where I keep the car. I'll park it with the two of you in it now, so that you'll know where to go. Keep up your act, signorina, and maybe your 'cousin' will go home alive."

"Of course," answered Chelsea.

"What did he say?" asked Anna.

Chelsea replied, "He wants to show us the garage where he keeps the car. I suppose that this is one more part of the tour."

Some ten minutes later, as the car pulled up to the shed-roofed building that seemed large enough to hold at least three cars, Antonino let the two out. The freestanding building was stone and stucco—not unlike the main house itself—with a clay-tiled roof. It had two sets of barn doors facing the gravel driveway that they stood on, and when one looked into the building through them, one could see two more sets of barn doors, the front ones staring on the left and center and the rear ones on the center and the right, so that one could enter and exit directly thought the center bay.

This appeared to be where Antonino normally parked the car, but there, on the left, partially under wraps, was what appeared to be a relic from the past: a horse-drawn carriage. The wheels were blocked from movement by bricks and stones, and the front assembly, although cleaned and polished, had been removed and was hanging on the wall, waiting patiently to someday be reattached and hitched to a horse.

Upon seeing it, Anna's interest was immediately aroused. She said to Chelsea, "Is that what I think it is?"

Chelsea, not expecting that this carriage, this memory from her past even existed, let alone had been kept and cared for, gasped a little in a mixture of fear and excitement, and followed Anna to the carriage. Antonino followed. Looking at Anna, he mentioned that the estate no longer kept horses, but the carriage was part of the estate, even if it really was just an old antique. As Chelsea translated, Anna looked a bit crestfallen. She remembered the story that her grandfather had told her those many years ago and wondered silently to Chelsea if this was, in fact, the carriage.

"Yes," came the single word reply.

After allowing them a short while to admire the coach, Antonino looked at his watch and commented that as dinner would probably be ready within the hour, they should go into the house and prepare. His mannerisms and speech did not appear to be as polite or cordial as they had been the previous few days, at least not to Anna. She sensed in him a feeling that he had something to do, some errand to undertake, and he could not achieve it as long as he was attending to them. Seeing this in Anna and sensing it also, Chelsea took Anna by the hand and strolled up the walk past the flowers toward the house.

Climbing the long curved stairway outside the villa, they both stopped midway, Chelsea touching the stone handrail, and gazed at the flowers in the vases and out across the grounds. Anna looked at her and said, "Did you ever think, in your heart of hearts, that throughout all of the amazing, uncanny things that have happened to you, that you'd ever return to Arcamo, let alone be standing here like this?"

"At first, I never would have conceived of it," Chelsea began. "But only when you came into my life—when I saw what our destinies were to be—did I realize that I had to come back. We had to be here, you just as much as me, although I suspect for a different reason. I have an odd feeling, Little One. I do not think that this is the end of our journey."

Anna tried to read her thoughts. They were a jumbled mess—entangled lines of mental images, mostly of someone of great age. She couldn't isolate any one particular thought but received an overwhelming sense of trepidation. Finally, just before turning to climb the stairs and enter the house, she caught a glimpse of a thought. It was a vision of Chelsea's that only one other had seen—Anna herself. It was of the two of them, changed, running through the woods, senses sharp, brisk breezes bristling their fur, picking up the spoor of others, joining with her clan, her family.

Anna stopped again and turned to Chelsea, who, looking at her, had tears in her eyes. Chelsea spoke the words that they both wore around their necks, but this time with a deeper meaning than ever before. "'Let Life and Death Dance on, Face to Face and Arm in Arm.' Whichever turn the road takes, my Little One, it is a road that we must follow." And with that, they entered the house.

Chapter XVIII
Resolution

Dinner that evening was far less elaborate. Chicken had been stewed as a cacciatore and served over a buttery polenta. It was flavorful, as was the Nero d'Avola wine that was served with it. The wine not only matched the tastes of the chicken dish but also helped to fortify Chelsea as she pondered her next move.

The overall tone of the meal was quiet, presumably as the next day would be New Year's Eve and some sort of interesting fare was being prepared for the event. Francesca Paola made a statement to this extent toward the meal's end, when she mentioned that she'd be setting out an early selection of cold and hot appetizers for Anna and Chelsea, as she and Carmela would be home with their families for "the bells," as the New Year's Eve celebration was referred to. Antonino would be on his own, but often preferred to keep it that way. At hearing the mention of his name, Antonino, who had been eating at the butcher block in the kitchen, rose, washed his plate and flatware, and left the house. Hearing the door shut, Chelsea asked Francesca Paola if she thought that he heard their conversation.

" Probably. He hears very well."

"Do you think that we offended him by not inviting him in tomorrow night? Even for just a glass of anisette?" Chelsea was hatching a plan, some means of getting into that garage without raising suspicion.

"Signorina, I would never tell you what to do, but he's a big boy. This is the life that he's chosen."

"But just the same, I'm going to talk to him. I hope that he hasn't been offended," said Chelsea, and with that she excused herself and left, but not before getting a sweater to wrap around her shoulders against the cool evening air.

Her footsteps in the gravel announced her arrival at the garage, which was lit inside by a single bright overhead bulb. The shadow that it cast grew longer into the corners and recesses of the car shed's interior, but directly underneath it stood Antonino, who had been removing the cloth covers from the antique carriage. The estate car was parked in exactly the same place that it had been in that afternoon, but the hood was now propped open, presumably for the handyman to perform some maintenance on. From where it was, Chelsea had to walk around it to meet Antonino, in the center, the open area.

He was using a rag to wipe his hands. As the light shone directly from overhead onto him, the shadows from above made sharp the lines that existed on his face, causing him to appear even older than his years. Taking his time, he finally looked up, and dropping the rag near the tool kit at his feet, he spoke.

"*Buona sera*, Signorina Gelsamina. You are right on time for our little 'talk.' I was just working here, thinking about some dreams that I've been having, ohh, for some time now. Shall I tell them to you? They always involve a man who has been tortured, by wolves I think. One would think that this is a grizzly sight, no? But this man is mentally tortured. You see, his parents were killed by wolves, and his life was twisted because of it. Have you ever seen those little trees that grow near the *Golfo Palermo*? How the ocean breezes slowly day by day bend them and push them until, if they grow at all, they grow bent and twisted? That is what the wolves did to this man in my dreams."

Chelsea said nothing.

"And then one day, signorina, the man turns and speaks to me. He knows my name. I think to myself, how can this man know my name? And then I realize, this man is the baron, my master. He is back, and he speaks to me. He calls me Antonino, and he asks me to avenge him. No, he doesn't ask, he demands, as if his immortal soul is hanging in the balance. He tells me of his torture, of his pain. He tells that he can no longer hunt them, but it doesn't matter, for they are stupid creatures, and they are only doing the bidding of their leader. 'Who leads them?' I ask my master, the man in my dreams. 'Wait,' he tells me, 'wait, and she will come to you.'"

Chelsea's muscles tightened as she stood facing him in the glare of the single overhead light. The hairs on her lithe arms tingled and rose. If she had changed, the fur on her back would be standing in anticipation of danger, yet Antonino still spoke.

"I think to myself, can the *Americana* be the leader of the wolves? This is preposterous. She seems smart, but she knows very little of who we are and where we are from, even if her ancestors came from here. No, I don't think that the *Americana* is the leader. Then, a thought comes to me. How is it that the younger girl knows how to speak Sicilian as clearly as me? I watch her as she looks at things in the town, almost as if she was looking for something else, something that maybe was there some time ago, maybe long ago. I see her sometimes look out of the window and I think, what sadness this little girl has for someone so young. It's as if she misses someone.

"And the man in my dreams, he even tells me your name, Signorina Gelsamina. Gelsamina is such a beautiful name. The kind of name one doesn't hear very often nowadays. In fact, if someone were to be named Gelsamina now, they would probably try to change it, or shorten it—maybe even Americanize it."

Chelsea's senses could not have been more heightened. She knew that Antonino was going to try to do something to her, possibly kill her if he could. She looked for an opening, a weakness. What she saw next was not what she expected.

" But signorina, this old man talks too much. It is better that I let my words stop now." And with that, he stepped over to the coach and, with a turn of the handle and the resulting "click," opened the door. A pant leg of dark brown, a color and cloth she'd not seen in over seventy years, extended out and onto the running board of the carriage; then, a gloved hand reached for a grip. Finally, out stepped the baron, looking older than she remembered him, yet still dressed elegantly in his period clothes. At first, she was overcome with emotion. Feelings from long ago, feelings that had been pushed into the back of her being, came flooding back. He approached her, gently holding her arms, looking into her eyes, almost as if he were looking for something in them.

"Antonino," he began, as his eyes pored over her face and hair, "you have done well, my servant."

"Thank you, master."

"Now you must leave us."

"As you wish."

Never leaving her gaze for a moment, he spoke to her, close and softly. "I have waited long years for this moment," he said.

She returned his deep regard, still looking up in silence. Mixed emotions filled her eyes—the embers of a love from long ago were now covered with the ashes of questions that were rising, phoenix-like—the way, apparently, he had. How could he return? Why did he return? Was it love? Was it love for her?

He began, "Gelsamina, I can still see the fire in your eyes." He sensed her astonishment. "Think of my absence as a state of limbo. When you disappeared, I will admit, I was distraught at first. I even looked to your pets for solace, but found that it was not for them to give. They seemed distant, untrusting of me."

Seeing the confusion in her eyes, he explained that from somewhere, a place that he couldn't explain, he was summoned. There, in the woods around them, wolves, dozens of wolves, brown, gray, approached him, tan, all real and yet not real.

"I can still recall the low growls they gave. I was surrounded." They set upon him, nipping and drawing blood from wounds, so many wounds. And yet, as they drew blood, they gave something of themselves. "After all of this, still I lived."

As they finished, they moved away, until only one wolf was left. And to his surprise, he himself was that wolf. "Clothed no more, having had the very things I wore torn from me, I stood clad now in fur, my own fur. I was a soul set adrift, no longer to inhabit my own body yet having been given a different one, that of a *wolf*." He spat out the word with a thinly disguised contempt.

"In time, I came to realize that I was also condemned to a life here at the villa, even to the point of learning to rely on the scraps that Antonino put out all these years. Yes, my dear Gelsamina, I have no power to remain either wolf or man until I get the same 'blessing' from you. Think of it, my love—we can rule all clans, all lairs. All wolves will be our minions. They will do our bidding. You could be their queen, and I would be your king. We have been given a great gift, and when you complete the final act, we will rule forever. Think of the power, my love."

The touch of his hands on her arms, a touch that was once tender, grew as he spoke. From gentle to firm to intense, now bordering on maniacal. This entity before her was an aberration. One who viewed the legacy, not as a responsibility, but as an opportunity to covet and abuse. How long would it take before their decisions would give way to his sole decision, before she became superfluous to his plans, and worse, before her family, her children, became his subjects? Didn't he just refer to them as his minions?

And what would this mean for Anna? To him, her "little one" would be an obstacle. She feared even thinking of what he might do to such an obstacle. "No one, *no one* will harm her while I live!" she heard the words in her mind that she had sworn to Anna what seemed like a long time ago.

She recoiled from his grasp. He stared at her, first in disillusionment, then in anger. He called for Antonino and ordered him to hold her. She tried to run, but tripped when her foot got caught on the edge of one of the carriage wheels. Antonino grabbed a wrench, something large, and held it to her neck, with just enough pressure to let her know that if she moved, he would crush her windpipe, destroying her ability to breathe. It was then that she heard the howling.

"See, my servants already cheer me on in anticipation," the baron began, clearly full more of his own desires than *l'anelito*. "If you won't give me what I need, I must take it." The baron crouched and changed before her. His wolf seemed more ugly, less wolflike and more satanic than the others, almost as if he were never meant to be what she and the *figli del lupo* were. As Antonino tightened his grip, the baron nipped at her legs, causing first drops and then little rivulets of blood to stop and start down toward her ankles.

Rising up, he pawed and ripped at her sweater and blouse, fully tearing the left half off. It dangled at her waist, exposing scratched flesh. Writhing to avoid him, she was powerless, even to change, as she could feel her head growing cloudy from lack of air. He bit at her side, just below her brassiere, again drawing blood. As if poured with some steadiness, he lapped it up, and then stood back on all fours, swallowing what his tongue had taken.

It was then that he heard the click. Before he could turn his head in the direction of the sound, a flash came from within the coach, visible through the still open carriage door, followed almost simultaneously by the cracking sound of a gun discharging. The baron looked to the flash and saw Anna slowly emerge from the shadows in the carriage, a spray of gunpowder still fresh on her blouse, holding the smoking gun that she'd remembered from the story that she'd been told as a teenage girl—the gun that the baron kept in a compartment at his feet in the coach, for hunting from the confines of his ride. The antiquated weapon had not been used in over seventy-five years, yet had been kept and maintained diligently, almost lovingly by the faithful servant who looked on aghast.

She had crept around and into the coach as the baron revealed his plan. As she listened, she thought only of the story, hoping that the weapon actually existed, and that she might in some way be able to use it. The baron realized none of this, for when he finally saw her face, he raised his hand to his head to feel the wetness at his temple. She had fired a single shot, miraculously hitting the fur-clad abomination as he stood digesting the fruits of his labors. The shot entered the right side of his head, traversed the skull of the beast that had once taken the form of the baron, and exited on the left side, still at a velocity sufficient to puncture the rear tire of the car that stood some twelve feet away.

He exhaled in a disgruntled curse and died on the spot, first transforming back into the form that was once the baron D'Arcamo, and then literally to ash, as if some great hellish heat finally completed its task of incinerating his soul.

Anna stared at the two of them as Antonino slowly loosened his grip on Chelsea. Still holding the wrench, he turned and ran as best he could out into the now darkening evening, in the direction of the grove of lemon trees. Anna looked at her great-aunt and said nothing. Clothing lay scattered on the floor of the garage as they changed and gave chase, two regal females, seemingly on the hunt, quarry in sight.

Anna got to him first. Unlike the calculated hunt that wears the quarry down and then moves in to finish off the exhausted kill, Anna seemed to be without boundaries. She leapt and attacked until, reaching the old man, she barreled into the back of his legs, toppling him in a heap. By the time Chelsea, finally regaining her breath and strength, caught up to them, Anna was atop Antonino's throat, biting and tearing in a vicious manner that left little wonder as to the outcome. He rapidly bled to a gurgling death.

He had not gotten too far away, as his blood lay in pools, slowly coagulating on the gravel not more than twenty feet from the garage. Anna had trotted a few feet beyond to lick her paws and muzzle clean of whatever blood she could. The scene was a horror. But as she addressed it, she saw a logic in what had happened. Perhaps one could consider it the logic of wolves, to kill or be killed.

Careful not to step in the blood, Chelsea spoke to Anna in their silent way, "Come." Changing, Chelsea walked over to a water hose that was coiled still inside the garage. Naked and shivering a little from the cold, she used the water to clean Anna. Calm once again, Anna returned to her form and dressed as the night air finally took hold. Chelsea was still hosing the blood into the gravel, allowing it to seep as much as possible.

"What can we do with the body?" asked Anna as Chelsea dressed.

"That is for me to take care of. For now, let us turn off the light but keep the shed door open," was Chelsea's reply. They walked a bit until both were sufficiently dry and then returned to the house. Only a few lights were on, and no one was up. It was hard to believe that hours had passed since Chelsea left the house. They climbed the stairs, washed, and retired for the night.

The next morning, they were awakened by the sound of Francesca Paola's weeping. Carmela knocked on their doors with the news that Antonino had not come back to the house last night. His body was found by the police at the end of the property, beyond the lemon grove. He had been attacked by wolves.

"It wasn't unusual for Antonino to stay in the shed till all hours, working on the car or the carriage, but when he didn't come in for coffee this morning, I thought that maybe he was sick. And now this ..." said Francesca Paola to Chelsea between sobs. The two women tried as best as they could to offer their sadness and consolation to Francesca Paola. Carmela had only recently met Antonino, so obviously she was not taking it as hard as Francesca Paola.

The police investigation was done over the next few days, as that day and the next all efforts were hampered by torrential rains that pounded the grounds. "Any evidence in the area, other than the body itself, has been washed fairly thoroughly," said one officer. "But from the claw and tooth marks, one could infer that the wounds were inflicted by a wolf, or in this case wolves; maybe foxes, but I think more wolves. Funny, I didn't think there were that many wolves around here anymore. Well, we'll have to notify the wildlife authorities."

After the funeral, which was held on New Year's Eve, the investigation pretty much died down, as animal-rights activists took up the cause for a dangerously sparse species that, for one thing, may or may not have been defending itself, and for another, had yet to be found within twenty kilometers of the villa D'Arcamo. Antonino, who had lived alone, was buried in the cemetery outside of town.

The events that the world was aware of—Antonino's death and the cause of it—were enough to account for the pall that enveloped Chelsea and Anna that New Year's Eve night. They had given Carmela and Francesca Paola the night off and were sitting in the upstairs parlor sipping a sweet muscatel and looking into a fire that Anna had built in the ceramic tile stove.

The events that they had experienced went far beyond any comprehension of severity. They sat there sipping and silently staring. The only sound was the occasional crackle of the wood in the stove. They had been quiet since the funeral, not even commenting to each other in their own silent manner.

Finally, in the distance, the howl could be heard. *L'anelito*, where no wolf had been seen, could be heard. Chelsea raised her head and sobbed a bit.

Anna spat out the words, "He was a bastard."

"He was loyal to his master. He loved him."

"As loyal as your pets were to you when you needed their help?"

"As loyal as you were to me when I needed your protection."

"I killed the bastard."

"Well, technically, I would say that you killed his spirit," Chelsea answered in a disingenuous fashion. "I don't know if it would stand up in a court of law." She chuckled madly.

"I've changed into a wolf and attacked a man. I've killed, and I am capable of doing it again," declared Anna, hoping to break the chuckling.

"I know, I have too," added Chelsea as the mad chuckle grew into laughter on the edge of insanity.

"We can change back and forth and hunt with our clan, and then dress up and go out on the town," said Anna, more loudly now as she began a nervous laughter. "And we probably won't die for hundreds of years." The nervous tittering grew into a rolling laugh. "And we can never have children or raise a family." The rolls of laughter were expanding unmercifully.

"Our children are the *figli del lupo*," roared Chelsea, holding her sides in guffaws.

"Everyone we know has either already died or will in time," said Anna as she slowly stopped laughing.

"Eventually it will be just us and the *figli*," chortled Chelsea, as her laughter, too, subsided. Then, as the quiet returned, it too came back, *l'anelito*.

"Let's go," said Chelsea. "Let's start the year running with them. I need to see them, to breathe in their scents, to roll and jump as one of them. Come with me. Let's go."

"No, I'm staying. In fact, my mind is made up. I'm going home. I need to go back to the farmhouse, and I need to see my family, all of my family. I can't stay here anymore."

Chelsea was taken aback. She'd really thought that they'd weathered all possible storms in their journey to join the *figli del lupo* here in Arcamo. As Anna spoke, it occurred to her that perhaps the journey here was hers and hers alone, and Anna's lay elsewhere.

"I'll come back from time to time, and I'll meet with Sagrigento to have papers drawn up so that you'll stay here and serve as my official representative. But while my parents are still alive, I want to have time with them. I want to look after my own clan in America. I just can't take the killing anymore." Anna had finished speaking. There were tears in her eyes.

Chelsea thought better of leaving. She stood up and hugged her. It was the kind of embrace that one gives a relative who has lived through a crisis. It was the embrace that says, *There now, things will be all right. You'll see.*

But at this moment, Anna didn't see. She was torn. The love that she kept for her family, from Nana and Nonno to her parents to Tina and her family to Zia Gelsamina, was a deep-rooted, rich tapestry of affection and food and stories and memories, but the journey had taken a toll on her. She had never been drawn to violence, and yet here she was, still coming to terms with the fact that she could and did fire a handgun, ancient as it was, and land the one-in-a-million shot that killed the demonic baron, in defense of her Gelsamina. And then the real killing, the savage, no-thought-involved, rage-filled killing of Antonino. This was all too much for her to digest. She needed to leave. If Sagrigento would meet her at the airport, she would even take care of the details there. She turned away from Gelsamina and walked into her room.

Epilogue
Gina's Story
2009

My great-aunt Anna never spoke that much. I can remember times when my brother and I would visit her at the farmhouse in upstate New York. She would greet us and, together, we would do things—summer chores and movies at night, the county fair or swimming at a nearby lake—but both my brother, Tommy, and I always felt that whatever she did say, it was all superficial. This became more and more evident as we got older. By the time I turned fifteen, it had gotten to the point where we really didn't want to be there, and that was a few years ago. Sure, this was different from spending another hot summer in San Antonio, but even last summer when we came here, it felt like she was just going through the motions. Tommy said it was like her mind was always on something else.

One day, when he had gone for a walk down by the stream at the other end of her property, I went out to the porch where she was sitting. She was staring out at the woods, past the rows of tomato and pepper that she had planted. Well, she didn't plant them. She had hired people to plant and take care of the vegetables in her garden. Aunt Anna had inherited a lot of money from my great-grandfather, and from that point on, she did a lot of stuff that I suppose wealthy people do, investing and traveling and all.

I went to the porch where she was sitting and staring out. She was in a wicker chair, wearing really nice tailored clothes, a stemware glass of wine in her left hand; from time to time, her right hand would finger that odd crest medallion around her neck. I don't think I'd ever seen her without it. She was pretty, slim and muscular, as if she ran a lot and watched what she ate. And she looked young. I don't know how old she was, but if my mother was in her thirties, then Aunt Anna must be in her sixties, and she looked like she was Mom's age. But she always looked sad, at least she did when she thought no one was watching.

She finally realized that I'd been watching her. She put down her glass and turned to me.

"Gina!" she began. "You didn't want to go down to the stream with Tommy?"

"No, Aunt Anna. It's too hot out there. I think it's nicer in the evenings." Something about my answer to her spurred an interest that I hadn't seen. Suddenly there was a sort of twinkle in her eye.

"Oh, so I suppose it's just we two girls here today," she said as she turned from looking out at the woods. "Gina, how old are you now?"

"Almost seventeen," I said. The sun shone warmly on the two of us as she stood up and began walking into the beautifully decorated house. As she opened the screen door, she said, "Have I ever told you about the chalk portrait of the young girl in the back room?"

CPSIA information can be obtained at www.ICGtesting.com
Printed in the USA
BVOW07s1014310714

361197BV00001B/124/P